Okay, he decided. *I'm probably going to die. But while I'm alive I'll get my act in gear and stop sniveling. And I'll give this craziness the best I've got . . .* then he remembered the old joke: I ain't much, but I'm all I've got. And he grinned.

As he lectured himself, Mark took off his jacket, folded it, put it on a small log, then removed his sweat-shirt. This level shelf of rock would be a safe place to wash and dry his clothes. He removed his pants, decided he'd wash them first, and then . . .

The log was moving . . . the one where he'd laid his jacket.

It was no log.

An alligator. A long one. Up on little stubby legs, headed for the river, carrying his folded jacket on its back. Mark stood rooted in shock, then yelled.

"Wait! Stop! No!"

He raced after the moving jacket just as the big reptile slid into the river.

Mark, close behind, instantly leaped in, clad in shorts and shoes. Water closed over his head . . .

SURVIVOR

ROBERT STEELE GRAY

St. Martin's Paperbacks

SURVIVOR

Copyright © 1998 by Robert Steele Gray.
Excerpt from *Afterburn* copyright © 1999 by Colin Harrison.

Library of Congress Catalog Card Number: 98-23930

ISBN: 0-312-96709-8

Printed in the United States of America

St. Martin's Press hardcover edition / November 1998
St. Martin's Paperbacks edition / January 2000

St. Martin's Paperbacks are published by St. Martin's Press, 175 Fifth Avenue, New York, N.Y. 10010.

10 9 8 7 6 5 4 3 2 1

SURVIVOR

ONE

Wet, dark Texas northers can be scary.

And dangerous.

The entire horizon, earth to sky, turns from gray to black, rolling ominously from the northwest. A dark and towering wall of weather, it sends out rain squalls, chilling rain, downs power lines and great trees.

Mark Lewellyn wasn't worried. He eyed the approaching mass of bad weather through his den window and knew he was right to stay home and watch the Cowboys' game on TV.

It'd be a mess out at Texas Stadium with thousands of Dallasites skidding about, banging fenders, ruining weekends. Not for him. Today, civilized people should stay indoors.

Mark snuggled into his deeply dented sofa, enjoying a full stomach. Only on Sunday mornings did he fully indulge his appetite. He and Eleanor had eaten at their favorite restaurant buffet. While she had yogurt, toast, and coffee, Mark gorged on eggs, bacon, sausage, grits, biscuits, pork gravy, and hash browns. Then seconds. Wonderful.

For the rest of the week he'd make do with fruit and cereal for breakfast. Unless he cheated. He knew now what the doc said was true: Food was his tranquilizer. Okay, so what? Maybe he'd taper off a little . . . soon.

He saw vertical, blue-white lightning streak along the advancing wall of blackness. Dull thunder muttered closer, wind began whipping treetops in Mark's yard. He smiled to himself. No chance for outside exercise today. He'd intended some walking. He really had. He began dozing off.

"Mark!"

Eleanor called from the top of the stairs.

"You see my yellow-handled screwdriver?"

"Um . . . the one on the drainboard?"

"That's it. Would you bring it to me? That silly screw on my computer console is loose again."

"I'll get it—except I put it in the workshop, and it's about to rain . . ."

"Wear your new tennis jacket," she called, irritated. "It'll keep the rain out."

Mark forced himself up off the couch, shrugged into his new jacket, out the back door. Damn. She always worked Sundays at that miserable computer. He shook his head. Eleanor was a driven woman, trying to make the big bucks in a hurry. Some Sundays they hardly spoke.

He hurried out into a cold drizzle. Thunder, louder now, vibrated through the trees as he entered his workshop, where tools and machines lined three walls.

Mark smiled with pleasure. It was a do-it-yourselfer's dream. He had every tool known: color-matched sets of screwdrivers, chisels, wrenches, pliers, hammers of all sizes, power saws, planers, sanders, drills. Thousands of dollars invested here. He loved its orderly look, the smell, the bright fluorescent lights. He just never seemed to have much time to work out here. Eleanor often reminded him of that.

Mark found the screwdriver she wanted, left, and shut the door securely. Black skies had opened above him. He zipped his jacket up as rain stung his face, obscuring the lake that fronted his property, and broke into a slow jog between the pines lining the brick pathway.

As he passed between the tall trees, an intense light blinded him. His eardrums were numbed by an explosion that sucked his breath from his body and lifted his feet off the ground. He only had time to feel intense pain in his head and wonder if this was a natural-gas explosion—then he lost consciousness, and the world Mark had known came to an end.

First, there was warm wetness against his face.

Then the fetid stench of moist earth and wet leaves pressed against the side of his head.

Mark awoke painfully, head aching. His left arm, flung out on the ground, had a strange tickle on the wrist. He raised his head in time to see the tail of a long, splotchy-hued snake undulate across his arm.

He froze with fear, watching in horror as the snake slid unhurriedly into nearby grass. Drenched in sweat, Mark gasped for breath. He sat up with a groan and looked around in silence.

Tall trees towered over him. Sun filtered down in circles of golden light on sparse green-and-yellow underbrush. Mark's hand came off the moist ground with damp leaves stuck to it . . . then he was shocked at the sight of his jacket sleeves. They were singed black, charred at the ends. And dark streaks ran down his white pants. He rubbed his face and eyes. His skin was hot, flushed. Felt like sunburn.

Then the explosion went off again in his mind . . . a blinding white sheet of flame, being lifted up . . . yet he was still alive. How could this be? And the weather . . . it had been a cold October day when he'd run into his backyard. Now it was warm, almost hot, here in the shade. Like late spring, early summer.

Pushing to his knees, Mark could see for hundreds of yards through open, shadowy woods . . . a tranquil, even lovely scene. How on earth had he gotten here? Was this a dream, or . . . oh, God, no. Was he dead? This, the afterlife? He rubbed his face. Couldn't be. He felt too awful. His head ached; he was sick to his stomach, exhausted. Nobody could feel this bad and be dead.

He staggered up, rolling his head around to ease the ache. Saw the huge height of these trees. All were hardwoods, that he knew, but he saw no pines. Only thing was, their size.

That hickory must be over a hundred feet high. Awesome.

Mark hugged himself, trying to quiet the shaking of his body, get his mind calmed down. This was no dream. He knew it couldn't be death. He'd wandered into some woods . . . but where?

One thing was sure: This wasn't near his home, fronting Lake Ray Hubbard. Somebody had to have brought him here, dumped him out . . . but why? He had no buddies who'd play such a dumb practical joke. Or did he? But this warm weather . . . how could it change so fast? Made no sense at all.

Mark took deep breaths and began stumbling up the gently wooded slope. He had to get hold of himself. Mustn't panic. He'd find a road, flag down a car, see where he was. Maybe he could get home in time for lunch . . . and he'd sure hate to miss the Cowboys' game kickoff this afternoon.

Dallas County Deputy Sheriff Joel Wiggins saw right off this wasn't your run-of-the-mill missing persons case. The attractive fortysomething female had herself tightly under control, not crying, just tense. She seemed positive about events of the past hour. He'd make sure.

"Lemme see if I got it straight. Your husband—Mark Victor Lewellyn, right?—forty-one, about five-ten, weighs maybe two thirty-five, blue eyes, brown hair, round face. Lotta hair on his arms, kinda slouches when he walks. He's got on a purple-and-white workout jacket, NIKE on one sleeve. White exercise pants, sweatshirt under the jacket, white jogging shoes."

"They've all got NIKE printed on them," Eleanor added. "It's tennis stuff I got for him. He likes to watch, not play."

"Should we call him fat?"

"Well, he's got some flab around the waist. Not fat, I guess, just . . . kind of heavy. He's had some health problems lately."

"Like what?"

"Doctor says his cholesterol is too high, and he's got

higher blood pressure than he should. Mark's got to lose weight, to make sure he doesn't have a heart attack. He doesn't smoke . . . and only drinks beer when he watches TV." *Which is most of the time*, Eleanor reminded herself.

"And about nine this morning," Wiggins read from·his notes, "he goes out to the toolshed for a screwdriver. It's raining, then you hear this big bang?"

"God, yes, it was tremendous. It shook the whole house."

"And you rushed out back, see those big pines on fire . . . and no husband. Right?"

"That's right. It was pouring rain then. Mark was gone. I looked in the toolshed, every·place . . ."

"You looked around the yard, out on the street, at the property on both sides of you. The man's disappeared. Is it possible that you were dazed by the lightning, maybe you passed out, went into shock for a while, and he wandered off someplace?"

"No, Deputy," Eleanor said firmly. "Not possible. I saw the flash of light, heard—and felt—the explosion, and fell against the sofa. I was outside in maybe ten seconds—no less . . . I was afraid Mark was dead from that lightning. I was conscious every minute."

Wiggins glanced out the back picture window at the shattered remains of the tall pines, now split and blackened by fire, one twisted down to the ground like a giant corkscrew.

Those pines, he had found, flanked the walk from toolshed to house, and the lightning strikes had ripped vertically down both trunks, toppling one, igniting bark on the bases of both. Rain had put out the fires.

"What if he'd gone around behind the toolshed, then headed down toward the lake?" Wiggins asked. "Could you have seen him then?"

"Of course. That was my first thought when I couldn't find him. I called neighborhood security, and they've spent the morning driving every street for a mile around, and down by the lake, and there's no way . . ."

"Even if he was running?"

Eleanor couldn't keep from smiling.

"Mark Lewellyn is not a runner. As I said, he gets almost no exercise. He hates it. I don't think he could run a hundred yards. Besides, everybody's home today. It's Sunday. Lots of people would have seen him going down the slope or in the streets."

"And in the other direction . . . east?"

"Well, you saw it as you came here. There's farm road 740—and then there's pretty much open prairie with a few trees. Friends of ours have been looking out there, too."

Eleanor covered her face with her hands.

Oh hell, thought Wiggins, *she's gonna cry.* He quickly asked whether anybody was coming to stay with her until her husband was found.

"Yes," she sniffed. "My son, Charles. He's a freshman at SMU. He should be here anytime now . . . he's not going to understand how his father could just . . . disappear. And all I've got to show Charles is *this*."

She pointed to the yellow-handled screwdriver on the table, part of the handle scorched.

"Mark must have dropped it when . . . when this thing happened. God, I wish I'd never asked him to go outside and get it for me.

"Besides that," she added, "I really needed a Phillips-head screwdriver. He went out there and got the wrong kind."

TWO

Two hundred yards up the forest slope Mark found fewer trees and more underbrush. He was winded, perspiring, thirsty. His pulse raced, so he stopped, knelt in the thick leaves, tried to think. This couldn't be. No way could he get knocked out in his own backyard and wind up in the middle of nowhere. Somebody, something, must have moved him . . . as crazy as that seemed. Now he had to find his home, wherever it was . . .

Two rabbits startled him as they broke from nearby underbrush, racing away. Then he spotted eyes staring, watching him. Deer. A whole herd of them, in heavy brush near a clump of trees. Led by a massive buck, they turned and trotted down the slope.

Mark realized he was holding his breath, fearing danger. He'd never been a hunter, hated it, knowing it disappointed his outdoorsman father. This was as close to a wild animal as he ever wanted to get.

Sweat rolled down Mark's nose, dripped from his chin. He wiped his face, smudged it with the charred sleeve end of his jacket. Eleanor would be furious when she saw its condition. Cost a bundle. He reached for his handkerchief but found his back pocket empty. Nor, he realized, had he worn his Rolex. Scratching his head, he wished he had his cap on. It helped keep his hair in place.

He dug into both pants pockets. Nothing . . . well, almost nothing. In one pocket he found a quarter, a dime, three pennies. At least he could use a pay phone.

Moving up the slope, Mark saw this was like a wilderness area in the national parks he and Eleanor had visited.

When Charles had been little, they'd taken him camping, at Eleanor's insistence. Mark hated sleeping bags and cold mountain streams. But Eleanor was grimly determined that their boy would camp out. Be a man and all that.

Charles accepted it all stoically until, as a teenager, he had gently told his mother he'd really rather stay home in summer to read his growing library on scientific subjects. Mark was secretly elated. Thank God. No more camping out. Well, not until now anyway. It wasn't yet noon, and he sure didn't intend to remain in this forest a minute longer than necessary. Shouldn't be any big problem. Just look around, find some people, get the hell home. Help shouldn't be far away.

His outer jacket and sweatshirt both off, Mark rested in the shade of a massive oak tree. He had finally staggered to the edge of the forest and was astonished at the spectacular panorama stretching away into the distance. He could hardly believe his eyes.

A vast, rolling prairie sloped down and away to the horizon from his vantage point. From his far left to right rippled an unbroken sea of waist-high grass, waving gently in a light breeze. Only a few bushes and clusters of trees dotted that prairie. It wasn't flat, though. He saw mounds and depressions, where tops of small trees appeared. And there were dark shapes in the distance. Wonderful! Must be cows or horses. Which would mean people and telephones.

But he needed to get higher up, to spot a road or bridge. Damn, he wished he had his new power-zoom binoculars. He carried them everywhere in his Volvo's glove compartment.

He looked up. Had to climb a tree to see better. It would further mess up his clothes, but what the hell—they'd need to be replaced anyway when he got home. The oak above him stood at least eighty feet high, but had low-hanging branches, so he could hoist himself up.

Mark folded his jacket carefully and put it on the ground, making sure there were no ant beds around. The lowest branch was five feet off the ground, another was about eight feet up. He figured to jump and catch the higher branch, then swing his legs up on the lower branch. An easy climb from there.

He bent, jumped, caught the higher branch, couldn't hold on, and fell to the ground with a grunt. He did a partial knee bend to limber up, took a higher jump, held on, swung his legs up, tried to push himself to a standing position on the branch, lost his grip, and collapsed to the ground.

Damn, he felt so weak, so inept. But he had to get up so he could see. There had to be somebody around.

Kneeling, Mark breathed deeply, rubbing his face and head. This was dumb. Lost, hurting, thirsty. It wasn't fair. He couldn't even get up into a miserable tree.

He stood erect, jumped, got himself up on the branch, began climbing, muttering to himself, breathing hard. By God, he wasn't helpless, he wouldn't let the panic in his mind and throat choke him down . . . and he would find a way to sleep in his own bed tonight!

For a while, Mark could barely see off into the distance. He had become exhausted during his twenty-minute climb up through the oak branches, resting often to gain strength for the next effort. Then he found a spot where he could see through the foliage. He didn't look down. Heights scared the hell out of him. He was thirsty, and his throat felt raw. If only he wasn't so damn fat. *Yes, fat*, he told himself. Not stout. Not heavyset. Fat. Two hundred thirty-seven pounds fat. No, that's a lie. With clothes on, he knew full well, his bathroom scale hit two forty-five. Every time he shaved in front of a mirror he could see that sagging gut, that sagging chest, and developing double chin. *You're fat, dummy!*

Forget that, he told himself. *Get your ass home first*. But something was making his tree shiver. It shook, then vibrated as he pressed his back to the trunk. Mark heard a low steady rumble off to his left. He moved around, saw nothing but waving grassland . . . and a thin spiral of dust. It rapidly swelled as he stared.

The sound, dull and guttural, grew. The tree swayed against his sweating back. Now a dust cloud filled the sky to Mark's left, the rumble increased to a roar. He turned and held on to the tree trunk, then, through the dust, he saw dark shapes coming toward his tree . . . many of them. Animals. Running in groups, hundreds of them, whipping a dirt cloud from the crushed grass underfoot. As they moved closer, his mouth fell open.

They weren't cows. Not horses.

Couldn't be.

Buffalo.

No doubt about it. He'd seen those great shaggy heads, tiny horns, little thin legs many times on television, running through cowboy epics. Only this was real, and Mark began to cough as the dust cloud swirled through his tree. Looking down, he saw shapes flash below him, sun glistening off brown-and-black hair, huge bulls appearing to herd the buffalo cows and calves as they went by Mark's tree and on to his right. Then he noted they weren't running hard. Simply loping along, in no great hurry. And it wasn't a huge herd at all. Maybe a couple hundred buffalo altogether . . . could this be somebody's private herd? Or was he in the midst of a government-controlled wilderness area?

Now he saw the buffalo slow, then turn into the edge of woods, hidden from his view. The dust-filled air brought both a choking fit and a revelation: Were those buffalo heading down into the woods for water? Was there a stream at the bottom of that ravine? Maybe if he went back the way he'd come, parallel to the buffalo, he'd find it. He knew he had to get a drink of something before his thirst made him really ill . . . so he let himself down through the branches, cursing and angry at the scrapes he inflicted on himself with nearly every move.

Then he noted a different worry. The sun had turned

weak, now it disappeared behind high, thin clouds. Looking northwest—or what he *thought* might be northwest—he saw low-lying rain clouds lining the horizon. Mark knew he didn't have much time to find water and shelter before dark. Damn, he hated camping out.

Mark found it impossible to get comfortable straddling a six-inch limb, perched twenty feet up. He kept telling himself all this was impossible, that it couldn't be happening.

Yet here he sat . . . your basic, unhappy camper, mind churning with the classic question: What the hell was he doing here? How could he survive with no equipment, no weapons, nothing to help him through the night ahead? The only good thing, he decided, was that he'd have one helluva good story to tell Eleanor when he got home. He even felt a little proud of himself for having finally found some drinking water.

Two hours of sweaty searching in the woods confirmed Mark's guess that the buffalo were heading for water. He found their river by late afternoon: a swift-flowing stream seventy-five feet wide, riding high in its banks, almost full. There had been recent rains, but the water looked clean enough to drink. Dusk was at hand, and a cool breeze ruffled the trees. Should he spend the night here or up on the prairie? Better the woods, close to water, but not on the ground, where there were snakes and crawling insects everywhere. Mark walked along the bank, looking for a tree he could climb: one that offered solid, easy-to-grab branches. Clouds darkened the sky, and the air smelled like more rain was on the way. Then he spotted a young cottonwood that he might be able to climb, right on the riverbank. Good. Or bad, he thought, as he'd sweated his way up into the lower branches.

This place couldn't be anywhere near Dallas. The weather was backward—and he'd finally become aware of something even more astonishing: No airplanes had flown over. No vapor trails. Certainly this was nowhere near Dallas or the giant DFW airport. And he had puzzled all day over the trees.

Exactly the same varieties he'd known all his life. This place was different but contained the same living plants he knew on sight.

He tried to put that out of his mind as he struggled through branches and found one where he could sit and anchor both feet on branches below. Could a man sleep like this? He doubted it. Turning around, Mark wrapped his arms around the tree trunk for safety. He zipped up his jacket, put his head against the tree, and tried to turn off his mind. Even as exhausted as he was, Mark remembered the worst thing about the day—he'd missed the damn Cowboys' game.

Chilling rain seeping down his back woke Mark from a light doze. He pulled the jacket zipper tight up under his neck, aware that branches offered little protection now that the rainfall was growing heavier. No way could he feel any more miserable.

Suddenly there were sounds below him. Growing louder.

Staring down, he waited for a lightning flash. When it came, he didn't believe his eyes. Below him, the stream was becoming a river. A *wide* river. It was up and out of its banks, and his tree was now *in* the river. Water swirled up around Mark's tree, growing more and more turbulent. The tree leaned slightly. Then he heard a menacing sound that he had only heard once in his life when, as a boy, he'd gone camping overnight with his dad above a dry, west Texas streambed. There was no other sound like it. First it sizzled faintly. Then moaned, and finally roared.

Flash flood.

Mark was stranded square in its path.

As realization hit, the tree itself confirmed his worst fears: It began to lean. All that upstream rain, swelled suddenly by a cloudburst, had turned this quiet river into a rampaging torrent. Thunder was constant. Lightning flashes revealed the river uprooting great chunks of the forest along its banks.

Mark watched brush, limbs, and small trees bobbing, rising, twisting, turning in the boiling water below him. He now knew that nothing could prevent him from being swept downstream by this living nightmare . . . drowned in a nameless river in a nameless place . . . no one would ever know what became of him. Miserable, terror-stricken, it crossed his mind to pray. But how? What to say? He'd never been a religious man but now felt sure he ought to say something appropriate to God and ask for help. Could he promise to be a better man? Better than what? Mark thought he wasn't too bad a man as he was . . . then again he knew God couldn't be paying much attention since his tree kept slowly toppling before the river's crushing force. The frantic man forgot about God and everything else as he scrambled higher, slipping, trying to get a secure foothold, before . . .

A thunderous rumble behind him twisted Mark around . . . just in time to see a four-foot wall of white, foaming water rushing down on him. The crest of the flood had arrived, seemingly alive, rolling and pushing everything before it, now engulfing Mark's lonely tree.

He barely had time to grab a breath of air before he was flung from his perch and plunged underwater, headfirst, arms and legs flailing, unable to control his movements. Choking, he knew he had no strength to fight his way to the surface. Then his head broke water and he was buoyant. Why? He felt air ballooning his jacket and pants. Those elastic ankle and wrist cuffs had trapped air inside his clothing. But a mass of vegetation nearly covered him as he tried to protect his head from dark objects hurtling by his face. He felt utterly helpless as the raging current seized him, tossing him hard against objects he couldn't see, making him a piece of river flotsam.

He felt, more than heard, the huge mass coming toward his back, and he spun around in panic . . .

Too late.

Mark could just make out—looming high in the water—a black and broken tree, jagged edges aimed straight at him, the instant before it struck. He threw up one arm as his head seemed to explode in a burst of crimson light, and everything went black.

THREE

Eleanor Witt Lewellyn didn't want to talk to this woman at all.

But she knew that publicity might cause somebody to find Mark. He must be wandering around, someplace, in an amnesiac daze.

So when the *Dallas Morning News* called for an interview, Eleanor decided—much as she distrusted publicity—it might help find Mark.

Already, a day after he'd vanished, Eleanor's ordered life was in turmoil. She couldn't sleep well. Suddenly, for no reason, she was constipated. Her boss insisted she take time off when she feared she shouldn't. Charles, carrying eighteen semester hours, needed to get back to school. Besides which, he was afraid his girlfriend might be pregnant. And worst of all, Mark's frantic mother and sister seemed to call every hour from Fort Worth, checking for news of Mark. Eleanor ground her teeth in frustration; this was not the even keel she wanted.

Reporter Hilda Harrison, tape recorder humming on the kitchen table, waited for Eleanor to stop pacing and sit down. "I read the police report, so I know pretty much what's supposed to have happened here . . ."

"Supposed to have happened?" Eleanor barked.

"Sorry, just a figure of speech. What I meant was whether the police report, and the first news stories about it . . . were accurate?"

"Yes, pretty much," Eleanor said, "though some of the

stuff on television made it seem like Mark disappeared under suspicious circumstances . . . you know, like he'd done something wrong. I don't think they understood what happened. 'Muddle' is the way it came through on TV."

"Well, you'll have to agree that the circumstances are strange, and that's why I'm doing a follow-up piece.

"You've stated," Hilda pushed ahead, "that perhaps your husband is now an amnesia victim. If that's true, we ought to give more details about what happened. And about him personally."

Eleanor shook her head in frustration. "It's awful to think that he might not even be aware of who he is, much less where he is. It's all a bad dream. . . ." Hilda glanced at her notes.

"What's really weird about this is the business of those two lightning strikes at the same time. I know you've been over this with the police, but has anything else come back to you that might help . . . anything at all?"

Eleanor shook her head in irritation. "No. It was just crazy. Both of those trees were hit at the same time, the police say it was two strikes, not one . . . those tall trees must have attracted the lightning."

"I've talked to an expert about the lightning," Hilda said, "and he's skeptical about two, almost simultaneous strikes. . . ."

"Then he ought to come out here and see what's left of those trees," Eleanor snapped. "Those pines were exactly twenty-seven feet, six inches apart, the police told me, and the brick walk Mark was on ran right between them. It's a miracle he wasn't electrocuted the second it happened."

"Yes, I've seen the pictures. But you're sure there wasn't a—an interval—between the two strikes? Enough time for your husband to run, or wander away?"

"No, I've been over that a dozen times. At first I thought it was one big lightning bolt but then I remembered there seemed to be two . . . a split second apart. I fell down on my couch for a couple of seconds, then saw flame and smoke and rushed outside. I was out there not more than thirty seconds, probably less, after the lightning hit." She grimaced.

"I *know* I was outside because it was raining and I got soaked, running around looking for Mark. But I was *not* hysterical. I'm not that way."

"Okay, tell me how people can most readily recognize your husband if they see or talk to him?"

"Well, he's an ordinary man . . . not ordinary to me, of course. I mean he's just under six feet tall, a little overweight. He has regular features, thick black hair, sort of slouches when he walks. Sort of ambles along."

"And he works at home?"

"Yes. Works for American Data Capture of Dallas. They allow people to work at home with computers. They relay data to Mark, and the others, by modem. It's stored, then, once a week, they turn in their disks for the database lists that the company rents out to customers."

"Has he had any kind of physical or mental problems that this experience might make worse, causing him to get amnesia?"

"No, he's been perfectly happy lately, as far as I know. My job makes me travel a lot, so I'm not here every night, but nothing lately seems to worry him much. Mark is settled and stable. Doesn't have any other business interest that I know of. He reads a lot, watches TV, takes his mother fishing when he can. He just leads a quiet life. Avoids problems, doesn't have anything to worry about . . ."

"Any special interest or hobbies at all?"

"No. Except . . . he does like all kinds of gadgets. He has no technical skills but loves electronic stuff. Labor-saving devices, stuff like that."

"Such as?"

"Well, new stuff on the market—he recently got that new VCR remote programmer. It gives you the time of day, a pick of different channels, and stores all kinds of programming. I don't understand it all.

"Then he has a fax phone answering thing that's wild . . .

it faxes, copies, doubles as a printer, a message machine, and even has an outside paper cutter, if you can imagine. He's got all kinds of electronic pest repellents, for indoors and out . . . and a California-style lifeguard stereo hat, with a stereo speaker system in the brim, and . . . well, you get the idea."

Eleanor smiled nervously. This all sounded so silly. She'd better shut up. She certainly wouldn't mention the last argument she'd had with Mark about those nutty gadgets. He'd bought a ceiling projection clock that projected the time, in huge letters, over their bed when he touched a button. It went, or *she* went, she'd finally told him angrily.

"I hate to ask this," Hilda went on, "but can you think of any reason why Mark might have *wanted* to disappear?"

"Why of course not! None at all. He's a well-adjusted man who simply likes his home, and . . . well, he's *happy*!"

Hilda knew she'd gotten all there was to get. She collected her things and rose to leave, knowing it would be tough to make much of this missing yuppie stay-at-home. A world-class goof-off, she decided, who'd flown the coop for his own reasons. Maybe good ones.

As she walked Hilda to the door, Eleanor also knew how Mark must sound to the reporter. He had a soft and empty kind of life, with little challenge to it. Mark seemed passionate about almost nothing, including her. But that's the way he was. And she couldn't change him. Nothing could.

This whole thing had ruined her immediate plans. She shut the door after the journalist and headed to her study. She'd try to focus on work.

There was the big company conference in Cincinnati the week after next. She simply had to be there to stand any chance of getting the territorial vice presidency her company would bestow on the soon-to-be-appointed Midwestern Manager of Southwestern Pharmaceuticals, Inc.

"Eleanor, we'll certainly understand it if you can't make the Cincinnati meeting," her boss had told her on the phone this morning. "So . . ."

"Harry, I will be at that meeting. I know it won't take

two more weeks to find my husband. I want that promotion, and Mark would want me to move ahead in the company. So go ahead and reserve me a room."

If I don't get there, Eleanor reflected as she hung up, *that bastard Cunningham in Houston will try to edge me out of my promotion, sure as hell.* She would not let that happen.

Mark choked, gagged, and came awake in a haze of pain and darkness.

Sharp points pressed into his body. He was in the water, somehow tied up, not moving. He felt sick, tried to vomit. Mucus clogged his nose, and his eyes stung.

Only a dull roar sounded now, from downstream. His head barely cleared the water, and he became conscious of dark shapes around him, jumping, shoving.

Carefully, afraid something would strike or bite him, Mark felt around his head and shoulders. He touched limbs, masses of vegetation, like a great web. They seemed to encircle his body, holding him against slippery bark. The remains of a big tree.

Then it came to him.

The tree that knocked him out must have also saved his life. He'd been caught in its branches, rushed downstream, and now was mashed against it, with the water level inches below his mouth.

Mustn't panic. Do one thing at a time, slowly. He lifted his chin, took deep, hoarse breaths and began pulling loose the branches that entwined him. The tree no longer moved. His clothes were heavy, dragging him down. To release that last vine from his chest, he pushed away from the tree and went underwater. . . .

. . . where his feet touched bottom. Quickly, Mark shoved up at an angle to the tree, and his head emerged in open water. He saw a dark line of woods ahead and struck out awkwardly, flopping arms and legs to get away from debris behind him.

Moments later he was stumbling up a muddy bank into

low underbrush. He slumped down, coughed up phlegm and water, fell forward, head on his arms. Mark knew there were probably snakes around him, but he didn't care. He was asleep the next instant.

Something warm and wet touched Mark's neck.

Low growls and movement behind him brought him awake in an instant. He struggled up to one knee, becoming aware of faint daylight around him.

And there, facing him, were two animals the size of large lean dogs, heads low, eyes staring. Coyotes.

They moved back a step, their whines and growls growing in volume. What they thought might be a meal was something alive . . . a strange two-legged animal.

Mark stumbled to his feet, looking around for a rock, branch, anything. But the coyotes moved back into the deep brush pile that bordered the river. Mark sensed that they waited there watching him.

In the dim dawnlight, he saw jagged, slatelike stones on the ground at the riverbank. He grabbed up two of them, hand-sized, but didn't throw them. Better wait and see what the animals did.

He bent over, trying to get mind and body together. He felt awful, stomach churning, still coughing up river water. A headache pounded at his forehead. He raised arms and legs and twisted his body. No bones broken, apparently.

Mark remembered nothing of his time in the water. He must have been like Captain Ahab tied to the whale—only he was tied to a broken tree, plunging down the river. A miracle he hadn't drowned. Now he had two predators tracking him, he was sick, drained of energy, with no idea where he was . . . or where civilization was.

He had to move, find a road, bridge, somebody. He needed food, sleep, and medical attention. His body was bruised and battered, he'd found blood on his hands, wrists, and neck where sharp objects had punctured the skin.

Mark noted where the coyotes had vanished and began

walking downstream along the riverbank, avoiding briar patches, skirting piles of logs and vines, hoping the sun would appear and dry his sodden clothes. He was sure his nightmare must end today. He didn't think he could survive another. He'd try to ignore the mystery of how he had gotten there. He just needed to get a bath, a good meal, and into bed. There had to be somebody around who could help him.

Mark didn't know where the energy came from, but he'd climbed another tall tree. The sun was just rising, and he'd become frantic to find a road that would take him out of this awful wilderness. Fifty feet up, he had a good view of the river in both directions. He sat on a limb, dozed a while, jerked awake. He was disoriented. He didn't know if he'd slept five minutes or thirty. Had to decide which direction he should go to find power lines, a bridge, any sign of life. Then he heard . . .

Voices? Yes, human voices, down below. He shifted positions, trying to find a spot where he could see.

Yes. Through the foliage he watched them, down on the river's opposite bank, some two hundred feet away . . . a group of men. But Mark caught himself as he was about to shout. Strange men. He gasped, swallowed hard, moved higher to get a better look, and listened intently.

Their voices were low, indistinct. Mark rubbed his eyes when he began to make out the men's appearance . . . their clothes. They were almost naked, except around the waist. Their skins were dark, bodies thin, wiry.

These people were Indians.

Small, hard-looking men . . . and they seemed to be struggling with something near the river's edge. Mark moved again to a higher position. He saw more clearly there were six . . . no, seven men.

The rising sun was still low, and they were all in shadow, but as Mark's eyes adjusted, he saw long black hair, tied behind their heads. Bare legs and arms, tiny shoes, and loincloths around their middles.

And there was some kind of trouble. Mark could see that they held another man down on the ground . . . he seemed to be a prisoner, struggling, shouting at his captors. They held him, talking among themselves. They had a leader who stood slightly away from the group as they pressed the captured man facedown on the ground. Now they stopped speaking. Mark felt as though he was watching a pantomine performance, with the small clearing a kind of theater and Mark in a high balcony seat.

It was clear that the Indians had some purpose in mind. Two held the captive's feet and legs, two more pinned his waist, the other two gripped arms and shoulders. His arms were held down outstretched, his head mashed into the ground. The leader then stepped forward.

FOUR

The Leader of the hunting party had no wish to do this. He was experienced in the errant ways of men. In this case he had no choice. This was a bad man. The Leader had been part of another hunting party in this same place at an earlier time when this same man had been caught hunting where he had no right to hunt.

Then, he had been sternly warned and sent away. This time he had again taken an animal in their forest. The fresh carcass lay nearby. If the Leader did not perform this duty, his hunters would think less of him, and so would his family at home. He sighed. No choice.

The Leader stepped between his men and straddled the body of the prone captive. He looked up.

"Spirit," he said aloud, "we send this man to you for your keeping. We must do this thing because he has broken our rules of life. You may judge him as you wish, and we ask that you know we do this because our lives must be guided by rules, and we seek only fairness in dealing with all men. We ask that you judge us with a good heart."

Then the Leader quickly raised his stone ax high in the air and brought it crashing down into the back of the captive's head. He quickly moved aside to avoid the spurting blood.

Nothing was said for a moment. None of the men, the Leader knew, had ever seen a man killed in this way before. Their faces were impassive, but there was no question they were shocked. They all seemed frozen in place.

The Leader hoped he had done the right thing. He would be judged on the circumstances and felt sure the Elders would understand his decision. He motioned, saying nothing. The six men knew what they were to do. They picked up the body—almost gently, it seemed—and carried it to the river's edge. When they stood in the water, waist-deep, the men positioned the body faceup and carefully guided it into the center of the stream. They released the body, and it floated downstream, faster, and disappeared around a curve.

The six men splashed back to shore. At a signal from their leader, they picked up burdens they'd been carrying. Mark saw them divide into three pairs, each pair carrying a long pole between them. It sagged under the weight of what looked like skins and meat secured to the pole.

They moved slowly off through the woods to the west, and Mark saw them more clearly as sunlight pierced the leafy canopy above, reflecting on their hard brown skins. Each man carried a short stick of some kind hung over one shoulder, and each wore a satchel at his waist containing what appeared to be short spears or arrows. They never looked back.

As they walked up the long wooded slope, toward the prairie above, the man next to the Leader turned to him. Neither had spoken since leaving the river.

"You saw the thing in that tree across the river?"

The Leader nodded.

"I saw him."

"He wore white skins. Feet covered in white. You have seen this before?"

"No. Never before."

"What must we do?"

"We will take our meat and skins to the families. We will tell the Elders what we saw. If they wish us to, we will come here again and find that thing, or man, and catch it. No one in our families has seen skins like that before, I think."

"What if we come back here and cannot find it? The families may think we lie."

"Yes," the Leader responded. "That's true. We must find out how many of us saw the same thing."

They talked together as they carried their burdens at a rapid walk.

Mark sat crouched in a state of shock. He could hardly believe what he had just seen. Murder. They had deliberately killed that man on the ground. He remembered gasping when the stone weapon came down and the blood, bone, and brains erupted from the man's crushed skull. He had caught himself just in time to keep from crying out. He was sick and weak and shaking, but all he could do was silently retch as he watched, horrified.

Just before the captive was killed, he had heard the guttural voice of the group's leader speaking a language he'd never heard. Mark had read of ancient Aztecs in Mexico making human sacrifices, ripping living hearts from victims on ceremonial altars. This was not that kind of ritualistic scene, he felt, since the entire killing had seemed so summarily carried out, as though it was an execution of a criminal. But any way he looked at it, it was murder.

His loss of sleep, lack of food, and close escape from drowning began to work on Mark as he slowly, clumsily came down the tree. He felt no physical reserves of energy left: Hunger clawed at his stomach. He could not believe that a town or farmhouse could be more than a few hours' walk away.

Yet those Indians committing murder here in the forest . . . could this be near civilization, or had he been taken to some barbaric land? Frustration boiled up inside him and he slumped on the riverbank. For the first time in his adult life, Mark felt like weeping from the enormity of it all.

He plunged his face into the flowing and snorting water, drinking some—although he knew it must still be dirty after the flood. Shaking his head, he got up. He must move, keep looking. There had to be people—civilized people—around here someplace.

Then, up the river, he saw a quick black line of something move from the river into the brush. Another snake. Moccasin, most likely. He'd have to be careful. Mark skirted a big brush pile at the river's edge, found a four-foot weathered stick, bulbous at one end. Looked like oak. He swung it and hit the ground. Better weapon than nothing, he decided.

Moving along the river's edge, Mark rounded a bend, saw that a tall tree had fallen across the stream—which now had sunk to its normal level. He would cross over, go back upstream, see if there was anything to the west.

Walking on the downed tree was tricky. His jogging shoes were still wet and clung to the tree bark nicely, but when he got near the end of the downed tree he still had to jump some six feet to the bank.

He backed up, took three quick steps, jumped—and fell short of the bank, landing waist-deep in water. Great. Now he was soaked again. *Tarzan I'm not*, he decided. *Can't run, can't jump, can't climb a damn tree. I'm as helpless as a baby out here. This is disgusting.*

Mark soon found the west bank of the river no different from the east. Through open forest he saw the land slope upward, but he wasn't about to follow where those Indians had gone. Then he came to the clearing where the killing had taken place. The underbrush was trampled, blood and gore still glistened on the grass. He turned away, nauseated and sweating . . . then saw more blood in the brush nearby.

And a carcass. Yes, a deer, its belly split open, blood staining the ground around it. And Mark realized this might have been why that man died. He might have killed this buck, those men found him, and they considered it some kind of poaching. Perhaps all this was a sort of game preserve.

But he shook his head. You don't kill people, just like that, for poaching. This man looked just like they looked. Didn't they know each other . . . or was he some kind of criminal? Why murder a man over a deer when the forest was full of them? They couldn't be that primitive. Mark shuddered. Or could they?

With his stick, Mark poked at the deer and found that the hunter who killed it had started cleaning it. The entrails were piled in a gray mass nearby. He looked more closely. Inside the chest cavity were other objects he could barely see. It was repulsive but the thought came anyway: food. He had to eat something to keep going.

Here was red meat, gruesome to look at but freshly killed. And available. Mark partially closed his eyes, gritted his teeth, and pulled open the deer's body. Blood coated the insides. Mark saw a large lump of meat. He seized it, pulled it free.

Looking carefully, he knew what it was. Liver. Ironic, he thought.

One of Mark Lewellyn's favorite dishes at home was liver and onions. Since his wife and son both hated liver, Mark sometimes went to a nearby cafeteria for lunch, and ordered a large dish of calves' liver, topped with a small mountain of greasy onions. Delicious.

Except for the fat. When Bernie the Doc had scared him into facing nutrition, Mark found that liver is one of the richest of all meats, with big-time cholesterol. He looked at the pound or more of flesh in his hand and realized that, if indeed it was liver, he was looking at, what, maybe a thousand milligrams of cholesterol? Dozens of grams of fat? Four hundred calories?

Then he began to laugh, quietly at first, then hysterically. Here he was on the verge of starvation and worried about fat in his diet! His laughter stopped abruptly as a moving shadow caused him to look left—and freeze. The shadow moved into sunlight, and Mark knew the long tawny shape was a big cat. Mountain lion, cougar, whatever . . . it snarled quietly, lashed its long tail, and waited to see what the man would do.

The man would leave the scene. Fast. Backpedaling down the riverbank, stumbling, falling backward into the shallows, his stick waving in his right hand, raw meat clutched in his left.

Mark sputtered to his feet, dripping, and hurried quickly along the shoreline as the mountain lion crouched, ignored him, and began to feast on the carcass.

A hundred yards upstream Mark stopped, knelt in the shallows to rest, take a drink, and wipe the sweat from his face. Damn, that was close. He felt his heart going twice its normal speed. Just one horrible event after another—and he wasn't prepared for any of it.

Blood from the meat drained down his jacket front; Mark was still clutching it his hand. He washed the meat in the shallows, then crammed it into one pocket, along with a rock. What a mess he was. He remembered how neat, how white this outfit had been when Eleanor gave it to him for his birthday. Eleanor would understand when he got home, and they'd laugh about this crazy business.

He decided to build a small fire and roast the liver. But as he moved up onto the stream bank, he suddenly realized . . . fire? He had no matches, no lighter. He was a nonsmoker and never carried either. Then Mark remembered his one Boy Scout camping trip with his father. Starting a fire with no matches, using friction, had been a big deal.

"Here, watch this," the Scout leader had said. "You drill with this stick into the other stick, the friction causes heat, then fire, and that ignites the tinder."

At the time it had looked easy, but Mark remembered that neither his dad, nor any other dad, had managed to get a flame all afternoon. It was frustrating for the adults, while afterward, in private, the boys laughed like crazy at the adults' embarrassment.

Now it was either start a fire with no matches or eat raw liver. Mark took a deep breath. Maybe he'd try a few bites— in a little while. After all, he told himself, he did like the taste of steak tartare.

*   *   *

Mark collapsed into short grass in the shade of a hickory tree next to the river. The sun, almost directly overhead, had forced him to take off his jacket and sweatshirt, and tie both around his waist—yet he was drenched with sweat and knew he could go no farther.

All morning he'd roamed up the river, taking detours through the woods, then back to the river—his only certain guide for going in a reasonably straight line. He saw nothing but wildlife. Two small deer herds, a distant view of what looked like coyotes, and snakes flushed from brush piles along the river. Once, a whirring of wings frightened him as he roused a family of wild turkeys from their brushy nests. They flew off low through the woods.

He'd eaten a few bites of the deer liver. It went down and, somewhat to his surprise, stayed down. He needed sleep in the worst way. He came upon a tiny stream that emptied into the river. Going up its shallow length, away from the river, he found that it widened into a small pond, about a dozen feet across. A pile of boulders had dammed up the little creek, creating a quiet pool. Mark could see the bottom clearly, the sand and rocks there. The grass around him was short, and there were no hiding places for snakes. He hoped.

He removed his clothing, laid each item in a patch of sunlight to dry, including his shoes. Naked, he edged carefully into the cold water where it lapped grass and rocks. He waded in up to his waist, sank down until water reached his chin. Wonderful. He splashed his head, then held his breath and went under. Hadn't felt this good—or clean—in two days.

Mark came up, eyes closed, took a breath, went under, rubbed his hands down his arms and legs, and luxuriated. He blew out his breath, surfaced, pushed the hair from his face, opened his eyes, and found himself staring into the coal black eyes of a large black bear, not ten feet away.

FIVE

On all fours, motionless, the bear stood at least five feet high at the shoulder. He was massive and clearly old. Waist-deep in the small, cold pond, Mark shivered, hugging himself with gut-wrenching fear.

Never had he been as close to a large wild animal as he was to this fearsome creature—which simply stared at him curiously. Then the animal saw Mark's clothes on the ground. Sniffing the pants, underwear, then the muddy white shoes, the bear took one of the Nikes in its mouth.

"Hey, no!" Mark shouted, before he thought. "Put that down! Leave it alone!"

The bear studied the naked man. These were strange sounds the bear had never heard. It growled and took two steps toward Mark, now crouching lower in the water.

For one of the few times he could remember, Mark got mad. Thoroughly outraged. This damn, stupid animal was about to chew up one of his shoes! How could he limp around this crazy place barefoot? Irrational fury boiled up in him as he felt a rock under his feet.

Mark lunged down in the water, groped frantically, found the long, heavy stone. He raised it quickly in his right hand, sensing it must weigh at least five pounds.

"Drop that shoe, dammit! Drop it!" Mark shouted, holding his rock aloft.

The bear, still holding the shoe in its mouth, rose on hind legs, sending its massive head at least seven feet high, towering over the terrified man.

Mark threw the rock with all his strength.

It caught the huge animal full in the middle of its chest. Mark bent instantly to find another rock.

The bear came down on all fours, dropped the shoe and coughed once. Shook its head and coughed again.

Mark threw his second rock, and it hit the bear on his right front leg, at the knee. Roaring in pain, the animal moved sideways, lifted the right paw, licked at its knee. Then, as Mark groped underwater for another rock, the bear grunted. And limped slowly away, downriver. In a moment, it had disappeared into the underbrush.

Mark, in shock, sank down in the water, up to his chin. He was spent, gasping for breath, his heart pounding. Never had he been so scared. If he was going to have a heart attack, he decided, this would be the time for it. He couldn't believe he'd thrown those rocks. Why didn't the bear attack? Mark knew he wouldn't have had a chance. His teeth began to chatter, partly from fright, partly from the cold pond water.

He reached down and found two more smaller rocks. He weighed them in his hand. Just right for throwing.

From now on, he decided, he would be a Stone Age boomer and never leave home without some. Rocks, that is. He almost laughed aloud. Mark, the Stone Age Rocky. Then his smile faded. He had an awful thought . . . but, no, that was too dumb to even consider.

Mark finally found something better to eat than the hickory nuts with their meager fruit: pecans. The first pecan tree he found after his bear encounter was almost stripped bare, but another nearby still had nuts on its lower branches.

Jumping, he'd gotten handfuls by bending the branches, then stripped them quickly. They were smaller pecans than he remembered in the stores—smaller and harder. Whacks with his stones opened them, but it took an hour of pecan breaking to get a few mouthfuls.

Next he brought out the last of the raw liver. Mark grimaced. He'd wrapped it in his dirty undershirt so it wouldn't stain his jacket pocket. But bloody streaks had drained all over the jacket anyway. He rinsed the meat in the stream, took a bite, chewed. Still unspoiled, he decided, and ate more.

Mark saved one small liver chunk, wrapped it in the undershirt, jammed it down in his jacket pocket. He could really be hungry by nightfall. Then he realized something: He had stopped expecting to find a road, a bridge, or any people. This sobered him. Was he giving up totally? He shook that idea away. He had to keep on. Had to find somebody to help explain what had happened to him.

Mark walked and stumbled upstream on the west bank of the river all morning, then turned west, up a long slope to where the trees thinned out. He came to the edge of the woods, and there to the west was the same sight he'd seen the day before, miles to the east: rolling prairie, covered with yellow, waving grass, tinged in spots with bluegrass of some kind.

It would be a beautiful sight, he realized, except for his desperate situation. Here, too, were no signs or roads or power lines—or vapor trails.

Which made no sense at all. Even in the most desolate reaches of the western United States, you would eventually see some high jet planes. Air traffic blanketed all of the country's skies. Yet here . . . nothing. The sheer immensity of the puzzle left him weak. Again he felt about to weep. Or pray. Mark lay down in the shade, put his head on his arms, and slept, emotionally and physically spent.

Understandably, Charles Lewellyn was worried about his father.

"Don't worry, dear," his mother told him, as he left home for school. "He'll turn up soon, I know it. It makes no sense that the police haven't found him yet."

"Mother, if he has amnesia, there's no telling where he may be," said Charles. "He could have hitched a ride anywhere."

"I know, honey. That's why we've notified the FBI, and they're searching all over the country. Then there's the reward we've offered . . ."

"It's hard for me to concentrate, Mother. I feel like I ought to be doing something to help find him."

"No, Charles. Wherever your dad is, I have a feeling he's okay, that he'll manage to take care of himself," Eleanor replied.

Ha. Charles smiled to himself. *Yeah. Sure.*

He looked upon his father as a really good guy, yet one of the most vulnerable people he knew. It was in no way a resentful thought. Charles loved his father, but Charles was no dummy. He categorized Mark Lewellyn as kind, compassionate, humorous—and wimpish.

"He's just not very apt," he had joked to one of his buddies recently. "Dad has all these tools and gizmos around the house, and he buys stuff that's supposed to make life easier, then they break and he never fixes anything. He loves high tech, but he doesn't really need it. He just likes having it."

"My dad," he summarized, "doesn't really do much except watch TV. I'm not sure he ever faced any real crisis in his life. He just kinda lets the world go by."

Charles then felt guilty. His father had been a good dad to him. He remembered the good times they'd shared as the boy grew up. Mark took his son to see Cowboys' games and major league baseball games—then came to watch and root for Charles as the boy excelled as a high-school athlete. Charles, six-two, 190 pounds, was beautifully coordinated. Mark could never quite understand how he'd produced a son who was a natural athlete.

Charles recalled that the only thing his father did well was fish. Mark had explained to his son that Charles's grandmother had insisted that Mark must know how to catch and clean fish. He'd hated it, he told Charles, but "It's the one thing she likes to do, so I still take her fishing. And I still hate it." Oh yeah, Charles remembered his dad could, in fact, throw a baseball well. But he knew that his father was too fat and lazy to have ever played the game.

Charles turned back to his books. No, his mother was wrong. He hoped that whatever happened to his dad was neither life-threatening nor involved any serious stress. Charles was sure Mark could never handle anything that posed serious physical danger. The old man would fall apart.

Almost in a daze, Mark stumbled down through the high-canopied forest until he found the river again. He felt disoriented, his mind in turmoil, aware that it was now late afternoon. That increasingly familiar, sick feeling in his stomach he recognized as hunger pangs returned. Never in his life could Mark remember actually missing a meal. He was ravenous and fell at the edge of the water to drink his fill. Then he ate his last bite of liver. He recalled something from his recent medical checkup:

"Mark, you can get by on very little food every day," Bernie the Doc had assured him. "You need water, and you need to drink lots of it. But you can cut way back on your protein, knock off the sweets, concentrate on fruit and vegetables. Keep your intake below eighteen hundred calories a day."

Bernie's overweight patient had tried. Sort of. But he knew that he rarely dropped below three thousand calories a day. He gained back each pound that he'd lost. And then some.

So Bernie would love seeing him out here, cutting way back on his protein. And on everything else. Fasting, you might say. Or starving to death, you might also say.

Mark began walking south. Oops. He stopped. That was the way the bear had gone. He turned upstream. Thinking of the bear caused him to check his jacket pockets. Yes, he had two hand-sized stones, in case they met again.

Ahead of him the stream curved to the left. Tall trees overhanging the river didn't quite meet over the stream's center, and slanting sunlight still illuminated the surface. But his path was blocked by a solid mass of vegetation.

He knew immediately what the plants were. Mustang grapevines, the most common wild roadside vine in east Texas. Some of his neighbors allowed the grapes to grow up the sides of oak trees or on their fences since the fruit made excellent jelly. Early Texas settlers, Mark remembered, made grape wine from the mustang. He poked inside the leaves and smiled. Lunch is served. Or the fruit course, anyway. But were these *eating* grapes? He'd find out soon enough.

He took a handful to the river and washed them. They were firm, bluish black, and unfortunately less than tasty. The one large seed within was surrounded by soft, tangy pulp. Mark spit out the first one, tried another. The outer skin was bitter, but Mark forced himself to bite into half a dozen grapes, spitting out the large seed, chewing on the pulp and skin, then spitting out the skin. He sat down by the stream, drank from it, and ate more grapes. The good part, he decided, was that the grapes weren't poisonous.

He ate as many as he could force down, felt a little better after drinking more stream water, then began to walk north, upstream. *Keep looking*, he told himself. *There just has to be some civilization here. Someplace.*

Mark's jacket was off, slung over his shoulder, his sweatshirt again plastered to his chest, his face streaming with sweat. His energy was gone, and he had seen nothing promising— except wildlife. The forest was alive with sound and movement.

Every few yards he flushed birds from their underbrush sanctuaries. Their beating wings flushed others. Wild turkeys seemed everywhere, and rabbits bounded across his path constantly. All of the big trees seemed to have their own squirrel families, and he spotted another large black snake, sunning itself on a log stuck in the river. He detoured hastily into the trees for a short distance.

*   *   *

Insect noises hummed around him as the forest grew darker by the minute. Maybe he had a half hour's light left. Then he spotted a large, decaying oak tree fallen toward the river. Its top branches had smashed down against a smaller oak alongside the riverbank. The fallen giant formed a sloping walkway, Mark saw, up which he might walk to where the dead tree merged with the healthy, live one. Otherwise, he'd have a half-mile hike through darkening woods up to the ridge. But there was no drinkable water there.

So this was his refuge tonight . . . after all, how much trouble could he get into while perched high in that tree?

Mark came awake with a start. There had been some noise and movement, maybe below him? He looked but could see nothing but blackness below and above. He reached out with the stick, hit all the branches within reach, and slashed at the closest leafy areas.

Then he heard distant howls of coyotes or wolves. His father, on their few camping trips, had made him listen carefully at night to understand what animal "night music" sounded like. His father had enjoyed those sounds. Mark hadn't.

Actually, he'd always loved animals, and took good care of the mongrel dog he'd been allowed to have as a small boy, and cried for days when it was hit by a car. He could never hunt wild animals, he had convinced himself, because he didn't enjoy killing. The thought repulsed him.

"Mark, you like meat," his father once told him. "Why is it that you don't care for hunting?"

"It's not the same," the boy had responded. "If somebody else kills it, then I can eat it. But I can't stand the thought of hurting or killing animals myself. I don't know why." Mark jerked back to the present.

Growling. Close by. Mark froze, fearing danger, looking hard into the dark branches below. Sounded like a big cat, and he realized that bobcats and mountain lions climb trees, too. Maybe he was surrounded by a whole family of animals who were about to attack? Heart racing, Mark flailed away with his long stick to his right, his left, beating branches below him and overhead. Sweat covered his face, and he began to choke and cough as phlegm caught in his throat.

Then a cramp convulsed his stomach, and he doubled over in pain, forgetting the threat of wild animals. He knew instantly what was wrong. He was getting a diarrhea attack, he had to have a bowel movement. Hell, what a mess. How could he do any such thing up here? He tried to stand up, his right foot on the branch below, and hit his head on the limb above. He sat back down and frantically began to loosen his pants. No choice, the pain was awful. Had to do it. Somehow.

As his bowels erupted into space below, Mark hung on to the branch, sweating and groaning as cramps convulsed— and emptied—his insides. Had to be those damn grapes, he moaned to himself. *Don't mix with liver and pecans* . . . He gasped. He'd never been so painfully miserable in his life. But as he sweated and strained, he knew there was at least one minor satisfaction: He'd quickly be alone in his tree. He heard flapping wings and the snarls of several animals as they fled from his body waste pouring down through the branches. He tried to grin a little. Whatever works.

Mark staggered like a drunk as he forced himself to the river's edge. He was dizzy, his clothing stank. He'd only gotten a few hours' sleep in the tree and was pretty groggy. He fell facedown at the water's edge. He noticed sunlight bathing the water as he dunked his head, drinking and washing his face at the same time. Two nights he'd spent in the wilderness, and still no real sleep, no real food, no hope of getting out of here alive.

The magnitude of it all hit him hard. His comfortable home, his family, all the good things in his life seemed so close and yet gone so fast, in a flash. He had never felt so totally depressed, so lost and without hope. He found himself sitting on the riverbank, sobbing into his hands. He rocked back and forth, tears flooding down his face, moaning. Again, he told God, *Please help me. I don't deserve this. Why is this happening to me? This is an awful way for some-body to die . . . it's just not fair. . . .*

Then he stopped and looked around. He was embarrassed. This was pitiful. If he was going to die, he decided, he could do it more manfully than this.

He washed his face, drank more water, and got up. He began to think more about dying. Yes, someday he was going to die. But he could just see his father and grandfather Henry—both brave men who had fought in and survived two wars. They would be ashamed if they saw him now, like this, blubbering and afraid of everything that moved.

Okay, he decided. *I'm probably going to die. But while I'm alive I'll get my ass in gear and stop sniveling. And I'll give this craziness the best I've got . . .* then he remembered the old joke: I ain't much, but I'm all I've got. And he grinned.

As he lectured himself, Mark took off his jacket, folded it, put it on a small log, then removed his sweatshirt. This level shelf of slate rock would be a safe place to wash and dry his clothes. He had good visibility up and down the bank, in case any big animals came to call. He could, after all, jump back in the damn river if he had to. He removed his pants, decided he'd wash them first, and then . . .

That log was moving . . . the one where he'd laid his jacket.

It was no log.

An alligator. A long one. Up on little stubby legs, headed for the river, carrying his folded jacket on its back. Mark stood rooted in shock, then yelled.

"Wait! Stop! No!"

He raced after the moving jacket just as the big reptile slide from the stone shelf into the river.

Mark, close behind, instantly leaped into the river, clad in shorts and shoes, directly behind the alligator. Water closed over his head.

SIX

Eleanor tried to cope with a new feeling: guilt.

And all because of one little remark made on the phone by her friend, Kathy Foulks. Kathy's husband, Brian, was an investigator in the Dallas District Attorney's Office.

"Brian spends his time tracing people who disappear," Kathy told her. "Some kids are runaways, some people get murdered and their bodies are buried . . . but lots of people leave home because they want to. Eleanor, is there any reason why Mark . . . well, you know, why he'd want to . . . just . . . disappear?"

Oh God, Eleanor thought to herself. How could anybody think such a thing! The idea was repulsive.

"Kathy, that's ridiculous," she snapped. "You know Mark. He's not in debt. He doesn't chase women. He's no drunk or dope fiend. This man has no problems at all . . ."

At least, I don't think *so*, she told herself.

Shortly thereafter, Eleanor had hung up, rattled, irritated with her friend. And wondering.

Had Mark wanted to leave her? Just vanish? It didn't seem possible. Her common sense told her theirs was a sound marriage, devoid of passion after twenty years, but still okay. Not great, but good. They actually seemed to like each other. But had Mark fallen out of love with her? Had she ignored his needs to the point where he contrived to disappear and start a new life? She thought back. No. Couldn't be. They'd had a good marriage, hadn't they?

They'd been compatible from the time they'd first met as

students at Southern Methodist University in Dallas. They were freshmen, both eighteen, good students. No drugs, no booze, busy with classes. They had English and algebra together.

Eleanor was attractive, if not beautiful. Mark wasn't handsome, but presentable and a good dresser. Eleanor was a straight-A student, and she intended to be a success in business. Her family, where entrepreneurship was a tradition, included very successful people, including her maternal grandfather.

William L. Jones had amassed a tidy fortune in "dry goods" stores that later became discount stores, catering to small-town residents. At his death, Jones left 4.8 million dollars in trust for Eleanor and his other two grandchildren. This meant Eleanor would be a money manager for the rest of her life, and she looked forward to building that tidy fortune into something much bigger.

She kept her private business to herself, leaving Mark clueless about his girlfriend's rosy financial future. She observed him closely over a period of time, to see what kind of mate he would be.

Obviously, he had little ambition. He was an average student, lazy about studying. He had no passion for the Vietnam protests of the seventies, watching curiously but never taking part. He registered for the draft, but drew a "high" number and was never called. She found him to be clean and tidy in his personal habits, generous with money, and honest in his dealings with other people. He did not smoke and only drank beer in small quantities.

Within a year of their first date, Eleanor decided that Mark would make her a suitable husband. She was slightly surprised that he had made no overt effort to sleep with her. He was an amorous kisser, but she never encouraged him to go into any further sexual exploration.

Eleanor's parents were not terribly impressed with Mark.

"Eleanor, he is so bland," her mother observed one weekend when the young woman was home from college.

"When I look in his eyes, I see a puppy wagging his tail, hoping for approval. Can this young man *do* anything?"

"Mother! Please. He's just a nice guy. He's uncomplicated," Eleanor protested. "He's pleasant, fun to be with, has a good sense of humor. He's no athlete, but he's interested in new things."

Then Eleanor laughed.

"I can just imagine your reaction if I brought home one of those wild-eyed hippies with me! A flake Mark is not, and I might really want to marry him."

And so it went. The nuptials were happily celebrated as the young couple completed their senior year in college. They honeymooned in Hot Springs, Arkansas, where Mark found out that Eleanor was not a virgin and Eleanor found out that Mark was not the world's greatest lover. They admired beautiful Arkansas scenery, ate delicious food and found they were comfortable together. Everything considered, their union was off to a good start, in Eleanor's view at least.

She also saw to it that Mark was offered a clerk's job at one of her grandfather's stores in Mesquite, Texas, just east of Dallas. She had already secured herself a position in a securities brokerage house in nearby Richardson. They moved into a small rented home in Mesquite, and in no time, it seemed, Eleanor was pregnant. It was not accidental. She decided, unlike many other young women at the time, to have her family early, so that she could concentrate later on her business career.

She thought she probably should have talked this over with Mark beforehand, but he seemed delighted with her pregnancy, if not surprised. The arrival of their son, a healthy Charles Lewellyn, was a difficult birth. Eleanor was in labor for nine hours, and she decided then in favor of a small family.

"Tie my tubes," she instructed her doctor at the end of the delivery, and it was done. She waited for several years to mention this to Mark, and he offered no particular objections. Certainly his son was all any father could hope for. Charles was big, healthy, and attractive. Eleanor had by this time explained to Mark that her trust fund meant they had no serious money problems, and so it was natural for Eleanor to manage the family's finances. She encouraged Mark to keep his own salary apart from hers, open his own checking account, and she would handle the family's basic living expenses.

With his first bonus, Mark bought a new Volvo station wagon, loaded with extras. Eleanor was pleased to cosign Mark's bank loan, at her bank. Within a year he was able to afford a fine Rolex wristwatch.

The years passed uneventfully, Eleanor remembered, and good things happened. She moved on to a better job as sales rep for a major pharmaceutical company, did well, and by the time she was thirty-five earned a salary and bonuses in six figures.

Mark moved on to a local firm specializing in "data capture." This meant he spent his work days at the console of a Macintosh, inputting raw data of all kinds. It was a sitting-down, all-day kind of job, so he got little exercise. Best of all, he could work at home.

A wonderful break came their way when Eleanor's parents, needing less space, decided at last to move away from their expensive, large home on Lake Ray Hubbard, east of Dallas, and into an apartment in the city. They invited Eleanor and Mark to occupy the big, four-bedroom lakefront home, since Eleanor would eventually inherit the house anyway. They had lived there now for eight years, their son attending nearby schools. It was in a growing, upper-middle-income neighborhood, and Mark seemed happy to have his own workshop, beyond the garage. He spent little time there, Eleanor realized, but was very proud of his power tools and other electronic devices.

This was, in fact, a bone of contention between them. Mark had the workshop air-conditioned. He put in a small darkroom in one corner, after he bought a costly Nikon, and explained that he wanted to experiment with developing his own black-and-white photos. At first Eleanor had little patience with this, and other expenditures on Mark's gadgets, but then took stock of what was important and what was not.

She consulted her bank balance and decided this was a small price to pay for a husband who, seemingly, had no real needs outside the home. He showed no interest in chasing other women. He had some buddies with whom he played golf every week or two. Mark told Eleanor he needed new clubs to help him break ninety, she remembered. And every day he watched sports on television and lived as quiet a life as a man reasonably could. Eleanor subsequently stopped objecting when Mark's latest electronic marvel appeared. She had no comment, for example, when he installed a wireless room-to-room intercom system, with a three-channel setup in their bedrooms, dining area, living room, and kitchen, with plug-in for the garage and workshop as well. With their son off in school, though, it did seem a bit much. The house was too often empty.

Mark also seemed genuinely pleased at Eleanor's steady rise in her company's management ranks. She told him that within a few years she would, in fact, be qualified to run the entire national operation—assuming she didn't fall prey to gender discrimination. She did not intend to let that happen, and worked very hard to ensure that her work was not merely excellent but demonstrably superior to everyone else's. *You don't succeed as a mediocrity*, she assured herself.

So, no, there was nothing in the past Eleanor could think of that would cause Mark to disappear by choice—even if such a thing could have happened. With that, Eleanor's anxiety eased. She had no reason to feel guilty.

She glanced at her watch. *Better go to the office for a while today*, she thought.

Life, after all, had to go on.

The speed with which Mark jumped into the river, chasing his alligator-borne jacket, was exceeded only by the speed with which he got out.

It took him only a few seconds to flail out with his stick and mash his jacket underwater, the alligator having vanished. He grabbed the jacket, lunged for shore, expecting that any second giant jaws would close on his arms or legs.

Mark fell on the stone shelf and looked around quickly to see if the monster had any buddies. Only a pair of rabbits looked at him from the embankment above.

He rocked back and forth on his knees, trying to stop shaking, lecturing to himself. *Mark The Idiot! You gotta think about what you're doing!* He shook his head. How could anybody possibly not *see* a world-class alligator right next to him? He clearly was not ready for prime time in the forest.

An hour's walk upstream brought him to another place where the flood had dropped trees into—and across—the river. He decided to cross to the east side, then go up to the prairie again for another try at spotting a road, sign, or other evidence of people. Increasingly, it seemed futile.

Balancing himself with his stick, he managed to cross on the downed trees without falling in the river again. He walked slowly into the rising sun, through a soft carpet of leaves, paying special attention to each step and every brush pile where something might wait to surprise him.

Then he came to a sunlit wall of vegetation where grapevines rose into the trees and small bushes blocked his path. The game trail forked and led both ways. He mentally tossed a coin and took the left fork. It led him along the vegetation, then seemed to go directly *through* the mass of leaves and branches.

Should he enter this dark portal? Was it where black bears and mountain lions holed up? He took a firm grip on his walking stick and decided it was the quickest way on the route where he wanted to go.

He stooped slightly and went carefully into the darkened passageway. There was plenty of elbow room if not much head room. He kept snagging his hair in low-hanging vines and branches and had to walk in a crouch.

Mark was about to turn back when he saw space and light

ahead of him. He pushed on and a moment later emerged
into a clearing. The place was beautiful. A small stream ran
along the base of a high rock wall. He saw pecan trees. Ponds
of fresh water. The full charm of the place came to Mark
slowly as he looked around at the lights and shadows of a
lovely glade. The rock wall was about twenty feet high,
topped by a thick mass of wet, glistening vegetation. Climbing grapevines partly covered the rock formation.

This was surely the loveliest forested spot Mark had ever
seen. There was no breeze to speak of, but the air was cool.
The overall effect was restful, and he suddenly decided this
was an ideal place to catch his breath, drink some water, and
take a short nap. He couldn't have had more than three or
four hours' sleep in the past two nights, and rest was what
he needed most.

He walked along the stream at the base of the wall, watching carefully for rotted logs or rocks which might well conceal cousins of that water moccasin he'd seen on day one.
The water was clear and fresh, and he enjoyed a long drink.

But where to take a safe nap? Like all of the canopied
forest, these trees didn't have any low-hanging limbs at all.
Then he studied the rock wall. It was the source of some of
the stream's water. Small rivulets coursed down the sides
of the wall every few yards, coming from springs in or behind the rock. All along the wall, water dripped into the
stream.

The rock face itself was horizontally rounded, in folds.
Looking up, Mark saw that about twelve feet above the forest
floor was a horizontal line along part of the wall—a kind of
ledge, although he could not tell how wide. Few details were
visible since dozens of thick, leafy vines hung down. He
needed some kind of cover or concealment. That ledge might
be a place where he could sleep. If he could get up there.

He pulled hard on one of the vines. It came straggling
down from its leafy connection high above him. He was
covered in leaves and vines for a moment until he shrugged
his way out of it all.

The next vine was stronger. He put his full weight on it,

and the vine sagged but held firm. He placed one foot on the wall face and began to pull himself up. After two steps up the rock wall, he fell back, irritated with himself. It was hell to be this weak. He hated it. As a kid he would have scrambled up there in nothing flat. *It's not that far up there,* he told himself. Mark took a deep breath and tried again.

This time he got four steps up the side of the stone wall before his foot slipped, and he slammed against the stone. But he held on, cursing and sweating. He swung himself around, facing the wall, and began to climb, hand over hand. His head reached the level of the ledge. Panting aloud now, angry, damned if he was going to drop to the ground. Another major heave, and he got one knee over the ledge, pulled himself up by the vine, rolled over on the rock ledge, and had a choking fit, coughing and spitting up phlegm, his face dripping with sweat and dirt. His hands were scratched and raw, but he'd made it.

He saw that he was in a strange little shelter. The grapevines, over many years, had attached themselves to vertical cracks in the stone wall, found drooping tree branches just above the rocks, and continued their climb up into their dense upper branches.

It was such a secure spot that he was suspicious. With his stick Mark began carefully sweeping back and forth under the rocky overhang area. There were no snakes—nothing but dirt, dead leaves, and small animal droppings. This seemed a natural refuge for a mountain lion, Mark thought, until he saw the extremities of the ledge. Both ends narrowed to nothing, and there was no place above him where large animals could get on the ledge, except the ever-present squirrels. Snakes could always reach this spot, and he again inspected the length of the ledge—some fifteen feet of it—but found nothing threatening.

He sat down beneath the rock overhang, cracked the few pecans remaining in his jacket with his pocket rocks, then folded the jacket for a pillow. He was so dizzy and exhausted, he hardly remembered stretching out.

*   *   *

As Mark slept, he turned over and flung out his right hand, palm up. In this hand a large bird, above him, made a sizable deposit.

Mark's eyes jerked open as warm poop plopped into his open palm. He sat up in disbelief, shaking the stuff out onto the ledge. Was he going to spend the remainder of his obviously short life as a target for every creature who came near him?

He rubbed his hands against the nearest stone surface, then cleaned them as best he could on his pants. Another little mess wouldn't make much difference now. He started to lie back down again, then thought better of it. Might be best to see if he could make some use of the rest of the day. He saw through the vines that the sun now slanted down at the edge of the glade at a sharp angle. Must be midafternoon or later. He had slept three hours or more.

Mark parted the vines and tossed his stick down to the ground below, then looked up at the glade. Half a dozen deer were drinking from the stream, and grazing on short grass.

Then, suddenly, they wheeled and shot across the glade, into the same game-trail "tunnel" that had brought Mark to the area. Moments later, a lithe, yellowish animal—a mountain lion, Mark decided—eased into the glade's shadowy edge and stood motionless. It padded to the stream, drank, looked around, listening, poised to move. Then it trotted quickly from the glade, tracking the deer.

Mark found himself holding his breath. Thank God he'd been hidden. It hadn't taken more than three minutes for the hunter and hunted to pass before him, and it focused his thinking.

This could not be anywhere close to civilization. This could not be a game preserve or an Indian reservation either. There were mountain lions only in west Texas now, and with all these familiar trees about him, Mark knew this was not west Texas.

Looking more closely at the trees, he saw pecans, plenty

of hickories and oaks, also the fast-growing cottonwoods. But no pines at all. It was the same kind of forest he'd known all his life.

Yet these animal species—bear, buffalo, the big cats—could be found now in city zoos or remote parts of western Texas, nowhere close to Dallas. He shook his head in frustration. It was maddening. How could he possibly have been transported to this wilderness from his home? Even if he'd had some kind of amnesia, he could think of no practical way he could have wandered or found his way to this incredible virgin forest.

Mark knew himself to be a fairly logical man. He had no illusions about how he appeared to others. He rather enjoyed the image of a soft and laid-back househusband . . . mainly because he was used to it, and it was so easy not to change. But he also wasn't stupid. There had to be an explanation for all this, and he knew that eventually he'd find it.

For now, well . . . he swung his legs over the edge of the stone shelf, then began lowering himself to the ground by the grapevine that earlier had proved strong enough to hold him. He washed his hands in the small stream. He'd always been fastidious about his hands. One of his small extravagances was the manicure he had once a month. Now his nails were ragged and filthy, with nicks and cuts up and down his bare arms. He'd hate for anybody to see him. . . .

Then he remembered: His job. This was what, Tuesday? Yes, and they would have missed him by now at the job. He checked in each morning by phone to verify with his supervisor, Bob Shamburger, what he'd be inputting that day.

A two-day absence on anyone's part was serious, and he hoped he wouldn't be in too much trouble for failing to check in. But then, of course, Eleanor would have been in touch with them by now. She'd explain everything.

He sat down by the stream in a sudden fit of melancholy. His wife, his son, his mother . . . they must wonder what had happened to him and be worried sick. They must have started a search by now. Eleanor would certainly spend whatever money it took to get private investigators, as well as the police, to look everywhere for him. *Meanwhile, get busy,* he reminded himself.

He looked more closely at the stream, to check it for fish. He walked along its entire length from where it came into the glade at the upper end, through an opening in the wall of vegetation, to the point where it disappeared from view at the downhill side of the large enclosure. In the late afternoon, Mark had less light by which to examine details, but it was clear that the stream offered two promising fishing holes. They were formed by rocks falling from the nearby wall in some past age, erosion by high waters in a spring flood, and fallen trees, whose exposed roots had opened large holes next to the streambed.

Each such pond, Mark figured, had to be five or six feet deep. One of them had a tiny shaft of sunlight on its surface. He knelt slightly away from the edge of the pool and watched the water circulate, looking for signs of life. He carefully removed the tiny remaining chunk of liver from his pocket, pinched off a piece, and tossed it onto the surface of the pond. A moment later there was a swirl of water, and the meat disappeared.

He sat as motionless as he could for some minutes, and deep within the pool he thought he saw drifting, shadowy shapes. Small fish, it appeared, maybe one- or two-pounders, but they'd be a welcome addition to his starvation diet if he could catch one.

That might be easier said than done. He had no hooks, no net . . . but, looking at his shoes, he realized that he did have a line of sorts.

He took off his left shoe and removed the shoelace. It was more than three feet long. He removed the last tiny piece of meat from his stained, now smelly undershirt, and carefully washed the liver in the edge of the stream, away from the pool where he intended to fish.

Mark found that the metal tip of the shoelace wouldn't punch through the meat. He picked up a short, sharp stick nearby, and used that for a punch. He threaded the shoelace through the small hole and tied a knot around the meat to hold it securely. Wrapping the other end around his right index finger, he tossed the meat out onto the surface of the pond and watched it sink slowly into the water.

Minutes passed. He felt sure the bait had reached bottom. He tugged at the bait gently, hoping to attract some attention. Again, nothing. Well, he'd have to toss it into another part of the pond, and he began to slowly pull in the bait.

Blinding pain shot up his right arm.

His index finger was nearly pulled from its socket as Mark was yanked headfirst into the pond by an incredibly vicious jerk on the shoelace. He went down into the water, choking, trying desperately to get the string off his finger.

SEVEN

"Claire, we're doing everything possible to find Mark," Eleanor wearily told her mother-in-law, "but the police haven't turned up a thing. It's only been two days, though, and there's a good chance somebody will spot him pretty quickly now."

"I don't understand," replied Mark's mother, who had been calling every few hours from Fort Worth. "How can somebody just disappear like this? It's been in the papers, on TV, everything, somebody must have seen him. You think he's been kidnapped?"

"No, Claire, I don't. We'd have been contacted by now."

"Well, his sister is out of her mind with worry, and I don't see why we don't offer a bigger reward. Money talks, you know. Besides, this Saturday was when Mark was going to take me fishing out on that lake of yours. I've been looking forward to it."

"You could be right about the reward. I'll see if his company will put up some money. But something else, Claire. Is it possible that Mark is wandering around with amnesia and might go someplace . . . a place he liked as a boy? Maybe a ballpark, or lake. . . . ?"

"No, he wasn't into sports or anything. He did like to go fishing with his daddy and me. Although Mark liked to wander in the woods more than fish."

"So there wasn't anyplace he wanted to go as a kid?"

"No, he stayed indoors mostly after school and watched TV. There was a big kid in the neighborhood then—a bully—who chased Mark a lot, so I kept him home. Made his daddy furious . . . but you can't change human nature, can you? Mark just never was very . . . um . . . bold? You know what I mean?"

"Yes," Eleanor said. "I know."

When Mark's free hand touched the pond's muddy bottom, he got his feet under him and pushed up, getting his head above water. He gasped for air, held the vibrating shoelace with both hands, waves of pain moving up his right arm with each jerk on the line.

Racing back and forth, the angry fish whipsawed the shoelace with increasing frenzy. Mark wrapped his left hand around the line to ease the pressure on his damaged right forefinger, then stumbled backward . . . scrambling up out of the pond, slipping and sliding as the fish hit the end of the short line with massive force. Then it broke water and Mark instantly fell backward, dragging the catfish up out of the pond and onto the grass bank.

Mark couldn't believe the size. Huge. Like a small shark. More than two feet long. Twenty pounds, anyway. He grabbed the closest stone he could get with his left hand, jumped on the fish, and pounded its head. He beat it until it lay still. Mark stopped, gulping air, and fell over on his side to stare at the long black body. His finger still throbbed terribly, but he marveled at the fish's size. If only his mother could see this whopper. She'd never hooked anything this big or tough.

Mark sat down to get his breath and puzzled over finding this big a fish in such a small pond. It must have been trapped when young, then grew too big to get through the rocky shallows downstream.

Anyway, he finally had something more to eat . . . but nothing to start a fire with . . . and nothing sharp to skin the thing. Unless . . . sure, stones. He rummaged among the small rocks in the shallow part of the creek. None looked like flint. He picked up a heavy stone, smashed it on another, and went through the flakes to find sharp edges.

He attacked the underbelly of the catfish with his sharpest stone edge, and after a while made a small rip . . . enough to tear the flesh apart, open the belly, and pull his shoelace from the fish's mouth. He carefully replaced his shoe. First things first.

Sunlight was now sloping into the glade at a lower angle. He'd have to hurry to get the fish skinned, cleaned, and ready to eat. He began cutting and chopping with all his strength, trying first one stone chip, then another. They only cut when he applied all his strength. Finally, he'd chopped out two big chunks of meat. Now, maybe he had time to start a fire . . . or at least try to.

He concentrated on remembering that one Boy Scout trip in his youth, and how the scoutmaster had finally shown the fathers and kids to use twine and materials in the woods to start a fire with bow and friction. He rummaged around in the underbrush.

Mark first found an oak branch that hadn't rotted—a short straight piece of limb, three inches in diameter, very dry. Using stone chips, he gouged a shallow depression in the dry branch, and another notch in a hand-sized wood chunk. Next, he broke off a two-foot length of green limb, half an inch in diameter, and limber. He removed the dry lace from his right shoe, tied one end to the end of the branch, bent it slightly, and tied the string to the other end, making a small bow.

Down on his knees, Mark took one twist in the bow's line around the small straight piece of wood, and fitted the sharp end into the large branch below and the hardwood on top. He began to work the bow back and forth, in a sawing motion, keeping one knee on the bottom branch, to hold it steady.

At first, the bow hardly moved. He lightened the downward pressure of his hand, and the small peg began to rotate in the depression he'd made.

Over the next few minutes, with practice, he generated a rapid drilling motion with the vertical peg, and friction caused it to start digging into the softer wood of the bottom branch.

Soon Mark saw smoke as friction generated a burning smell that both surprised and delighted him. Almost there. He stopped long enough to pile dried leaves and bits of wood around the friction hole, to catch fire at the proper time. Then he resumed the sawing motion, his right arm growing tired from the need to keep the peg spinning rapidly.

Smoke. Mark could hardly believe it. Real smoke, a thin spiral of it, drifted into his eyes and nostrils. Fantastic. He sawed faster . . . saw a tiny red spark, but it faded. He found sweat running off his nose but he couldn't stop. Almost there . . .

The shoelace snapped.

Exhausted and angry, Mark fell on his side. Friction of the lace against the wooden peg had worn it through. Tying it back in a knot, he realized, would prevent a smooth, sawing motion. He cursed his ineptness. How the hell had the Indians done this, anyway? Then it came to him. He knew very well how: with tough strips of animal hide, sliced thin. The kind you could only get with a knife or some kind of cutting edge. Even if he killed an animal, how could he cut up a hide with these dull soft rocks? No way.

Looking at his fresh catfish meal, Mark sighed. No entrée choices tonight. He took a bite. Tough, chewy. Luckily, he had good teeth. He forced himself to swallow, eat more. Had to have something in his belly to stay alive. He paused. Was it worth it, to live like this, out here . . . alone, defenseless? He shook his head in despair. He'd lost his appetite. Whatever he did seemed futile. Maybe death wasn't that bad an option, after all. Mark climbed wearily up to his sheltered ledge and stretched out, his eyes moist, his strength gone. Maybe he'd stay right here . . . until death, in some form, came for him.

Exhausted in mind and body, Mark slept until daylight caused his eyes to blink open. When he remembered where he was, he didn't want to wake up. Depression overwhelmed him as he tried to think of what he might do to find civilization again.

He couldn't shake the knowledge that this forest wasn't that foreign to him. He knew every tree, most bushes, the river. Only the wild animals were new to him. It was as though this had been his home before but he'd been reintroduced to it in an earlier time . . . no, he had to stop thinking like that. Ridiculous.

His face rested on his right arm, and he watched as daylight began dimly to etch outlines of trees beyond his vine barrier. Birds flew across his line of vision. Then Mark's eyes widened, he stopped breathing, and tried not to cry out. This black outline . . . a great, rounded silhouette rising up before him, up above the level of his ledge . . . becoming humanlike.

It was a man . . . almost naked . . . swinging up his vines, looking for him. Mark watched in horror, his left arm finding his long stick. He raised it, quivering above him, swinging it with all his strength.

The whack of wood against flesh and bone shattered the glade's stillness. And then a human cry as the man fell away.

Looking down from his ledge, Mark could make out the body—it was one of those Indians—draped across the narrow creek. He saw blood on the head. The man didn't move. Grabbing jacket and stick, Mark swung down the vines, bent over the prone figure, and felt the man's wrist. There was a pulse. Thank God. He hadn't killed him, but the head wound looked bad. Mark cupped his hand and splashed creek water on the man's open wound. He grabbed a handful of leaves, washed them in the creek, laid them on the open wound. Might stop the bleeding.

Mark's mind raced. Those other Indians would come looking for this man. If they found Mark there, he'd die just like that other man they'd killed. Panic consumed him, but he forced himself to stop and think. He made sure he had rocks and his remaining raw fish stuffed in the jacket pockets. Then he grabbed his stick and jacket and hurried out of the game trail tunnel. It didn't matter which direction. Had to get out of this place. His mind replayed that gruesome sight he'd seen . . . the hatchet smashing open the back of that Indian's skull . . . it could happen to him minutes from now if he didn't escape and keep running. Crouching low, he flew through the vegetation tunnel and raced up the wooded slope toward the open prairie. He was winded immediately but didn't stop running until he was well out onto the prairie, the rising sun in his face.

He collapsed into the waist-high grass, gasping for breath, hoping no one had seen him from the edge of the forest. Moments later he had a terrible thought and poked his head up to look back. Oh, hell.

Just as he'd feared: His race through the grass had spread it apart and tamped it down. His path was clearly visible. Those Indians would have no trouble at all tracking him down with that kind of trail to follow. Mark put his head in his hands. He was going to die anyhow. Just a matter of when.

EIGHT

At midmorning the hunting party Leader found his missing companion.

He was awake and bathing his head in creek water when the other hunters entered the glade. He removed leaves stuck to his head, trying to understand how they'd gotten there.

"I found him," the hunter told the Leader. "He struck me with a weapon. I fell." The man tried to stand, and it was clear that one ankle was hurt. He then explained in detail what happened, including the wet leaves he'd found on his head which stopped his bleeding.

The Leader asked no questions since he did not wish to embarrass his hunter. The strange manlike thing was gone. If they had the time, he knew, they could track it down. But with the sun well up, they needed to be about their business to return to their families with meat and skins before nightfall.

It was enough that they had found the creature, had done combat with it, had had one man injured. But those leaves . . . had the thing tried to help his hunter? Was it human after all? This would provide the Elders with enough conversation to last a long time.

As Mark ran, jogged, and walked away from the forest, he kept telling himself he'd done the right thing. He knew those Indians could find him and trap him in the forest. They could be invisible there. He stood out like a white elephant.

So his one chance was the prairie, due east—since that

was the only direction wide-open to him. At least he could see his would-be killers as they approached. Given his head start, by moving constantly he might have a slim chance to escape.

His rapid walking and trotting was even more tiring than the stress test he'd taken a year ago, when Bernie the Doc got him on that damn treadmill. Mark had been hooked up to machines that showed his body reactions to exercise, minute by minute.

Bernie had written on a pad for nearly fifteen minutes as Mark walked the treadmill. It speeded up, inclined, up to fifteen degrees, left him dripping with sweat, finally forced him to call a halt, exhausted. Bernie smiled thinly, Mark remembered.

"Mark, that's not bad. Your signs are okay. If you'll do that every couple of days, it'll help you lose some weight." Mark saw he was kidding. Or was he?

"Bernie, that was awful. My heart feels like it's out of control. This can't be good for me, can it?"

Bernie tried not to laugh outright. Mark was a friend as well as a patient. *How do I convince this clown that his life might depend on turning off the TV and getting off his ass?* he thought.

"Mark, seriously, if you'll exercise like this three times a week, it'll help you. You don't have to kill yourself. Just do it regularly. I'll set up a routine for you. There's that health club at the shopping center you can join. Doesn't cost much. It'll only take three or four hours a week to sweat some. Why not give it a try?"

"Try" is what he was doing right now, Mark thought. Trying to stay alive. Trying to keep ahead of those crazy killers back there. So far he'd seen no sign of them. But they might know how to track him without his knowing it. They were the toughest little men he'd ever seen. That man he'd struck this morning was all bone and muscle. Maybe five-six, barely a hundred pounds in weight, yet so formidable that Mark shuddered when he thought of how helpless he would be in a physical contest with those people.

He hurried through the tall, dry grass, worried that he couldn't see where his feet were falling. There must be snakes out here, maybe other creatures, but he had to keep moving although his breath came in gasps. His jacket was tied around his waist, his sweatshirt already soaked even though the sun had barely risen.

More than anything, Mark wanted to sit down and rest. Already he was thirsty. Why hadn't he filled up with cool creek water before he'd fled? Dumb. As usual, he wasn't thinking ahead.

He knew he must not stop, though, since by now the Indians would have found their injured man. Lord, he hoped the man wasn't hurt bad. Or worse, dead. He slowed for a moment to get his breath. If he wasn't going to collapse, he must set himself a pace he could maintain, not run blindly until he passed out. Mark saw the grass getting taller around him, almost at eye level.

Soon it was over his head and within minutes he was pushing through tall stems that towered a foot or more above him. He could only walk directly toward the morning sun to know he was going east. It was frightening not being able to see ahead of him, yet he had to go forward, not back.

He'd had no chance to eat anything this morning. He slowed, pulled out his dirty, stained packet, and took a few careful bites of fish. It tasted awful, but it was all he had, so he finished the remaining chunk. The slight moisture in it helped to keep his growing thirst down a bit.

Mark knew he had covered at least three miles or more. And pushed himself to his physical limit, wanting to put as much distance between himself and his pursuers as possible early in the day. They could stay on his trail all day long, he thought, if they wanted to really kill him.

He began to fear he couldn't last until day's end. His face was constantly draining sweat, and he had no head covering. He knew his body would soon be out of salt. He had to smile, remembering how Bernie the Doc had warned him about his salt intake.

"This stuff just isn't good for you, Mark. I've eaten with you, and I've seen how much you use that saltshaker. If you were a manual laborer, sweating all the time, you'd need a lot of salt. But most of us use too much for our bodies to handle. It can kill you if you overdo it," Bernie had warned him. He wished now Bernie had told him what do to when he ran completely *out* of salt. Would he weaken suddenly, collapse? And this tall grass seemed to be closing over him, trapping him. He seemed to choke, trying to get air in his lungs. His anxiety level grew until, he suddenly realized, he wanted to scream and throw himself on the ground. He stopped, dropped to one knee.

He told himself it was only grass around him. He wouldn't suffocate with air above him. He knew this was pure self-pity, and he had to stop feeling sorry for himself. He shrugged, stood up, began to walk a little faster, with more determination. Regardless of what happened, he had to keep moving forward.

Within ten minutes or so he found the grass getting shorter. It was down now almost to the top of his head. Before he showed his head above the grass, he had to rest. His body, under sweatshirt and pants, was wet, all the way down to his ankles. He simply had to sit down awhile. He dropped to the ground, swinging his stick in a wide arc to scare off anything that might be at his feet.

Then he lay down, his jacket under his head. Sleep came immediately.

Mark forced himself awake, remembering where he was but having no idea how long he'd slept. The sun was higher, almost midday.

Looking back at the trail behind him, he could see which direction he'd come from. He got up and began walking toward what he assumed was east. He wondered why his pursuers hadn't caught him. He thought of all the possible reasons why they might not want to kill him. It didn't help much. He still feared they were coming along his trail, getting closer.

Within a few minutes the grass was shorter, and he went up a gentle incline. Then he saw above the grass a pair of dark shapes.

They materialized into buffalo, grazing quietly less than a hundred yards in front of him. As he moved forward more carefully, he saw there were other buffalo beyond them. And on both sides of him. Then an awful thought hit and he looked behind him. Oh great.

He was standing in the middle of a buffalo herd, surrounded by dozens of the great, shaggy animals. They were spread out, heads down, grazing, the tops of their bodies visible above waist-high grass.

Except for the big bull of the herd.

Even Mark could see he was the male, by his size and big horns. Standing motionless, head up, muzzle thrust forward, the leader of the herd pawed the ground with his right foot. . . .

Staring at Mark.

The bull began moving deliberately toward the shocked man, viewing Mark as an enemy to be eliminated.

NINE

The rocks in Mark's pocket felt useless, his walking stick puny in his hand. His mind groped for a way out . . . maybe he could jump aside when the buffalo charged . . . then he remembered something and slowly turned his head. Yes, there it was to his right rear—a small tree he'd noticed moments before he'd seen all the buffalo. But he winced. The distance might be too much. Sixty, seventy yards away. Low branches, though. He'd never be able to outrun the giant animal that far, but if he could just dodge one time, he might have a shot.

Mark gathered himself, took a deep breath and got ready to run for his life. At that moment, there was a snorting noise off to his left. The bull buffalo wheeled in an instant, looked, then ran off at full speed. It appeared that some of his females had run into a disturbance, and the male had to find out what it was.

The next instant, Mark was running hard for the small tree. He looked back once and slowed down when he found the buffalo wasn't hot on his heels, but had in fact disappeared in the tall grass behind him. Mark got to the tree, hauled himself up onto the lower branches, and sat, breathing hard, wondering what other disaster could confront him today. The day was young. Not even noon yet.

There was little foliage in the low tree where Mark took refuge. But it was thick with limbs, so he had no trouble climbing up twenty feet, once his pulse stopped racing. From

that point he could see for at least a mile. He twisted around
back to the west, where he'd come from that morning. *Good,
no sign of any pursuers. God, what a relief.*

To the east, waving yellow grass stretched to the horizon,
broken by one faint line of green. More trees, hopefully con-
cealing another creek. But tonight, if he could muster the
strength to go that far, he knew his thirst would be painful.
His only food now was the handful of nuts in his pants
pocket. He counted them: seven pecans for the rest of the
day. Slim rations.

His other major problem was direction. The sun was overhead. It would not be easy down in the tall grass to know
whether he was going east or had veered off in another direction. He'd need to stop on each rise of ground, make sure
he had a distant reference point to guide him. Easy to get
lost in this immense sea of grass.

Mark was glad to rest while the buffalo grazed nearby.
They paid him no attention now that he was not conspicuous,
and the giant male boss of the herd moved restlessly in the
distance. Buffalo calves were almost invisible as they followed their mothers about, so tall was the grass. The treed
man found a firm position astride twin branches, leaned back
against the trunk of the tree, and closed his eyes.

Eleanor would never believe he could sleep in trees and
on stone ledges, after all the time they spent last year picking
out expensive new mattresses for their twin beds.

"Mark you know you like a softer mattress than this,"
she'd instructed him as they each stretched out on the show-
room model. "This one's too hard for you." As usual,
Eleanor was right. The softer mattress was more to Mark's
taste. One of the reasons he had never taken his son camping
much was that he hated to sleep on the ground, even on an
air mattress, and was cranky when he did not get a good
night's sleep. As he thought about his bed at home, Mark
wondered if he would ever enjoy such comfort again. He
dozed.

*   *   *

Mark was almost ready to drop.

His clothes were plastered wet against his body, and the afternoon shadows were lengthening. He no longer worried about the killer Indians chasing him. Buffalo still grazed off in the distance but didn't threaten him.

It was the awful endlessness of that huge prairie that formed his horizon in all directions . . . there was no limit to it. He still headed east, the sun now at his back. He had no idea where he was going, no objective. There was no sign of any civilization anywhere. Even in the one wooded glade where he'd found a tiny trickle of water in a nearly dry streambed, there was no sign of man. Or woman. No candy wrappers. No beer cans. No empty plastic bottles. It was like this was truly virgin country . . . unsettled. . . .

He stopped walking. Stood there, staring at nothing. He didn't want to think about the possibility, but he must. It was mind-numbing. But, face it: no roads, no power lines, or vapor trails. No trace whatever of civilization . . . and all these animals . . . Indians in a primitive state with odd, short spears.

Mark sank to his knees, holding his head. It just *couldn't* be that . . . could it? He was sure his thinking was messed up.

Did that explosion yank him away from his own time, his own century . . . into some earlier time? *Oh God. This is preposterous*, he thought. He had to stop thinking like this . . . had to think about today only. He needed water, a safe place for the night. He got up quickly. There'd be wolves out here after dark, and he knew he wouldn't survive a night alone on the prairie. Had to keep moving.

Mark leaned on his stick and knew he had a chance. There, less than a half mile distant, was the tree line he'd been approaching all afternoon. He knew he could make it. Had to: If there was no water in there, he might not see another dawn. Out where he was, he was a dead duck.

He looked up at the half dozen buzzards that had circled

him much of the afternoon. "Sorry, boys," he said aloud. "Not today."

"Maybe," he added grimly, "tomorrow."

Twenty minutes later, Mark hurried into the line of woods, through trees and low underbrush, trying to move in a straight line as the light grew dim. He could barely see the other side of it.

There was a glint of light off water. Within a minute, Mark was facedown at a small creek, barely ten feet wide, drinking too fast, choking it down.

He washed his hands and face and lay back on the grass of a sloping bank. His mind sounded a small alarm, but for a minute he couldn't figure out what it was. Then he heard grunting, moving bodies.

Quickly on his feet, he saw the first members of a buffalo herd as they moved toward him through the grass at a trot. It dawned on him: This was their watering hole. They must come here at dusk to drink. The thin forest wasn't more than two hundred yards wide, paralleling the little creek. He hurried upstream in the lengthening shadows. Within minutes, he could see there would be at least a hundred of the big beasts milling around.

Underbrush scratched his hands and clothing, but he kept forcing himself to the north for a full ten minutes before he stopped. There was a small pool in the stream caused by the uprooting of an old tree that had fallen across the creek, partly damming it at that point. Then he spotted an oak with branches low enough for him to climb. Even better, he found, was the big pecan tree alongside. Instantly, he was on his knees searching for nuts. He filled his pockets immediately, and decided to crack some with his stones before he "retired" to his tree for the long night.

Mark could barely see the branches above him as he finally began his slow and tiresome climb up into the tree. And for a place seemingly uninhabited by day, he found his thin grove of trees a busy, noisy place at night.

Before it was fully dark, he heard a virtual orchestra of

howls and barks by coyotes or wolves—or both. He still could not tell the difference. He heard a rustling movement below him, and in the distance he heard the snapping and growling of two animals fighting over something. Distantly, he could also hear the buffalo herd as it moved around. Insects provided a steady cacophony of background noise as Mark tried to find some position on a group of limbs where he could sleep without falling.

He knew that in the morning, if he survived the night, he must eat—even if it meant killing an animal to do it. That made him a little sick. He didn't like the idea of killing a rabbit or a squirrel, but if there were no fish in that stream, he would have no choice. It kept coming down to one thing: survival. *Well, of course*, he told himself, *nobody wants to die.* But what could he do out in this empty, hostile wilderness to protect himself and keep going . . . but going where? What good is survival if your own world is gone, totally lost to you, and there's no hope of return?

That word "survival" triggered something far in his past . . . a conversation he'd had with his father when Mark was about fifteen. Yes, he remembered it now . . . there'd been a big school discussion about World War II. Mark's dad, John Lewellyn, had been a fighter pilot—an ace—in Europe. He'd been shot down, taken prisoner, his knee badly hurt.

Yet Mark remembered the pride he'd felt in telling the class how his father later escaped from the German prison camp and made his way through hostile, enemy-held territory to the Swiss border, more than eighty miles, with a bum knee, no food, and only a pocketknife, living like an animal of the forest.

He also remembered clearly his father's simple explanation of what drove him constantly, made him a survivor in the face of terrible odds and constant pain.

"Mark," he'd told his son, "what I learned from that was kind of simple. Don't give up if you've got a problem. Don't ever, *ever* give up. Simply as a matter of pride."

Yeah, sure . . . pride. Mark half smiled as he closed his

eyes, head against the tree trunk. Did *he* have any pride, like his father? Good question. He doubted it. He doubted himself, felt empty inside. He was almost helpless. What good would pride do here, scratching for food, expecting to die every day? And the worst indignity of all . . . having to sleep in a goddamn tree. . . .

TEN

By dawn, Mark was so foul-tempered and distraught that he was ready to do battle with any animal in the forest.

He would especially love to throttle those damn coyotes. Every time he dozed off, they woke him with their howling and barking. And no matter how high he got in his tree, there were mosquitoes. He'd tried to escape by zipping up the jacket over his head. Which made it too hot inside to sleep. His hands and face were puffy with bites. At first light, he was red-eyed, hungry, incensed at the fickle fate that had landed him here. He gazed with disgust at the black shapes roosting in the lower branches below him. Wild turkeys. Mark had heard them gobbling and moving about during the night.

Then he focused. Could he get one . . . for food? With the thought came determination. He eased down the tree, pausing to see if it spooked the birds. None moved. He held his walking stick by its smaller end. Had to get close. He'd get no second swing if he missed. So Mark forced himself to go slow and moved to the branch above the bird nearest to him. He measured the distance with his eye. Close enough.

Holding tight to an upper branch with his left hand, Mark leaned down and drew back his stick. There was just room enough to strike without catching the tree trunk. He paused, then swung with all his strength.

The turkey exploded in flying feathers and squawks, flopping out of the tree, down to the ground. Mark followed the bird—but not by choice.

As he swung his stick, Mark's right foot slipped off the branch. He dropped the stick, grabbed for another branch with his right hand, missed—then fell from the tree. He landed on wet, soft earth next to the flopping, screaming turkey. It instantly flew into Mark's face. He rolled over, grabbed for his stick.

He had fallen on his left side, leg bent under him. He'd hit his left elbow on the ground, numbing it. But his immediate problem was getting untangled from the injured thrashing turkey. He couldn't tell whether it was attacking him or trying to get away. He found his stick and began beating at the turkey with all his strength. It took fully two minutes before the bird lay dead.

It was big. Twenty pounds, maybe thirty.

Mark was winded, sore in every muscle, face scratched. He wondered if he had twisted his ankle. He tried to stand and, although sore, his left ankle seemed to support his weight.

Limping to the stream, he carefully knelt down and drank as much as he could. Then he washed his face and head.

The sun now sent its first light into Mark's spot of woods, reminding him that the day's heat was not far behind. He contemplated the dead turkey. This was the last thing he wanted to think about this morning. But he had to eat something, and he couldn't look at another pecan right then.

He picked up the bird by its feet and carried it to the stream. What would happen when the bird was immersed? Not much, except it got heavier and looked messier. Then an idea hit him. It would be easier to eat something *inside* the bird than to remove a lot of feathers. He had no wish to try and start a fire. Mark selected a big stone and spent several minutes crashing it down on other stones in the creek, breaking some, chipping off flakes with sharp edges. He scraped feathers away from the turkey's breast. It took him a few minutes to get the hang of it but then, with a sharper chip and by sawing hard, he managed to open the skin. With both hands he pulled the bird open, using all his strength.

It was nauseating work, covering Mark's hands and arms to the elbows with blood and guts. With no breakfast, his stomach rolling, not sure what he was doing, the effort made him feel like a true savage. He grew angry at this madness— a civilized man forced to act like an animal! The madder he got, the more viciously he ripped into the turkey's body cavities.

Mark stopped to calm himself. Piled between his knees was bloody pulp, organs, chunks of flesh of all kinds. He rose shakily, washed himself off in the stream, and tried to stop trembling. Then he swallowed, almost ready to throw up.

But he didn't. He needed food too much. Mark got down on his knees, felt through the pile of meat, identified what he thought were liver and heart. And some . . . giblets, as his mother would call them. He washed it all in the creek, pulling away bits of stringy tissue, then wrapped it up in his undershirt, crammed it all in one jacket pocket.

He couldn't eat any of it now, his stomach was too upset. He'd walk some, calm down. The very idea of killing anything had always been anathema to Mark, and this experience was totally unsettling. But at least he now had a pound or more of meat to chew on, when his stomach permitted.

He walked along the creek, drank, realized he must start across that endless prairie again. He simply dreaded it.

Why was he going east? Did he actually know why? No, he admitted to himself . . . except there were distant tree lines he could identify to the east, where there should be creeks. He had to have water to stay alive, and he wouldn't go back to the west.

He sat down for a moment. Must think, calmly. No emotion, he warned himself. Had to be logical. But was it logical to think that he was out of his own century? Of course not. That was only crazy . . . but, well, think crazy for a minute. Won't hurt to make believe this is a fantasy, maybe a walking nightmare. So assume this is another century. Maybe the nineteenth, maybe even earlier. Say, the eighteenth . . . or even sixteenth century, when all those Spanish explorers got here from Europe . . . then that must mean there was probably some early settlement someplace in this wilderness . . . where people spoke some language he'd recognize. . . .

Oh, hell, he thought. *This is just dumb. I'm here. This is real. I'm flat-ass lost . . . but there's gotta be a sensible explanation.* He'd put that crap out of his mind. Push on. Somewhere, somehow, he'd find an answer to where he was, maybe even why he was here.

Mark grabbed up his stick and jacket and walked vigorously through the prairie's tall, waving grass. One thing he now knew for sure was how he had to plan each day to cross this sea of grass. He had seen how the huge prairie was well-watered with tiny streams coming south, with trees thick along each stream. These green strips were from two to ten miles apart, and he could stop for midday rest while the overhead sun no longer gave him a sure sign where east and west were located. And he needed to reach a creek by nightfall to sleep in a tree, away from predators. So he had to time his walking between these life-giving creeks. His future seemed to depend on it.

He found no creek at noon but did find shade under a lone scraggly oak tree on a rise in the prairie. He'd walked steadily all morning, slower and slower as his strength ebbed and the sun parched his head. Now he must force himself to eat some turkey meat, with no water to help it down. He ate, then slept, his head and back pressed against the tree trunk. Ants biting his neck finally woke him. He staggered, scratching, to his feet, then began walking toward another distant tree line. It was one more of the longest afternoons of his life. It was, pure and simple, a crapshoot whether he'd get there before dark, and before prairie wolves found him. Soon every step was a major effort. The blazing sun in an azure sky kept him drenched with his own sweat. And then he stopped sweating and grew dizzy. What saved him from total collapse, he realized later, was a slow change in the weather.

First came thin high clouds, then thunderheads out of the west eased over him, blocking the sun. A cool breeze made him feel better and began to whip the grass around him. Everything was dry, Mark noted. No rain here for some time. He cleared a rise and almost shouted with joy . . . a tree line, green and inviting, only a mile distant. He broke into a stumbling jog, fell to his knees, got up, and walked rapidly. He had a shot at one more night, anyway.

Mark choked, breathed deeply, and tried not to drink too fast. Water had never tasted so good. He drank more, then rolled over on the ground. Closed his eyes.

Then he sat up with a jolt. Wait a damn minute!

He stared at the far bank, two hundred feet away. This was no stream. It was a river and he knew it! Hell, yes. It was right where it ought to be—the first major river east of the Trinity.

The Sabine. Flowing from the northwest, down through east Texas. What it meant was . . . he put his head in his hands. His mind was in chaos. No, it couldn't be . . . but, it must be . . . nothing else fit the facts. He was in virgin country, the land untouched, native plants growing as they had for centuries, wildlife roaming free.

Face it, he told himself. *You've got to accept it, deal with it.*

Now he was certain: He was gone from his own century. This was an earlier time. Worse, he'd never get home again.

It took a major effort of will for the exhausted, unstrung man to get to his feet after sitting almost motionless on the riverbank for an hour. He felt completely defeated. Gone was the lift he'd gotten from his father's own survival story. His pride? Hell. What difference did that make? He was *alone* out here. Him, wild animals, and killer Indians. The truth overwhelmed him.

How could he, an average twentieth-century man, hope to stay alive and healthy in these primitive surroundings? He had no weapons, no survival skills, no objectives even. Where would he go? What was the point of surviving hand to mouth in this wilderness when there was nothing here of any value to him?

The darker his mood turned, the darker the skies became. It would soon be night. If he was to live until morning, he must have another place to roost. Mark cursed and began moving along the stream bank.

Soon, the evening predators would appear, and he knew himself to be a highly visible, helpless target. Yet the giant cottonwoods and oaks that lined the river's banks had no branches low enough for him to reach.

Mark continued walking, more rapidly, looking everywhere for a tree where he could find safety. *Survival for one more night*, he told himself, *is only sensible. Bullshit,* he corrected himself. *You're simply afraid to die, like any other intelligent human.*

ELEVEN

Heat lightning flickered across the southern sky through most of the long night·as Mark shifted from one position to another. All his walking the previous day had made him so sore that if he stayed in one position long, he felt cramps start in a leg, foot, or thigh.

Once during the night he pulled out the turkey meat and ate what was left. It was bitter and made him thirsty. There was no way, however, that he was going to descend into the blackness below for a drink.

It had been virtually dark before he'd found an oak with low branches, growing next to a tall cottonwood. Now a fairly adept tree-climber, Mark quickly clambered up the oak to where he could shinny out a large branch into the bigger cottonwood branches. His final perch was thirty feet above ground, and more than fifty yards from the riverbank. He wanted no more risks from flash floods.

This seemed a safe distance from the river, a safe elevation above the noisy nighttime woodland below him. He could see no other shadowy shapes in the tree with him, by the light of a partial moon that dimly lit the overhead cloud cover.

Threatening skies produced no more than a fine drizzle during the night, but thunder continued to vibrate through the forest. Lightning threw long black-and-white shadows on the ground below. Mark, huddled against a tree trunk, dozed off, jerked away repeatedly, finally awoke to a strange smell.

Something burning.

From the south it came, a faint odor of woodsmoke. He climbed up on his branch, turned the other way, and faced south. Saw a flicker of red.

Fire. A thin line of it, in the distance. A mile off at least.

He watched, fascinated. Had Indians set fire to the tall, dry grass? He'd heard of that being done to enrich the earth, for planting crops. But were these Indians an agricultural people? So far he'd seen only hunters. And they wouldn't start fires in the middle of the night.

The fire line grew brighter. And longer. Red-and-orange sparks danced across the prairie, going both east and west. Through dark cloud masses, Mark saw vertical lightning flashes from sky to earth. That must be it. Lightning had ignited some dead tree. Ideal tinder, it had set fire to prairie grass. Now it was spreading.

As Mark watched with mounting worry, sections of the fire grew in height, the line now stretching up across rises in the prairie, over hills, down into hidden valleys. In places, the flames exploded up from the ground, and a pall of smoke turned into a dark cloud, which grew larger by the minute.

The fire was coming north, toward the river. Toward Mark. This was no isolated grass fire that would burn itself out. It was too widespread, moving too quickly. He saw it crop up on a distant hill, still spreading into the distance, and he began to wonder whether he should move, climb down, try to cross the river, move to the north. Certainly the Sabine should be a firebreak big enough to contain the fire, he thought. Or was it?

He hated to leave his safe perch. Already below him he could hear sounds of movement as animals began stirring. Then he heard the fire's distant crackle. Some of the fire line, it seemed to Mark, moved as fast as a man running, devouring tall grass, bushes, small trees, everything in its path.

Hesitating no longer, he slid down the cottonwood, moved into the oak branches, lowered himself, jumped the last eight feet to soft earth, rolled, and came up trotting toward the river.

He found himself part of a busy, chaotic migration, as a stream of wildlife erupted from the forest and prairie, running from the fire.

In semidarkness, he made out wolves coming from the south, dark shapes hurtling through low underbrush. He was almost knocked down by smaller animals—coyotes, he sensed—that brushed by him, never stopping. Groups of deer ran parallel to the river, wild-eyed. Tiny ground animals ignored predators in their dash toward the river.

From the evening before, Mark remembered seeing an old dead tree sticking up from the bank at a low angle, more than halfway across the river. It had been downstream, he thought, and he hurried through the brush where the Sabine made a sweeping curve.

Twice he was nearly run down by flying deer plunging straight at him, but instead they swerved at the last minute, continuing toward the river, splashing headlong into the shallows. The advancing fire line, over his right shoulder, now cast flickering light into the forest as it ate its way closer, sweeping through grass toward the line of woods. Mark moved faster, infected by the fear of the wildlife around him. Then he saw the tree hulk, arching out from the riverbank, only a few feet above the moving water. He also saw what was sitting on the very end of the downed tree: a mountain lion. Huge, it seemed to Mark, its tail lashing back and forth, snarling as it contemplated the noise and confusion around it. Smoke swirled across the river's surface, hiding the far bank.

The mountain lion eyed Mark, then the river, as the acrid stench of woodsmoke and grass smoke stung the man's eyes and caused the great cat to blink, shake its head, and turn around. There was more light in the forest as fire ignited the edge of the woods, less than two hundred yards away, and the noise of the blaze's movement became louder, a savage roaring conflagration that would reach the river in minutes.

Coughing, his mind numbed with fear, Mark knew he must get out on that dead tree, as close to the far bank as he could. He stood up on the leaning trunk, whacked at it with his stick, and took a tentative step forward, toward the cat, twenty yards away. Oddly, he found himself more afraid of the fire than of the lion.

The animal crouched, turned, took a step toward Mark, then another. Mark whacked the trunk repeatedly, began shouting incomprehensible threats at the mountain lion, hardly aware of what he was doing. Then the cat pivoted, crouched, and sprang away into the smoke. Mark heard the splash of water, and quickly picked his way to the end of the sloping tree trunk.

He glanced over his shoulder, saw the fire was now tree-high, an all-consuming wall of seething flames, furiously burning up and down the river as far as he could see. The riverbanks were like a scene from hell: the air filled with shrieks of small, terrorized animals, scurrying along the banks, some throwing themselves into the water. Birds of all sizes floundered through the smoky air, some wild turkeys barely missing Mark's head as they whipped by him. Deer threw up great plumes of water as they raced into the river, wolves and coyotes alongside them. Shallow water teemed with tiny trails of rats as they left the riverbank, swimming for their lives.

Then came a tidal wave of buffalo, thundering just ahead of the fire wall. Some of their hides were smoking, others had tiny points of flame on their bodies where fire had ignited thick bunches of hair.

Front-running buffalo tried to stop at the river's edge, but the ones behind smashed into them, pushing hundreds of great bodies into the water, as more buffalo roared up and trampled those already swimming. Mark stopped for a moment as hundreds of buffalo poured into the Sabine River, trying desperately to reach the far bank before drowning, under assault of those coming from behind.

Burning trees boomed and cracked as the dry forest virtually exploded into the tree area where Mark had spent the night. He shielded his face with one arm, searched the river, knowing he must jump to survive. He would be plunging into every kind of animal hazard he could imagine, including alligators. Yet here, he knew, he would simply burn to death within minutes.

His decision to jump was spurred by what he now saw on his sloping tree trunk: dozens of snakes of all sizes and colorations, slithering quickly out along the tree, coming straight at him.

Quickly, he zipped up his jacket all the way, clutched his stick, and jumped into the river.

Mark hit the water feetfirst, went under, then surfaced. As he'd hoped, his pants and jacket trapped air, as they'd done in the flash flood, and he was buoyant for a few minutes. He whipped around to see what creatures might be close to him, then remembered the rocks in his pocket and threw them away instantly. Too heavy.

Smoke hid everything but those objects closest to Mark—branches, leaves, chunks of charred trees. He began paddling to the north bank, away from the fire wall. His face and head felt hot and scorched as he heard, rather than saw, the blinding incineration of the last trees on the south bank.

Something struck his right leg, and he recoiled, paddling furiously away, holding his breath to see if he was stung or bitten. Nothing. He had struck a limb, then saw it attached to a log and tried to get a handhold—until he saw, on top, a thick, coiled snake. Had to be a rattler, he knew, as he splashed off a few yards.

As the air in his clothes leaked out, Mark moved toward what he hoped was the north bank, away from the fire, although thick smoke blocked his view. Three buffalo came splashing in front of him, squealing and snorting. He saw which direction they were going and followed. Mark also could dimly make out deer antlers on his right, going the same way.

Then a noise behind him caused Mark to swivel about, in time to see a tall tree, aflame from top to bottom, topple slowly into the river from the south bank, crashing into the water with a great blast of steam and smoke.

Now he was certain of his directions and struck out quickly. He felt something touch his feet and jerked them up in panic. Putting one foot down slowly, he touched bottom. Paddling harder, he got both feet into the muddy bank and felt the water grow more shallow.

With the smoke clearing, Mark could now see downstream. Some treetops were still flaming, but the river had served as an effective firebreak, and only isolated bushes and small trees appeared to be burning on the north shore. Then he became aware of a steady rain he hadn't noticed before. It must have helped check the raging fire at the river.

For a moment, Mark was afraid to leave the river. He stood there, waist-deep, wondering if what was waiting on shore was worse than what was in the water. He had to chance it. Any minute he could be attacked by a big gator or some of the snakes sliding ashore near him.

He splashed across an area of rocky bottom, pulled himself soggy and spent onto a sloping grass bank. Finding a clear area he fell down and closed his eyes. He could hardly move. Finally, Mark forced himself to roll over and saw the first signs of light in the east. He stared in horror at the devastation on the river's ravaged south bank. As far as he could see in both directions were burning trees and brush. Beyond the fire were the ghostly outlines of a dead forest, smoke billowing high into the air, virtually nothing left of what had, only minutes before, been a lush woodland, full of life.

As the flames died down, Mark saw not only the wreckage of the woodland but its decimated population. Carcasses floated downstream, bodies of deer, buffalo, and smaller creatures half-submerged. Surviving scavengers, he knew, would feast today . . . and already buzzards circled high in the early dawn light. Mark wanted to get away, far away, from this sad and desolate place, and he felt drained of all energy, all emotion.

If Eleanor could see him now, he forced himself to smile, she might consider him in terms of his investment risk. Okay for the short term, considering what he'd been through, but for the long term?

Bearish. Definitely bearish, for the long term.

Mark unwrapped himself from around the tall cedar tree where he'd slept, on the ground, oblivious to snakes or anything else. He looked up at an overcast sky, the day already warm. He'd slept for an hour or more, and his clothes were wet, uncomfortable, plastered to his body.

All around him was the stink of disaster. Even on this north bank there were smoldering tree stumps washed ashore, piles of burned vegetation, and blackened animals floating in the shallows.

He got up, looked around in almost total silence. On the other side of the river lay absolute desolation. Stubs of great trees were shattered, leaning at odd angles. Smoke eddied up from the blackened forest floor, and shimmering steam drifted along the shoreline. There were big mounds on the ground to mark the remains of the largest animals caught and killed by racing flames.

Mark's throat was raw, and he craved water, but the Sabine this morning resembled a wide garbage ditch. He found his walking stick, amazed he still had it, and moved downstream, through the edge of the woods, around smoking piles of brush that had been deposited by the river overnight.

He felt better moving and encountered few live animals. An alligator launched itself into the river as Mark circled a brush pile near the shore, and downriver he could see coyotes back in the woods. He tried to walk through open areas, where he would not be surprised by snakes or wolves.

He came to a small creek that emptied into the river. Mark followed it upstream, away from the Sabine, to a point where its water was clear, cold, and undisturbed. First, he drank, long and slow. Then he removed his clothes, put them on a bush, stood ankle-deep in the creek, and washed his body. Cold and refreshing.

Shrugging back into wet clothing, he continued walking up the creek. He rubbed his growth of beard and tried to imagine Eleanor's horror if she could see him now—dirty, bearded, hair matted, clothing stained and torn. He was skinnier too, Mark noted, as he tied the thick string tighter in his waistband.

As he'd hoped, he found both hickory and walnut trees but no pecans. With rocks, he broke nuts and nibbled at the bits of fruit inside. A lot of work for a small breakfast. He wished he had more of that turkey meat even as bad as it tasted.

Trees thinned out on his right, to the east, as Mark walked, and he saw partly open grassland in the distance. So it appeared that the Sabine had in fact stopped the fire, and most everything on the north side was undisturbed . . . very few birds, no rabbits, no squirrels.

His eye caught movement out in the grass.

Mark froze.

He focused on those dots, hundreds of yards away. Not animals. People.

They were Indians.

Should he hide or run? He had only seconds to decide.

TWELVE

Lying prone behind low creek rocks, his face pressed against sharp stones, Mark went numb with panic before he got his mind together.

He couldn't run back into the woods. He'd be spotted. Here, there were a few trees between himself and the approaching Indians. He might remain unseen if he made no sudden movements.

Slowly, he raised his eyes above rock level. There were at least a dozen of them, their movements taking them down the slope toward the river rather than directly toward Mark. They would enter the woods, it appeared, well below his position. He heard barking. Coyotes? And then he saw small thin dogs jumping through tall grass, running ahead of the taller human figures, perhaps chasing ground animals.

All the people carried baskets or other burdens of some kind. Mark saw some were dressed in long tunics that reached from neck to knee. Women, it appeared. These must be Indian families.

Of course. They would be after warm meat, hides, waiting to be gathered from that big devastated area below. The charred smell still drifted through the trees, reminding Mark of how awful it would be there in a matter of hours. The Indians would want to collect all they could carry before the dead meat turned foul. And before it was picked over by four-footed and winged scavengers.

Tracking their movement down the grassy slope, Mark noted that some men carried coils of rope and long poles.

Others had the spear device over their shoulders, with a waist pouch carrying small spears.

All of the men were bare to the waist, wearing thin headbands above eye level. They were lean and hard-bodied but not like those grim-faced killers Mark had seen the week before. These people talked and laughed with each other, called to the barking dogs, and appeared to enjoy themselves.

He thought for an instant about revealing himself, approaching them . . . for what? They would think of him as an intruding stranger, not somebody in need of help. He could easily be killed. Better to stay hidden.

He remembered the wind. Would those dogs catch his scent? They seemed headed directly toward the burned area, and nobody looked in his direction. He sank down in relief as they vanished, going away from him, to the south.

He moved north, through the thin edge of woods. If he hurried, he could go behind the Indians, turn east beyond the first groundswell, and be out of this area before they returned.

As he walked rapidly, something bothered him about what he'd just seen. Something about what they carried . . . it was at the edge of his mind, but he began to perspire, hurrying up the slope, and he put it aside to concentrate on his path, avoiding rotted logs that might conceal snakes, looking in all directions to be sure there were no more Indians following those who'd just passed.

Turning east, Mark made good time through waist-high grass. Seeing no buffalo or deer, Mark felt totally alone as the prairie stretched off before him, more hilly now, with another dim line of green-tree clusters perhaps two miles away. They would offer shade. Maybe another creek. Only above him was there visible life. Hundreds of buzzards circled, crowding the sky above trees that flanked the Sabine River.

Mark walked quickly to the northeast, praying he would not encounter Indian salvage parties coming back from the fire-blackened area. Hot sun burned off the morning mist, and soon his jacket was tied around his waist and his sweat-shirt wrapped around his head. Something kept gnawing at his mind.

Then he stopped in his tracks. It dawned on him what it was that seemed so curious about the Indians, what had struck him as important, but he couldn't identify.

It wasn't what they carried . . . but what they *didn't* carry. Bows.

They had no bows and arrows. Only spear-throwers.

The awful significance hit Mark hard. His mind and his memory churned as he sat down in short grass, hoping some-how he could be wrong about the absence of bows. He re-membered too well the things his grandfather had told him.

Mark Lewellyn got to know his father's parents when he and his younger sister had visited them on the Lewellyn farm just west of Nacogdoches, in east Texas. At first they were bored with Grandpa Henry's lectures on nature, animals, and In-dians. It was his private passion. He loved Indian lore and artifacts. He'd taught them to make crude bows and arrows, like the one he used himself to hunt small game.

The children's interest perked up when they found they could actually shoot small arrows into the hay bales out be-hind their grandpa's barn. And on one occasion they were goggle-eyed when the older man shot a rabbit to demonstrate his homemade bow's accuracy. He showed them how the bow was made, how he had fletched the arrows himself, how a crudely fashioned flint tip was fitted to each arrow. The children paid rapt attention.

"The Indians were no Robin Hoods," he explained. "Most of their kills would have been at forty yards or less. In the case of buffalo, maybe closer." He also emphasized that the bows must have dramatically altered the Indians' lives, per-haps even their culture.

"What did they use before they got bows?" Mark remem-bered asking.

"They used a sort of primitive spear-thrower called the

atlatl," said their grandfather. "I can show you a picture of it."

"Did Indians around here invent the bow?"

"Oh, no, bows were used all over the world in ancient times. Our Texas Indians got bows, oh, sometime around 500 A.D., according to what I've read from archaeologists."

Mark recalled his sixteen-year-old confusion. "When was that?"

Grandpa Henry smiled. "Well, you've studied some history. You've read about ancient Rome, the Roman Empire? Well, about the time that the Roman Empire fell—roughly five hundred years after Christ—that's when the first bows got to this area. Before that, Indians here just had the spear-thrower."

Mark went over that conversation of twenty-five years past, and knew he was not mistaken. His Grandpa Henry read all there was to read about early Indian life. He visited archaeological "digs" in Arkansas and Texas, Mark remembered, and even wrote a couple of articles on early Indian life for the local newspaper. He knew his ancient history.

Which could mean but one thing: Mark Lewellyn now lived in a prehistoric time, somewhere prior to the fifth century A.D. The whole idea was ridiculous, yet he knew it must be true, and he must force himself to face it. This was the Stone Age in North America. There was simply no civilization, as he knew it, anywhere in his new world.

THIRTEEN

It was an alligator that helped Mark decide where he must go to survive this trackless wilderness.

That decision came soon after his shock of realizing where in time, roughly, he now lived. Mark's reaction to that revelation sucked all the energy from his body. He finally stood up, rubbed his face, and scratched his itching scalp. Tried to keep from crying out, screaming aloud, in anger and frustration.

He wanted to wallow in self-pity, curse the fate that had taken him from home and comforts . . . but it all seemed so pointless. Nobody could hear him. Nobody cared what happened to him. His old life was over. Finished. Zip. He had to start all over . . . with a new life, in a savage land. He could count on nobody for help. Nobody . . . except him.

Mark found himself stumbling into the line of trees ahead of him, where he found a tiny creek. He drank and moved south, down toward the river again, to see if he was beyond the burned area. He still could not decide what direction he should go . . . keep moving east or go south, since he knew the Sabine would eventually turn down toward southeast Texas.

He stopped and sighed with relief when he saw the river. All was green again on the far bank. He'd walked past the burned section. Mark knelt and splashed water on his face. Then a sudden frantic movement caught his eye . . . downstream.

He hurried forward to see, but also got ready to dash into

the trees lining the bank if any movement spelled danger.

It was a deer, he saw, a young buck, struggling to reach shore . . . its hindquarters held fast in the long jaws of a massive gray alligator.

In a frenzy of motion, the deer tried to jerk free, but the great mouth was clamped tight. Mark grabbed up two rocks and ran along the bank, stopping a dozen yards from the injured deer and its attacker, and quickly threw both rocks. They missed, and he grabbed more from the rocky bank, aiming carefully. One stone thunked into the side of the long gator body—and got its attention. Relaxing its jaws, the alligator turned slightly, and for one awful moment, Mark thought it was coming for him. He half turned to run.

In the next second, the reptile was gone, slipping silently underwater, leaving a broad ripple. Mark grabbed the deer's antlers as blood gushed from the animal and swirled dark red around his feet, making the rocks slippery.

Overhead, buzzards circled lower, ready to join the party. But he was a scavenger, too. He hadn't helped the deer to save its life. He'd seen it as food, without even thinking about it. He shook his head wearily. Only one week out in the wilderness, Mark realized, and he was quite ready to kill for something to eat. His main concern was beating the buzzards to dinner.

He then saw he would not have to kill the deer. Its eyes glazed over, the body jerked once and was still. Mark dragged it into the leaves under low-hanging trees. He didn't want to fight off the buzzards, and there was always danger an Indian party might come down the river.

He again became a rock-breaker, smashing large stones onto smaller ones, to get chips with a cutting edge. He finally got three hand-sized rock fragments with edges.

Mark sawed at the white underbelly of the limp animal, managing to make only deep indentations at first. He persisted until finally he made a cut through which blood seeped.

Then he noticed the deer's splintered leg. Two bloody

bones sticking out had sharp points on them where the gator
had snapped the lower leg. Mark managed to break off the
sharpest bone six inches above the splintered point. Now he
had something to pierce the deerskin. Blood covered his
hands and arms as he jabbed a series of holes into the deer's
belly, about an inch apart, in a straight line. Then he took
his sharpest stone chip and sliced, hard, from hole to hole.

When he'd cut six inches open in the deer's belly, gray-
and-white intestines began to ooze out, but he kept hacking
at the hide. The thought of reaching inside that mass of flesh
and blood turned Mark's stomach, and he worried that he
might vomit.

He forced himself to keep working as sweat poured down
his face, getting into his eyes. He wiped at it with one wrist
and managed to cover his face with animal blood. Before
him on the ground were intestines and other fleshy parts.
Mark knew he'd have to empty the carcass interior, and he
shook his head in despair. The sight of blood had always
unnerved him. Now he knew what he had to do, and it repulsed him.

Trying not to think about it, Mark jammed his bare right
arm into the carcass and hastily yanked all the interior body
parts out onto the ground, just as he'd done with the turkey.
Only this was bigger, messier.

He pawed through the mass before him and found the
liver and heart. There were other edible organs, he felt sure,
but he'd reached the limits of his patience and strength. He
wanted to leave this place, quickly, and not smell any more
blood or fecal matter, get himself clean somehow.

Mark wrapped the meat in his stained undershirt, gathered
his clothing and stick, and hurried along the riverbank. Looking back, he saw the first buzzards alighting near the deer
carcass.

After dark, Mark had fantasies about knives. Sharp knives,
long ones, light shining on smooth, steel blades, knives that

sliced effortlessly through hot beef roasts and large, succulent hams.

Straddling his customary foot-thick branch, darkness around him, Mark thought lovingly of his big, multibladed Swiss knife. The one he'd failed to pick up the morning he left home for the last time. He would never, never, ever—he told himself bitterly—see the likes of all that cutlery again.

Opening that deer today by ripping the skin with dull rock edges, focused his attention now on only one thing. He had to have a cutting edge. A piece of flint or sharp rock from which he could make a knife . . . tools to use in cleaning game and scraping hides. He had no idea how he'd fashion such things from stone, but there had to be a way. He nodded off, so exhausted he barely heard the chilling wolf and coyote sounds.

Memories from his subconscious woke Mark before dawn. His thoughts about knives stirred other recollections . . . the time in Hot Springs, in southwestern Arkansas, when he and Eleanor had a close-up look at the area's prehistoric Indian culture and their many stone quarries.

It was on their second vacation visit to the place, he remembered, when they'd joined other tourists on a mountain hike. Their forest-ranger guide told them how the valley's hot springs attracted Indian settlers, who had found rock outcroppings a fine source of arrowheads. The rock, explained their guide, was known as novaculite. Mark and Eleanor poked around the Indian quarry in wonder, walking over thousands of chips of the multihued stone, quarried by Indian hunters hundreds, perhaps thousands, of years before. Their guide cautioned them about the hazards.

"You wouldn't believe how sharp this stone can be," he smiled. "I suggest you not pick any of it up . . . you can sure cut your fingers around here."

* * *

Mark had made his decision as he carefully climbed out of his tree when daylight arrived. He'd leave these woods and plains, turn northeast, toward the Ouachita Mountains. A long hike, he knew, maybe two hundred miles or more. He'd have to dredge up memories of all those trips along Interstate 30, from Dallas to Texarkana toward Little Rock. Hot Springs was tucked into its long mountain valley, just a few miles west of the freeway. He sighed. No roads now. No maps. Just memories.

But damn sure better than no objective, no purpose in life at all, he knew. He'd have to steer clear of Indians. He wouldn't try to build any fires, nor attract any attention. Move carefully. Be patient. Learn to make friends with this wild and primitive land. He was an educated man. Not a wilderness expert to be sure, but intelligent. If Indians could learn to live out here, why couldn't he?

Oddly, he felt cheered up. He certainly knew his handicaps. But he had to focus on his strengths. He now knew danger when he saw it, smelled it, heard it. And he knew when to run like hell.

He stuffed more rocks in his pockets, to reassure himself. They'd have to do until he got where he wanted to go.

If he could only find it.

FOURTEEN

Mark knew how Columbus must have felt on first seeing the New World.

Or Balboa when he spied the Pacific Ocean.

Or Whatsisname at the North Pole . . . or any of the other great explorers who'd conquered distance and danger as part of their personal odyssey . . . to someplace.

Mark practically glowed with pleasure, standing on a bluff overlooking a wide river of slow-moving reddish water. This had to be the Red River, and he could hardly believe it. It was right where he had assumed it would be.

Until this moment, Mark never had been sure if he was going consistently in the right direction. Even if he did have a big target to aim at. He knew the mighty Red River came down from New Mexico, across the top of Texas, along its borders with Oklahoma, Arkansas, then Louisiana, curving south, becoming part of the Mississippi River system. Big Red was more than thirteen hundred miles long.

Mark couldn't guess exactly where he'd intercepted the wide river with its distinctive red current. He could be facing Oklahoma or Louisiana, but most likely it was Arkansas. One thing he knew for sure, though: He had walked more than one hundred miles in seven days, headed northeast. He laughed aloud, shouting with joy, at finding himself able to navigate trackless prairie and arrive, in one piece, to a reach checkpoint. It was almost as good as a road sign. Or like making an A-plus on a geography test.

The past week had been one long crapshoot with hunger,

thirst, and animals. The trick, he found, was to get enough sleep in a tree at night to have the strength to get across the prairie from one forested creek to the next, avoiding his greatest hazards: animals. He could not survive on the prairie at night. Prowling wolves, coyotes, and the ever-present snake population made that obvious. Only a few big cats inhabited the thin strips of forest that bordered all these north–south streams down across Texas—but the few cats could climb trees. Mark knew he had to face their nighttime company on occasion. Three nights ago he'd had to throw his pocket rocks at a wildcat too close to him in a tree. One rock had connected, the cat had snarled and screeched at him, but then slunk away.

On the prairie in daylight Mark's biggest danger, besides wolves, was a buffalo herd moving together. Once he almost was trampled, and got behind a tree just in time to avoid the great bison as they loped past him. He ended up covered with dust and mud—it had just rained that morning—but he was unhurt.

His food continued to be nuts, fish, and small game.

Day before yesterday he had killed his first rabbit. The animal had run into Mark, and he'd grabbed it by the hind feet. He then killed it with his stick when the small creature sank its teeth into Mark's hand. He hoped the thing wasn't rabid.

Skinning a rabbit, he found, was harder than cleaning a fish, especially since the rocks he could find were of poor splinter quality, with few sharp edges. Eventually, he got enough rabbit meat to satisfy his appetite for one night. He no longer thought about making a fire. It would attract wolves and maybe Indians. He had seen no more humans since the hunting party after the forest fire.

However, Mark did have one scare. He awoke one morning before dawn to the faint smell of smoke . . . and, the aroma of roasting meat.

He climbed higher in his tree and saw a tiny light in the distance. Fire. Someone was burning something, and as his eyes probed the distance, he made out tiny plumes of smoke drifting up. It was too far away—at least half a mile—and he could identify no figures. Mark had no doubt that these were Indians cooking game. The smell was faint but tantalizing.

That signaled his prompt departure. Just before dawn, while fearing he might be the target of wolves, he nevertheless hurried out across the prairie. He still carried a vivid memory of that Indian being murdered. He would take his chances with wild animals before he'd get closer to any more Indians.

That day he noted, with relief, how the land was changing. The prairie began to shrink, with wooded areas more numerous, as he walked east. Then he spotted his first pine tree. Soon there were others, then the forests became a mix of pine and hardwood. Those predominantly pine forests had thick carpets of pine needles on the ground and very little underbrush. These were virgin trees, some well over one hundred feet high and as much as four feet in diameter. Every few miles he found small creeks with good water.

Mark's nighttime problem now was the lack of branches by which to climb the tall pines or big oaks. One night, fearfully, he had to spend on the ground, leaning back against a pine tree, his stick at the ready. He was not disturbed except for the ant bites on his legs the next morning.

Now, looking down at the Red River, Mark realized this was his fifteenth day in the wilderness. He'd started making notches on his walking stick to keep track. His clothing was filthy, and he knew he stank. He also winced at his reflection in a still pool of water.

A vagrant was what he looked like—hair going in all directions, matted, filthy. His beard, growing black and heavy, soaked daily with sweat, made his face itch, and he scratched often.

His beautiful new Nike tennis workout clothing was smeared with a mixture of meat stains around the pockets, mud, blood, and scratches from thorns and sharp underbrush.

His Nike shoes were still in one piece but scarcely a patch of white showed through dust and dirt.

It no longer mattered. Finding this river was such a huge relief that his elation put him on a "high" he had not experienced before. If he'd gotten this far, he decided, surely he could find the Ouachita mountain range.

Mark was almost jaunty as he moved down the embankment and prepared to cross the Red River. It would have appeared impossibly formidable to him two weeks ago, but now it was just another obstacle to be surmounted. Even if he didn't quite know how yet. Then he spotted a weathered log in the brush nearby, a foot thick and about eight feet long. He pulled on one end, and it rolled over, down to the water's edge. It was dried-out and should float well.

He slid his walking stick down his back, beneath the jacket, which he zipped up to his chin. Making sure his shoes were tied securely, he pushed the log into the river, walking in after it. The water was cool, refreshing. An overcast sky promised rain later on.

Mark was able to walk a third of the way across the river before he had to swim. There were still air pockets trapped in his clothing, and he took a firm grip on the log, hoping there were no water snakes or alligators close at hand.

He angled the log clumsily to his left, pointed toward the spot where the bank curved to his right. Kicking heavily, to get out of the stream's center, Mark nearly missed the point where he could get ashore, and only the river's shallowness saved him a long float downstream. As the current swung Mark to the west, his feet sank into the soft river bottom. He let go of the log, thrashed out with arms and feet going at once, to the east bank shallows. He went under twice and swallowed water, but finally his feet got some traction on the bottom. He struggled up into waist-deep water, spitting and wiping his face.

Mark found it hard to stand erect because violent physical activity still left him exhausted. He needed rest, decent food, and relief from the stress and fear of each day. That, in fact, had been one of the topics Bernie the Doc kept reminding him of. Although Bernie, Mark recalled, seemed to favor stress. Which didn't make sense at the time.

"Mark, it's like this," Bernie had said. "If you went to an office every day, you'd be under stress to compete and do a good job, right? And if you're out there on Interstate 30, driving into Dallas, you are *sure* under stress just to avoid the maniacs that can kill you with their bad driving.

"But there's all kinds of stress," Bernie went on. "A surgeon doing a delicate operation is highly stressed, but the surgeons I know tell me they do their best work under intense pressure.

"And look at the professional athletes. With a minute to go and trailing by two points, you can imagine how a quarterback feels. That, my friend, is pressure, *real* stress. But look at how often that produces an incredible performance, a play that wins the game.

"So what I'm saying, Mark, is that stress can work *for* you. If you get into decent shape, lose that weight and all, stress shouldn't hurt you. Depending on what you want to do, it can even help you—especially if you're trying to do something that's really hard to accomplish."

Mark flopped down on the east bank of the Red River and sighed. His earlier "high" was ebbing. *Okay, Bernie*, he complained to himself. *I've just crossed a big river with no boat. I got no food, no friends, no future. If stress can help me, I'm waiting. Any little thing at all would be nice.*

Mark pulled out pecans and hickory nuts and began to crack them open. He'd long since found out how little meat he could get from a hickory nut—but something was better than nothing. But not by much. He got up and moved upstream along the river's mud flat, which extended out from the bank a few yards.

He stepped on a small shell and picked it up. Kind of oysterlike. He couldn't pry it open with his ragged fingernails, so he found a chip of stone, then tapped the chip into the bivalve to force it open.

Then he remembered. Of course. This was a mussel. They were common along east Texas and Arkansas rivers. Inside the two shells was a tiny lump of meat. He pulled it out, washed it in the water and chewed it. Not bad. A little tough, but with enough of these, he could add something more to his diet. Pushed by his empty stomach, he searched for more shells along the mudflat.

Mark never thought he would miss that beautiful but terrifying prairie he crossed in upper east Texas. The Indians, the fire, the wolves . . . all were threats he planned never to see again.

But his first hours above the Red River made him almost long for the prairie's open vastness. There, at least, he could usually see where he was going. Here, almost never.

This was different country. Open meadows, big rocks, and an awful lot of timber. He spent the morning trying to walk to the left of the rising sun—northeast—but he constantly had to detour around big stands of underbrush, skirt the edge of dense forests that slowed him down. Now the sky was overcast.

He was not going to make good time, that was painfully obvious.

Mark sat in short grass at the edge of a dense wood. He had slept for an hour after he had eaten the mussels and realized it was no good trying to go any farther until the sun got low enough to be sure where northeast was. It was going to be pure guesswork, whichever direction he took.

But he knew where he had come *from*, as he climbed up on a low rise in the meadow. That much he could see behind him where the land sloped down toward the Red River's shallow valley. If he could just climb up on the big rock outcrop ahead of him, Mark decided, he might be able to see what lay beyond.

He grabbed the rock projection nearest his path, started his right foot up to a ledge . . . then froze. That telltale sound rang bells in his head . . . there was no other sound in nature

quite like the sound of a rattlesnake when he shakes his rattles. Mark had heard it only once before in his life, on
Grandpa Henry's farm, but you never forget how a rattler
sounds.

In an instant, Mark caught sight of the big, coiled reptile,
just inside a rock crevice, barely a yard away. There was no
time to think, only act. And fast. Jumping from his left foot,
Mark tried frantically to shift his right foot up onto the low
rock projection, above the snake.

He almost made it. But not quite.

Before he could even realize what had happened, the rattler had flashed through the air and embedded his fangs into
Mark's right foot. Or, as he then realized, into the soft upper
fabric of his jogging shoe. He winced in horror, expecting
pain, but feeling none . . . then watched in shock as the big
snake—more than six feet long—coiled around his feet and
legs, thrashing its body like some giant whip.

What happened next came from instinct alone. Mark
raised his left foot and rammed it down with full force on
the head of the rattler, now clamped to his right foot. He
sickened as he heard the nauseating crunch of the snake's
head under his left foot, and the simultaneous pain that shot
through his right foot and up his leg.

Mark collapsed to the ground, the snake's body still whipping around him. Mark grabbed the tail with both hands and,
with all his remaining strength, jerked the snake's crushed
head from his shoe, then whirled the reptile as far from him
as he could throw it. It was brain-dead but continued for long
minutes to coil, whirl, and flatten the grass around it.

Mark was sick, his eyes blinded by sweat, his heart ham-
mering. He knew that if he could have a heart attack, this
would be a perfect time for it. He fully expected his body to
revolt in some way. Instead, he grew drowsy and felt himself
on the verge of fainting. Struggling to his feet, Mark groaned
at the hot pain in his stricken right foot. He hobbled to a
spot where there was little grass, sat down, and carefully
removed his right shoe. He looked in wonder at the gash the

rattler had made in the soft, strong fabric mesh alongside the shoestrings.

He carefully massaged his right foot, feeling for anything that might signal a broken bone. The foot was sore all over, swelling, and it seemed to Mark the ligaments inside his right leg still vibrated. He would not be able to get much farther this day. He found his walking stick, then hobbled over to look down at the awful size and menace of the snake. At least three inches in diameter. He'd never seen any reptile this fearsome outside of a zoo, and again he realized how close he had come to a lonely, painful death out in the middle of . . . then Mark grinned, weakly.

Welcome to Arkansas.

Two hours of hobbling through open woods brought Mark to a small creek. Thick underbrush lined the far side, and he knew he'd have to go upstream or downstream to get around that bushy barrier. He also knew that his injured foot wouldn't carry him any more today. He took off his shoes and soaked his feet in clear, cold water. Around him was a mix of oak and pine, with a few hickories. He sighed. Another night for a nutty dinner, unless . . . he picked up a couple of hand-sized rocks and began watching the rabbits that chased each other through the brush, only a few yards away. After his close escape from snakebite, Mark felt sure he could survive the night better if he dined on something substantial . . . he began to wonder if any of this lush grass was edible . . .

FIFTEEN

At the time, Mark was irritated when Eleanor had insisted she drive on their vacation trips.

"You're a better map reader than I am." She smiled at him. "I'll drive, you navigate."

Now he was very glad for that arrangement.

Three times they had driven into southwest Arkansas to Hot Springs; first on their honeymoon, then, on vacations. They'd taken side roads, avoiding the busy freeway—and Mark learned the roads, rivers, and geography on their trip.

Now he knew how he could find the valley of hot springs. The Ouachita River should lead him to it, he told himself, recalling the road map. Running roughly northeast, parallel to Interstate 30, the Ouachita finally swung west, and Hot Springs Creek emptied into it, coming down from the north.

Find the river, follow it, find the creek, follow the creek, and you're there, he decided. *Easy to decide, tough to do*, Mark thought, as he limped through the woods, his foot aching, swollen and discolored. He had breakfasted on raw turkey eggs and was still swallowing hard—just to keep them down.

From the daily notches he'd scratched on his hickory stick, Mark knew he'd been gone from the twentieth century for twenty-two days. He looked like it, smelled like it . . . above all, he felt like it. His attitudes were different. So was his body. When he washed himself in a stream this morning, he'd been surprised to look down and see his feet. His belly was smaller.

He now moved warily through the forest, watching every spot where he put his foot, examining every downed tree before he got to it, every creekbed where some animal might wait in ambush. Funny, though . . . he really didn't *think* about doing those things, but did them instinctively. Bad things could happen to him if he wasn't alert every waking moment. He still jerked and was prepared to run at each woodland surprise, but now he knew what could hurt him and what wouldn't . . . probably.

He saw black bears, usually at a distance. They wouldn't attack him, unless provoked, he decided. And hoped. The deer herds and the occasional elk he'd seen were clearly no threat. Even the wolves and coyotes wouldn't attack him in broad daylight, he suspected . . . he just had to be sure not to get between them and their next meal.

Mark's biggest, constant danger was the snake he might step on as he waded through knee-high grass and through scattered, prickly underbrush. He considered his next biggest life-threatening hazard to be the large wildcats that did much of their hunting at night or at dawn. They liked trees, just as he did, when the sun went down. But they preferred lower branches, where they could wait for kills. Which meant Mark was now accustomed to sleeping much higher in trees.

He slept differently, too. He found he could get by with only a few hours' sleep, if it included relaxed periods when he was half-asleep and half-awake. Rarely did he sleep soundly more than two hours at a stretch. He could sleep sitting up with his back against the tree trunk, or curled around the tree trunk. Possums were among his worst night-time aggravations. They were nervy little creatures, often sneaking up on him and nuzzling his clothing until he awoke in terror, striking out with his stick.

Mark no longer was intimidated by the wildness of vegetation around him. He skirted thornbushes and took pains to avoid the poison ivy and poison oak that he'd encountered as a boy. He did not touch or eat any berry or plant that he couldn't identify. He was especially glad to find large patches of ripe blackberries and dewberries in sunlit portions of deeper parts of the forests. No longer did he fear that he would actually starve to death. He had stopped thinking in terms of "meals," and now simply grazed on wild fruit, nuts, or small game whenever he had the chance.

He discovered another change. A modest and fastidious man, Mark now found himself almost indifferent to the calls of nature. Each morning he would walk into a nearby creek with his shoes on, drop his pants—sometimes in the water, if he wasn't careful—squat, and move his bowels. He splashed water on himself in place of toilet paper. He found his energy level higher each morning. He was confident that he could, in fact, find the Ouachita River. It happened unexpectedly.

Heading due east, knowing the river must be someplace in front of him, Mark thought at first the shrill noises might be birdcalls. He hurried up a slope, through dense pines, and spotted both river and people. Women. On the far bank. No, girls, he corrected himself, as he drew closer and knelt to hide his presence. He could see their tiny, bronzed bodies, shining in the sun, as they splashed through shallows across the river from where he crouched.

Indians. And Mark felt the nausea of fear.

He kept well back from the edge of the woods, peering through tall weeds. There were seven small girls playing in the green water, all naked. On shore sat four adult women, talking together and watching the little girls. The adults seemed to have long garments on, from neck to knees. They were small people, barely five feet tall. The playing girls looked to be about eight or ten years old from their flat chests and thin legs.

Mark noted that the women appeared relaxed, not at all apprehensive about any dangers to their children in swimming. Which must mean they were close to their homes—their village, if that's what it was—and felt secure from danger. He feared being seen. He also felt like a Peeping Tom.

Mark eased back into the deep forest, turned, and began

to walk parallel to the river. He'd have to be very careful and not stumble into an Indian settlement. He could just imagine how these small, primitive people would react to somebody who looked as he did—huge, dirty, bearded, wearing clothes they'd never seen.

Just as he would have, had he encountered a giant Bigfoot in the woods . . . shoot first, ask questions later. At all costs, he must avoid these people.

Mark made good time for the next three days. He stuck to the west bank of the Ouachita River, finding wild fruit and nuts, and catching a small fish in one of the river's shallow tributary creeks. He never entirely satisfied his appetite but neither did he experience severe hunger pangs. The weather stayed warm and clear.

Nights were his bad time. Wolves and the big cats were audible and uncomfortably close at hand. Mark slept as high up in trees as he could climb. On day twenty-five—by his walking-stick notches—the river took a sweeping turn to the west. This change of direction was what he'd hoped for. It's got to be where the river comes down from the mountains, he reasoned. All he had to do now was find a big creek— which must be Hot Springs Creek—where it empties into the Ouachita . . . assuming that it looked in ancient times as it did in Mark's own century. Chancy, at best, but he had no other options.

In his haste to cover ground, Mark very nearly encountered another group of Indians. As he came around a bend, almost directly across the river from him were two rough brown shelters—obviously man-made. They had rounded tops, looked to be about six feet high. He heard voices from that direction, and he quickly ducked into head-high brush that ran along the river—nearly stepping on a mottled dark snake in the process. Another water moccasin. He jumped quickly away before the snake could coil to strike.

Mark stopped to get his breath. These close encounters left him panting and sweating, his heart racing. He bent over, put his hands on his knees, and took some deep breaths. This was his way of life now, and he had to stop feeling so wiped out every time something unexpected popped up.

He pulled himself upright, made sure he could not be seen from the far side of the river, and moved slowly through the high brush. For the better part of an hour, he worked his way up on the higher ground of the river's south bank, then, up-river, he waded and swam across, fully clothed. Constantly, he feared being seen.

Mark had hoped, by going into the mountains, to stay well clear of these Indians. He thought of them as primitive savages, and, from what he'd seen, they thought nothing of killing another human. If he could isolate himself in the depths of mountainous forests, then he could cook food, fashion flint tools, and weapons, give himself time to adjust to this total lack of civilization. It would *take* time . . . but then, he reminded himself, he had the rest of his life. What there was of it.

This had to be it.

The creek mouth was maybe forty feet across, and emptied clear, cold water into the darker-colored river. He had to assume that it was Hot Springs Creek and led north into the mountain valley he remembered. He couldn't see beyond the trees and brush around him, but felt sure those mountains had to be there someplace. Mountains that offered cover, concealment, and time.

Time to train himself. Right now, he grimaced, he wasn't ready for Stone Age living. Then he laughed out loud. He had to take Prehistoric Hunting 101. If you flunk, you get eaten. Well, at least he was recovering his sense of humor.

Mark didn't know he'd reached the mountains until the trail inclined at an angle. He'd followed game trails from the Ouachita River and now, surrounded by taller timber and less undergrowth, he knew he must be close to his target area. The hill rose more steeply on his left, the trail narrowed . . .

and there, on his right, below his level, he glimpsed a narrow valley. Another mountain, perhaps a thousand feet high, was visible just beyond the valley.

Yes, this must be it. If he could stay out of sight now, find a remote spot to hide, he might have a better chance to survive. He began to hurry up the path.

It was midafternoon: The sky had turned overcast, the air cooler. It began to drizzle, and the chilly breeze caused Mark to put on his outer jacket and zip it up. He rested, ate nuts, inspected the trees. At another time, he'd have admired the beauty of the place. Oaks and pines coexisted here, along with other species he couldn't name. The woods were "open" in the sense that he could see hundreds of yards up and down the mountainside.

He saw a few deer in the distance, and the undergrowth abounded with rabbits and squirrels. The woods were wet and quiet, soft rain easing the heat of the day. It would have been a good place for a nap had Mark found any shelter.

His trail led him along the bottom face of a rock cliff, covered with vines, that extended almost to the tree branches overhead. Then it wound up a sharp incline by large boulders. Underfoot, the path had grown slippery with rain, and he could feel points of sharp rocks embedded in the ground. Was it smoothed by animal traffic . . . or humans? If he could just get to the mountaintop, he might better plot a course for the densest forest he could find. Out of sight, away from all human contact.

His rising trail took a sharp turn—a cutback to the left—ahead of him, around a large stone outcrop that blocked his view ahead. He picked his way along more carefully to be sure there were no snakes at the base of the outcrop. That, he knew, was where they were apt to nest.

As Mark climbed the steep turn, up around the massive rocks, he had his eyes on the ground. When he looked up he was looking into the startled eyes of a little old man. An Indian.

Alongside him crouched a wolf. Ready to spring. Snarling. Teeth bared.

SIXTEEN

Shocked and frightened, Mark fell sideways against the rock wall. The old man, barely five feet tall, had his spear-thrower poised as if to throw, and Mark could almost feel the stone point rupturing his body.

He took a quick step back, struck a projecting rock in the path . . . tripped himself . . . both feet slipping . . . and flopped to the ground, squarely on his rump.

To his astonishment, the old man smiled. Mark realized he must have looked both clumsy and funny. He smiled, too, in spite of himself.

Lowering his spear-thrower, the old man stood erect, waiting. His wrinkled brown face was framed by wisps of gray hair. He wore a dark band around his head, his frail body bare, except for a kind of folded leather strap around his waist and between his legs, and rough sandals on his feet. His thin, hard body made him look like a wet bronzed statue in the drizzling rain. Unwavering brown eyes stared down at this massive, seemingly helpless creature on the ground before him. At first, the old man had thought to run. His pride wouldn't let him.

He spoke sharply to the wolf, who stopped growling and sat down on his haunches.

Mark's mind raced. It was life-or-death time. The future meets the past. This guy could kill him right now. What the hell do you say to Prehistoric Man?

First he smiled. That couldn't hurt. Then he crawled slowly to his knees. No sudden moves, he decided. Better act more hurt, more helpless than usual. He scratched his head, got slowly to his feet, hands empty. Wanted to make sure the old-timer saw he had no weapon.

He knew he mustn't look threatening. Be friendly. You're an innocent traveler, he told himself, as emotions and conflicting ideas clogged his mind. Buy some time. You mean no harm. Smile. Mark held up one hand, palm toward the Indian. He grinned more broadly, trying to think of something to say.

"Hi," he announced. "Peace!"

Mark, you fool, he told himself. *That's stupid. He doesn't understand. Maybe identify yourself. . . .*

He pointed to himself and spoke distinctly.

"Mark," he said. "I'm Mark."

There was a long silence as the old man considered this. He had lived a long life but had never seen anything like this. It must be a man, he decided, but it was ugly, huge, bearlike.

He knew this was no dream, that the big man was real. But was he seeing some kind of spirit from another world? Was his life now over and this being had come to guide him to another place?

Never could he have imagined any living thing so tall, on two legs, and so wild-looking. It wore loose skins, but from an animal he'd never seen. The mass of hair on the face and head was incredible. And those eyes—the color of clear water. He had never seen a man with blue eyes in his life, although he knew other members of his family who had heard of strange people with eyes unlike their own.

And those coverings on his feet . . . would anyone believe him if he survived this experience and tried to describe it later? He felt more reassured now of his own safety, having seen the clumsy way the man—if that's what it was—fell down on his rear. He knew also that his animal friend would attack and help defend him, if necessary.

So he would find out more about the strangest creature he'd ever seen. Its name was . . .

"Mock," he said aloud, pointing to Mark, who vigorously nodded.

Putting his hand to his chest, the old man said, "Um-see."

It came out as an unintelligible mumble to Mark, who cupped his hand behind his right ear and raised his eyebrows in question.

"Hmm?"

"Um-see," the Indian replied more slowly, and Mark understood.

"Um-see," he nodded, smiling broadly. Mark pointed to himself, and said "Mark" again, then to the Indian, and repeated "Um-see."

There was silence for a five count, as Mark tried to think of something more to say. Then he remembered the big wolf, still sitting, staring silently. Mark motioned to it.

"Wolf?" he tried.

Um-see heard the word and shook his head.

"Seebo."

Then there was silence as Mark debated his next move. They now all knew each other. *Great. Now what? If I turn and run,* Mark thought, *I'll get nailed in two steps . . . somehow I've gotta make some great conversation with a savage.*

Mark deliberately sat down on the wet trail. He smiled and motioned for the Indian to sit down facing him. It took a moment for this to sink in, but then the old man folded his body down in a single motion, but slowly. Mark noted how stiffly the Indian moved. Maybe the old-timer had arthritis. He then saw the Indian staring in fascination at Mark's shoes, now dirty, scuffed, and almost unrecognizable as the fashionable jogging shoes of a month earlier.

Mark took one shoe off and held it up.

"Shoe," he said.

After a moment, the Indian responded.

"Soooo."

Then the Indian slowly reached out and felt the fabric of Mark's pants. He rubbed the material together between his fingers and looked up, questioningly.

"Pants," Mark explained, and repeated the word.

"Panz?"

"No, pants," Mark repeated, emphasizing the T.

This, it seemed, was a new sound for the old man. He tried to say the word again, but the T-sound was indistinct.

Um-see had other thoughts as well. He stared fixedly into Mark's eyes. The old man always had trusted his own judgment, and he knew he could read men—and their nature—in their eyes. This great hairy man had a clean, honest look in the way he returned Um-see's stare. There was no hostility, only friendly curiosity. And uncertainty.

Yes, this was a man, not an animal. He was too clumsy to be a hunter, too obviously tired to be a threat. No longer did Um-see feel the desire to get away from this man. He knew Mock must be intelligent . . . could he talk to him? One thing Um-see knew: Mock was more afraid of him than the other way around. And he did need help, it was plain. He must come from some far-off place where men grew big and grew hair, like bears. Very well, he decided, so be it.

Stiffly, the Indian got to his feet. He motioned for Mark to rise also. The younger man took a moment to put his shoe back on, lace it up tight, and tie it. He looked up in time to see the old man's look of total fascination. Mark saw the Indian was impressed by all his shoelaces and his instant tying of the bowknot. Um-see stepped carefully around him on the trail and motioned for Mark to follow him back down the wet path along which the younger man had just come.

Um-see called to the silent animal and Mark saw it follow them at a distance, ears erect.

This was surely a wolf . . . and yet, he was bigger than those Texas wolves he'd seen. Lighter in color, although his hide and fur were drenched dark from the ongoing drizzle. The animal must be at least three feet tall at the shoulder, Mark guessed, and had to weigh a hundred pounds. Like some massive, tawny German shepherd, with a broad chest, white feet, and a bushy, white-tipped tail that curved up over his back. Mark shook his head. A big wolf, certainly, but it seemed almost doglike in some ways. One thing Mark knew for sure: The big animal could jump his back at any time. His other fear was that he was, in effect, being captured. What would this old man's tribe do with him? He'd have to watch carefully and find some chance to get away before he reached any big encampment or village.

Mark followed as the old man picked his way along the rocky trail, noting that the Indian limped, favoring his left leg. *He really needs a crutch, or something*, Mark decided.

"Um-see," Mark called.

The Indian stopped and looked around. Mark offered his long stick to the old man, motioning to the Indian's gimpy leg. There was a moment's silence as Um-see considered this, then shook his head curtly. He turned and limped down the trail.

That gesture puzzled the Indian. If he had wanted to carry a stick, he thought, he would have one. This strange man must think him helpless, and the thought made him resentful. He was determined not to give in to his injury, not become helpless. The leg did hurt sometimes. It had never mended properly after that fight with the black bear so long ago. Some days he felt more weak and helpless now that he was old. But the gesture made it seem this big man wanted to be friends. Was it a trap of some kind?

All the more reason, Um-see decided, why he should try to know this man and find out his way. He told himself that he was now very old anyway, and certainly this was the experience of a lifetime. He would do what he could to know this strange man, and find out anything he could to warn the families if Mark intended harm.

Besides that, Um-see was lonesome for human company. Even such an awful-looking man as Mark might also help him. Especially if Um-see fed him.

They stopped at the foot of the rock cliff that Mark remembered passing earlier. It rose straight up, arching out so that the tops of the great rock face was not visible from below.

Vines and weeds grew from cracks in the rough stone face.

Um-see pointed up, and said, "Ee-Uh." He waited for Mark's reaction.

Mark nodded dumbly, not understanding. Was this where the old boy lived?

Um-see moved to one side of the rock wall and reached into a fissure, pulled out a tangled length of vine that angled up the face of the rock. Looking up, Mark saw the vines disappear from sight about fifteen feet above his head.

Mark now found that while Um-see might have leg problems, there was nothing wrong with his upper body. He stepped back, pulled himself up the vines, and "walked" up the face of the cliff within seconds and disappeared from view. The muscles in his arms stood out like cords of bronze rope. The old man was solid muscle from the waist up.

Um-see looked down from the ledge above and motioned. Mark was expected to climb up . . . and this, he knew, was his chance to escape. Until he glanced to the side and found Seebo silently staring, not ten paces away. If he ran, the animal could nail him in three steps. Mark sighed. No escape . . . at least for now.

He wearily grabbed the vines, put his right foot against the rock face, and tried to emulate the Indian. He didn't fall or hurt himself—but it was a hard, sweating climb, and he rolled up over the ledge out of breath, hands raw and scratched.

Um-see squatted before a large opening in the cliff face. He now was sure. Mark was big, fearsome-looking, but not too strong. He had thought the big man would be powerful. But his face was covered with sweat, his breathing was rapid. Was he sick or just tired from lack of food? Perhaps he had come a long distance and needed rest.

When Mark rolled to his knees and looked up he saw what appeared to be a cave with a high entrance in the face of a rock outcrop. He climbed stiffly to his feet, moved closer. Two vertical rock faces rose from the rocky ledge, creating a kind of "front porch" roughly twenty feet deep and about forty feet wide. Dense walls of vegetation flanked both ends. But it wasn't really a cave, he realized. Heavy timbers stretched across the top. Someone had spanned a wide rocky crevice with trees, then piled dirt on top.

As Mark looked, Seebo came trotting around the end of the stone ledge from the underbrush. The animal must have his own way of getting up to the ledge. Seebo sat on his haunches near Um-see and studied Mark. It was disconcerting to the man. He had lived in fear of these hungry predators for weeks, and now had one looking at him as though planning its next meal. But Um-see seemed to control the beast.

Through trees still misting with rain, Mark made out dim outlines of a mountain in the distance—to the east, he thought. Walking to the edge of the rock face he'd climbed, Mark also saw the same green color of a level surface a hundred feet below him. It was a small valley between the two mountains.

He was sure now that he had actually found his destination.

This must be the valley of the hot springs, the place where he and Eleanor had come for their honeymoon. Hot Springs Creek must run down the far side of that valley. It had been in another lifetime when they had walked up and down Bathhouse Row and the city's historic area at the base of that far mountain. He recalled the warm baths they'd taken at their hotel, and wondered if there were pools of hot water nearby where he could clean himself.

"Mock," said Um-see behind him.

He turned and found the old Indian going into his shelter, motioning Mark to follow. He hesitated, then went inside.

It was dark and smoky. Rock cliff faces on both sides of the shelter were light in color and reflected illumination into the place. It smelled musty. Overhead, log roof supports were about six feet above him. High ceiling. And black, from what must be years of soot from wood fires.

Um-see bent over a circle of stones where embers glowed

dimly. Underfoot, Mark felt a firm, slightly sandy floor, swept clean.

There was a pile of furs along one wall, a large stack of kindling near the fire. As Mark's eyes grew accustomed to the gloom, he saw objects hanging from the logs of the ceiling. He could not make out how far back the shelter extended, but it must be more than thirty or forty feet deep. Um-see got a fire going. Mark wondered why, since the day was warm and the drizzle outside had stopped. Then he saw that the Indian was cooking something. He had a dark clay pot resting on large stones that circled the small fire. Mark moved to see what it was. Smelled good.

Then he became conscious of Seebo's dark outline silhouetted at the entrance. The big animal had quietly seated himself and sat looking inside. Mark realized that he was, in fact, a prisoner, if Um-see and the wolf chose to make him one.

He tried to shake it off. He was so tired from his ordeal, so glad to have some companionship, that he'd try not to think about that fearsome animal. Then the strangeness of all this hit him. How come he trusted this little old man? Somehow, Mark felt, Um-see meant him no harm. Was this just wishful thinking? He'd find out soon enough.

Um-see was cutting something into small pieces, dropping them into the pot over the fire. Fluid began to bubble. Um-see used a short-bladed knife of some kind. It appeared to be black, flintlike stone, with a shine to it. The Indian sliced up the material in his small hands quickly and expertly, then used a piece of hide to lift the hot open pot and securely fix it in the rocks, over the fire. Mark felt aware of intense hunger.

He stretched, then began to take off his jacket. Just as he unzipped it, he saw Um-see staring at him. Again, the Indian's mouth was open. He had seen the zipper open, Mark knew, so—to demonstrate—he zipped it up again, then opened it once more.

Um-see knew now this man had great magic. He had

never seen such shiny objects before, and the sliding thing must be a trick of some kind. Anyone who had such a thing, and could make it work for him, was a special man, one with other powers as well. Um-see's mind was filled with both shock and intense curiosity.

He pointed to the zipper and said, "Mock?"

Mark understood. He knelt down by the fire and showed Um-see how the zipper went up and down, opening and closing. He said, slowly and clearly, "Zip-per."

These sounds were foreign to the Indian's tongue. He could only mutter "Zim-puh.".

"Close enough." Mark smiled. He finished taking off his jacket, folded it carefully, putting it next to the rock wall away from the fire. Um-see stared at Mark's dirty sweatshirt. He stared at the writing on it: NIKE, stitched in letters three inches high. The Indian reached out his hand, and Mark moved closer so Um-see could run his fingers over the fabric. It seemed to entrance him.

Mark knew the Indian could never have seen fabric like this. Or metal on the zipper, or writing. It must be a lot for him to handle on short notice, and he could understand Um-see's shock. Mark had been out in this wilderness now for more than three weeks, he reminded himself, and he sure wasn't used to the Indian's world either.

Mark took the sweatshirt off over his head and handed it to Um-see. The Indian took it carefully, ran his fingers over the cloth, squeezing and turning it in his hands. He looked inside the garment, smelled it, and shook his head. It was beyond his understanding how it could have been made. Um-see was used to the simple weaving done by the women of his family, using plant fibers. They made light garments to cover the body, and in winter they made hide garments to cover feet, legs, and arms. But nothing like this. He would show this to his grandson's woman, and the other women. They would not believe it either.

Um-see was further surprised to see yet another garment on Mark's body—the stained undershirt. It had carried his meat, grapes, and berries, and there was a rainbow of smudged color all over it. The Indian noted, too, all of the body hair on Mark's chest, clearly visible through and around the undershirt. No man he knew had such hair. It was black and curly. Um-see shook his head again. This had been a day of surprises for him, and nothing in his life could compare to what he was seeing now.

He turned to the fire and used a hide scrap carefully to lift the hot pot off the rocks. He poured its contents into two small bowls. Then he handed one to Mark. Mealtime, at last. He was starving.

Yet he wasn't all that eager to dig in. The small bowl held a warm liquid with lumps in it . . . of something. Mark wasn't sure what. He smelled it. Not beef stew, for sure. He held it to his lips and took a tentative sip. Hot, spicy, but no familiar taste. The gravylike fluid was sweetish, and the lumps—he bit into one—seemed like some kind of meat. Venison, maybe? Chewy, but good . . .

Um-see watched him intently. The Indian sipped from his bowl, and food ran down the corner of his mouth, dropping onto his folded legs. He didn't appear to notice. He was sitting by the fire to eat while Mark leaned back against the opposite rock wall.

Mark was too hungry to worry long about what was in the stew. He sipped it hungrily and finished the full bowl quickly. It was then that the Indian turned to a basket near him and took off the top. He produced a small cuplike object, dipped into the basket, and handed Mark the cup. Sniffing first, Mark took a sip. Water, cool and clear. He drank, then examined the cup. Of course, he knew it now: a small gourd, or half of one anyway, complete with the stem to serve as a handle.

Mark couldn't take his eyes off the basket. He had to get up and go see it. How could a basket be waterproof enough to hold water? Must be a liner inside it. He knelt and felt the ground alongside the basket. Yes, there was some moisture but not much. He looked inside and, in the dim light, could see a faint coating of what looked like a white material on the inside of the basket. It appeared the basket weavers had found some kind of pitch material for a lining that made the thing waterproof. Mark sat back down, astonished at this display of ancient skills and applied technology.

Um-see held out the pot then and offered Mark more of the stew. When Mark held his bowl out, Um-see gave him all that was left.

"Oh, no. Keep some for yourself," he protested. Then he motioned to Um-see's bowl and offered some of the food to him. The Indian smiled and shook his head. He turned to a basket behind him and pulled out a handful of nuts—pecans it appeared—and began to crack them on one of the outer fire rocks. He offered some to Mark, who shook his head and ate the rest of the stewlike soup. Um-see cracked nuts and ate them in silence, watching Mark. This was an experience to remember.

In his weariness, Mark had nearly forgotten the wolf sitting in the entrance. Then he heard a soft sound . . . "woof." Not a bark. More like a coughing sound.

Um-see rose and went to the rear of the cave, reached into one of the hanging baskets above his head and took something out, came to the entrance and put it in front of Seebo. The big animal took it in his jaws, turned, and disappeared outside.

Mark saw it was growing dark. Rain no longer fell. A fresh breeze pushed tall pines back and forth, beyond the entrance. It felt wonderful to be in a dry shelter. For the first time since leaving his home, he felt real comfort, a full stomach, a sense of well-being. He knew he had to trust the old man, like it or not, and he grew sleepy as he tried to imagine what would happen to him the next day. He hoped the Indian would let him sleep here tonight. He put his sweatshirt back on.

For his part, Um-see assumed that Mark would sleep in his Ee-Uh, and he hoped that the big man did not have some sly, treacherous plan that would spell death for Um-see during the night. To be on the safe side, he would encourage Seebo to sleep inside the shelter this night. He rolled the man's strange name around in his mouth. *Mock.* He felt he'd never say it like the man did, with those odd sounds.

He got up and rummaged through some large skins in the back of the cave. He found three in good condition and offered them to Mark. This, it was clear, was bedding for the night. Mark had been prepared to sleep on the ground. The skins were soft and pliable, with hair on one side. He rolled up his jacket for a pillow and stretched out on the skins. He smiled, remembering how different this was from his own bed at home. But it was sure a lot better than what he'd known for nearly a month. He was asleep within minutes.

One thing concerned Um-see. The big man smelled bad. He must never wash himself. First thing tomorrow, the Indian decided, they would go down to the stream and get clean. Um-see didn't like bad smells. He hoped Mock's odor didn't keep him awake all night.

SEVENTEEN

Mark awoke to find the wolf sniffing his face. Inches away. Growling deep in his throat, Seebo watched unblinkingly as the horrified man shrank back against the rock wall, struggling to wake up. He was speechless. His hands scrabbled around the ground, trying to find a rock—anything with which to defend himself.

Pulling back, Mark watched as the green eyes stared with more curiosity than threat. He winced from the animal's rancid breath, found that his own mouth was open and he was holding his breath. Waiting for his fate to be decided.

Then came a shout from outside the shelter and Seebo turned and moved through the entrance. A bright morning sun illuminated the long body, and Mark saw him fully for the first time. Dried-out, this was a different animal than he'd seen the day before.

Seebo was golden. The sun sparkled on his head, back, and flanks with an intensity that made him glow. As he moved, Mark saw the underside of the tail, the insides of legs, and stomach. All were a light tan color. A dark line of gray outlined Seebo's tawny, peaked ears. Across the shoulders was a band of copper-colored hair. The rest of his hide, pure gold in the intense light, contrasted with white feet and the white tip of his bushy tail.

This was, Mark knew, the most awesome four-footed animal he'd ever seen—in strength, power and sheer beauty. But was he wolf or dog? Or some of both? Seebo resembled the thin, reddish wolves he'd encountered so far . . . sharp ears, short muzzle, rangy length, floating movements. Yet, now, with his upturned tail waving slowly across his back, at this instant he seemed a huge domesticated, friendly dog. Um-see's companion and protector, certainly . . . but his pet? No, Mark decided, this was nobody's pet. He was a hunter, with wolf's eyes, wolf's movements, the power in those jaws to kill anything in the wilderness.

Um-see stood on his rocky porch and put his hand gently on the animal's head. Then he produced a small animal body from a basket he carried and tossed it to one side. Seebo walked to it, sniffed, took it in his jaws and disappeared into the underbrush alongside the porch. Mark leaned against the rock wall.

He wiped his hand across his face, found sweat running down into his thick, matted beard. God, what a way to wake up. He had a dull headache, he was hungry, and he needed a bath in the worst way. He must smell awful. And to wake up looking into the eyes of an iron-jawed killer, inches from his face!

Um-see came inside, looking at Mark in a new light, and was disappointed. He had hoped this strange traveler might have miraculous powers, might indeed be able to make magic in some way. But now Um-see knew he was just as other men. He had been scared out of his mind upon awakening, as any stranger would. Mark had to eat, to sleep, he showed fear when facing danger. Very well, perhaps it was for the best. Since he was a man like any other, Um-see would treat him as one and not a spirit.

Mark pointed outside and raised his eyebrows with a question.

"Um-see wolf?"

The old man shook his head slowly, not understanding.

"Seebo yours?" Mark tried again, pointing to the Indian. Um-see would try to explain.

"Seebo," and he held his hand close to the ground. Then he repeated the animal's name as his hand rose by stages, until it was almost to his waist. Mark understood.

Um-see had raised the beast himself, possibly here in this shelter. He lived here . . . Mark was the intruder. Would the big animal tolerate his presence? Then he became aware he had to urinate, immediately, his swollen bladder made worse from his wake-up shock. He pushed upright, looking at Um-see, and held himself below, with the obvious query.

Um-see pointed out the doorway, then around to the left. If Um-see needed any more evidence by which to judge whether Mark was man or spirit, he now got it.

As Mark stepped into the doorway, the rising sun bathed his face, momentarily blinding him. He stumbled over a small rock and fell down onto the rocky porch, catching himself with his hands, and on his right knee. He rolled over, cursing furiously, and grabbed his knee, rocking back and forth.

"Oh, goddammit. That miserable . . . oh, shit. Now I've broken my damn knee. Ahh."

When Mark fell, Um-see had the nervous impulse to laugh. The big man did look funny as he fell. But his pain was real and understandable, and the Indian knelt down quickly to look at the damaged knee. It was a little bloody, and scratched but no real damage done—although Um-see noted the rip in Mark's pants. He felt of the material, and wanted to examine it more closely, but the younger man lurched to his feet, now in pain from both his fall and his need to relieve himself.

Mark limped to the left side of the porch and saw a narrow rocky path that disappeared into underbrush at the side of the rock formation. He took several steps, then could wait no longer, and urinated into the foliage, being careful not to touch it. All he needed right now, he decided, was poison ivy on his penis. It was going to be that kind of day.

Um-see held out a gourd full of water and a long strip of something brownish in color. Mark took them both, sipped the water, and looked at the meat . . . meat? Um-see sat down, chewing on the same kind of strip. He dunked it into the water, stirred it around and chewed on it.

Mark did the same. It was tough, salty, hard to chew, but he finally knew it was a kind of dried meat. Venison, most likely. He could see why it needed soaking. That made it a little easier to chew and—eventually to swallow.

Then Mark remembered seeing what looked like black-berries the day before. The berry vines went up the same side of the rocky porch where he had just urinated. Great. He'd have to go see if he had pissed on the rest of his break-fast.

Um-see made it clear that it was time to get busy. Doing what, Mark wasn't yet sure. The little Indian stood near the edge of his front porch, obviously ready to climb down the vines to the path below. He held two coiled ropes and two baskets. Mark saw curling ends of fiber sticking up out of the rope coils. Must be made from plants, he concluded. Um-see handed him a basket and rope, without a word, and then motioned for him to climb down the rock outcrop.

Still limping, his knee covered with blood and aching slightly, Mark wanted to lie back down in the shelter and feel sorry for himself. He still quaked from that eye-to-eye encounter with the wolf-dog.

Um-see motioned again. He was anxious to get this strange man moving. It was an hour since dawn; the Indian had been up for two hours and was having doubts about the wisdom of his inviting this stranger to his home. Mark did seem to get upset about small things.

Mark slung the rope over his shoulder, hesitated, and tossed the basket down to the trail below, then began to lower himself down the vines, trying to avoid hitting his injured knee on the rock . . . Damn! Hit it again. Mark dropped the last two feet from the vines and sat down to massage his knee.

He had left his outer jacket in the shelter since it was already a warm morning. He took off his sweatshirt, then took off his stained undershirt to wrap around his knee, which was oozing blood. He tied it securely, put his sweatshirt back on, and staggered to his feet. This was embarrassing since he knew the Indian regarded him critically now, and he hated to appear inept at every turn.

Um-see motioned, and Mark followed him off down the trail, descending steeply down the mountainside. Mark saw that it was more than a game trail. The footing was hard, studded with well-worn rocks. Thousands of people had walked this path. It had to be near an Indian settlement, and he became more nervous about where Um-see was leading him. He regretted now leaving his jacket in the shelter . . . if he was led into a hostile village, he'd want to run, try to get away. Surely, they'd see some sign of human life shortly. Mark felt certain that Um-see was no hermit . . . there were other Indians along the river, only a few miles distant. He liked the old man, wanted to trust him, wanted to stay and eat again . . . but safely. He shrugged and followed the limping figure down steep pathways, out of the forest, into a gentle sloping area with fewer trees. He stopped in shock and his eyes widened in disbelief.

Facing him across the valley, only a hundred yards away, was a scene of such power and magnitude that it took Mark a full minute to look and slowly comprehend.

It was a huge, wide waterfall, stretching off in both directions. The mountainside—and it must be Hot Springs Mountain, he realized—rose from a smoky, shadowy valley. It was covered with a massive sheet of shimmering, gold-colored rock of some kind. Steaming water cascaded down from more than a hundred feet up the mountain, down over a glistening surface, to fall hissing into pools and ponds at the base of the mountain.

Mark guessed the waterfall to be at least a quarter mile high, and some of the upper reaches—where water came from the mountainside—were just below the tree line. There was little vegetation where the hot water smoked its steaming way down to the vapor clouds below.

Mark tried to take in all the detail, standing in awed incomprehension. Um-see waited patiently, seeming to understand the astonishment that this spectacular sight had caused. Finally, he moved forward, onto the valley floor, toward the wall of steam and falling water.

Mark knew that bright surface lining the mountain's face must be some sort of sediment caused by the gushing springs above. Closer, he saw dozens of mounds high up on the mountainside, where water poured up out of the ground, then fell through steam clouds that obscured the creek bed beneath.

Um-see led him across the narrow valley, where there were few trees, and to the edge of the stream. Mark remembered then: This had to be Hot Springs Creek. Looking around, he smiled. Here would be downtown Hot Springs, centuries in the future. Bathhouse Row, with pedestrians, tourists, traffic, twentieth-century civilization. The time he'd come from, and where he wanted to be. Now they were the only humans in sight.

They waded through knee-deep water toward the vaporous area ahead, the creek turning warm around their legs as they splashed to the opposite bank.

They stopped at a wide pond, about twenty feet in diameter, a steamy mist rising from it. Um-see pointed into the pond. Mark understood, but first he leaned down and put his hand into the water.

Hot . . . but not too hot. Fair enough, he decided. If Um-see wanted to bathe here, Mark was ready. By this time the Indian, naked, was easing himself into the water. Mark saw how frail the Indian's lower body was. He had very little rump. His legs, like his arms, were stems of knotted muscle.

Mark removed his shoes, began to push down his boxer shorts, then changed his mind and decided to keep them on. They needed washing worse than he did. He eased down in the water and found large boulders just beneath the surface. He lowered his body down between them, and let the water come up to his chin. It felt wonderful.

Um-see was seated, too, splashing himself and dipping his head underwater. He had removed his headband and was rubbing it in the water. Then he settled down to his chin and closed his eyes.

This was about as close to really feeling good as Mark could remember since he left home. The only other thing he'd like to do right now was shave. He always enjoyed shaving in a hot shower—and he kept an array of fine shaving tools next to the shower, as well as his new fog-free bath mirror that let him see to shave as the steam swirled up around him.

Another world, another life. For now he was content to stay here as long as Um-see wanted to.

Mark's knee had stopped hurting in the hot bath, and he felt almost cheerful as he and Um-see waded up the creek to the north. He had finally washed all the clothes he had on, including his shoes, and with the sun now at midmorning level, the damp clothing was not uncomfortable.

Crayfish is what they sought, it soon became clear. Um-see showed Mark, by example, how to spot the shrimplike creatures as they darted about the shallows. This is what their baskets were for, and they spent the better part of an hour grabbing crayfish that swarmed in abundance in the chilly upstream water.

When they had nearly filled the baskets, Um-see motioned them back toward the shelter. These things, Mark decided, must be what he'd had for supper the night before. They probably tasted like shrimp, although he'd been too tired to notice.

Well upstream from the valley's waterfall area Mark saw animal life all around him. Rabbits bounded everywhere. They spotted a small deer herd farther north, near the base of a mountain blocking the valley's upper end. They spooked two dark-colored snakes along the river's edge. Um-see seemed unconcerned and made no effort to kill the snakes, detouring around rocks and logs where they'd appeared.

There was yet no sign of Seebo, and Um-see did not seem concerned about the animal's absence.

He had not brought his spear-thrower, so Mark concluded this was not a hunting expedition but a morning bath and resupply of easily available food.

Even if Um-see could have communicated with Mark, it is doubtful whether he would have told his visitor that Seebo was off sulking. Um-see saw that another person in the shelter had upset Seebo's rhythm of life, and the wolf-dog was upset, resentful, and jealous. He always accompanied Um-see on even the shortest trips about the valley. This morning he had taken his meat and disappeared . . . probably watching from a distance right then.

It worried the older man. He valued the animal's friendship and respected his feelings. It came to him that Seebo might try to harm Mark . . . no, that was unlikely. He was a deadly hunting animal, but he never killed or attacked prey unless it was necessary. Um-see began to think it might be a good thing if his guest moved on into the wilderness after a few days.

As they neared the shelter Mark understood why they carried the ropes. Near some fallen trees, Um-see stretched his rope on the ground and began to gather dry, broken branches and short tree limbs. He motioned Mark to do the same. Firewood was everywhere since it was obvious, even to Mark's untrained eye, that the valley was the path of annual floods, which sent underbrush and small trees coursing down between the two mountains . . . probably in springtime, Mark guessed. Now there were limbs and wood trash along both sides of the valley, caught in underbrush and small trees, piled well above the height of a man.

He followed Um-see's lead in wrapping up a large bundle of firewood in the rope, and was astonished to see how big Um-see's burden had become. He must have sixty pounds of firewood on his bony shoulders, and carried the basket of crayfish in his left hand. It was all Mark could do to move the same load, and he knew he'd have to stop and rest every few hundred feet. Mark stumbled along behind the agile Indian, limping as his cut knee began to throb. He told himself that Um-see, old and frail as he was, would surely plan some R&R for the afternoon.

It didn't seem unreasonable to Mark that a midday nap might be on the program, considering the morning's exertions. Um-see, at the shelter, saw to the hauling up and storage of both bundles of firewood. He cleaned the fresh supply of crayfish with a little water poured into one of the smaller baskets, as Mark watched. Um-see then produced two round, thin objects from another basket. He handed one to Mark and filled two gourds with water. The Indian broke his round cake in two, dipped half into the water, bit into it, and began to chew.

Lunch, Mark decided.

He took an exploratory nibble and found it rocklike. He'd read of a nineteenth-century sailor's ration called hardtack. This stuff certainly fit that name. He dunked it into his gourd, and it was still hard.

By soaking the cake in water and chewing vigorously, Mark was able to eat the thing down to the last bite. At least it was filling. He could see why Um-see and his people—wherever they were—would find this a handy way to keep food dried and ready to eat for long periods. Crumbled up in that good stew they'd eaten last night, it wouldn't be too bad.

Mark watched Um-see chew the hardtack and saw again what good teeth the old-timer had. There seemed to be but one gap in his lowers. They were white, even, and looked well formed, although some were worn and came to a partial point. It had to be eating tough material like this that wore one's teeth down, Mark concluded. He hoped his own were in good shape. There'd be no dentists out here.

Um-see leaned back against the rock wall on his front porch, his eyes closed.

Nap time, Mark concluded. He, too, relaxed against the rock wall and was dozing off when he felt his shoulder being nudged. Um-see was up and getting ready to go someplace else.

Damn, Mark thought. *This old guy needs some lie-down time, too. Why can't he relax awhile?* The younger man hated the thought of climbing down that rock wall again. Besides, he realized, glancing up at the sky, it was about to rain again.

Nevertheless, within minutes, they were lowering themselves down the rock wall to the trail, each with a coiled rope and one basket. This time Um-see carried his spear-thrower, and Mark saw three spears in a thin sack that Um-see wore over his shoulder. It also contained short, stone-tipped projectiles that appeared to fit into the ends of Um-see's spears.

Mark then knew. This was a hunting trip. Oh, hell. He was already tired. He began to watch the trail, and picked up hand-sized stones for his pockets. Some defense was better than none. He was glad he'd worn his jacket.

Um-see concealed his annoyance. Where was Seebo? He had counted on his animal friend hunting with them. This was an important opportunity Um-see had not had in many weeks: another man to help bring home their game.

Repeatedly in the past, Um-see had tried to fit a harness onto Seebo so that the animal could carry meat and hides, but the four-footed hunter would have none of it. Even as a puppy, he had resisted any restraints being put on him, growling and fighting. Which meant that Um-see could bring home only a small portion of the meat he needed for himself and his shelter.

Now with Mark to help carry home their kill, Um-see was determined to hunt this day, whether it rained or not . . . whether Seebo joined them or went hunting on his own. One thing Um-see knew: If the wolf-dog wanted to find them, he would. The old man kept glancing around. He would much prefer to hunt with his powerful four-footed friend than without him.

Um-see signaled Mark to stay behind him. He did not

want him scaring any deer they might find before he threw his spear. Um-see shook his head in amusement as he watched the big man pick up rocks from the trail. That wouldn't help much . . . unless Mark could hurl those stones like a spear. The Indian chuckled to himself.

His pocket rocks not only gave Mark some sense of protection, but brought back memories. Among them was the one he most cherished, along with some he did not cherish at all.

Mark's father, hoping his boy might love competitive sports as he did himself, tried everything in his power to instill a love of athletics as the youngster grew up. At twelve, Mark finally agreed to try out for a Little League team—having declined until then to go near a ball diamond. For what seemed hours to Mark, his dad had played catch with him in their large backyard. John Lewellyn could see that his son, although chubby, could throw well. So he took him to Little League tryouts. Mark did what he could. He was slow running the bases because of his weight. He caught the ball well, and it was immediately apparent he could throw with speed and accuracy for a twelve-year-old. But the weight he carried in his upper body and waist kept him from hitting the ball. He swung late and rarely connected.

"Dad," he told his father on the way home after three days of practice, "it's not my thing. I like baseball, but I don't think I can make the team."

John had to face the fact that maybe his son was right. The kid wasn't going to be effective unless he really wanted to be—and he just didn't have any desire. So in succeeding years, John had to be satisfied with Mark's younger sister, Cleo, a natural athlete, filling up her room with ribbons and trophies from swimming and tennis.

Mark, however, had made an important discovery. He could in fact throw the baseball. Hard and accurate. A junior in high school, he went out, without his parents' knowledge, for the baseball team. He was still overweight but knew he had strength in his right arm. The coach was impressed, and for several days had Mark working with one of the team's catchers, then pitching batting practice.

Again, however, Mark saw the handwriting on the wall. He couldn't run with any speed and had never batted enough to develop an eye. If he did connect, he was an easy throw-out at first.

"Mark, I'm sorry," the coach finally told him. "You can pitch, no doubt about it. But we have two other guys who throw almost as well as you do, and they can also run and hit. So if you want to stay out, you can probably get some playing time as a substitute. Otherwise . . ."

Mark didn't fight it. He also didn't mention this to his dad but resigned himself to daydreaming about being a major-league pitcher and never played the game again.

He avidly read newspaper sports pages. Mostly he followed the career of an up-and-coming pitcher named Nolan Ryan. By the time Mark was married and had a twelve-year-old son himself, Ryan was well on his way to one of the most spectacular careers in the game's history.

Mark thoroughly memorized Ryan's statistics, read avidly of the man's straight-arrow reputation, his mind-boggling workout routines, and, as Ryan got older, his defiance of time by pitching no-hitters when other men his age had long since retired.

It was one of the great thrills of Mark's life when he took Charles to the ballpark that memorable night of May 1, 1991, as the Texas Rangers played Toronto. The excitement was electric for 33,439 fans that night as Ryan held Toronto scoreless and hitless going into the final innings. It was pure magic for Mark Lewellyn since he knew how it must turn out. And it did: Ryan scored the seventh no-hit game of an amazing career, at the ripe old age of forty-four, some five years older than Mark himself.

Next afternoon, Mark suggested to his son that they "throw a few" in the backyard. Charles, sixteen, was starting catcher for his school baseball team, and they were having a fine season as school neared its end.

Charles and his dad had played catch before in their backyard, but this day was somehow different.

Charles watched his father pace off the distance from the pitcher's mound to home plate—sixty feet, six inches. This was farther apart than they usually stood to play catch. Charles was curious to know why his dad wanted to measure off the exact pitcher-to-catcher distance.

As they began playing catch, he saw his dad was throwing harder than he usually did, and began "winding up" before he threw. With his high knee action, it looked much like Nolan Ryan—the knee coming almost up to the chin, before the stretch and delivery. To Charles's astonishment, his father fired a fastball straight into the pocket of his catcher's mitt with surprising force.

Then his father did it again, and again, the ball smacking leather with real power. *For crying out loud*, the boy thought, *this man can throw!* Charles squatted down and got set, in wonder, as his dad threw a succession of streaking fastballs directly into his mitt. One pitch in particular nearly rocked Charles back off his feet. He stood up, shaking his head in wonder. It was a side of his quiet, pudgy father he'd never seen. How could a man with a big gut throw a baseball like this?

"Dad," he said, "you've been holding out on me. I didn't know you could throw like that. Why didn't you ever play ball?"

His father fairly glowed with pleasure. He tried to be cool and offhand. "Oh, I just never could hit the pitching, and they had guys better than me.

"Son"—he shrugged, knowing how phony that sounded—"I was too fat, and I just didn't have the desire. I wish now I'd forced myself to lose weight and that *my* dad had kicked me in the ass a few times, to make me stay out there."

Mark remembered going into the house then, feeling better about himself than he had in years. He knew he didn't have Nolan Ryan's ninety-six-mile-an-hour fastball, but his arm felt good and he felt, well . . . apt. The next day his arm and shoulder would be so sore he could hardly move them. But he almost sang in the shower that particular evening. For once in his life he had impressed his son, physically. It would probably never happen again, but for tonight it was a splendid feeling.

So much for history, Mark reflected, as he trudged along behind the limping Indian. Baseball . . . another lifetime, another world. He'd never see another game, he sadly reflected, but he still savored that wonderful moment in his backyard, when he found he could make the baseball go exactly where he wanted it to, and at great speed. He'd always remember that.

After an hour's walking, both men were drenched and tired. Um-see's sparse hair was plastered to his head. Mark sweated inside his outer jacket but kept it on since a cool breeze had come up as they climbed higher up the mountain, toward the top. They had come two miles or more, and the woods were silent, with only the hiss of rain spray dripping through the wet oaks and pines. Underfoot, the trail was muddy and slippery. Mark couldn't figure why the Indian didn't turn back. What the devil were they out here hunting, anyway? It would take forever just to walk back to the shelter.

The sharp crack of a branch to their left, up the slope, caught both men's instant attention. A herd of a half dozen white-tailed deer ran at them, full speed, veered away, and disappeared in the trees. Um-see raised his spear-thrower, but it was too late. They were gone before he could throw. Um-see moved up the trail, motioning for Mark to stay back. The Indian knew something had frightened the deer.

There was a rock outcrop on the trail just ahead of Um-see, blocking his view. He stepped carefully to his right, into knee-high weeds, peered around the rock . . . then began backpedaling, raising the short-handled thrower. The Indian backed directly into a bush, caught his balance, but dropped his spear. As he stooped to pick it up, a black bear came loping, head down, around the rock outcrop.

Mark heard the bellowing growls before he saw the bear. The animal was limping but still moving fast. Blood streamed down its back and it weaved slightly as it lumbered into view, the bear's glistening black hair soaked with rain, wounded and killing mad.

Um-see had retrieved his spear. In one fluid motion, he raised it and threw. The four-foot projectile streaked into the bear's left side, causing a howl of pain and anger. The animal paused less than ten feet from the Indian. Um-see raised another spear as the bear lunged forward, moving its lower head back and forth.

This was the biggest bear Mark could even imagine. He stood five feet high, even down on all fours. Mark unconsciously took the rocks from his pocket as Um-see threw hurriedly. The spear flashed past the animal, and the bear, with one great forepaw, knocked the Indian flat on his back. He lay there, dazed.

"Hey," Mark shouted, "look here!"

The bear stopped as its jaws moved toward the Indian's throat. Mark was twenty yards away and he had no conscious plan of attack. He wrapped three fingers around the largest of his rocks, and began a pitcher's windup. As the bear paused, watching, Mark threw as hard as he could. His rock passed three inches wide of the bear's head.

Mark quickly began another windup as the wounded bear moved toward him. He forced himself to be deliberate. This was his last chance. His left knee came up toward his chin and he concentrated on the bear's eyes. The animal was growling hoarsely, eyes on fire, saliva at the corners of its jaw.

When Mark threw, taking a long stride with his left leg, he put all of his weight behind the rock, which weighed slightly more than a baseball. It struck the bear squarely in its left eye, with a sickening thunk. The big animal staggered, lost its footing on the muddy trail, fell to one side. Great paws plowed the ground as it tried to get up.

Um-see, now alert and watching, moved instantly. He drew his small knife and leaped directly on top of the struggling bear, plunging the five-inch blade squarely into its damaged left eye. The thrust penetrated the animal's brain. In a mighty convulsion, the bear jerked up and over, hurling Um-see into the air as it roared, grunted, then lay quivering.

Um-see, on his side in the tall grass, looked up and then lay back to get his breath.

Mark sank to the ground on his knees, his heart pounding, mouth dry, trying to get his breath. He could not believe what had just happened. This was some awful nightmare, and it was not over yet.

A jagged flash of lightning illuminated the forest. Mark jumped, then heard growls and snarls of other animals nearby.

Rain began falling in sheets, almost blinding them, as the two men stared intently into the gloom, just beyond the dead bear. They saw the floating outlines of four wolves, moving back and forth, snarling quietly, clearly intent on claiming the bear carcass as their own. Mark sensed that they were the animals that had wounded the bear earlier and put it to flight. Now the wolves intended to get rid of these humans, who stood over their quarry.

Um-see watched the wolves as they circled. His weapon was useless for the moment. When the bear knocked him down, his spear tips went flying. He held his left shoulder, where blood seeped through his fingers and colored his arm to the elbow. He did not think the wolves would attack.

Mark, still on his knees, acted from instinct he didn't know he had, whipping off his outer jacket, wrapping it around his left arm while kneeling. Only much later would Um-see tell him that, crouching low, Mark looked like another animal to the wolves. Seeing the dark, hairy figure close to the ground, the nearest wolf charged, lunging directly at Mark's throat.

The terrified man got the jacket-wrapped arm up in front of his face just as steel-like jaws snapped together, burying long fangs in layers of fabric. Mark felt the bite penetrate his skin and he staggered to his feet, the wolf growling and pulling at him.

With no thought, Mark grabbed a handful of the wolf's skin at the neck with his right hand and pulled the animal around him. In desperation, he clung to the wolf's skin, pivoting fast in a complete circle, the animal stretched out in the air. As he came around a second time, Mark flung the wolf with all his strength against the sharp face of the rocky outcrop.

The wolf slammed into the rock headfirst, and dropped without a sound. The next instant, something slammed into Mark and he was rolling on the ground, aware that another wolf was on him. He tried to keep his wrapped arm above his face.

An explosion of sound and fury swept the animal off him. Mark quickly rolled over, staggering to his feet. A dimly seen but vicious fight went on almost at his feet between two wolves, snarling and screaming as they bit and slashed at each other. But the bigger one . . .

It was Seebo, and as he attacked the wolf that had been on top of Mark, the man found his pocket rocks and threw hard at another wolf closing in. The rock hit the animal's leg, and, with a yelp, the animal veered off, limping.

Mark watched Um-see fire off the only spear he could find, aimed at the last member of the wolf pack. It snarled, screamed at the impact of the stone spearpoint, and raced around a rock outcrop. Mark saw it was not a killing wound. But the wolf did not reappear.

He'd been hastily backing away from the fighting animals near him, but now the noise of their struggle stopped. Seebo stood panting over the wolf's body, his jaws covered with blood. Then Mark saw his injuries.

Seebo bled from at least three raw wounds on his back and hindquarters. He held a bleeding left forepaw off the ground, then limped to Um-see, who had sat down by the dead bear. The fight was over.

There was silence then, except for thunder muttering between the mountains and rain slanting through tall trees. Darkness was near. Mark sank to the ground near Um-see and wiped his face. He was exhausted, spent, his mind numb with relief. He unwrapped his left arm, and when the jacket came away he found a row of bloody spots on his bare arm. The wolf's teeth had broken the skin but had not penetrated deeply. He let the driving rain wash his arm as he inspected, almost clinically, the dripping teeth marks. Strangely, he felt no pain. Maybe he was still in shock.

He felt Um-see standing beside him. Mark looked up to see the Indian with a tight grin on his wet and weathered face. Um-see said nothing, but reached out and put his hand on Mark's shoulder and squeezed gently.

Mark smiled and nodded. No words were needed. It had been a very close call. He climbed to his feet and touched the old man's arm. It was a good moment for them both.

A lightning flash showed Seebo nosing around the wolf he had killed, a growl rumbling deep in his throat. The big animal must have trailed Mark and Um-see through the forest and found them as the wolves attacked. Mark shook his head. He didn't know whether he could have survived the second wolf's attack without Seebo's help. He doubted it. He owed this animal his life.

But Seebo did not seek either man's approval. He almost ignored them, walking over the bloody ground, favoring his forepaw slightly. He sniffed at the dead bear, the wolves, then sat on his haunches and stared silently at the two exhausted men. They both felt lucky to be alive. It was the first time in Um-see's long life he'd heard of wolves attacking men, without provocation. Then he realized—it was the bear. Their quarry, and they wanted the meat bad enough to kill men for it.

Um-see wondered even more at Seebo's attack . . . this came as a total surprise. He had raised this wolf-dog, had seen the big animal bring down deer many times, even once, with another dog, he'd seen Seebo attack and kill an elk. But wolves . . . they were part of his blood and, well, he admitted to himself, Seebo was hard to understand. Something else troubled him more.

Um-see made a silent appeal to the Spirit that rules all animals. He wanted to explain that he would not kill any wolf needlessly. Surely the valley Spirits would understand. It was considered bad luck among his people to kill wolves, unless the people were starving or threatened.

Wolves always had been a part of Um-see's life, the same as deer, elk, turkey, all the living things of the forest. They were respected as hunters, they protected their young, they killed only for food, even as man did. No, he told the Spirits, he should be considered innocent of wrongdoing, and he apologized to the Spirits of the dead wolves, if they should be near.

EIGHTEEN

Um-see knew what Mark did not.

Their danger wasn't over. Far from it. The wolf pack didn't give up so easily. And it was almost dark.

Lightning continued to split the dark gray skies with jagged blue-white explosions. Rain pounded the mountainside as both men shook off different reactions to near disaster.

Um-see knew how close death had been. But he always had expected—even hoped—to die in a fight like this one. It was how a hunter's life should end.

Mark's mind was too numbed to think clearly. What caused him to do what he'd just done? It was as though he'd been watching some other person, outside himself, someone who knew exactly what he was doing. Mark could not imagine where his nerve, and actions, had come from. He must have momentarily gone mad from fear and excitement.

The Indian knelt on the bloody bear carcass and with quick knife strokes, cut into the animal. It was hard going, Mark could see. Sharp as it was, the obsidian knife required repeated slices to penetrate the bear's thick hide. Mark wanted to help but knew this was up to Um-see. So he began looking in the weeds for the Indian's lost spears and points. He found two each and put them into Um-see's spear sack. Then Mark looked at the carcasses of the dead wolves. He couldn't believe he had killed them. *I'm no killer*, he told himself. *How can this be happening to me?* He wanted to sit down, put his head in his hands, and pretend this was all some nightmare and he'd wake up soon. Then he found himself shaking and felt hot all over.

He glanced at the rock that he'd thrown at the bear. He picked it up, examined it. Better save this. He didn't want to think about where he'd be now if this rock had missed.

"Mock," the Indian called and pointed to the two baskets they'd flung to one side of the trail. Given one, Um-see put bear meat inside, chunks at a time. He had managed to cut most of the hide off the bear's side and belly, and continued slicing away, inside of the carcass, to get the organs. Mark found himself pleased to see both heart and liver pulled out and put into the basket. It was deeper than Um-see's other baskets, obviously designed to carry burdens long distances. There was a heavy, wide strip of hide woven around the bottom, which ended in a thick carrying strap at the top.

Now Um-see paused and looked around for Seebo, then tossed a chunk of bear meat. The animal sniffed it, paused, looked around, then carefully took it in his mouth and walked a short distance away before stretching out, full length. He began eating carefully, facing the forests and not the two men. Seebo, Mark saw, expected more trouble.

Um-see motioned. The Indian held his hands so as to form a circle, then held them wide apart, vertically. It took Mark a moment to realize the Indian was trying to tell him they needed a pole. Of course! Something to carry hide and meat. He remembered that grisly scene weeks before, those Indian hunters killing the other Indian, then walking off with their meat tied to long poles carried between them.

Mark rummaged through the sodden forest debris. Most long branches were too rotten, the smaller ones too willowy. He finally found one with no bark, attached to a fallen oak. He bent, twisted and kicked it, and the weathered limb finally broke away. Seven feet long, he judged, and three inches thick. Maybe too heavy—but he pulled it to Um-see, who nodded. The old man had managed to roll the bear's body over and was cutting into its other side. Both baskets were full of sliced bear meat. Heavy, Mark noted, as he picked one up. He hoped they could carry everything.

Um-see was breathing hard as he sheathed his knife and stood up. He motioned to Mark to grab one edge of the bear hide. They pulled together and got the hide from under the animal's remains. Um-see had sliced off a long section of the bear's skin, from neck to haunches, all around the bear's massive body. What was left sickened Mark as he stared at it. He clumsily helped Um-see pick up the bloody mass of hide and wrap it around the pole. Their ropes were blood-soaked and slick, but they finally got the hide tied on securely. Then Um-see picked up one end of the pole and put it on his shoulder. Mark did the same. He estimated that both pole and skin must be at least eighty pounds. Each man picked up the handle of a full basket of bear meat with a free hand. *Another thirty pounds or so,* Mark thought . . . *how far can I go with this load?*

They heard Seebo growl behind them. Um-see knew the sound. Danger. He hurried onto the trail, pulling Mark along at the rear of the pole.

Mark knew Um-see was in a hurry and, glancing to one side, knew why. As the two men staggered away with their load, Seebo stood glaring and growling behind them. He turned and followed the men down the trail as five snarling wolves huddled over the remaining bear carcass.

More than once, Mark mentally gave up and decided he could go no farther. Every fifteen or twenty minutes he called a halt, put his burden down, and sat in the muddy trail. Um-see was tired, too, and did not protest. They sat with heads down and eyes closed, rain dripping down their faces. After a few minutes Um-see would stand, look at Mark, and wait. The younger man wanted to refuse to go on. He wanted to lie down and sleep right there. But when he looked at the thin old Indian, he could not bring himself to quit. He wanted this man's respect—and quitting was not the way to earn it. So he repeatedly staggered to his feet and trudged on.

By the time the trail wound down to the rock cliff below

their shelter, it was dark, the forest illuminated only by lightning flashes, as rolls of thunder pounded their eardrums.

Mark leaned against the rock as Um-see climbed up the vines to the porch above. Moments later a rope snaked its way down and Mark attached it to a basket of meat. Within minutes, Um-see had hauled up the baskets, then Mark attached the rope to the pole and hides. He wearily climbed up the vines, scrambled over the edge, and rested a moment. He helped Um-see pull up the heavier hide burden from below.

He could hardly remember, later, getting into the shelter and on his hides for sleep. Mark vaguely recalled Um-see wrapping the bearskin in fresh hides from the back of the cave and suspending the meat baskets from overhead hide strips.

The Indian revived their fire, pulled out one strip of bear meat, roasted it over the open flame for a few minutes, calling Mark's attention to it. The exhausted younger man sat as though dazed, leaning against the rock wall. Finally Um-see handed him a stick spearing about a half pound of roasted meat. Half-asleep, Mark nibbled it, found it edible and, without thinking what it tasted like, must have fallen asleep as he lay down, still chewing. He was not even aware that Seebo came by him, sniffed at the sleeping man, and moved on into the rear of the shelter to sleep.

Dawn sent a pale shaft of light across Mark's face, his bladder reminding him it was another day. He groaned, his muscles complaining at every move as he tried to get up. His knee ached where he'd fallen yesterday. He could hardly lift his right arm or shoulder, so stiff was his entire upper body from last night's rock-throwing and weight-carrying. The line of brown spots on his left forearm reminded him of possible infection from that wolf.

Then he remembered yesterday morning and the shock of Seebo staring into his eyes, inches away. Mark staggered outside. Seebo was nowhere in sight, Um-see was already busy at work, doing something with sticks. Mark headed quickly around the corner to the urinal area, looked up, pleased to see a clear sky. Maybe the sun would ease his black mood and aching body.

Um-see was erecting some sort of circular shelter on their rocky porch. He had six flexible poles, perhaps eight feet long, stuck into holes and crevices on the flat rock, wedged in stones to keep them in place. He pulled the tops of the poles together and tied them with hide thongs.

The result was a round skeleton hut, slightly taller than Mark. Inside was a circle of stones, and in the circle Um-see had started a small fire. Bits of wood had been burning for some time, it appeared, and Mark knew Um-see had been up working for hours. The sun began to redden the tops of the tall trees over on Hot Springs Mountain, to the east.

Um-see dragged piles of folded hides out of the shelter, and he beckoned for Mark's help. Each hide had lengths of rope tied to slits in two edges. As Um-see motioned directions, the two men secured the hides, one after the other, to the vertical poles of the hut framework, enclosing it. Soon smoke came out of the hut at a small opening at the top.

Mark now saw what this was about: Um-see intended to smoke the meat they had collected the night before. He left a small flap opening loose on one side of the hut, so he could get in and out. Peering inside, Mark found the Indian hanging hunks of bear meat on lengths of hide tied to the overhead pole framework. A small opening had been left around the base of the hut, so fresh air could get in to feed the fire.

Um-see added more branches and built the fire to a higher level, but not high enough to scorch the hanging meat. He finally closed the flap, got some gourds of water, and offered Mark one.

Hunger pangs made themselves known then as Um-see offered Mark another piece of the tough dried meat he'd first seen yesterday. He ate hungrily, then sat down against the rock wall, cracked a few pecans. Breakfast.

He remembered that he had not taken his walking stick with him last night. When Mark found it, he scratched two more notches on the side of the stick, one for yesterday, another for this day. He counted: His twenty-seventh day since leaving the twentieth century.

Well, old boy, this is your life, he told himself. *Forget home, forget the past. From now on, you're out with the wolves, bears, and Indians. You'll be bitten, bruised, and hungry most of the time. At least I don't have car payments anymore.*

While Mark had been daydreaming, Um-see had spread out the bear hide on a part of the rocky porch. It was still damp with blood. Um-see began scraping it with a sharp stone, a scraper about six inches long, sharp on one edge with a point on one end. The scraper's other end was thick, so it could be grasped firmly.

Um-see scraped at big globules of meat that clung to the hide's fleshy side. He stopped repeatedly to pull up long fatty ligaments and cut and lay them aside. He quickly was covered with bear blood up to his elbows.

Sweating, he looked at Mark, got up, went inside the shelter, and returned with another rock similar to his own. He offered it to Mark, then turned and went back to work. Mark grinned.

He had been gently asked to help out. So he knelt by the Indian's side and began to scrape with the stone, as Um-see was doing. *Yes*, he told himself, *you've got to earn your keep in this outfit.*

An hour later, Mark's knees were raw, and the bear hide was fairly clean of fleshy material. Um-see seemed satisfied. The skin still had a whitish layer of meatlike matter on the underneath side of the black hair, but it was smooth.

Um-see carefully collected all the fatty material they had scraped off in two clay pots. One appeared to contain only fat, while the other held chunks of meat.

The Indian placed both pots inside the smoking shelter, between the circle of stones where the fire blazed and the outer hide wall. From time to time, Um-see added green branches to the fire within the hide shelter. It created thicker smoke.

Um-see was pleased at Mark's willingness to help with the scraping. At least the big man wasn't lazy. Nevertheless, Mark was delighted when Um-see pointed toward the hot pools on the far side of the valley, and raised his eyebrows, smiling.

Mark nodded vigorously. A bath? Absolutely!

If Mark thought this would be a short workday, after their hunting adventure, he was disappointed. After a quick lunch of crawfish stew, Um-see gathered baskets and ropes and stood waiting for Mark to get slowly to his feet. He'd been hoping for a short siesta.

Instead, Um-see led the way in scaling the jagged face of their shelter, a height of some twelve feet above the "front porch." Um-see had two of the tough fiber ropes tied to a small tree above them, and they climbed this with ease. On the shelter's roof, soil sloped up the mountainside through dense underbrush and thorny thickets. Some of this had been placed there deliberately, Mark thought, as Um-see moved tall bushes to one side, allowing them to get through.

This, he smiled to himself, was Um-see's rooftop security system against marauding animals that might approach the shelter from above.

They soon encountered another game trail that led north along the upper mountain, and came to a wet place where a trickle of water had eroded several feet of the trail down to bedrock. Here was a clear pool of water, in a rocky receptacle at the base of an outcrop. Mark cupped some of the water with his hands and found it cold and delicious. Both men drank at length, then filled baskets nearly full. They retraced their steps to the shelter roof, trying to spill as little of the water as possible. Mark went below, and Um-see lowered the water baskets to him on the ropes.

Overnight, Um-see had done a great deal of thinking about this unusual blue-eyed stranger. He had been impressed the previous night at Mark's courage and his ability to stun the bear with a stone. Then his killing of the wolf was so unusual he knew that his grandson would hardly believe the tale.

He also had noted Mark's reaction to these events and knew the man was not an experienced hunter. It had bothered him to kill animals, and he knew little about taking skins and meat.

Now the Indian was satisfied that Mark was a man with no evil intent. Um-see still could not imagine how such a different kind of man, dressed in these unbelievable skins, could be here—but he decided that Mark was welcome. And he would allow the stranger to help him with all of the things that Um-see formerly had to do alone. He might even enjoy teaching Mark things he clearly did not know about life in these mountains, if the younger man chose to stay.

As he thought about these things, Um-see decided on his next housekeeping task. He spread out a large hide on the porch, alongside the smoke tent. He handed Mark one of his black knives. Mark noted the length: about eight inches. Some three inches were rough, stone handle. It was two-edged and very sharp.

Reaching inside the smoke tent, Um-see began to bring out chunks of bear meat. They were hot to the touch, but much of the fat and blood had drained away and were grayish in color.

Um-see began to slice the meat into long strips. It was slow cutting since the meat contained gristle. Mark followed suit, watching to see how Um-see handled his knife.

Um-see poked a small hole into one end of each strip. He then fed a thin ribbon of old, cured hide through the hole, and tied a knot in the hide strip, to keep the slices apart. He added more meat to the string until there were a dozen or more slices suspended on it, and this he hung from the topmost members of the poles inside the smoke tent. As fat dropped from the hanging strips, the fire leaped and sizzled.

Green twigs and branches began to smoke, and Um-see closed and tied the entry flap.

Um-see looked closely at Mark, seeing that the younger man still suffered from the effects of the previous night's hunt. He glanced up at the sun. Yes, he decided, there was time for what he wanted to get done this day.

He motioned Mark inside the shelter and pointed to his sleeping skins. Then Um-see stretched out on his own skins, closed his eyes, and seemed asleep immediately.

Mark sank down thankfully. He needed this.

Mark woke up as Um-see gently shook his shoulder. He started up from his hides, fearing some emergency, but it was just a wake-up call.

He was stiff and sore—as usual, he reflected as he climbed to his feet. Where on earth would the old guy want to go now? he wondered, expecting the baskets-and-ropes routine again.

Um-see was pouring something like melted fat into three small clay pots. This was the bear fat that the Indian earlier had put inside the smoke tent. Um-see added small chunks of meat or gristle to the liquefied fat. He sliced up thin pieces of old hide, dunked both ends into the fat, then went inside the smoke tent, returning with a small piece of burning wood.

Within a few minutes, the old man had ignited what was apparently the "wicks" of hide that stuck up from melted fat in the pots. Mark understood. This was illumination. Um-see handed one of the lighted pots to Mark, took the others in each hand, and moved into the dark, rear portion of the shelter.

With three flickering flames, it was possible to see what was back there. Mark looked around curiously.

The place was an absolute mess. Old, crumpled hides were thrown about, there were many short lengths of wood, poles, dozens of baskets of various sizes were tumbled together. Mark could not count the number of pots—some broken, some whole that were underfoot.

Why was Um-see showing him all this? After a few minutes, he realized it was clean-up time. The Indian gathered an armload of hides and took them out to an open space on the porch. Mark did the same. They repeatedly picked up armloads of everything in sight—baskets, pots, sticks, rectangular wooden frames, ropes, baskets, both new and old, some loaded with rocks, chips, stone implements. There were baskets full of small stone pieces that, on closer inspection, turned out to be rough spearpoints designed for Um-see's spear-thrower. And there were two racks of deer antlers plus a bigger set, covered with dust, that must be from an elk. Leaning against the rearmost wall of the packed-earth shelter was a crude ladder of thick tree branches, some ten feet long. Its "steps" were short branches, tied on with hide thongs.

This answered Mark's question about how Um-see could hang those baskets of food from the ceiling. The flickering pots of oil revealed that just below the high ceiling timbers were two stout poles, stretching from one side of the shelter to the other, black with soot. They were stuck in holes gouged into the two rock walls that formed the shelter's sides. It was from these poles—reached by that ladder—that Um-see was able to suspend his food in baskets.

Um-see himself carried out a bulky, rolled-up bundle of hides. Unwrapped on the front porch, they proved to be garments of all kinds. Mark saw long leggings, obviously to be tied on the legs with hide thongs, and a poncho affair with a head hole in the middle, for the upper body. There were shapeless woven garments, but Mark couldn't tell how they were used. He did recall that it got cold in these mountains in winter, with occasional snow. This must be cold-weather gear.

It took them nearly an hour to get everything out of the shelter's depths and into the open. Mark was surprised at the huge cache of supplies that Um-see had stored away. All this for just one man? Or was it some kind of tribal warehouse?

It was also throwaway time. Um-see went over the piles of material, picked up a rope here, a pot there, rotted pieces of wood, and laid them in a different pile. He intended to get rid of the old stuff, Mark assumed, and so the younger man pitched in and began to examine everything. He found cracked pots, held them up for Um-see's inspection. The Indian shook his head and pointed to the throwaway pile.

Mark followed him back into the shelter depths as they collected the last scraps of debris. The old man took a length of old hide, dragged it over the sandy floor surface, and tidied its appearance.

They then took the salvageable material back into the shelter and stacked it carefully. Hides that were clean of animal hair on both sides went into one stack, hides with hair on one side into another. Pots were neatly arranged, as were baskets, by size and shape. They worked steadily, as the three pots of bear fat sent tiny spurts of flame and smoke up to the blackened roof timbers above. Mark sensed that Um-see's shelter must have been in use for generations. It was large enough to allow a big family to live there, although the circulation of air left something to be desired.

Family occupancy must once have been the case, Mark noted, as he found that Um-see placed the lighted oil pots on flat areas of the rock walls that had been chipped away for just that purpose. He saw at least five places where oil lamps had blackened the stones above, all the way to the roof.

It took all afternoon to arrange Um-see's supplies in the rear of his shelter and stack everything in neat piles along the walls. As for the throwaway stuff, Um-see tossed it over the vegetation on the urinal side of their front porch. This, thought Mark, was their garbage dump.

After feeding the smoke tent fire again, Um-see made clear his intention to go on another errand: He picked up rope and basket, motioning Mark to get his, too. Sighing wearily, Mark got up and did as ordered. Why was he letting this old-timer work him like this? He knew the answer: It was a place to stay. With security. Food. Companionship. Mark knew what was out in that wilderness: death by violence, slow starvation . . . or loneliness. This was better, even if he was working harder than he ever had in his life.

They had collected crayfish from the upper stream, north of the hot-water area, for more than an hour, almost filling both baskets. They stopped at a wild plum tree, where Um-see climbed up and dropped dozens of the tiny fruit to Mark, who wrapped them in a soft hide Um-see gave him. They picked up the usual large bundle of firewood on the way home.

Mark fell on his sleep skins and watched as Um-see now did one more chore. He laid out the still-damp bearskin and, with a large gourd, ladled out cold ashes from his circular interior fireplace. The entire skin side of the bear hide was covered when he finished, to a depth of two inches or more. He mashed the ashes flat, then carefully rolled up the bear hide, ashes inside it.

Mark assumed this must be some sort of preservation process, as Um-see wrapped an old hide around the roll of bearskin and stored it in the back of the shelter.

Then he turned to rekindle the fire, and when Mark saw the stew pot he knew it was suppertime. Whatever it was, he would eat it. It didn't matter. He was starving. He marveled at the way the old man moved, in his steady way, from one chore to the next.

Where did Um-see get all his energy? *He's gotta be sixty anyway*, Mark judged, *and he had me going dawn to dark. He's still cranking, and I'm pooped*. What was worse, Mark realized, Um-see was shamelessly exploiting the younger man for his work potential. Then he shrugged. He'd wanted some hideaway where he could learn survival in the wilderness . . . now he had it, but there was a work price to pay. He knew he had to convince the old Indian that he was a handy monster to have around the cave. Otherwise, he could be out the door.

NINETEEN

Mark looked into Um-see's basket and found himself staring into the glazed, dead eyes of a deer, its head severed from its body. It rested in a pool of thick blood and raw meat.

Mark's stomach recoiled, and he swallowed, turning away, then hurrying into the cave for a gourd of water.

Um-see had climbed up the vines from below and motioned for Mark to pull up both baskets. One contained the deer head and edible organs, the other held much of the deer carcass.

The older man was tired from carrying both heavy baskets, but he went about his chores briskly, stoking the smoke-tent fire and laying out clean hides on which to prepare the venison.

Mark had been allowed to sleep while Um-see was up before daylight to hunt and kill a doe. Mark was puzzled, his stomach still upset at the sight of that severed head.

Why would Um-see take another large animal when they had all the bear meat, crawfish, and nuts they could possibly eat? It made no sense. Was Um-see trying to put in a large supply of smoked meat for the winter? It was still summer, and too early for that, it seemed to Mark. *But*—he shrugged—*what do I know about such things?*

What he did know was that Um-see now had another four baskets of deer meat on the porch, plus a bloody hide, waiting to be cut up and worked on. Another day off to a sweaty start, he sighed.

*   *   *

Mark and Um-see butchered the venison into strips and hung it inside the smoke tent, removing some of the dried bear meat and storing it in baskets hanging in the rear of the shelter.

Mark sat down to drink water and crack nuts, but Um-see had another chore in mind. He came out of the shelter with his stone ax in hand. It was little more than a heavy rock, sharp on one edge, secured by hide strips between split ends of a heavy, wooded handle. Um-see also carried the rolled-up bear hide, which he now unrolled, shaking out the ashes over the front side of their rock porch. He cleaned the skin side of the bearskin with a soft hide that had been soaked in water.

Then Um-see pulled the deer head from one basket, laid it down on the bear hide, and carefully began tapping it with his ax. He made an obvious decision, then quickly chopped down twice with the ax, splitting the skull open. Brains and blood splashed out on the bear hide. Um-see held the deer head up, so that all the contents drained out on the hide. He tossed the shattered head aside. Then with his hands, he began to rub deer brains all over the bearskin's inner, fatty surface.

Mark was horrified as Um-see massaged the grayish material, streaked with blood, into every square inch of the bearskin, then went back over the surface a second time. As Mark forced his stomach to settle down, he saw there must be a method to this madness, some sort of curing or tanning process. But why brains? Why not fat from bear meat? It seemed bizarre. Then a thought occurred to him: Protein? A kind of preservative?

Now Um-see came from the shelter, dragging a wood frame made of short poles, and motioned for Mark to help him.

With his skinning knife, Um-see made tiny slits in the edge of the skin, and laid it across the frame. Mark held one side of the frame for him while Um-see stretched the bearskin taut—with the skin side up—and tied it in place with hide strips. He stood the frame up against the rock face next to their shelter entrance, so that the rising sun's rays hit it.

Um-see then took two handfuls of remaining venison into the shelter, and Mark guessed the Indian's intentions. He revived the inside fire, pierced the venison slices with green sticks, and positioned them above the fire.

Mark would have to force himself to eat anything, so shocking had the brain-smearing process been to him. He pushed himself up and walked out of the shelter, and around to the urinal side. It would be a little while before he could face the enjoyment of this morning's à la carte special. The rocky front porch had the strong aroma of rotten eggs.

Um-see was glad things had worked out well that morning. He did not like to hunt large game so close to the shelter, since dawn was when the wolf packs did their hunting also. With Seebo alongside, Um-see had speared the young doe near his spring, and Seebo brought death quickly to the animal with his powerful jaws. It was the kind of teamwork Um-see had worked long with the wolf-dog to perfect. And he rewarded Seebo with a large chunk of the best meat as he began to skin the deer.

Seebo guarded the carcass, while Um-see made two round trips to the shelter, carrying hide and meat. He was glad to see that Mark had finally arisen. The young man slept too much, in Um-see's view, and it seemed unhealthy to him.

He gathered ropes and baskets and waited at the lip of the rocky porch for Mark to join him. It was well past sunup, most of the hunting animals were asleep in their dens, and it was time for men to be working.

Um-see was glad to have Seebo's company this morning. Coat glowing golden in the morning sun, he had joined the two men quietly as they began their trek, appearing suddenly from brush ahead of them. Now Seebo ranged through the open underbrush on their uphill side, stopping occasionally to smell the cool morning air.

In one respect, it was a melancholy journey for the old man. He hated to dwell on the past, but today he couldn't help but remember a time long ago when he and his son, and his son's best friend, had walked this path together. It was a painful memory. The two boys, young men really, were in high spirits, had chased birds and deer just for the pleasure of seeing them fly and run. They felt as close to this fine, open forest as they did their homes.

Um-see's eyes misted over as he remembered the bad end to that day. The young men had tugged and grappled with each other on the tall rock, in a friendly way, enjoying their youth and strength. Then one had slipped, grabbed the other and they both fell from a great height. Um-see found his son alive, but the other young man had broken his head open in the fall. Then the great bear had appeared, hunting, and Um-see did not have his spear-thrower. The bear approached, and Um-see threw his weight against it. They rolled down the mountain, struck a tree, bounced off, and landed in a rock-strewn gully. The bear was dazed, and Um-see killed it with a great boulder. But his leg was hurt. He could hardly walk.

By the time the injured man got back to his son, the young man was dead. It was the worst day of Um-see's life. Suffering his own pain, he stayed at the spot all that day and night.

Next morning, weak and barely able to move, Um-see struggled back to his village. He knew that the animals would devour the young men's bodies. He thought he would die on the trail but managed to reach the families' shelters down the valley. When a search party reached the young men later, there was little left of the bodies. Um-see wished to die since he knew he should have prevented the accident. No one blamed him, but he knew the other young man's father felt differently toward him after that. He had failed his duty as an elder man, and he blamed himself.

There was also his son's woman, who was with child. She

now had no man. He moved to her shelter, since his own woman had long since died, and helped care for the young woman until she gave birth to his son's son. Later, she selected another young man, and they moved to their own shelter.

Um-see watched proudly as his grandson grew to manhood, not only tall and strong but wise as well. It was clear to all that he would become a fine hunter. Now, Um-see decided, he could spend his remaining years helping others. He would, if the Elders agreed, become Helper in the valley.

This was an honored post, one always held by older, respected men. It came from the age-old tradition that these families were keepers of the hot springs valley. The caretaker families lived nearby on the mountain slopes in winter, then along the great river just south of the valley in summer. The Helper lived in the valley year-round, aiding visitors who went there to visit or to die. Many came because they heard the hot water would cure problems of their bodies. Um-see was not sure of these cures, but he respected the waters and loved to bathe in them.

After the elders agreed for him to be Helper, Um-see moved to the mountainside shelter overlooking the valley. His grandson and his friends helped clean and improve the old shelter, built long ago between two stone walls protruding from the hill.

Um-see found the work of Helper to be hard and lonely. He could not hunt large animals alone since he could not carry the carcass. So he took small game and prepared hides and spearpoints while the families were all away. Few visitors came in the warm time. Most came when the snow flew and the valley was protected by its steep hills. He looked forward to that time since his grandson and friends would return. For diversion, he raised the wolf-dog and explored all of the mountain trails. He sometimes was sad and felt sorry for himself and the limits that age constantly told him about. Now, with Mark's appearance, he had someone to help him . . . although he did not understand this strange man. All that laughter last night, when Um-see could see nothing to laugh at. But Mark was helpful to have with him.

The teacher in Um-see was fascinated to see what such a strange, crude man could be taught about living among peaceful people.

After Mark's stomach stopped growling from the fresh-meat breakfast, and his muscles stopped complaining, he began to feel almost energetic walking along the mountain trail. He knew this must be an important mission since both men carried two baskets each, with their ropes. Um-see had his spear-thrower while Mark had shouldered one of Um-see's hide sacks that contained nuts and four hand-sized rocks. They must be going somewhere to get something special, he figured. He was even glad when Seebo joined them.

They stopped once to drink from a spring outcrop, and another time to relieve themselves. Mark had found that Um-see never fouled the paths they walked. The older man moved several paces off the trail, dug a small pit in the leaves, and squatted there for his bowel movement. Mark followed suit, and brushed leaves over the waste when he finished.

With warm weather, Mark wore only his boxer shorts and shoes. He felt less conspicuous outdoors now, virtually undressed, and he had to smile at the thought. *Who's to see?* he asked himself.

It appeared they had reached journey's end when the trail stopped amid an area of boulders, on a mountaintop. Mark found a steep drop-off beyond them, to a valley he estimated to be hundreds of feet below. Um-see motioned him away from the precipice.

Suddenly, Mark knew the place. That old Indian quarry, of course. The same place he and Eleanor had visited with other tourists and a guide, so many years before. It was different, yet the same. Now he found more and taller trees. But the rock outcrops and boulders were much the same: novaculite. Most was gray, some streaked with red and pink.

Underfoot, as he'd remembered, were countless thousands of stone chips of every size and shape . . . the result of long years, perhaps centuries, of work by these prehistoric peoples, getting the stone they needed to survive.

He stood fascinated as Um-see went to work at a broad stone face, near the drop-off, using a hand-sized hammer stone to chip at the stone face.

Mark felt drawn to one formation in particular. At the cliff's edge stood a tall, single tower of rock—on top of which was perched a long, massive boulder. It appeared to be balanced precariously, and was so heavy that Mark could not imagine any men putting it there. He knew his recollection came from guidebooks he and Eleanor had read on their Hot Springs visits. One showed a large illustration of Balanced Rock. Local guides explained that the horizontal rock itself was no longer there in recent times. Here, now, it was as pictured, just as nature designed it.

Mark soon understood why they'd brought four of the deep carry baskets. For the rest of the morning, Um-see hammered away at large stone boulders, chipping at first one surface, then another. The old man knew what he was after, Mark could see. The baskets began to fill with stone "slices," four or five inches in diameter, from a quarter inch to a half inch thick. This must be raw material Um-see needed for tools and weapon points.

When Mark tried also to strike larger stones against the rock chunks, he could not seem to extract the same kind of stone chips as the Indian. Clearly, there was a technique involved. First, Um-see would pound out a large piece of the stone, weighing five to ten pounds, and then he would bring his hammer stone down sharply along the edges, chipping off the thin stone slices along a grain line that Mark could not see, even on close inspection.

It was hot, tiring work, and Um-see stopped twice to rest and once for water from a nearby spring. For his part, Mark got down on his hands and knees to sift carefully through the carpet of stone chips, hoping to find something resembling a blade. He failed, realizing that what was here were all rejects from other Indian stone chipping.

Mark sensed this must be late summer. Leaves were falling from the big oaks, and some of the pines had carpeted the ground with needles and cones. Even at midday there was a coolness to the breeze, a slight chill to the air at the top of the mountain. Mark could see nothing but low green mountains in the distance, unbroken save only for a thin silver creek in the valley below. This was primeval country, sparsely populated, with room aplenty for its few occupants. They had clear, abundant water and an almost unlimited game supply for food.

Seebo spent his time sniffing underbrush or resting in the shade. Then Mark watched him move slowly, quietly—then spring into brush, from which two rabbits scampered. Seebo was on one of them in a second, and Mark winced as he saw the wolf-dog's powerful jaws crunch into the rabbit's neck. Seebo vanished into the brush to feast on his midday meal.

Um-see also stopped work for a time so they could chew on dried meat and nuts, then rest in the shade. He dozed off immediately, and Mark wished he could catnap like that. Then he did, lulled into a doze by a cool wind and the low buzz of insects that roamed through the red, yellow, and gray cracks of the great stone outcrops.

When Mark awoke, Um-see was nearly finished with his chipping. The four full baskets were heavy—at least thirty pounds each, Mark estimated, as they left the mountaintop.

He marveled at the fact that Um-see, even limping as he did, carried his two baskets with ease. Only a fine film of sweat coated the Indian's nut-brown shoulders, and he did not seem to be breathing hard.

The younger man was wet with sweat, as usual, his beard itched, and his arms ached.

Mark could hardly move his arms and shoulders two hours later when they deposited the load of stone chips inside the shelter. He watched in surprise as Um-see spread out an old hide, then began digging handfuls of ash from the indoor fire, out on to the leathery scrap. In a few minutes he had dug up much of the ash heap, down at least six inches deep.

Um-see spread all the stone chips inside the circular depression. The fire ring was about five feet across, ringed with stones, and the pile of stone slices covered the circle to a depth of several inches.

Then the Indian replaced the ashes on top of the stone chips. Mark got down on his knees to help him, wondering what on earth they were doing.

When all the ashes and dirt were back in place, Um-see kindled a new fire. He ignited it with a smoldering stick from the smoke tent, and soon the inside fire leaped and crackled higher than Mark had seen it. The Indian put all his remaining firewood on it to build it up as high as possible, and smoke quickly filled the shelter, making it too warm for comfort. Mark stepped outside.

It was still early enough to have a hot bath before dark— and there was something in the valley he wanted to look at more closely.

He got Um-see's attention, pointed to himself, then across the valley to the hot steam, making it clear where he was going.

Um-see nodded, then handed Mark two coiled ropes. He smiled slightly. As long as you're going, he made clear, bring back more firewood.

This guy's always thinking ahead, Mark noted. *Carry something. Don't waste time, don't sleep much, get up before daylight to work or hunt. No damn rest for prehistoric man.* He grimaced. *Well, at least the hot water never runs out in this place.*

In a straight line, their shelter was only about a quarter mile from the spring. Mark eased down the steepest paths, across the narrow valley floor, and was soon in the hot water. He left his shorts on and removed only his shoes. The valley was partly shaded as the sun sank lower, and it was all Mark could do to avoid drowsing off in the warm pool he'd selected.

The sun warmed and dried him as he got out and walked north for a few hundred yards to the point where the creek, beyond the springs, turned to the left. Here were raised piles of brush, left from what must have been a big spring flood. Small timbers, limbs, and rotted logs had been swept downstream and piled up where the swollen spring had turned south toward the hot, steamy area.

Mark circled the brush piles and saw what he'd noticed yesterday—a pole, about five feet long, with a slight curve at both ends. He climbed up on the piles of trash, got one end of it, and pulled it free.

By bending and twisting the long branch, he assured himself it was not rotted. About two inches thick in the middle, it was weatherworn and smooth, tapering at both ends. Oak, most likely.

He decided he had found himself a bow.

As usual, Um-see was mystified by the big, hairy man's actions. He saw that Mark did not take any rocks with him to the spring. Was he no longer afraid of wolves, snakes, or bear? Um-see concluded he must be brave, or foolish. And he seemed fascinated by the hot water. Through the trees, Um-see could see Mark getting into the pool. Perhaps, like some of his own families, Mark had religious feelings about the water and the steam that rose in smoking clouds above it.

Um-see had noticed that other visitors had been awed by the vapor and the high wet wall shining in the afternoon sun. Some families, he had found, seemed to feel a bond between the hot springs and the invisible spirits that ruled all people.

Being a practical man, the Indian gave little thought to such things. It was enough for him that the hot water was close at hand for cleaning things, scraping skins, and keeping the valley warmer than other places beyond the mountains. He had heard of such places but never wanted to visit them.

Later, he saw that Mark had brought home yet another long stick with the firewood. Why did he find sticks so interesting? Would he seek to make a spear-thrower? Um-see hoped so. He could protect himself with well-aimed rocks, but the Indian worried that Mark needed a better weapon if he ever intended to take animals at greater distances.

Then Um-see sighed when he saw the size of Mark's curved pole. Wrong size. Too long. Too thick. Ah, well . . .

That night for the first time, Mark had enough energy left before sleep to sit outside the shelter after supper. It was cooler tonight, and he had put on his sweatshirt. The night was clear, and he admired the blanket of stars that blinked through waving branches overhead. Night noises were tuning up. Wolves, both far off and close by, created their own blend of mournful harmony. There were barks from coyotes. Every insect in the forest tried to speak at once.

This, Mark realized, was no longer strange to him. He could relax after dark, with a full stomach, in no fear for his safety, and enjoy the magic of nighttime in these low mountains. He thought sadly of his family, wondering how they were living in his absence. His eyes misted as he thought of not seeing Charles again. Never had he fully appreciated his talented, stalwart son. The boy was mentally tough and focused, just like Eleanor, Mark reflected. He would shake off his father's absence and get on with his life. But it was sad to think of leaving such good people behind.

He sighed, yawned, and went inside to sit on his pile of bed skins. By the light of firelight, reflecting off both rock walls, Mark turned his new pole over and began planning how he would try to turn it into a bow. He must thin it slightly in the middle for a good grip. The limbs must be shaved in thickness so it would bend but not break. It must be slow, careful work.

First, anyway, Mark would need cutting tools from that novaculite buried under the big fire. Um-see had used most of the firewood Mark had lugged home to keep the fire high all afternoon and evening. Already, he saw, they'd need more firewood in the morning. Why was it important to get the stone hot? It must have something to do with the way it flaked, Mark finally had to conclude. Otherwise, this was dumb, and so far he hadn't seen Um-see do anything dumb. The more he thought about it, the more impossible it seemed that he could actually make a real bow.

He shook his head. It seemed hopeless. He felt as though he could never learn fast enough what he had to know to survive in the wilderness—especially alone. Um-see had provided him with refuge, for the moment. What if he had to leave here? He still would have no tools, no weapons. After all, he was forty-one years old, still overweight, felt weak much of the time, and had virtually no future to look forward to, here or anywhere.

Mark put his head down on his knees. So far, he was not a smash hit as Stone Age Man. He still couldn't do much except sleep in trees and sponge off an old Indian's generosity.

Besides that, it bothered him that Um-see's wolf-dog seemed to avoid him. Seebo had appeared briefly that night, stared at Mark, taken the meat put out for him, and left. Mark sensed that, before he came, Seebo slept at the shelter. Now he didn't.

Yet the animal had virtually saved Mark's life in their bear–wolf encounter. Why would he have intervened . . . unless, it came to him, Seebo attacked on Um-see's behalf, to chase the wolves away?

Mark decided he would understand if Um-see wanted him to leave. Clearly, he had upset the rhythm of the older man's life . . . at least as far as Seebo's valued friendship and protection were concerned. Mark sighed. That deadly four-footed companion was of far more value to Um-see than he himself. Tough to admit, but there it was.

TWENTY

She could walk no more and sank to the ground, exhausted. From before dawn the woman, carrying her small child, had been following her man through valleys, winding through forested pathways, always seeking water and places of refuge. She began to worry that they were lost.

Her man, she could tell, shared her fears.

This trip, both knew, had been a mistake. The man, feeling a deep debt to his father, had agreed to accompany the older man back to his ancestral home, some nine days' walk to the south. It meant bringing the woman and their son with them, but it was very important to the old man, since he knew that his time to live was brief. He had been coughing up blood for two days and increasingly seemed confused as to the directions they should take. Now he lay down in the grass, dropping off to sleep at once, while his son and the son's woman tried to decide their best course of action. It was late in the day, and they must soon find refuge for the night, where they could defend against predators if need be. It was clear to the man that his father could not help them. He was barely able to walk. Another day on the trail, and his end might come far from where he wished to die.

The woman looked up quickly, hearing a sound behind them, and then her man grunted, alarmed.

Down the slope from the nearby woods trotted five men they had never seen before. They were not smiling or friendly and had not shouted some customary form of greeting. The leader of the men was tall, wide, and fearsome in appearance, his black hair hanging loosely to his shoulders. He, like the others, carried a stone ax and a long spear. He stopped two paces from the apprehensive travelers and glared at them, but did not speak. The woman's man tried to be friendly.

"We need your help," he began, "since dawn we have come far and . . ."

He got no farther. The big leader of the group motioned with one hand, and the woman felt herself seized from the rear, both arms pinned to her sides, lifted up, and held tightly. Her little boy began to awaken at her feet. She cried out, and her man quickly grabbed up his stone ax.

He was too late. The big man who led the group already had his knife in motion. It ripped into the traveler's midsection in the blink of an eye, and the woman screamed as her man fell to his knees, clutching his stomach, his intestines dripping through his fingers. Groaning, he fell forward as the woman cried out in hysteria, and the boy began to whimper.

The older man on the ground, now awake but unsure what had happened, tried to rise, but the leader of the group shoved him back to the ground with a kick of his foot. "You and you," he shouted to two of the men behind him, "kill the old man!"

Uncertainly, the two men stepped forward with their long spears and hesitated, looking again at their angry leader. "Now!" he thundered. "Kill him, or I kill you!" Quickly, they began jabbing at the old man as he understood his plight and sought to stumble away. One spear thrust caught him in the side, and he fell down and rolled over. The other man, aiming carefully, then drove his spear directly into the old man's heart. Then the second spear pierced his neck, and the two killers gasped for breath as their victim jerked twice, then grew still.

Beside herself with grief and fear, the woman pulled from her captor's grasp and threw herself, clawing, at the great brute who had killed her man. He roughly slapped her, hard, and she fell rolling on the ground. He brandished his knife over her and knelt close to her face.

"Listen to me, woman," he hissed at her. "If you fight me, I will kill your boy. If you do as I tell you, both you and the boy can live. You have seen what I will do. Do you understand my words? Speak!"

Choking and sobbing, the woman could only nod as she began trying to gather up her child, now shaking in fear.

"Very well, we go now," the leader of the killer group announced. "Gather up their things. We must move quickly if we are to reach our camp by dark. Search the bodies for knives and bring their other weapons. Move!" he shouted, as his men still stared at the two dead men.

He turned and motioned for his men and the dazed, stumbling woman to follow him into the woods. He was not happy with his four men. They had not behaved as he had expected them to. They were all hunters and knew how to kill animals—why did they seem to fear killing men? Must Kuh-moh teach them everything?

TWENTY-ONE

Mark couldn't believe he was making six notches in his walking stick. Six days of constant work. He'd never get used to this kind of dawn-to-dark activity.

Um-see was like a man possessed. He was up long before dawn. At night he lighted his little pots of fat for illumination and worked until he began to doze off. He found that Mark ate everything fixed for him, so Um-see fed the big man small meals whenever they took a break. Usually it was a mix of dried meat, soft roots in a thick greasy soup, and always nuts. Bland stuff, Mark thought, but filling.

He had little time to feel sorry for himself. Each day there were basic chores: More firewood. More water. Scrape and rub the damn bear hide. Keep the smoke tent going, since Um-see now was putting their daily collection of rabbits and the occasional possum and squirrel into the tent for smoking.

When Um-see got the chance to kill another deer early one morning, he recruited Mark to help carry the entire carcass to the shelter. It was a backbreaking load. Soon after dawn they were skinning, cutting up meat, and had the smoke tent nearly full of hanging venison within three hours.

Which meant they were running into a major inventory problem. Baskets hung from the overhead rafters in greater numbers now, as Um-see stored the smoked meats in them, with tied-on hide covers. He was running out of baskets. Only five of the storage kind remained, and the venison would likely fill those within a few days, Mark could see. Why was Um-see stocking up? He was either planning one helluva banquet for somebody or else he feared the coming winter to be so bad that he would not be able to hunt . . . which didn't seem likely.

There was no time to wonder. The weather stayed clear, and Mark tended the smoke-tent fire, cut and stored dried meat in the baskets, and hauled things in and out of—and generally organized—the back end of their shelter. Under Um-see's direction, Mark installed another cross timber up close to the ceiling timbers, to hold more hanging loads. The ends of a long pole were jammed into overhead rock crevices, then other sharp stones were tapped in around the ends to hold them in place.

Mark found that Um-see had coated the support timbers with a thick layer of animal fat to discourage insects. The baskets and pots hung from strong animal sinew, twined together to form a strong, braided rope. These, too, were coated with animal fat. Mark was startled sometimes to find Seebo, sitting in the entrance of the shelter—usually in the early morning—staring at him. But Seebo's visits were short. Um-see gave the wolf-dog a chunk of dried meat, and he would leave, reappearing only when Um-see and Mark set forth on some errand. Then Seebo followed them at a distance—circling, watching the nearby brush, visible but not companionable.

Which saddened Um-see. He knew how Mark had upset the animal's life, and changed his routine. Seebo had a tiny den farther up on the mountainside, Um-see knew, but he missed his presence at night in the shelter. He felt helpless to know how Seebo could be persuaded to accept Mark into his life. Yet he'd never tried to make this fine animal into a captive dog-like creature, because he knew he could not. Seebo was half-tame, half-wild, and needed his freedom. Um-see knew he was the animal's friend, not his master. Now the old man feared that, at any time, he might simply disappear, never to be seen again.

If that happened, Um-see knew, he would have little defense against wolves or the great cats when he himself went hunting. He didn't want to think about that.

Mark almost dreaded the evening's work. Sitting on his skins after a supper of crawfish soup, meat, and a hard cracker, he felt like he still had cramps in his right arm. Um-see last night had given him a new assignment with a new tool—a bone scraper. It had been sharpened on one end, with the other end rounded. Um-see had demonstrated how he wanted Mark to massage the bear hide with it.

The brain tissue on the hide was dry, forming a slightly glazed surface. Mark's job was to run the bone edge firmly into the skin side of the hide until it turned a whitish gray and became more flexible. It was dull, boring work and took all afternoon.

Tonight, however, was to be different. Um-see sat down on the largest rock in the shelter—a two-foot-high boulder well away from the leaping fire, and he lighted two of the fat pots for more light.

He opened his basket of stone chips—washed clean by Mark in the hot pools—and picked out one about six inches square and a half inch thick.

"Finally," muttered Mark, "we get down to business."

Um-see's right hand held a rounded rock, much used. It was egg-shaped with tiny pits all over it. A hammer stone.

Um-see began tapping the big stone chip with this egg-shaped stone around the edges. The blows were light, exploratory, and grew stronger as he chipped off edges, reducing its size. It began to assume a long, triangular shape, about three inches long. *Rough,* Mark thought. *Is this the finished point?*

Hardly, it turned out. Um-see rubbed another rougher chunk of stone along the stone's edges, dulling them, blunting the sharpness.

Then he picked up two old pieces of hide, dark and weathered. They fit into the palm of his left hand. He held the rough spearpoint on the hide in his palm, gripped with folded fingers.

In his right hand, he took a sharpened antler tip, then applied it to the stone's edge.

Mark looked carefully at the antler tool. It was a Y-shaped piece of antler, and Um-see's thumb and forefinger straddled the crotch of the Y, with the foot of the Y being sharp.

The Indian pressed the antler tip against the rough edge, then, with a quick downward motion, he snapped a tiny chunk of stone away beneath the point. He lifted the point and showed Mark the thin flake that had come off the bottom of the stone. Then Um-see turned the point over and repeated the flaking motion on the opposite side, along the same edge.

Now Mark remembered what this process was called: *Flint knapping* was the term his grandpa Henry had used in explaining how he'd shaped his own arrowheads. It was an ancient art, he said, that made prehistoric mankind the master of all species, the world's most successful hunter.

But in the flickering shelter light, Mark had to look closely to understand what Um-see was doing. He finally saw that the Indian was forcing chips off the stone's edge below the stone—but not by arm and hand muscle alone. He sat, with left-hand palm up, fingers closed inward on the stone, arm against the inside of his left thigh. His right hand, pressing down on the antler tool, rested hard on the inside of his right thigh.

As Um-see made the downward flaking motion, his two legs added pressure by coming together at the moment of the cut. Mark saw that the combined movement of legs and the hand-twist were needed to unseat a small, long flake from beneath the stone's edge.

After a few minutes of steady flaking, Um-see held the point up in the firelight—at arm's length—and turned it, the pale stone catching reflected light from the flames. It seemed near-perfect to Mark, but the Indian was not satisfied. He grunted to himself, shook his head slightly, and handed the stone to Mark as he poked through his basket for another piece to work on.

He was not proud of that point, he admitted to himself, but it would help to teach Mark what he seemed interested in learning. Um-see found a good "blank" in his basket and moved off the boulder, motioning for Mark to sit there. Then the Indian demonstrated how to use the oval stone to strike the thin edges and rough out the shape of the point by percussion. Mark tried it, breaking off too much in some spots, not enough in others. He finally got the stone into a rough triangular shape. Um-see took it, delivered a few careful strikes to smooth out the long edges of the point that would eventually be cutting edges. He then used his rough-edged stone to vigorously sand those edges, blunting them.

Um-see motioned for Mark to take up the hand pads, showing him how the pads fit in the palm of the left hand, then the fingers curled down to hold the stone in place on top of the protective pads. Mark picked up the elk antler, and Um-see showed him how to put the rounded point down near the bottom of the stone's edge, the back of his left hand resting against the inside of his left thigh.

Mark tried it. Pressing. Pushing down to apply more pressure.

Nothing happened. Again he went through the motions. Nothing, the stone unyielding. Um-see took the tools and went through the motions. Mark told himself there was some trick to this. Not strength alone . . . but leverage, somehow applied, and technique. Um-see did it once more, to show him. The Indian could not imagine a full-grown man who couldn't seem to do such a simple thing. Where had Mark grown up? Had no one ever taught him what all men must know to live?

But Um-see sat patiently and motioned Mark to keep at it, correcting his aim at the stone's edge, his arm and leg movements.

Time passed and sweat dripped off Mark's nose. His left hand was numb where he kept pressure on the stone, his right grew slippery as sweat dripped onto the antler tool. Mark was ready to give up in frustration, doing the same thing over and over, when he saw—astonished—a half-inch stone flake in his hand.

"Hey," he shouted, "I got one! Look, Um-see, isn't that a flake?" The Indian smiled and nodded, not understanding the words but knowing full well what had happened. He motioned for Mark to continue. *A small start*, he thought.

For yet another weary hour, the younger man worked to get more chips from the stone's edge. He finally got to where he could get the flaking motion to work nearly every other time he applied pressure. He began to understand why Um-see had him turn the stone over each time he got a stone flake, in order to work the reverse stone face. Where there was a flake gone, he realized, the stone was thinner, so you next attacked that thin area.

Finally, when both of Mark's arms began to cramp, Um-see called a halt. He looked at the point. "Ump," he commented and nodded slightly. Mark leaned back and grinned. He'd been certain he couldn't do it. Yet he had.

But the day wasn't quite over.

Um-see picked up a stick and motioned to the smoke tent outside, indicating for Mark to put more wood on the tent fire. That drying meat should be finished by morning.

Massaging his arms, Mark went into the dark, felt around for small logs he had gathered that afternoon, then dumped them on the smoldering tent fire. His work with that stone had captured his mind, and he felt the glow of having done something difficult, although he knew he hadn't yet mastered that art, not by a long shot.

Um-see stretched out on his skins with some feeling of satisfaction. Mark, while clumsy, would learn. He might even make acceptable hunting points. He remembered with pleasure how, as a young man, he found he loved the stone that made him a good hunter. Soon, his work was admired by other young men, then by older men. They showed him their prize points, and he showed his own. They did not always agree on which stones in the valley made the best points.

Some liked the light gray material, others the dark gray-green stone, while others regarded the dense, black stone with favor. It was a personal matter, Um-see concluded, since all men of the families measured their ultimate success by the animals they took and the meat they brought back to the shelters. Um-see himself was convinced that the light gray stone made his own spears fly truer and kill game better than any of the other kinds.

The old man was drifting off to sleep when his nose warned of an odd smell in the air. He stirred, rose, and moved out the shelter entrance.

Mark had taken a drink of water from his gourd and was getting comfortable on his skins when he saw Um-see go outside. Then came a shout.

"Mock, Mock!"

"Damn, now what?" Mark grumbled as he moved to the shelter opening, then stopped in horror.

The place was on fire.

TWENTY-TWO

parks and flames leaped from the smoke tent as Mark
rushed onto the rocky porch. Um-see swung an old hide,
beating at the fire, jumping up and trying to smother it at the
top, near the smoke hole.

Mark grabbed another hide and did the same. They circled
the tent, flailing at the fire as billows of foul-smelling smoke
engulfed both men. They choked, coughed, withdrew for a
moment, then stepped in again to try to contain a ring of fire
that circled the tent's very top.

Um-see hurried into the shelter and returned with a basket
half-full of water. He opened the tent flap and splashed the
water on the fire inside. It sizzled out, sending more smoke
rolling out of the opened tent flap.

It took another five minutes, but the two choking men
were able to beat out the last of the flames that charred the
tops of the tent hides. Again, the stench was like rotten eggs,
only stronger now. Mark retched and turned away quickly.

Um-see now knew what had happened: A wood knot
within the fire had exploded, sending up sparks to ignite the
inside of the hides above. But why would that happen? . . .
unless . . .

He went inside the shelter and returned with a piece of
burning wood from their fire circle, pulled open the smoking
tent flap. By the light of his torch, Um-see inspected the
firewood inside the smoke tent that must have exploded and
shot the first sparks upward. Then grunted.

"Mock!" he said angrily, and motioned.

Mark looked at what Um-see was pulling from the smoky interior of the tent: pieces of the partly burned wood that Mark had put on the fire a short time before.

Um-see thrust one of the blackened sticks at him, and Mark inspected it by light from the shelter that spilled out onto the porch. Ordinary firewood . . . except . . . and then he realized. It was pine. Softwood, not hardwood. In the near dark, on his return from the hot springs, he had gathered wood rapidly, not noticing what kind it was. His bundle had included pine, and the pine knots had blown up, setting the tent on fire. Something his grandfather Henry long ago had warned him about!

"Mark, we never use pine in our fireplace. It produces too much smoke, and those pine knots can explode all over the front room before you know it."

Now he had half destroyed Um-see's smoke tent. Damn. What could he say? Nothing, it turned out. At least for the moment. The old Indian was furious. Muttering, he limped around the fire tent and examined the damage. Scorched midway down, ruined at the top. He glared at Mark, went inside the shelter, and came out with baskets. Following his lead, Mark began to take the drying meat from the inside of the tent to store in the baskets. The meat, at least, looked nothing worse than scorched.

They stored the baskets inside the shelter. Then Um-see, with very little light to see by, began to unfasten the thongs that held the hides in place. Mark tried to help, but Um-see grunted and motioned him aside.

The Indian stripped the upper circle of hides from the skeleton of poles and stacked them to one side. It was all that could be done tonight. He limped back into the shelter, and Mark followed, feeling like a convicted criminal.

They sat on their skins.

"Um-see," Mark said, "I'm really sorry," and he held up his hands in a gesture of sorrow and resignation.

"Umph," Um-see replied, lying down on his skins, face to the rock wall.

He had already started blaming himself. For some time now Um-see had intended taking the old hides off the smoke tent. They were dried-out, stiff, and would burn when a spark touched them. It could have been a spark from hard wood as well as soft wood. Mark was at fault for picking bad wood—how could any sane man put soft wood on a smoke-tent fire?—but Um-see had seen this happen before, usually when children were left to tend fires. No, Um-see told himself, he himself had gotten careless. He should have tended the fire himself, before going to sleep. He would try to make this clear to Mark—sometime. Somehow. He felt worse because he had lost his temper. He did not like to let himself do that. A shameful thing. But, he assured himself, it was one of the things people did when they got old. It was expected. Or should be.

Mark slept poorly. He was awake before Um-see, before dawn. Um-see was soon up and had the inside fire kindled from coals. He had saved the heart from the deer they had recently killed, stored submerged in a pot of water. He let water drip off of it, looked at it closely, and smelled. Still fresh, he decided, and rammed a sharpened spit through it, then positioned it above the fire. He knew that Mark liked the organ meats of animals, and the deer heart should start the day off properly. Mark, seeing this, sighed. *Exactly what I need*, he told himself, *rare venison for breakfast*. Was this Um-see's punishment, or a peace offering?

Their morning's work waited for them on the porch. The old, burned hides were put to one side, all of the hides were taken from the tent skeleton, and one of the scorched ribs replaced. Then they brought out fresh hides from the inside storeroom and tied them to the tent framework. By late morning, Um-see had restarted the tent fire, the meat was back in place within, and they both were filthy from the blackened hides they'd been handling. Um-see picked up the ropes, handed one to Mark, and headed off down the mountain. First stop: the hot springs. Both men washed themselves in the steamy water as best they could. It was a cool, crisp morning, and Mark felt chilly after the hot bath. Accustomed now to wearing only boxer shorts and shoes, he saw that it was time for his sweatshirt. Fall was in the air.

On the way back they collected their bundles of firewood. To make his point, Um-see picked up a length of pine branch, got Mark's attention, and shook his head emphatically. He cast the branch aside. Mark smiled and nodded so Um-see knew that he got the message. No pine for the fires, period. Um-see smiled, slightly. His mad, it appeared, was over.

Mark counted the notches on his walking stick—forty days had passed, five since he last did any notching. He put the stick aside and picked up his bow. Finally, he was making progress. He now had crude cutting tools, a result of his work every night to master the stone chipping. His fingers had small nicks and cuts on them and one real gash in his palm. The stones often had razor edges, and, at first, he was totally clumsy. His skills improved slowly and, with Um-see's help, he now had a crude knife. It had a five-inch blade, sharp on both edges, with a four-inch stub for a handle.

He found he could not cut deeply into the surface of his hard bow wood, but the knife was good for scraping thin layers of the wood, short slices, a little at a time. Over the past three days he had managed to thin the two bow ends, leaving the handle area its original thickness.

Um-see began to show interest after Mark found a way to illustrate what he was doing. It was the night after their tent fire that Mark got his knife far enough along to start scraping bow wood.

"Mock?" said Um-see, motioning to the limb. He raised his eyebrows questioningly, as they both had started doing, to ask what the other meant by something. Then it hit Mark: He'd draw Um-see a picture.

Smoothing a dirt patch on the shelter floor, Mark used his finger to draw a vertical line, indicating the bow with its slightly curved tips. Then he drew another curving line, showing the bow bent back, as it would be when strung. Now Mark drew a line from one bow tip to the other, indicating a bowstring in place, with the bow fully strung. Um-see watched, puzzled yet fascinated.

Mark held up the rough bow limb, and pantomimed it being bent back. He then motioned to one of Um-see's spears and drew a horizontal line in the dirt from the taut bowstring out across the front of the bow. Um-see shook his head, unsure what this meant. Mark pantomimed the drawing back of the bow. He held the feathered end of the short spear in his right fingers, then drew it back against the bow limb, supported by his left fist holding the bow. Then slowly he "released" his fingers and motioned, pretending that the spear was shooting forward rapidly.

Um-see stared, and shook his head slightly. He understood that this was some new kind of spear-thrower, but he didn't yet understand what would propel the spear.

Mark went through the procedure again, pointing to the different parts. This time he walked back to one of the hanging storage baskets and took hold of the supporting tendon above it.

"Bowstring," he said, and pointed to the string drawn in the dirt, holding the bow in its bent position. Then Mark pretended to fit the spear nock into the tendon, and pantomimed the pulling back of the spear against the tendon, held by the bow tips.

On Mark's third try, Um-see began to nod. He had it now. The limb was taut, bent back, held by the tendon, and the spear was thrust forward when pressure was released. He could imagine how it might work—but would it have any power? The Indian could not visualize the flight of the spear. But Mark seemed to know what he was doing. He would have to wait and see how this odd thing worked. One thing Um-see was sure of: It had to work better than the crude cutting blade Mark had made himself. The Indian was surprised Mark could even shape his limb with it, so rough was the stone he'd created. Um-see decided that he'd have to help make the younger man a decent cutting tool.

Meanwhile, he had some spear work of his own to do. He might as well take Mark with him to be sure he knew how to prepare spears, and that meant he needed glue.

Um-see led Mark down the slope from their shelter to where a group of young pines had been slashed at several spots. Mark saw that the tree cuts were deliberate. Each pine tree slash oozed pitch, and Um-see went from tree to tree, scraping it off with a piece of sharp stone, into a pot. When he had collected several ounces of pitch, they went back to the shelter, where Um-see crushed an egg-sized chunk of charcoal from the fire pit. When it was powdered, he poured the charcoal into the pot on top of the pitch, then put the pot on the fire, supported by rocks on three sides. Soon the flames were heating, then slowly melting the pitch.

From his bundle of reeds, Um-see selected one about four feet long and a half inch thick. He tapered one end with rapid strokes of his black knife. In the other end he drilled and gouged out a deep hole, using sharp-pointed bone tools and stone fragments. When the hole was more than an inch deep, he fitted one of his foot-long short spear tips in, to be sure it was a snug fit. The tips were slotted, and a stone spearpoint attached to its end.

Mark now saw, close up, how the spear-thrower worked. It had three parts: the two-foot-long handle with a hook on the end, the long spear itself with feathers at the rear where it was slotted to take the hook, and the smaller-diameter reed shaft that fitted inside the spear, forward end, to which was attached the stone point.

To use the spear-thrower, the hunter held both handle and spear, hooked together, until the throw, allowing the spear to slip from the fingers as he propelled it forward with a sharp snap of the handle. The small spearpoint embedded itself in the animal, and the hunter could then pull the larger spear loose from the tip, and insert another point in its place for the next throw. In this way, Mark realized, Um-see only needed to carry two or three of the longer spears and many of the smaller, lighter projectiles with stone points.

In the next hour, Um-see demonstrated how he slotted spear tips to receive the stone points, then wrapped them tightly around with lengths of brown tendon from his basket. He coated this joined point with the hot, soft pitch.

Soft pitch also formed the adhesive for feathers that Um-see used to put on the spear's back end. But Mark noted he used only two lines of feathers. Odd. Why not three? Mark had never seen any arrows that didn't have three feathers . . . and then he grinned. Hey, if it works, don't fix it.

However, there was a major, obvious problem. Those four-foot spears were too heavy, too thick, to be used with the bow Mark had in mind. His arrows had to be more like a quarter inch in diameter, and no longer than about thirty-five inches or so. Somewhere he'd have to find thinner shafts, straight like these long reeds, but lighter. Where? He didn't have a clue.

When Mark finished notching his day-count walking stick, he was depressed. Again. Nights were his bad times. He leaned back against the rock wall and shut his eyes. When he thought about his former life, his wife, son, his mother, all the people he cared about, his eyes grew moist.

They were good people, and he loved each one in different ways. He had been a contented man, he knew, wanting nothing more from life than to be let alone to enjoy the good things he already had. It was simply maddening, beyond understanding. *Why me?* he asked yet again. What had he done to deserve such a weird fate? Did he really want to live like this—in a smoky cave, eating primitive food, scared much of the time, with no weapons to speak of? No. He shook his head. He might as well be dead. This wasn't living as he knew it.

Then he stared at Um-see, bent over near the fire, creating more spearpoints from the dark gray stone. Mark liked the old man, knowing that he wanted to help him adjust to this strange, rough life, but having no idea about Mark's origins or intentions.

You'd have to call that blind faith, Mark acknowledged. Um-see had taken him in, fed him, taught him some skills, shared everything he had with a total stranger. He had no idea where Mark came from or what his intentions might be. Mark then resolved to stop his self-pity. He had better thank God for the old man's faith in him and Um-see's generosity in all things.

For the moment at least, he wasn't wet or cold or hungry, or threatened, Mark reminded himself. Not everybody in twentieth-century America could say as much. So maybe he wasn't that bad off. He didn't see how he could ever get home again, but he'd just have to make the best "home" for himself that he could find. He rubbed his hand along his half-finished bow. For now, he had to concentrate on some means of defense that would help him stay alive. Remembering the ferocity of that huge black bear and those hungry wolves, Mark resolved to follow the old maxim: The best defense is a good offense. And it was up to him to provide for his own survival. He picked up his "sanding stone" and began rubbing the bow limb with renewed vigor.

TWENTY-THREE

Only Um-see's quick reactions saved him from the cotton-
mouth moccasin.

He and Mark were stepping carefully over half-sunken,
rotted logs when the dark reptile erupted from a weed clump
alongside.

The Indian had been eyeing those weeds, and he jerked
back just as the snake shot above the log's scaly surface.
Um-see whacked his spear-thrower down in the water where
the moccasin disappeared, but it was gone. It missed Um-
see's thigh by inches.

Both men stood quietly for a moment. Mark's body was
dripping and not entirely because of the sudden snake attack.
They had been splashing through this fetid swamp for half
an hour, and finally ahead of them was what they'd come
for.

Um-see pointed forward, and he moved carefully through
the knee-deep water. There they were: thin, straight reeds,
the size Mark wanted for his arrows. The Indian now was
fed up with this low-lying backwater. He never would have
come here if Mark hadn't shown him, by motions and pictures, what it was he'd wanted to find. Um-see remembered
seeing them here, long ago. Why would Mark want such thin
reeds?

Rising four feet out of the water, the reeds were half-
hidden in a mass of vegetation where the west side of the
swamp ended at a high, overhung dirt bank.

Both men were muddy all over and barefooted. Um-see

had hung his hide sandals on a brush pile when they'd entered this area, and Mark followed suit—with misgivings. His feet felt vulnerable in the soft mud of the swamp, and he stepped deliberately to avoid underwater stumps and rocks.

It had taken a lot of pantomiming on Mark's part originally to show Um-see what he wanted. By drawing tiny circles in the dirt of their shelter and marking off a shorter spear in the dirt, Mark pictured for Um-see what an arrow would look like. The Indian thought about it, then nodded. Yes, he seemed to indicate, there are smaller reeds. He also felt that the younger man was foolish to try anything so light and flimsy against large game. Nevertheless, he got two deep carry-baskets from the shelter, and they set out, heading south along the valley floor.

It took them a short hike, to the west of Hot Springs Creek, to find the swamp. Mark knew they'd arrived from the oppressive stink, gloom, and the tiny bugs that swarmed around their faces. Stagnant water rippled away from the movement of their legs. Mark was glad he had worn his sweatshirt. Mosquitoes had arrived in force, and soon he had welts itching on neck, face, and arms. Um-see stooped and applied handfuls of swamp mud to his upper body and thighs for protection.

With a shudder, Mark did the same. Soon he was a brown man punctuated by a stained, white sweatshirt. He tried to forget his smell and discomfort by hurriedly pulling at chunks of the thin reeds. It wasn't that easy. They clung to the bottom tenaciously, and Mark had to thrust his hands down into the ooze and grab the very roots of the plants to wrench them free. Dripping with mud, foul water, and sweat, bedeviled by insect swarms, both men stomped rapidly out of the swamp when their carry-baskets were finally full of reeds. They put their shoes on muddy feet and headed directly, by unspoken agreement, for the creek, only minutes to the east.

There, cold, clear water was a welcome relief for the slime

on their itching skins. Mark sat down in the stream, washed out his shoes, lay facedown in the water, and was thankful the sun was out. But a cloud then obscured the sun as Mark dried out on the creek bank, feet in the water. It was no cloud, though. Tens of thousands of birds winged over them, hundreds of feet high, going south. They were not ducks, Mark could see, but looked like . . . oversized pigeons. He had seen pigeons in parks before but never so many in such a concentrated flight. It took at least five minutes for the giant wave of flapping wings to fly over them. Could these be passenger pigeons? He had read of their incredible numbers prior to the coming of the first western settlers, and by the twentieth century they were gone. Hunted to extinction. Um-see watched the birds fly over but seemed disinterested. It must be a common sight for him, Mark concluded.

He very much wanted to ask Um-see questions, and this triggered an idea. There might be a way he could eventually communicate. It would be worth a try. He would start that night.

After their dinner of squirrel stew, Um-see noticed that Mark was doing strange things.

The big man had climbed to the blackened overhead beams and scraped off a cupful of smoke soot up there. Then Mark had crushed some brittle embers from the fire, ground them up . . . and mixed them with some cooking grease. Was Mark about to *drink* the mixture? It would kill him!

But Mark wasn't finished. He heated the smelly pitch mixture Um-see had used for his spear fletching, then put some on the stub of a broken arrow-reed and—of all things—attached short chunks of animal hair to the pitch.

"Mock . . ." Um-see began, trying to puzzle out some explanation for all this, but his friend held up one finger and nodded. Yes, he pantomimed, he would explain in a little while. Um-see shook his head and smiled. Mark was one surprise after another.

It took fully an hour before Mark was ready to start his

effort to communicate. He'd thought about how he would do it, and now that his crude "paintbrush" was dry, the pitch hardened, he was ready . . . Time for language class to start.

He lighted all three of the fat grease pots so that the big, smooth stretch of wall close to his sleeping area was brightly lighted. By reaching up at arm's length, he could get his brush nearly eight feet high on the wall.

Dipping into the black paint pot, he stroked MARK on one side of the wall, and UM-SEE about three feet to the right. Then he looked at Um-see, who sat watching, and puzzled. These black marks on the wall . . . did they have special meaning for the younger man?

"Um-see," said Mark, pointing to the Indian's name he had painted on the wall in letters four inches high. "Mark," he said, pointing to his own name and himself. Um-see raised his eyebrows. Mark meant something by this, the Indian knew, but he could only shrug.

Then Mark remembered their very first meeting, in the rain, on that slippery mountain trail. He pointed down to his shoe, then wrote on the wall, under his own name, SHOE. He turned and printed what Um-see had called his own tiny slipper: NO-SO. Again he pointed to his shoe, then to the word SHOE on the wall, and to Um-see's foot, then to the name, and pronounced "*No-So*," pointing.

The Indian's brow furrowed slightly. Was Mark trying to show a connection between what they said and these wall markings? What sense would that make? Um-see shook his head slightly.

Mark tried again. He pointed to himself, then to the fire. "Fire," he said, pointing to his own chest. He pointed to the fire, and then to Um-see, questioningly. The Indian paused a moment, then said, "*So-ah*." Mark nodded and wrote on the wall FIRE under his name and SO-AH, under Um-see's. He then pointed to the fire, then to SO-AH, and said "fire," then to his own FIRE and repeated that word. Um-see stared, concentrating. Was Mark trying to picture fire on the wall?

Yes, he reasoned, Mark *was* trying to connect the names

of things to those wall marks. He failed to see why. Was it
some kind of game?

Mark persisted. He picked up a persimmon, called it *fruit*,
and learned that Um-see called it *Main-see-ah*. He wrote both
words under their respective names, pointing to the persimmon. Pecan turned out to be *Mah-suh*, and was printed on
the wall. Then *basket* became *So-ee-mah*. Within minutes,
Mark had translated five of his words and their Indian equivalent. He carefully repeated Um-see's words, to be sure he
was saying them right.

The Indian found it hard to believe, but he did understand
now. For the first time in his life, Um-see considered the
idea that words he spoke could be shown by markings, by
odd figures on a stone wall. Those black marks, lighted by
flames flickering from smoky fires, took on new meaning.
They *meant* something. He found the thought astonishing.
And . . . why do this? He shook his head and looked questioningly at the bearded man who stared at him.

Mark was quietly elated. It looked like Um-see had a
glimmer of what this was all about. But he knew he'd have to
somehow personalize this thing a little more.

Mark sat down facing Um-see, close to him. He used
hands to pantomime words coming out of their mouths.

"Um-see," he said. "You speak to me. I speak to you. I
know what you say." He pointed to Um-see's words on the
wall. "I learn your words, I speak to you."

Mark got up to illustrate. "Um-see," he said, "this is *So-
ah*," he said, pointing to the fire. "This is *Mah-suh*, this is
Mah-see-ah," he said as he pointed to pecans and
persimmons.

Then he put both hands on his chest and spoke slowly.
"*I speak Um-see.*"

The Indian's eyes opened in astonishment. Mark was saying he wanted to speak Um-see's own language. And learn
it from these wall markings! Never could Um-see remember
being so surprised. Over the years, talking to travelers who
spoke different tongues, he had picked up a few bits of other

men's languages, but this . . . this marking on the wall to show words . . . this was a new thing!

Um-see breathed out, trying to adjust to the shock of a lifetime. Could this man so different, with these strange body coverings, looking almost like a two-legged animal, could Mark learn to speak as Um-see spoke . . . with paint on the wall?

Then he nodded slightly.

Yes, he told himself, *Mock might. And I will help him, if I can. In this way, too, I might learn where Mock came from and why he is here. And where he is going.*

Mark shivered as he came awake. It was chilly in the shelter and raining hard outside. Um-see, for the first time Mark could remember, was still asleep at dawn. Not surprising, he smiled to himself. They had been up half the night, saying words and marking them on the wall. He looked up. The entire wall, eight feet up, was covered with clumsily printed words, more than three dozen English words and their Indian equivalents alongside, in two full columns. It had not been easy. Mark ran out of nouns, of physical things they could actually see around them. They named the parts of the human body, identified animals whose hides were represented in the shelter, named rock, dirt, smoke, everything in fact that was visible to them.

Mark found there were a lot of sounds Um-see did not seem to use. His words seemed heavy on vowels—a,e,i,o,u words were easy to spot. But that left a lot of letters unaccounted for, in terms of English sounds. It was slow work, and Mark had to ask Um-see to repeat many words for him. He decided that he would take each of Um-see's words, divide it into two or three syllables, so he could say them all clearly, then write them on the wall, hyphenated, so that he could more easily memorize each word and its meaning.

The old Indian loved it. He could hardly wait for each word to go up on the wall, and he began to try and pronounce some of the English words, with Mark's coaching, but the sounds felt strange in Um-see's mouth.

Verbs, Mark could see, were going to be a problem. How could he get some Indian equivalents for words denoting action? It would have to take place as they did things together, then he'd have to remember them for the wall record. *Go* and *return* were easy enough to find out from pantomime but more complex action verbs would take time, he realized.

For now, he was exhausted with words and language. He would try to revive the fire himself and get something cooking for breakfast. Then he had to get on with his bow-making and arrows. Lucky it was raining hard. They could stay indoors, he hoped, and work on his big project. But there were possibilities he hated to think about: What if his bow didn't work? Or broke on the first shot? Or had no range?

Mark laughed aloud as a nutty thought hit him. He visualized the front page of a *Prehistoric Times*: Strange Man Invents Bow. Bow Doesn't Work. Man Is Expelled From Valley.

The madness of it all made him want to burst out with a wild cry of both outrage and laughter. Here he was, trying to prove the practicality of an ancient weapon that had helped mankind rise from barbarism, had helped feed and clothe people for thousands of years. *Well, the damn thing had better work, right here and now, or else it might be back to the wilderness for Old Mark.* He put his hands to his head and tried not to think about it.

TWENTY-FOUR

It looked rough. It felt rough. It also looked like a bow.

Best of all, it was finished. Or as finished, Mark decided, as it was going to get.

He was proud of his handiwork but nervous about it. He had narrowed the limbs of the bow, but not to thin points. He was afraid the tips would crack off if they were as pointed as Grandpa Henry's bows. He had raked his memory to remember how those bows were grooved, at the tips, to secure the bowstring. Lord, why didn't he pay more attention then? His grandfather would have shown him exactly how to finish a bow, if Mark had only asked. Now he must guess at every step.

So he scraped out a shallow groove around the bow's two tip ends to hold the bowstring, long strips of deer tendon, glistening with fat. It seemed thicker to Mark than it should have been, meaning that the nocks in his arrows must be larger.

Using rough chunks of novaculite, he had rubbed and sanded carefully, to be sure both limbs were thinned down to the same size, to get an even "pull" from the string. With one foot in the middle, or handle, of the bow, he pulled up on both ends simultaneously to see if he could detect any difference. They seemed the same.

Stringing the bow was hard. He dimly recalled Grandpa Henry stepping through the bow, one tip on the floor against his right foot, then sliding the bowstring up into position with his left hand as he compressed the bow. It took Mark a dozen tries to do it before he found the combination of moves needed to seat the bowstring in both tips' grooves. He pulled back carefully, and the tension was so great he wondered if he'd have the arm strength to pull an arrow all the way back to his face. Good question.

He wanted to try it out in the shelter, but dozens of hanging baskets in the rear prevented any indoor practice.

What helped him finish was wet weather. For three days, warm rains and high winds kept Mark and Um-see mostly indoors. For his part, Um-see was more fascinated with the rock wall full of black marks than by Mark's work with the bow. The Indian frequently interrupted Mark's work, motioning him to say some of the words on the wall, and their English equivalents. He clearly was excited by the new sounds in his mouth, as he tried to duplicate some of the strange noises that Mark made, and he couldn't. He tried particularly hard to say the R in "Mark," but didn't manage it until the younger man suggested that he growl. "Rrrr," Mark coaxed, getting down on hands and knees to imitate a wolf. Um-see smiled and tried it, and began to feel the way an R works by using his jaws. He finally got an R out by growling out of the corner of his mouth.

Putting it together, he carefully pronounced "Marrrrk," with a lengthy growling sound, which caused Mark to burst out laughing. Um-see looked hurt, so Mark quickly stepped over and patted the Indian's shoulder, nodded, and smiled, and repeated what he understood was approval in Um-see's tongue, "*Moh-kah*."

Once Mark went outside for another supply of pine pitch. As he walked down the mountain, he realized he actually enjoyed being drenched, wearing nothing but thin boxer shorts and shoes. He turned his face into the driving rain and opened his mouth. It was like an outdoor shower, if a little chilly. There was an exhilarating freedom here he'd never felt before. He went from tree to tree with his clay pot, cutting off the pitch lumps, listening to the clash of branches above him, the steady sizzle of rain on the leafy hillside. It felt wild and wonderful.

When he got back to the shelter, dripping, he sat down to dry off by the fire, and thought that he hadn't felt so alive since he was a boy. Yes, this might be a terrible way to live, filled with danger and uncertainty. But there were advantages.

He didn't have a job anymore, but he didn't need one to support himself. If he could become a hunter, he could live, like Um-see's people, off the land. His only responsibility was to himself—to stay alive. Nobody cared whether he lived or died, excepting possibly Um-see. This was about as "free" as a man could get. Then Mark grinned to himself. If he could go home again, he'd give this life up in a second, freedom and all. He knew he had changed since the accident that put him here . . . but he also knew he still thought and perhaps acted like a twentieth-century, civilized man. He didn't want to become—or think like—a true savage. He hoped he could remember that.

A cool breeze whipped the trees above their shelter as Mark and Um-see, facing a rising sun and clear skies, moved down the mountain. Mark carried his untested bow and ten newly finished arrows. The stone arrowheads and turkey feathers felt heavier than he thought they should. He dreaded the possibility that the bow would simply break on being fully drawn. He hated to appear an incompetent fool in Um-see's eyes. The Indian carried his spear-thrower and three spears.

Mark spotted a knee-high bush up the valley a short distance. They walked to it, and Mark pointed at the bush, and with an arrow he indicated to Um-see they should use the bush for a target. The Indian nodded. Then Mark turned and paced off forty yards. He found himself a little short of breath, his heart beating faster than usual.

He tested the bowstring with his right hand. It was a tough pull, certainly as hard as his grandpa Henry's bow had been.

But he was only a kid then, he reflected. He was stronger now. Or should be.

No point delaying. He made sure that the hide protector was in its place on his left forearm—he remembered that painful slap on the arm the bowstring delivered at the moment of release.

He turned the weapon horizontally, fitting arrow to bowstring. Carefully, he moved the bow almost vertically, the arrow riding on a small piece of wood he'd shaped and glued to the bow's center section. Then he deliberately, slowly, pulled the arrow back until his three bowstring fingers were lodged against the right side of his mouth, his arm muscles trembling. He stared a second at the bush, then released.

The arrow went two feet above the bush, good for direction. Mark was elated. It worked!

He stared down for a moment at the weapon. He actually had made this thing himself! He wanted to shout, yell, something. But he carefully nocked another arrow. *The bow might yet break. Don't celebrate just yet,* he warned himself. His second arrow in place, he aimed lower, concentrating on the bush. His arrow thudded into the earth five feet short. Still it was amazing to him. He had produced a high-velocity projectile that he, personally, could control! It was hard to make his movements slow and deliberate.

Trying to act unconcerned, Mark took a deep breath and nocked his third arrow. It would take hours of practice, he knew, to develop the shooting skills he had seen Um-see display. This was only a warm-up. To make sure the bow was sound. But he did need to hit that damn bush.

The third arrow came closer, slightly right but good elevation.

Um-see could restrain himself no longer. While Mark selected another arrow, Um-see stepped up beside Mark and in an instant he threw a spear. It passed directly through the bush. He said nothing but a muttered grunt.

Oops. He doesn't think much of my bow, Mark said to himself. *He hits the target and I don't. Gotta try harder.*

Mark shot his fourth and fifth arrows before finally, with his sixth, scoring a direct hit on the bush. He walked up and retrieved his arrows, Um-see his spear. Mark was glad to find all of his arrows intact, having landed in soft earth. He knew now, roughly, how to aim. And he knew his shoulders would need conditioning. It seemed to him that this bow was as strong, perhaps stronger, than Grandpa Henry's fifty-five-pound bow. And he already felt achy in his upper body.

Mark turned from the bush and paced off sixty yards. He knew from weeks of watching Um-see throw spears that this was just past the Indian's killing range for larger game. Mark had never seen him throw at a target more than about forty yards away. But that, he remembered, might be because of Um-see's eyesight beginning to blur.

Mark's first arrow at sixty yards was short. His second was a foot right of the bush, his third directly through the bush's center. He stopped and looked at Um-see inquiringly. The Indian smiled slightly and shook his head. He saw no need to waste a spear at that distance.

That's not how you take game, it seemed to indicate. You have to get up close. Mark nodded.

He picked up his remaining arrows and turned around, pacing off another twenty yards. Eighty yards now to the target. This, he knew, was out of killing range, but he had to see what the bow would do. He got lucky. His first arrow landed a foot to the right of the bush, the second slightly short, but the third went directly into the bush. This, he knew, was good shooting, especially for him, a beginner, with a brand-new bow. It was luck, in part. He hesitated. He had to find out the bow's true range. Grandpa Henry had told him of an archery event—did he call it *the clout*?—in which archers shot at targets spread on the ground at distances of more than one hundred yards.

He turned around and paced off thirty more yards. That put him one hundred ten yards from the bush.

Mark drew the arrow as his left arm elevated to approximately thirty degrees, then released. To him, the arrow's flight was marvelous. He could not believe it when the arrow fell beyond the bush. Um-see on his right side nodded his head. It was clear that he was impressed. He laid down his spear-thrower and opened his hand to Mark, who put the bow in it. Um-see held it in his left hand, as Mark had done, pulled at the bowstring slightly, felt the weapon's balance, and tension, then handed it back.

Mark could almost see what he was thinking. Um-see would want a bow of his own. He must see what difference it would make in hunting. He had seen its power. Now he must *feel* its power.

But Mark wanted to know the bow's maximum range. He remembered reading of the great medieval battles at Crécy and Agincourt, where English longbowmen defeated armored French cavalry at ranges up to two hundred yards or more. Those Middle Ages archers had great skills and made fine, tested weapons for such long-range work, but he must know what his crude weapon could do. He paced off another forty yards, putting himself one hundred fifty yards from the bush.

He elevated his arrow to about forty-five degrees, held for a second to line up with the bush, and released. The arrow went nearly out of sight. When it fell, he noted with excitement, it again was beyond the bush. He shot one more arrow at maximum elevation and it, too, went well beyond the target. Um-see, Mark noted, was silent, but his eyebrows were up. This was a new experience for him, too.

When he had retrieved his arrows, Mark found them about thirty yards beyond the bush, close together. So his range was at least one-eighty. He found himself thinking, as they walked toward the shelter, what if he used smaller arrow-heads to lighten the weight? Or shortened the shaft slightly? It could be an inch shorter, he felt, and still allow maximum pull.

Um-see had no such thoughts. He had never seen anything made by a man hurled so far. *But*, he asked himself, *can this new weapon be used to kill the great elk or bear? What use will all that distance be for each day's meals of squirrel or rabbit? I'll wait to see whether Mock*—or Marrrk, as he now tried to say it—*can hit anything. Except the sky.*

The three middle fingers of Mark's right hand were so sore he could hardly touch anything with them. All day, after trying out his new bow, he had to favor those fingers in doing the shelter's various chores. With the weather fair and cool, he and Um-see had hauled water, gathered firewood, then took time to go fishing. Up the creek, in the cold waters, they used meat bits on hide lines to catch half a dozen small perch for their supper.

Mark's finger soreness stayed with him all afternoon, making him aware of every movement with his right hand. He felt the discomfort was worth it. He was convinced now his bow was a good piece of work. He could not recall ever making anything that had given him so much personal satisfaction.

He practiced with it in the valley again in the afternoon, spending an hour shooting at long and short distances, discovering the line of sight and elevation needed for targets as close as five yards and as distant as sixty yards. He also found out that the "release" was key to his accuracy. A sudden snapping open of his bowstring fingers could cause the arrow to veer right or left. What was important was a smooth release of the fingers.

Um-see watched alongside him part of the time. The Indian clearly wanted to try out the bow. When his fingers became so inflamed that he could pull no more, Mark handed the bow to Um-see, with an arrow.

Mark smiled to himself: Prehistoric Man tries out a new weapon. Would it sell?

Um-see fitted the nock to the bowstring and followed Mark's example of holding the bow slightly to the right of vertical. Slowly, testing its strength, he pulled the arrow back with three fingers.

Mark was surprised that the Indian drew the bowstring easily, mastering the strong tension with little visible effort.

This guy is flat strong, Mark thought. *He'd probably pull a hundred-pound bow, if I could make one.*

However, Um-see's first arrow went off to the right. Mark saw why. The Indian had jerked the arrow at the moment of release, so the younger man demonstrated in slow motion how to release, to avoid influencing the arrow's direction. Um-see got the hang of it immediately, and the next arrow was good for direction, just short of the target. He shot all of Mark's remaining eight arrows, two having been broken in the morning's practice, and three of them hit the target bush at fifty yards. They retrieved the arrows, and Um-see turned to Mark.

"Marrrk," he growled, and then he began to pantomime, pointing to the bow, then to Mark, then to himself. For a moment, Mark thought Um-see wanted him to make a present of the bow to the Indian. Then he saw, as Um-see pantomimed cutting and polishing, that he wanted Mark to show him how to make a bow.

Relieved, Mark nodded and grinned.

"You got it," he announced, and Um-see shot another group of arrows at the bush, from farther away, about sixty yards. He scored one hit. The Indian saw that this was a powerful weapon, but it would take time to master it. He studied the bow, realizing that tension coming from the bow-string created great power—the power that men now had to supply by throwing a spear—and once he learned to control that power, he could kill the bear, elk—maybe even the giant buffalo to the south—and do it with less danger. Too many men, he grimly recalled, had lost their lives through foolish bravery, getting too close to animals that could kill them. Now, he felt, this weapon might change that. Everything about hunting could be different. If Mark would help him make a bow, he could convince the rest of the families of its value.

For his part, Mark had to prepare more arrows, which meant he had to chip and flake more stone for arrowheads. And he had to have something in which to carry them . . .

some kind of quiver. Both men were silent as they went to the shelter, thinking of their own plans, trying to imagine what it would be like to hunt with this weapon.

Mark chuckled. It was ridiculous. Here he was hoping Um-see would adopt the weapon that he knew full well ancient man had used for centuries to feed and clothe himself. It just hadn't been used here.

So maybe, he realized, he was launching a little revolution. And he hoped it wouldn't get out of hand. The bow could be dangerous if it wasn't used properly. Then he remembered: That's what people in the nineteenth century said about gunpowder. And, later, about atomic power. Oh well. He shrugged. The bow couldn't be all that bad. Um-see's people would never use it to kill people, he was sure. Or would they?

Closing his eyes, almost dozing off, Mark floated in hot water, only his face above the surface. This was heaven. Clouds of vapor swirled around him, and it was easy to visualize himself in some elegant Turkish bath instead of in a shallow pool at the base of a shiny cliff of tufa stone that rose high above him.

Steaming sheets of water, some of it too hot to touch, poured down the face of the rock formation above, falling into a whole line of such pools. Mark had found one favorite pool that was hot but not too hot in which to bathe. He had removed his shorts and shoes and was luxuriating sleepily when he heard noise.

He looked off to his right, to the valley floor. He heard it again.

Voices. Human voices, coming closer. The heated mist thinned, and he saw them. People. Several of them, coming closer. Not Um-see. Then he made out details.

They were Indians. They carried spear-throwers, and they were coming toward him. He'd been spotted. He didn't know them, they didn't know *him*, for sure.

"Um-see," he shouted, as loud as he could. "Hey, Um-see, come quick. Over here!"

Approaching the pool in which Mark lay stretched out and naked, the Indians stopped and stared. They could hardly believe their eyes. It appeared to have the body of a man but the head of an animal, with hair all over it. Would it attack them, or should they kill it?

They turned to each other and muttered something.

Even more disturbing for Mark were the other figures he could see just beyond the two men. Two females, one grown and one small. They, too, were staring at him. He didn't dare stand up or they would see his nakedness.

This was really embarrassing. Life-threatening, too, he immediately discovered. These hard little men were about to use their spear-throwers. On him.

TWENTY-FIVE

Anger and frustration filled Kuh-moh's mind as he looked at the men around him.

They were lazy. And surly. They could not be trusted. But they were the only men Kuh-moh had to achieve his goal. They did have one quality that he needed: Most were hard men, willing to kill anything in their way . . . even other men.

He was the leader of the group, and he eyed the other men carefully to be certain they all knew it. Kuh-moh was larger and stronger than anyone else present. His face was scarred from an ugly incident in his past, which no one questioned him about.

Deliberately, Kuh-moh wore no headband, and his thick black hair fell on both sides of his head—he wanted it to stream behind him in the wind when he ran. His black eyes were set close together in a broad face, dominated by jutting cheekbones and heavy dark eyebrows.

He had thick, muscular arms, strengthened by many winters and summers alone in the forests. He knew these men did not like him, and most feared him, but also depended on him to lead where there was good hunting, water and—in time—women for every man.

Kuh-moh had come a long way from the day, long ago, when he had left his families, far off to the west. He had not wanted to go but had been forced to. It was humiliating and fired the anger that would boil within him all his life.

He had grown to manhood among those people, losing his

father and mother when he was very young. Relatives who raised him saw he was headstrong. Once he was suspected of stealing—a crime almost unheard of among families of decent people.

Once he attacked another young man for some forgotten reason and had received the slash across his face from a sharp knife. He had seriously injured the other boy, and only his youth kept him from being banished then.

Grown, he took a woman, and it proved to be his undoing. She was a plain girl but seemed to like him—at first. When she displeased him, however, he struck her, and she cried out. This happened often after a while, and a group of Elders came to see him. They were formal and polite. He still recalled their old, lined faces telling him stiffly that many among the families had heard his woman cry out in pain. It was against all their traditions to mistreat one's woman, they said, slowly and carefully. It must not continue, or he would have to leave his village and find another place to live. He would only be told this one time, they emphasized, and now he burned within to think of how he had been forced to sit there, hearing such insults and not be able to strike them down.

For a time he and his woman lived quietly. Until she again displeased him. He could not now recall what she did. She screamed when he struck her repeatedly, sounds heard by everyone, since their shelters were all close together, for safety against animals. So it was that Kuh-moh was told next morning by three messengers from the Elders that he could no longer live among them. He must be gone, with his possessions, by the time the sun had gone down. His woman could go with him, or stay, as she chose.

She immediately moved to her sister's shelter nearby. He tried to think of some way to get revenge on these people, but the three strong young messengers, whom he had known all his life, stared at him with cold eyes as he gathered his belongings. He abandoned his shelter and walked into the forests with only a supply of hides, food, and spears. He had never seen those people again, although he dreamed about the revenge he would one day take against them.

Kuh-moh, a good hunter, was at home in the forests. He found the game he needed and walked steadily east. He knew he must start a new life, but he skirted other settlements of families that he came to. He knew they would suspect any young man, alone, of being an outcast, and would not accept him among them unless he could prove that he was innocent of wrongdoing.

In time, he found other men like himself. Twice, he had to fight—to prove his superior strength over other outcasts. They then agreed to follow him and become a new family. They would seek others—also banished from their families— and form their own community. And Kuh-moh would run it, by force. He would be the acknowledged leader of them all, or else he would kill them, he assured himself.

Summers and winters went by as Kuh-moh's band grew in number. He had heard stories about a valley where the hunting was good, there was good water, and the mountains formed a protective shield against winter.

It was said that weak people lived there. He decided he would seize that valley. If the people stayed, they would have to obey him. There would be no Elders. He himself would decide how families lived.

He sent some of his men to find other outcasts, so he would have enough men to do his bidding when the time came to occupy the valley. They also sought to find women. So far they had captured only one woman and one young girl. He had lost some men killed in raids they conducted on groups of travelers. But he counted his men and found he now had almost three times the number of his fingers. More still were needed, and he would find them. Soon he would be ready to move toward the valley of the hot springs. He would wait for the cold period, so that few men would be abroad, and he could move noiselessly and take what he wanted from men less strong than he.

It was a satisfying time for Kuh-moh. He could not think

of a word to describe the power he felt within him. He only knew his desire was to rule other men, to take what he wanted where he found it. . . . This was a kind of revenge that he savored when memories returned of being banished. Now he would decide such rules, and the word would spread of his strength, his cunning, and the influence of his own new family. All the world would know of his greatness, and future generations would remember his name, forever.

TWENTY-SIX

His distance vision might be fuzzy, but there was nothing wrong with Um-see's hearing. Mark's shout for help reached him across the valley, and the old man knew there was trouble.

Grabbing spears and thrower, he hastily slid down the vines to the mountain trail, then raced, limping, down to the valley.

"Marrk," he shouted, to let him know that he was on the way. Almost instantly, Seebo, too, flashed down the mountain and moved along beside him.

Mark, meanwhile, sat straight up in the hot pool, and raised his arms high in what he hoped was a gesture of non-violence or surrender. Horrified, he saw one of the three men draw back, aiming his spear-thrower . . . the other two in positions of readiness . . . about to attack.

Then he remembered one of Um-see's words he'd written on the wall. "*Moh-hah-mo,*" he called out, and repeated the phrase.

It might have saved his life. The tallest of the three Indians stopped the youngest from throwing his spear. Had the hairy creature called out "friend"? They approached Mark slowly, saw his raised arm covered with black hair. Then, through the drifting hot vapor, they made out his features, marveled at all the whiskers on his face—and his eyes! They were blue, the color of the sky. And this man—for surely that's what he was—seemed to be visibly frightened.

Um-see's answering shout to Mark's cry spun them

around toward West Mountain, and they saw Um-see's small brown form hurrying down the valley slope, a huge dog trotting beside him. The three men relaxed. This must be the Helper. Perhaps he could explain this odd creature . . . this man . . . who now got out of the pool. But he had turned away from them as he did so, shielding himself. Very strange.

Mark hurried inside the shelter, peeled off his wet shorts, put on his stained white pants, sweatshirt, then decided not to wear his outer jacket. He knew he'd have to face those strangers again, and he was conspicuous enough as it was. The stained jacket, with zipper . . . he hated the inevitable questions.

By now, Um-see probably was trying to explain to the travelers who he was and why he was here . . . if he could! Mark realized, however, that he was almost glad to see other people, even if it had been mortifying to him for the woman and girl to see him naked, scurrying quickly out of the hot pool and across the valley to the shelter. They'd all said nothing, but simply stared in shocked wonder.

Um-see was indeed having difficulty explaining to the travelers about Mark.

"He comes from a distant place, beyond the big river . . . that way, to the south," Um-see told the group. "He stays in my shelter. His name is Marrk, an odd name. He's different from other men."

They nodded agreement. Different, yes. Much different.

"Why is he here?" the oldest man asked.

"He comes for our sharp stone, to make tools and weapons. He has only rocks to throw at animals. He saved my life with a rock against a black bear."

"He killed a black bear with a rock?" two voices asked together.

"He hit the bear in the eye, it fell, and I killed it with my knife," Um-see replied. "He helps me with my work . . . and he has made a weapon I have not seen before. It throws a short spear better than this." He held up his thrower. "I will ask him to show you this weapon, if you wish. I am making one now for myself."

"He looks like an animal," the young man spoke up. "That hair, on his head and body. No man has hair like that. Can he speak as we do?"

"He speaks," Um-see said carefully. "But not our tongue. Much different. He now learns our tongue, a little."

He could see that the men were still skeptical, nervous about this fearsome-looking stranger.

"Marrk is my friend," he stated firmly. "We help each other. He is strong and honest."

Um-see now recognized the oldest man of the group, a man about his own age. Yes, he remembered him, from his youth. They had known each other as boys in this same valley. The other man had gone off when his mother, whose man had died, joined another man, to live with his families. Now this woman must be the old man's daughter, the boy her son. Her man, strong and square, was about Marrk's age, Um-see judged. He thought they might be here in hopes of joining the valley's families, if given permission.

They could not travel much, it was clear to Um-see, since the older man was hurt. He walked with help from a long stick, forked at one end. His leg had been ripped open, the open wound red around the edges. Um-see shook his head. A bad sign. The man could die if it got worse. He asked how the wound happened.

The old man's son spoke up.

"We had a fight with some bad men three days ago. They came to our camp, at night. They tried to steal my daughter, Mee-oh." He glanced toward the shy little girl, seated next to her solemn-faced mother. Around them were piled their carry burdens and shelter poles.

"Why would men do this thing?" Um-see asked. He had heard of children being taken from their homes, but never close to his valley.

"They want new families, I think," the man said. "They were cast out of their own, I have heard. They have few women, so they try and steal young girls to take away with them.

"We fight them. My son"—and he indicated the tall boy next to him—"killed one bad man with a spear. My woman's father killed one more after the man tried to kill him with a knife. I hurt one, and the others ran away. We made the hurt man tell us what they wanted . . . before we killed him." He shook his head sadly. "It was a bad thing. It was not like this before."

So true, thought Um-see. All of the families he knew—his own and others he knew about—cast out men who did not follow rules for proper living. Outcasts were forced to take their weapon, food, whatever they owned, and go to live in forests far away. From what this man had said, some of those men had banded together—outcasts all—and tried to steal a child. Perhaps they would try to steal others. He must warn his families by the river.

First, though, he had to see what could be done to help the wounded older man. The hot waters might help. He motioned toward the vapors rising from the base of the valley's long, glistening wall of stone.

"Put your leg in the water. The water could make it better," he said. "We will get your shelters up." He looked around, hoping Mark would come and help. He had seen how upset Mark had looked as he hurried in his wet garment up to their shelter.

Maybe he did not want to meet these strangers. Was he afraid of them?

Mark forced himself to walk to the valley and meet the travelers. They were at the hot springs, with the oldest of the group sitting in a hot pool.

They saw Mark coming and stopped to stare. None had seen so large a man before. And those skins he wore—what animals could they have come from? The woman knew instantly they could not have been made from plants, as Mark walked up to them. She wanted to reach out and feel the fabric but restrained herself.

"Hello," Mark smiled. Then he remembered the greeting word he'd written on the wall. "*I-ee*," he added, and smiled again. Um-see nodded. Good. Mark had remembered one of his words.

Then Mark saw the terrible gash in the older man's thigh. He knelt and stared. Looked bad. The warm water was flaking away the dried blood, but the red lips of the open wound might be infected. He looked at Um-see's face and knew how serious this was. Everyone knew. The old man could die from this wound if it was not treated. Yet he seemed resigned to his fate. Um-see pulled the lips of the wound open so the hot water could get into it, and the wounded man shook his head slightly, wincing.

"Let your leg stay in the water for a time," Um-see said. He got up, followed by the other two men as they picked up long saplings and began to find soft spots in the ground where shelters could be erected. Mark understood what they were doing and helped assemble the round-topped shelters, much like the smoke tent Um-see had put on their rocky porch.

He could see that the two younger men—father and son—had carried the saplings on their shoulders, with hides and other belongings hanging from the center of the wooden poles. Both the woman and child had carried shoulder bags of other possessions, while the older man carried a hide satchel containing spear-throwers and spears. He knew they must all be tired and hungry.

Um-see motioned, then led Mark at a quick pace back up to their shelter. He got their fire going and heated a pot of stew, then began to pack a basket of food for the travelers—venison, bear meat, their last persimmons, some hard crackers, a gourd drinking cup.

Then Um-see carefully opened a small pot Mark had not looked into before. It was tightly bound with a hide cover and had been placed inside another hanging container. Mark saw, and then smelled . . . honey.

That old rascal, Mark thought, grinning to himself. *He's been holding out on me. I love honey, and here he's had this stuff squirreled away. . . . it must be rare. Or valuable.* Mark followed as Um-see hurried back down to the valley and knelt by the injured man, who smiled and nodded when he saw the honey pot. He understood what Um-see intended.

Motioning, Um-see had the wounded man carefully pull the wound open with his fingers, while the honey was poured slowly into raw flesh. The reclining Indian clenched his teeth in pain, but made no sound.

Mark remembered now. He'd read of ancient Egyptians—or was it Greeks?—who used honey as a wound treatment for their soldiers. Here it was obviously the quickest medicine of choice. Perhaps the *only* choice.

From the basket in which he'd carried the pot, Um-see took out a length of tan hide. It was deer hide of soft texture that Mark had not seen before, and Um-see wrapped it loosely around the man's thigh, securing it with two long strips of thin hide. The wounded man nodded his thanks as Um-see appeared to be giving him low-voiced instructions.

"Um-see," Mark spoke up, as the Indian appeared ready to head back to the shelter once more. Mark pointed to himself, said his own name, then to Um-see and said his, then motioned questioningly to the other Indians. Introductions?

Um-see hesitated but then nodded. Yes, he understood that Mark did not know these people. He also did not know why Mark should be so curious about their names. Um-see shook his head, hoping the travelers would not be offended, and he went ahead, with help from his old friend, to tell everyone's names to Mark.

Um-see decided that at some future time he would try to make it clear to Mark that it was not considered proper to ask people personal questions, such as their names, until you were acquainted. Mark, he sensed, must come from a place and a people where personal things were not so important.

If Mark learned his language, Um-see told himself, he must do what he could to teach the younger man good manners.

This was Mark's first chance to see Um-see talk to others of his own kind . . . and it was absorbing. All of the people spoke with animation, and they gestured as they spoke. Something then came to Mark.

These people seemed to have words for everything—yet they used all these gestures and hand motions. It dawned on him that they must be using hand and finger movements to lend nuance and special emphasis to some ideas, much the same as Italians gesticulate for added meaning. He realized it would take a lot of work on his part to fathom that extension of the native language.

Mark also saw the men clenching and unclenching their fists, and he recognized the motion from his language sessions with Um-see. It had to do with numbers.

Um-see could count and had words for numbers up to ten. Beyond ten it appeared that larger numbers were expressed by use of the hands . . . two fist-clenches must mean twenty, three meant thirty, and so on. Also, Um-see readily had understood when Mark had put scratches in their shelter's dirt floor, showing numbers one through four, then a diagonal line through them to indicate five. He'd entered Um-see's words for one through ten on the walls. As he learned more about it, he'd probably find others.

So it appeared now that the travelers were telling Um-see how long they'd been on the trails and their adventures. The conversation, he saw, then turned to him. They stopped talking and stared, mostly at his clothing, and especially at the big NIKE on his sweatshirt, his stained pants with the elastic cuffs at the bottom, and his running shoes.

Um-see motioned for Mark to come close and he did so, if slowly. The woman could restrain herself no longer. She smiled up at Mark and hesitantly reached out her hand to touch the sleeve of his sweatshirt. Then she rubbed the fabric together between long, slender fingers.

She was no bigger than Um-see, perhaps five-two, with dark hair that hung in a circle around her shoulders. She was attractive in a plain way, he noted, and wore a loosely woven garment that hung on her much like a sack, reaching to her knees. Her daughter, close behind, glanced up quickly at the big man, then looked down when he caught her eye. She seemed to be ten or eleven, he thought, and was dressed in a shapeless garment like her mother. All of the men were clad much the same as Um-see, except the older man. Besides a loincloth and thin, slipperlike shoes, he had a roughly fashioned vest made of hide on shoulders, chest, and back.

The men looked at Mark's garments closely but did not touch them. To be helpful, Mark held out his right arm, so they could inspect the fabric. They said nothing although, clearly, they were impressed. Um-see spoke to them rapidly.

"I do not know what hides his clothes come from," he told the men. "Those marks you see are like those he puts on my shelter wall . . . they show words we speak . . . I mean . . . he has special marks for what he says . . ."

Um-see realized how this must sound. The men's eyebrows went up. Was this something from the Spirit world? Something people should not be involved with? Clearly, the idea of marks representing spoken words was not merely mystifying but frightening . . . adding to their suspicions of the big man, who tried to keep smiling, yet saw only fear in their eyes.

Mark knew their fright was even more troubling for Um-see. He wound up the conversation, and motioned Mark back toward the shelter.

The old man was worried as he led the way back up the mountain. He had to do something about how Mark looked. If he didn't, he feared, others might attack and kill him because he was so different and looked so threatening.

He decided then what he must do. And soon. Mark would not like it, he was certain.

TWENTY-SEVEN

Without saying anything to Mark, Um-see made his plans that night to change the younger man so that he could be more acceptable among civilized people. He found some clean hides and cut them into specific shapes.

Um-see's plans were interrupted. Arrival of that first family yesterday seemed to open the floodgates to travelers. Daylight brought more voices and the muted woofing of dogs from up the valley . . . Seebo was soon pacing, with obvious irritation, along the rocky porch, growling, waiting for Um-see to investigate.

When he did he found that two more families had arrived and had started erecting their shelters. Yet another two families came into the valley before nightfall, sending Um-see into a day-long routine of taking food to the newcomers, helping them erect shelters, talking at great length, as Mark stood uncomfortably nearby. He was, as before, the object of much discussion . . . and concern.

Mark found Um-see especially agitated after he had welcomed the last family to arrive, just before dark. It included one adult man, two women and four children. This group, clearly, had problems. Both women seemed distraught, as Um-see, followed by Mark, went to meet them. One woman dropped to the ground and lay motionless while the other two adults held to the children around them and spoke with difficulty. They had only meager belongings in shoulder bags they carried, and no poles or hides for shelters.

After a few minutes of conversation with the one man,

Um-see turned to Mark, shaking his head. "*Moh-nee, moh-nee*," he repeated, leading the way back to the shelter for food to give the travelers. Once inside, Mark looked at the wall.

"Wait," Mark held up his hand as his eyes raced up and down the wall, as Um-see spoke more slowly. There'd been a bad fight . . . a man was dead . . . a child, stolen? "My God," he breathed, his eyebrows going up in question. Um-see nodded. He knew now that Mark understood his agitation, the pain of that little group. The woman's husband had been killed, Mark realized, their child kidnapped. It meant this wilderness had more than wild animals to protect against. There were human predators out there too.

As he sharpened his knife, Um-see worried about two dangers.

One was the threat of those bad men who were trying to steal women and girls. Another traveling family that came today had reported seeing those men. They told Um-see the men were on a distant hillside, moving generally toward hot springs valley, perhaps thirty of them.

"We saw mostly men," he told Um-see, "and only two women. It was not a proper family, I think. So we came here as fast as we could. We hear they've stolen women."

Accordingly, Um-see had sent two young men, members of the visiting families, hastening down the valley to the river so Um-see's own families could be warned of this. They were due to return to the valley for the winter, and perhaps they should come back early, he instructed the young men to say.

Another thing that bothered him was the danger Mark was in, although the younger man wasn't always aware of it. When today's late-arriving visitors saw Mark, Um-see had to quickly intervene to prevent the youngest man in the group from throwing his spear. Mark had been down on his hands and knees, gathering acorns beneath a large nearby oak tree. The young man, like so many nowadays—and Um-see shook his head—wanted to kill that strange animal before even finding out what it was. Um-see stopped him, and Mark didn't know what danger he'd avoided.

It was all the hair on his head, Um-see felt. He looked too much like an animal, especially with that white hide on his upper body. So, he decided, he must save Mark's life by cutting the hair off his face.

He knew Mark would not like this. It would hurt. But if he didn't make Mark look more like other men, it was only a matter of time before an impulsive hunter killed him out of surprise or fear.

For his part, Mark was enjoying the good feeling of a warm fire on a cool night, after having had a splendid supper. One of the families in the valley below had sent a son up to Um-see's shelter carrying a basket of freshly cooked turkey meat. They were pleased to share it with Um-see because of all his help as they made camp. On top of that, Um-see also had a fine venison stew, containing the small, white roots or vegetables that Mark had come to like. Now, with full stomach, he reclined on his skins, practicing his memory work.

Each day he had tried to memorize some words he'd marked on the wall. Words like *I, you, we, they, go, come, hurry, stand, sit, good, bad* . . . all the basic everyday words he knew he must learn to carry on even the simplest conversation. It had not been easy to get definitions for them all.

Today, listening closely as Um-see talked to different visitors, Mark had been able to pick out some words he knew and some of the hand movements. He watched now with interest as Um-see labored over his black obsidian knife, one of the old man's personal treasures.

To sharpen it, Um-see was knapping a sharp new edge, flaking off tiny fragments the length of the blade. His elk antler was busy and Um-see grunted with each flake that dropped off the blade into his hand. Mark also noticed two pots bubbling away on rocks at the side of the fire.

"Marrk," Um-see finally announced.

"Umm?" Mark replied.

"*Mah-mee fah-moh*," Um-see replied.

Mark sat up and began searching his lists of words on the wall. He found the first:

"Cut . . ." And then he found the second word. "Hair?"

Um-see was smiling and feeling of his face, as though he fingered an imaginary beard.

His meaning was clear. *Omigod*, Mark thought. *He wants to cut my beard with that hunk of stone! No way, José.*

Mark emphatically shook his head. He pointed to the knife, then his face, and winced, as though in great pain. Um-see understood. Yes, it might hurt a little. He pointed to the two pots on the fire, and then he made circling motions across his face, as though massaging the skin. Mark looked into the pots. One seemed to be boiling water, the other had a thick, greasy look about it. This was lather? Had Um-see ever shaved anybody in his life? Well, of course not. This was madness! He'd be a bloody mess . . .

Mark understood now, Um-see saw, and was alarmed. He was afraid the knife would hurt him. Somehow he had to understand the alternative.

"Marrk," he said slowly, "*Ee-sah hah-mo-oh* . . ." And Um-see then raised his right arm as though throwing a spear. "*Ee-sah fah-moh ho-dahn oh-san.*"

Um-see repeated his words slowly, as Mark's eyes raced up and down the wall dictionary. "I die, you say?" Mark replied. "I look like a . . . bear?

"Oh," Mark said, and sat staring at the Indian. Um-see was telling him he was in danger because of the beard, that some hunter—like that boy the other day—would spear him, thinking he was a bear.

Then Mark remembered something else. He recalled how, as a boy, his father had read aloud an article in the paper about hunters seeing a huge "Bigfoot" in the Pacific Northwest, and had tried to photograph it.

"Man, if I came on to that thing," his dad had said, laughing, "I'd shoot first and take pictures later on."

That was it, Mark realized. Um-see was worried that an

impulsive hunter would think he was a prehistoric equivalent of Bigfoot, and nail him for good. They could do it, too. He shrugged and slowly nodded, reluctantly.

OK, he indicated. *Time for a shave. God help me.*

And maybe he'd better help himself, he decided. Reaching into his rolled-up outer jacket, Mark extracted his worn and stained undershirt. He'd washed it only the day before, so at least it was clean. He pointed to the bigger pot and asked Um-see, *"Fuh-mah?"* Yes, Um-see nodded. Water.

Mark slowly lowered the undershirt into the pot, squeezed it out, popping it from one hand to the other since the water was almost boiling. Then he lay down on his skins and wrapped the steaming undershirt over and around his bearded face. He held up one finger so Um-see would know this would take a few minutes.

While Mark's face was covered, Um-see decided his thick mass of hot fat probably needed something more to soften that thick hair, so he took several pinches of fresh ash from the fire and stirred them into the mixture. He'd heard women say this was a good way to clean a pot that was too dirty. Maybe it would help make that hair easier to cut.

When Mark unwrapped the undershirt, Um-see went to work. He carefully smeared the hot mixture over the younger man's face while Mark kept his eyes closed tightly. The smell was pungent, acrid, and his nose itched. He helped by massaging the grease into his face, under his chin, on his throat. He decided then he would not let Um-see shave his upper lip. He'd rather have a moustache than cuts all over his mouth. Strange, but the mixture had a gritty feel about it.

Um-see slowly scraped a small patch on Mark's lower cheek to see how easily the hair would cut. He had to press deep into the flesh for the knife to cut any hair. It was slow going. Mark pointed to his upper lip and shook his head violently, saying *"Moh-nah,"* several times, to be sure Um-see knew he was saying "No" to shaving the upper lip.

Mark tried to relax. Um-see applied pressure and scraped

the knife repeatedly over the same spot until the hair was gone—mostly. Within ten minutes he had done all he could, and Mark's face was relatively free of hair on cheeks, chin, and throat. The bush on his upper lip was still thick but he'd had enough of that knife. Blood seeped from his face at four points where the stone blade had nicked him.

Mark wrapped his face again with his water-soaked undershirt, then cleaned his face thoroughly, took the knife from Um-see, and tried running it over his face where he could still feel stubble. A little more hair came off. Then he tried taking a little off his upper lip. Oops. Another nick. He did not attempt to remove the moustache but tried to cut the stubble down so it didn't fall over his mouth.

He found Um-see smiling and nodding at him. "*Mohkah*," the Indian pronounced.

"If you say it's good," Mark replied, "I'll go with that. Now if I just don't bleed to death."

The nicks were scabs on his face next morning, and Mark sponged them carefully with his wet undershirt.

"Uh . . . Marrk," began Um-see, pointing to his hair. Mark realized his hair was standing straight up, growing wild in all directions, uncombed for some two months now.

He was not about to let the older man cut *that*, however. Mark nodded and then looked into Um-see's pots. He found one that appeared to have clean, light-colored animal fat in it, and he dipped his fingers in, then rubbed the grease into his hair and scalp. And no comb, he immediately realized. Well, there was one solution to that. He stepped out of the shelter and picked up one of the large pinecones that fell on their rocky porch.

He ran the prickly cone across his hair, and its rough surface reached his scalp, slicking the greased hair down in a rough kind of way. He turned to Um-see, who smiled at a totally different-looking Mark than he'd seen before.

The big man looked younger to Um-see now that the face hair was mostly gone. Um-see still found that hair on his upper lip repugnant. And he worried about those strange garments on Mark's body. As well as the huge things on his feet. How could he run while wearing those? Then the Indian motioned to his own scrap of hide, circling his waist and genitals, and he pointed to Mark's middle with an inquiring look. It was clear that he was being asked to wear a loincloth, Mark saw, instead of his long exercise pants.

Oh come on, he groaned to himself. *I'd look like a damn fool walking around with a piece of hide around my ass . . . and it's getting colder every day.*

Mark had grabbed his head and rolled his eyes when Um-see's motion made his meaning clear. The Indian kept a straight face, however, and Mark soon saw he was serious. He really wanted him to dress as he was dressed, like other men in the valley were. It seemed important to the old man, and after a few minutes of agonized expressions, Mark shrugged and nodded. He had no earthly idea how to wrap that hide around himself, though, and make it stay.

Um-see did, and showed him. He quickly produced soft deer hide from the skins that he had cut up.

Mark took off his pants and shorts, then Um-see showed him how to secure the rolled-up hide between his legs, tie it in back to a piece that went around the waist, and wrap it snugly in front.

Mark felt naked. And foolish. Eleanor would fall down laughing if she could see him now. Especially with the big jogging shoes on his feet, and his Nike sweatshirt now stained so bad it looked like a camouflage jacket.

He took off the sweatshirt, and Um-see frowned. There was still Mark's body, that thick mat of chest hair, solid black with a few gray streaks, and more hair sprouted from the shoulders on his back. Mark also had much dark hair on his legs. Um-see shrugged. It was the best that could be done. He had seen a few men with some body hair. Perhaps the people could get accustomed to it. He would have to warn Mark not to get down on the ground like an animal, though. It could be fatal if any nervous young hunters were around.

For his part, Mark was noticing something about himself. Looking down, he saw—and felt—that his belly was about gone. He wasn't skinny, for sure, but he thought he weighed less than two hundred pounds—a weight he could hardly remember from his youth. He had been going around for weeks in only his boxer shorts, so his skin was tanned—although not nearly as dark as Um-see's. He found all this sort of funny.

So, he kidded himself, *I've joined their club. I'm too big and soft to be a real Indian, but if clothes make the man, I am on my way to fame and fortune as a Stone Age fashion plate. All I need now is a pair of those leather slippers.* Um-see, looking at Mark's large shoes, was thinking the same thing.

There were now six traveling families camped in the valley. More arrived each day, while some left after thanking Um-see for his help, heading south.

After making sure his shave wounds weren't bleeding, Mark followed Um-see and Seebo down to the valley floor to look in on all the visitors. They all registered visible surprise at Mark's changed appearance, and he became conscious of all eyes on him as they approached. At each shelter, men looked at him with eyebrows raised, but with no other expressions, and no one said anything to Um-see.

One small boy, however, broke the ice and began giggling as he saw Mark walk up in loincloth and large jogging shoes. The boy's father instantly took the boy firmly by the shoulder, and the boy quickly looked serious, biting his lower lip. One of the grown men also looked away to avoid, Mark thought, showing a smile.

Yeah, I know, Mark agonized to himself. *I look totally ridiculous . . . out here in a leather jockstrap trying to look like an overweight Tonto, or something. Damn. This is embarrassing. I just wish to hell they'd all laugh out loud and get it over with.*

But they didn't. For an hour, Um-see and Mark made the rounds of the visitors, to see what they needed in the way of food or assistance. Nobody laughed, although Mark did see some of the young girls look down as he approached, to conceal their smiles. He groaned inwardly, but Um-see pretended not to notice and diligently did his job.

Some of the new arrivals had dogs with them, and it became clear to Mark that Seebo dominated them, almost at first sight. The golden wolf-dog sniffed at two of the males but growled deep in his throat if they approached him first. These were short-haired animals, with long muzzles, uniformly brown, some with black-tipped tails, most with very little white on their bodies. One large male barked twice at Seebo, who sat on his haunches and simply stared silently at the other animal until it moved away. Seebo stretched out in the sun and waited for Um-see to finish his work.

Then Um-see caught sight of a newly arriving family starting to erect their shelter at the north end of the hot springs area, beyond the cloud of water vapor. He jumped up and hurried toward the newcomers while Mark followed. He realized now that Um-see was showing him off, making sure that everyone saw Mark was not an animal but a man—and one who would not harm them.

Um-see jogged as fast as his limp permitted and signaled to the two men of the new group. He pointed up the mountainside, and spoke rapidly. Mark understood words that translated as *bad* and *fall down* and *kill*. He studied the mountainside where Um-see pointed.

Some of the hot spring vents were as low as sixty feet up on the mountainside, while others erupted at elevations of more than one hundred feet above the valley floor. At the north end of the springs, Mark now saw, was a great swell of stone, an outcrop, of the same tufalike material as the rest of the shiny, pinkish wall of rock formed by centuries of cascading hot water. The outcrop bulged out from the mountain like a giant boil, formed by calcium-filled water that had stopped flowing in that section.

That big stone outcrop had captured Um-see's attention, since the newly arrived family was camped directly beneath it. As Mark watched, the two men nodded their understanding and began to pull up poles they'd planted to erect shelters. They gathered their belongings and moved south along the creek that ran through the valley to a spot closer to where other visitors were camped, well away from the base of the mountain.

When Um-see came back to where Mark stood, the younger man pointed up, inquiringly.

"Moh-nee Koh-dah?" Mark asked, meaning bad, or dangerous, Um-see nodded, and added, *"Ee-fee-moh,"* or *kill*, as Mark understood it. From the valley floor, though, the outcrop did not look that threatening. He could see it, certainly, but it seemed no more dangerous than other protruding rocks visible on both facing mountains. He looked skeptical, and Um-see decided it was important to show him what he meant. Everyone in Um-see's families knew about that hanging rock, and so must Mark, that he, too, would avoid this spot. Someday, and Um-see shuddered to think of it, a terrible thing could happen because of the bad rock.

He motioned for the younger man to follow him, and hastened up the wooded slope, onto the mountainside.

They took a game trail upward, toward the gushing springs. Ten minutes of climbing and turning put them on a horizontal trail north and south along Hot Springs Mountain, a hundred feet above the valley floor.

Going toward the rising vapor of the springs, Um-see arrived at the swell of the rock outcrop, which formed a broad platform, thrust out from the earth around it. Mark started to step out on the rounded surface of the outcrop, but Um-see caught his arm.

"Marrk, no."

Mark was astonished and delighted. Um-see had learned one of *his* words. Um-see smiled at his surprise, then knelt in the dirt and began to hollow out a trench where rock came out of the earth. He dug with both hands until he had an excavation three feet long. He stuck his arm down into the crevice, pulled out more leaves, then stood up. With one hand, he traced the line of his trench for some fifteen feet in the dirt. He held his hands about a foot apart, and motioned along the trench line.

Mark got down on his knees and ran his hand down into the crevice that Um-see had uncovered. His arm kept going down into the earth until his fingers encountered . . . nothing. There was empty air, down in the ground, beyond the length of his arm. He understood then. Very little rock connected the huge overhang to its mountainside support. Um-see was right. Any unusual weight or vibration out on the surface of the outcrop could cause this gigantic stone to break off and thunder down the mountainside crushing everything in its path. It had to weigh twenty tons or more. Understandably, Um-see wanted no one camped under it.

They then walked south along the mountain path, above where most of the hot water erupted from cones that dotted the mountainside . . . but there still were some springs higher up.

They had to walk carefully through muddy areas where centuries of boiling water had eroded the path down to bare rock, mixed with occasional slides of dirt. One bad step, Mark saw, and he could slip off the mountain to certain death below.

Um-see knew all the safe spots, and Mark tried to walk in the old man's footsteps. He also tried to count the number of springs that belched steaming water. By the time they'd covered a quarter mile, Mark counted more than sixty active springs. He marveled that so much thermal activity could be confined in so small an area. And there was no apparent order to how the springs had erupted.

Old, closed-off cones were mute reminders of the water produced in ages past. He decided that as deposits built up around the mouth of the cone outlets they finally sealed themselves off as calcium solidified at the springs' mouths. Some of the cones were small, which meant that new springs were being created as old ones sealed themselves. Clouds of vapor rose from the valley below, as hot water cascaded down into pools alongside the cold creek water.

He saw something else. Visiting families were already bathing in the hot pools, and in one he clearly saw three women, standing naked as one of them bathed a small child. Mark stared, fascinated, as a bright sun glinted on wet bodies, highlighting firm breasts, small waists, and slender legs. One of the girls lay down full length in the water, stretching out arms and legs, her body beautifully formed, dark hair spilling out in the water around her head. Mark found himself surprised somehow that she looked like any twentieth-century maiden would look, even to the triangle of dark pubic hair between her legs. The other girl dipped a basket into the steaming water and poured it over her head, clearly enjoying the warmth as it cascaded down her chest, dripping from her nipples. Then more vapor swirled up in front of the bathing women, and Mark could see them only faintly.

These were not children, Mark realized, but rather young women whose innocent sensuous movements aroused him immediately. He remembered how long it had been since he'd been in bed with Eleanor. He found himself alive with desire, before reason asserted itself. He could not—should not—think of sex with these young women. They were of a different culture with totally different lives than his own. He'd try not to think about it, he told himself . . . but it had been a long time.

Um-see, observing the young women, sighed. Then he grunted, turned, and hastened back down the path the way they had come. He understood what Mark was thinking. Natural thoughts for a younger man. This could be a problem he would have to solve. Mark would need a woman, in time. But first, he knew, there was another question. Would Mark be accepted by the Elders to stay with the families in the valley? The answer would come soon. Families would be coming back from the river camp at any time. Um-see hated the thought of Mark leaving the valley. He thought of him now almost like a son. He wanted, more than anything he could think of, for him to stay and become a member of the families. But it would not be an easy thing to make happen.

Only the Elders could approve of Mark staying in the valley. Um-see would appear before them and speak. He only hoped that in the meantime he could keep Mark alive, and that everyone could accept him as a man and not as half-man, half-animal. He shook his head sadly. People could often be unfair in how they judged others, if they looked different.

TWENTY-EIGHT

As tired as he was, Um-see forced himself to work late each night. There was much to be done, to see that Mark looked as much like other men as possible.

He would start with the shoes.

After the evening meal, Um-see found the thickest piece of cured hide he had and cleaned it carefully. Marrk had big feet, but this should cover them. He had the younger man stand on the hide barefooted, then used sharp, blackened sticks from the fire to draw a careful outline of Mark's feet onto the hide.

Mark noted that the outline was drawn more than an inch away from his feet. Did Um-see plan to make the things too big on purpose? But the Indian seemed to know what he was doing, so Mark said nothing.

Mark saw, however, that this was taking Um-see's time away from work on his bow—something the older man obviously wanted to finish. So Mark picked up the bowstick and, as Um-see cut the hide in the shape of Mark's feet, he started rubbing the bow limbs with roughened rock, to pare them down to size. Um-see noted this and smiled. He did want that bow finished, to show the families when they returned from the river. He even hoped to be able to use it well by that time.

The weather cooperated. It began to rain during the night and continued, off and on, for two days—a hard, chilling downpour and brisk wind that whipped the mountainside, bending small trees almost to the snapping point. Seebo did not appear for morning handouts, and the visitors in the valley stayed mostly in their shelters. With two days and nights of worktime indoors, the men completed their projects. Mark understood now why Um-see had cut the shoe soles much bigger than his feet. As the Indian worked, excess hide on the sole was folded up, to be stitched along the side of the shoe to the covering on top. That, Mark surmised, was to keep the stitching from coming into contact with the ground at every step. Um-see punched holes along the edge of the soles with sharpened bone points. He forced twisted tendon through the holes, to form a line of stitches. It was slow work, and Um-see had to sit close to the fire to see well—which meant that sweat dripped from his upper body in a steady stream. Mark, concerned that the older man might get dehydrated, frequently handed Um-see a cup of water.

Mark did his own thing on the tough surface of the oak limb that was turning into a bow. He cracked small rocks off the walls to try out their sanding qualities and found some rough enough to dig into the wood surface. His arms and shoulders ached each morning from scraping the night before, but the bow took shape. By the third day, Um-see's bow was ready to be strung—and Mark was ready to wear his moccasins. Or loafers. He wasn't quite sure what to call them. The important thing was, they fit.

The sun rose behind them as Um-see and Mark climbed the mountain behind their shelter. Both wanted privacy in which to practice with bows.

In his last practice session, Mark found himself "holding" his arrow too long, trying to aim, when he had pulled the bowstring to his mouth. Holding was necessary to track moving game but he still had to learn the almost instant, instinctive shooting that seemed natural to Um-see.

Mark's first arrows missed by a foot or more as he tried to track the rabbits that were moving everywhere at dawn. In two dozen shots, he lost two arrows, broke three others, hit nothing but rocks. Besides which, his feet hurt. Not from the new shoes but the pointed rocks underfoot. Centuries-old game trails had worn down to pure stone, and Mark felt tiny rock points digging into his feet. His next chore would be to cut another set of inner soles for his thin shoes. The soles of Um-see's feet, he decided, must be like leather.

The older man ended their practice with a rabbit he'd shot at short distance. He'd been throwing a spear all his life and did not appear to aim at all when he quickly drew and released his arrow.

"Terrific," Mark growled, grinning. "Already he's making me look bad." He knew he'd need hours of practice to be as accurate with a bow at forty paces as he was with a rock at twenty.

Before they left the summit, Um-see gave in to a dream he'd been having. He remembered Mark's long-distance shot during that first bow demonstration. Now Um-see faced west, toward an area he knew contained no people. He nocked an arrow, slowly drew it fully to his face, aimed up at a forty-five-degree angle, then released. Because of their high vantage point, both men could keep the arrow in view for a long time, early-morning sunlight glinting off the turkey feathers and stone tip. Finally it fell into trees at least half a mile from where they stood.

"Ahhhhh," breathed Um-see. Never had he expected to send any kind of spear, large or small, on such a journey. He felt new power in his arms and back, jubilant as though he were young again. Mark, smiling, knew that high arrow flight had made the older man's day.

Finally, Um-see headed off down the trail. Turning, he asked Mark "*Mah-ee-ah?*"

"Yes," replied Mark. "Eat. Let's do breakfast."

It was the sound of excited voices and high-pitched shouts of children that woke Mark and Um-see simultaneously. They were groggy from too little sleep since they'd worked late on fletching arrows and knapping stone arrowheads.

Every day for three straight days, the two men had prac-

ticed their archery—morning and afternoon—until they both
could come close to a moving target with some consistency.
It was a costly exercise in lost and broken arrows, however,
and each night they'd had to replenish their supply. Now
Mark wanted to roll over and go back to sleep, but Um-see
grunted at him and motioned outside.

Um-see knew exactly what the sounds were. They walked
out onto their stone porch and breathed deeply of the cool
dawn air. Through the trees were distant moving figures,
coming from the south, and within minutes they had a caller.
A tousled black head appeared at the lip of the porch and
pulled himself quickly up on the vines with a happy shout,
"Um-see, *I-ee!*" The lithe little boy, perhaps ten years old,
ran up and grabbed the older man around the waist, and Um-
see hugged him, grinning. They talked together for a moment, then Um-see pointed to Mark, and said simply,
"Marrk. *Mo-kah-mo.*"

Mark was glad that he'd been identified since the boy's
smile faded at sight of him. Mark put on his widest smile
and nodded. It seemed from the exchange that the lad was
related somehow to Um-see, but the older man gave no clue
just how as the youngster disappeared down to the path below.

Instead, Um-see motioned to the people moving up the
valley. "*Ah-ee. Oh-ee-ah.*" It took Mark a moment to trans-
late, but then the words fitted into his growing vocabulary.
The families of the valley were returning.

Um-see's first impulse was to hasten down to the valley
floor and welcome his friends. Then he caught himself. It
would be important for Mark to be with him, to establish
Mark as friend, not enemy, so that everyone could get used
to how he looked. It had been seven days since Um-see had
cut the younger man's whiskers. Now he again had a dark
shadow across his jaws—and his hair. It stuck out in all
directions, giving him a slightly crazy look. At least, Um-
see reflected, Mark was now wearing the shoes he'd made

for him, and he seemed to have gotten accustomed to the hide that protected his private parts.

Otherwise, Mark's body was not covered, and for a moment Um-see wished it was. All that black hair—on chest, legs, arms, even on his back—made him look too much like an animal. He sighed. He hoped his earlier message at the river had gotten around to everyone. He would have Mark stay close to him, to show the families he was under Um-see's protection.

Um-see went into the shelter and got their fire going. They would eat something, allow the families to occupy their usual shelter positions, and visit after some of the confusion ended. In the meantime, Um-see found the pot of clean fat and handed it to Mark, pointing to his unruly hair.

Dress-up time. Time for him to go on display, Mark knew. It was clear that Um-see was going all out to make him presentable, get him accepted, keep him alive. *OK*, he decided, *I'll buy that.*

Mark rubbed rancid fat into his hair and scalp, then went outside to find a pinecone to slick his hair down. He laughed out loud. All his life he'd been a private person. He hated crowds, hated drawing attention to himself. Made only a few friends. Now he was to be a public spectacle, a kind of tame Bigfoot on display. He then remembered that movie comedy he'd seen, where the family adopted a Bigfoot, and brought the giant man-animal home to live with them. Now he knew just how the monster felt, as well as the family he descended upon. He was sure this was going to be a rocky relationship.

By the time sunshine had warmed the chill off the mountains, returning residents had congregated at the upper end of the small valley.

Mark and Um-see paused as they came down the mountain path and found Seebo behind them, silent as usual. They could see, up the valley, nearly a hundred people erecting shelters at the edge of open woods, just beyond the hot-water outcrops. Mark tried to picture this scene as it would look centuries later in his own time. On his three visits to Hot Springs with Eleanor, this was the area where they'd spent most of their sight-seeing hours.

This stretch of the creek would later be covered over with Central Avenue, and right where the falling water created those giant steam clouds, that's where Bathhouse Row would be built. And that little park at the upper end, it was right across the street from where they'd stayed, the Arlington Hotel. It was there, just about, where he saw the returning Indians had set up their camp.

As they drew closer, people recognized Um-see and waved to him. He responded with nods and smiles, and an occasional word of greeting. Mark quickly concluded that the messenger Um-see had sent earlier had also told about his own presence in the valley.

Everyone simply stared at him silently, without hostility but with no smiles either. All about them was feverish activity. People were unpacking their carry poles, moving into shelters being erected. On the slope everyone had a commanding view of the south. Most of the shelters were positioned beneath trees that would give some shelter from rain or, later, snow.

Mark quickly saw this was no hasty campground. It had been here for years, perhaps centuries. Shelters were going up on cleared sites with hard-packed trails leading to them, wildflowers growing on all sides. This was the valley people's longtime winter home, only a few minutes' walk from the hot pools down the valley, and less than a hundred feet from the cold creek water upstream. The shelters varied in size according to the numbers of children there, it appeared. All shelters had openings at the top, and some already sent wisps of smoke drifting up into the crisp morning sunlight.

Around some of the shelters Mark could see dogs, although there was almost no barking. Seebo stopped at one shelter, woofed, and went nose-to-nose with a smaller dog that he obviously knew. Then the big animal did an odd thing: He stretched out on his stomach, whined slightly, and the smaller dog sniffed at him. Mark would never have guessed their ferocious wolf-dog could ever be subservient to any other four-footed animal . . . yet he was witnessing it now. He'd have to ask Um-see to explain Seebo's behavior.

As Mark and Um-see watched the moving-in process, Mark felt a sudden sting on the back of his left leg. He jumped, whirled around, thinking he'd been stung by a bee. He found a small child, seated on the ground, wailing. Mark had knocked the toddler down as he spun around.

He quickly knelt to comfort the child, and saw then what caused his sharp pain: The little boy had a tiny handful of black hair that he had plucked from the back of Mark's leg. His wails caused only a few people to look around in the general hubbub of noise and conversation. But one young woman hurried to the child, snatched him up, and hastened away from Mark, without making eye contact. He started forward to try and make some apology, but Um-see—who'd seen what happened—laid a hand on Mark's shoulder and gently shook his head.

Um-see smiled and ran his hand over the black hair on Mark's chest. It was his hairy body and legs that had attracted the child, and which caused a number of the busy Indians to glance at him as they worked.

They'd been told about him, Mark knew. He also saw that most of the people were trying not to stare, and he hated it. He felt like a walking wildlife exhibit. He ground his teeth but continued trying to look pleasant. Um-see clearly had a destination among the shelters being erected. They entered the pine grove that fringed the slope, and Um-see waved, then called out to a slim young man who smilingly waved back.

"Um-moh," grunted the older man. "*Ee-oh-kah.*"

Mark had to concentrate to remember the last word. This man was Um-moh. Who was . . . Um-see's grandson?

The two Indians hurried to each other—and quickly embraced, smiling. It was the first time Mark had seen adults show open affection. They were relatively alone here, the nearest shelter being a hundred feet away, which could mean that public displays of love were rare.

Mark stood a few feet from the men and waited while they talked rapidly. Then Um-see motioned to him, calling Mark's name, then pronounced Um-moh's name slowly, to be sure Mark understood it. Mark smiled broadly, and started to hold out his hand for a shake, quickly thought better of it. He had seen no handshakes, so far.

Um-moh called out to his shelter, and a young woman quickly emerged, smiling at Um-see. This must be the grandson's wife—or woman, Mark corrected himself. He hadn't yet found a word for *wife*. Simply *woman* and *man*. Um-moh smiled at the young woman, looked at Mark, and said "Mee-new." She was a small, well-formed girl, probably still in her teens, and visibly pregnant. She nodded to Mark, but he noticed that her smile was hesitant.

Um-see's grandson was slightly taller, at about five-seven, than the other adult Indians Mark had seen, his body well muscled. He wore his hair tied behind his head and did not wear a headband. Like Um-see, he had a prominent hawk nose, high cheekbones, and wide-set dark eyes. He spoke with animation and good humor. It was hard to guess his age, but Mark felt sure the lad could not be more than twenty, if that. Mee-new was silent and listened as the two men talked. She glanced repeatedly at Mark but looked away as he caught her eye, nervous at his presence.

Mark sighed. He had a lot of ice-breaking to do, and they might never get used to him. One thing, for sure: He must memorize more words, quickly, if he was to communicate with them. Maybe if he could talk to them—even haltingly—it might take their minds off his great hairy body.

TWENTY-NINE

Kuh-moh jerked his knife out of the dying man's chest and stepped back quickly to avoid spurting blood.

Men standing nearby were frozen in shock and silence.

They had known that Kuh-moh was a violent, unpredictable leader, but this was the first time they saw how fast his irritation could cost a man's life.

He himself had not wanted to kill this man. He could not even remember the man's name. Kuh-moh had sent him with three others to attack a party of travelers, kill the two men, and seize their women and children.

But this man had let one of the travelers get away. One of his men had been killed. One of the women—in resisting the attack—had been hurt, which sent her half-grown daughter into hysterics.

It had been a poor effort, Kuh-moh knew, and he told this dead man of his contempt. He had called the man's father a snake, said that his mother smelled like a skunk. When the man grew angry, so did Kuh-moh, and, in front of eight of his men, they fought with fists and knives. Within seconds, the bigger, stronger Kuh-moh had clubbed the smaller man into unconsciousness, then stabbed him repeatedly with his long green knife that tapered to a fine point.

It was a waste, Kuh-moh reflected, as he stood up. Strong men, desperate men, were hard enough to find. He should have conducted the raid himself. He would have killed both those men, and nobody would have known that he had taken their women and children. Now he knew the escaping man would carry the tale . . . perhaps to the same valley he intended very soon to command.

He pulled his hide jacket closer around him. He was cold and nervous. Kuh-moh glared at the other men, who stood mute, his cold eyes black with fury.

"This man," he said, "did not follow my orders. He was careless. You"—he pointed to another man—"help me."

The two carried the dead man to the top of a ravine nearby, and, at Kuh-moh's direction, they swung the limp body out in the air, and it bounced down the steep slope to disappear in leaves and brush at the bottom.

Then Kuh-moh signaled and led his men down to a small creek sparkling in the afternoon sun. He would clean himself and talk to the other men. They must understand how they could seize the valley. He wanted to control them by fear, but he understood that his men had to want to set up their new home in the valley, to enjoy the plentiful game there, to have women to serve them, and to enjoy a good life. Outcasts all, few of them had even known a stable life. If he could make them know the rewards of what he wanted, then perhaps they would not talk among themselves over his killing of this man today. So, he decided, it was time to move closer to the valley, to scout out its surrounding mountains.

Kuh-moh had fewer men than lived in the valley of the hot springs, yet he knew there was a way for him to defeat those men. They were probably weak from easy living. He was strong. And determined.

Now he must, very quietly, go there, observe them and how they lived. They must have no warning when he struck.

It took three days for the villagers to get accustomed to Mark's presence and looks. He now walked with Um-see by the families' shelters without comment. Men and women glanced up at his approach, some nodded, then they resumed their work.

Most of the adults were seated, some on the ground, others on low stools, all involved in handwork of some kind.

Older children worked, too, while the toddlers stayed close to their parents.

In all, Mark counted thirty-seven shelters, not including those of the transient travelers, who were camped farther down the valley, toward the hot springs. Perhaps ninety people in all, he estimated, including children. Of the roughly three dozen men, Mark spotted some who were elderly, a few who were infirm.

With few exceptions, the adults worked on domestic chores. Some women shook out soft leather clothing. Mark recognized long trousers, vests, shirtlike shifts for upper body, soft deerskin boots—all being aired, cleaned, and repaired. Winter was on its way, the work made clear, and people were getting ready.

It was cool, and Mark had started to put on his muddy white workout pants today, but Um-see restrained him. "No," Um-see said. He wanted the younger man to appear as he did, it was obvious. And to use those words of the valley language which he knew. "You speak," he instructed Mark. "You know Um-see words." And he smiled broadly. They'd been working long hours at night to be sure Mark learned the most common words. Um-see tried out short sentences, to see if Mark understood, talking to him as though to a child.

"You like hunt big black bear?" Um-see asked.

Mark grinned. He suspected Um-see was kidding him gently about their memorable bear encounter. So he shrugged.

"Bear good. Mark like hunt small animal. Deer, rabbit, squirrel," he replied, slowly. Then added, teasingly: "Um-see bear man. Um-see and big knife."

The Indian chuckled. He recalled with pleasure how he had finally killed the bear—something he planned to tell in more detail when he was able to talk at length to his friends and family. Every man was expected to have his exploits become matters of village history, to perpetuate his fame and memory.

Now, though, Um-see was doing his job as Helper. Mark carried a loaded basket in each hand, and they made the rounds of families who needed some kind of assistance. One family's shelter had caught fire their first night in the valley, and they needed replacement hides, which Um-see carried. Mark's baskets contained dried meat, nuts, and dried fruit.

Mark was fascinated by the work going on at each shelter, and wanted to watch. He was glad when Um-see paused to exchange a few words with most men and a few women. The men were either knapping stone for spear tips, repairing their hide garments with sharp bones and tendon or working on new weapons. Also, it appeared to Mark that every shelter and male adult kept one or more long spears, taller than a man, for protection.

Some of the women were also making baskets and pots. The yellow-and-green reeds they used for baskets were several feet long, and the work began at the bottom of the basket. Six or more reeds extended up as the women worked other reeds cylindrically around the vertical reeds, their nimble fingers obviously strong and capable.

Older boys at several shelters scraped and cleaned fresh-killed animal skins. Already, hunting parties were returning from nearby forests with deer carcasses and wild turkeys.

Um-see, meanwhile, held long, serious conversations with some older men at the uppermost line of shelters, in the wooded section of the mountain slope. Mark started to go up and join him, but Um-see saw him coming and held up his hand. It appeared he wanted to talk to these senior citizens privately. *That's odd,* Mark noted. *This must be private business of some kind. About me? Probably,* Mark thought wryly. He'd begun to feel a little like an albatross around Um-see's neck.

He was almost too weak to move, yet he knew he must reach that creek only a few yards in front of him. He must have water or die. Again, the injured man rose up on hands and knees and began to go forward, but the action took his last ounce of strength, and he fell forward, unconscious.

This was where the hunting party from the valley found him, more dead than alive.

It was Um-see's grandson, Um-moh, who found the prone figure near the creek. He and his fellow hunters saw that the man was gravely injured. His head was bloody in back, and there was more blood on his arm and shoulder. One leg seemed twisted in an awkward way. But when Um-moh listened at his chest, there was a beat within, and he appeared to be breathing.

Within minutes, they had rigged a litter from poles and hide strips, and an hour later they hurried into the village, calling out for assistance as they neared the first shelter. The injured man was soon being looked at by a small older woman, who knelt by his side and ran her fingers around his wounds. She ordered him carried to a nearby shelter, where she bathed his face with water, after pouring some of it carefully into his mouth. He choked but swallowed most of it.

"He needs rest and food. His leg is broken. Get wood strips," she said to Um-moh, holding her hands two feet apart. He hurried to do her bidding. As he left the shelter he sent one of the younger boys to tell the Elders about the injured man. They would need to know that the threat to their safety was still in the mountains. Those Bad Men had hurt and perhaps killed, again. Everyone must know . . . and be aware of the danger.

Um-see could not remember any meeting of Elders before like this one. When he had been a member of this select group, their business had concerned small things . . . the misbehavior of an unruly young man, or two men wanting the same woman and fighting over her. Or suspected theft.

Now two important matters were before the Elders, and Um-see regretted this. He wished to make a case for admitting Mark to be a permanent resident of the valley. Mark sat behind Um-see so that he could hear the discussion, but the Indian worried that Mark didn't seem aware of how serious this was. If the Elders refused his request, Mark would have to leave the valley and go away.

Yet he also knew the other matter was more pressing: Serious danger to everyone was close. The wounded man brought into camp showed how real it was. The man had finally gasped out the story of his friend being killed and their women and children stolen. He'd lapsed into unconsciousness before being able to tell more of his ordeal. Whatever threatened them was less than one day's walk away.

Um-see heard the details immediately. The old woman who nursed the injured man was Mee-soon, a lifelong friend. She told Um-see the sad tale that now had everyone alarmed.

Um-see then told Mark of the attack and killing, but at this moment their primary concern was how the Elders would react to the unprecedented idea of accepting an alien person into their midst. The five Elders sat in a semicircle on one side of the fire stones; Um-see and Mark sat on the other side. Light shone directly into their eyes from the open entrance flap. The Elders obviously wanted a clear view of Mark's face during this talk, he realized.

In deference to his years and status, Um-see was invited to speak first. He explained he would talk slow in order that Mark might understand his words. The Elders' eyebrows went up slightly.

"This man knows our tongue?" asked the senior Elder, clearly surprised.

"He speaks some but not all," Um-see replied. "He has worked hard to learn, and has marked out words—in his own tongue—on the wall in my shelter. You must come and see this. It is a new thing, and shows that Mark has a good mind."

Then came the questioning: How Mark had first come to be in the valley, where he came from, what his skills were—and had he been banished by another village? Um-see's answers were short and truthful. He knew little of Mark's past life. But he came from a place with fine craftsmen and materials for hides never seen here before. He held up Mark's jacket and one of his shoes, which the older men examined with barely concealed astonishment.

Um-see told of Mark's help at the shelter, his hard, uncomplaining work in preparing and dispensing food and help to travelers. Um-see saved for last the story of their encounter with the berserk black bear, the attack by wolves, their difficult escape.

Like everyone he knew, Um-see considered the truth an important rule of life. He had never, to his knowledge, told a serious untruth. However, tale-telling was an important, respected verbal skill, and Um-see was proud of the way he could hold an audience when he told stories.

So the tale of their brush with disaster had dramatic overtones that Mark understood: It was the largest bear Um-see had ever seen. Never had he felt the hot breath of the wolf pack so close to his throat. He was sure he was about to enter the Spirit world when Mark saved him with the well-aimed rock. And then he told of Seebo's timely attack that held the wolves at bay and allowed them to claim their meat and hides.

The Elders' eyes were bright with excitement and respect.

"A man who can do all this is a man we want here in the valley," Um-see concluded, looking each of his old friends carefully in the eyes. This was no small thing. He was, in effect, staking his reputation on Mark's being a solid, contributing member of their community. If not, the shame would be on Um-see's head.

"He is so different," offered Um-fon. "Will our young men accept a stranger who looks so, ah, so strange? Almost like an animal."

"Yes," agreed Um-see. "I felt like that also when Mark first came. I did not know if I could trust him. Then, as time went by, I asked myself—should I judge this man by how he looks, or by how he lives? Does he have courage and does he respect other men?"

Um-see paused, and there was silence. He continued.

"Mark can help us. He has offered to show our men how

to use his new weapon, which throws short spears better than our weapon."

"Better?" two Elders asked in one voice. "How so?"

"It shoots longer. You can aim your spear with more care. The small spears are lighter to carry."

"But have you seen this man kill large animals with this . . . what do you call it . . . ?"

Um-see pushed out his lips, to make a "B" sound he breathed out. It was a sound he'd rarely made.

The Elder tried the word and got out "Po." He smiled and shook his head. That sound was difficult.

"No," Um-see answered their question. "I have not seen Mark kill a large animal. Only smaller ones. The bow he made is new, he needs practice. I have made one for myself, and I have felt its power. Soon I expect to kill deer, elk, turkey . . . and wolves, if they hunt too close to the village . . . and if they kill some of our dogs as they did last winter."

There was skepticism in the air, Um-see knew. If Mark's skill as a hunter depended on his killing animals with a bow, Um-see thought, then he was not judged properly. He made this point, and others, as Mark listened carefully, trying to pick up as much of the exchange as he could.

My man is flat going to bat for me, Mark thought, as Um-see spoke long and earnestly, although he couldn't make out all that was being said. He wondered if they'd want him to say anything.

Indeed, the time came when all eyes turned to Mark. Um-see asked him, "You speak with Elders?"

Mark knew he must say something.

"I like valley," he said, choosing simple words he knew, speaking slowly. "I like Um-see people. Good people here. I work, hunt, be helper. I wish stay here, if Elders agree."

Good, Um-see thought. *Marrk did well, and the Elders were impressed, although they each found his accent strange.*

They sat silent. None wished to hurry a judgment. Um-see saw that two of them clearly were unsure whether it was wise to let such a different man into their community. And he knew why.

How could they allow Mark to stay if then they turned away other travelers who wished to join them—people of their own tongue, appearance, and customs? There was a limit on how many families the valley could support.

As Um-see well knew, every child here grew up knowing that the valley was a special place, its people responsible to the Spirits for its beauty, its bounty, and its availability to all travelers. The giant hot-water mountainside that sent vapor clouds into the skies showed each day how the Spirits smiled on this place. Too many people, it was believed, would hurt this place and cause the mysterious forces that created it to be upset with the valley people. Elders had to decide who could stay and who must travel on, often an agonizing decision.

Which was why the valley population was larger than it had ever been. Many were allowed to stay.

The Elders also knew they must do the right thing by Um-see, a man of great worth. Might the decision, the presiding Elder finally asked, wait for a brief time? The other four old men glanced at each other and slowly nodded.

"We must think and talk about this," he told Um-see and Mark. "This is different, and we must respect the feelings of everyone. Mark is a good man, we believe. Yet the wishes of others are important, too. We want nothing to cause deep division within the village, now that we face great danger."

That ended the discussion, and Um-see motioned to Mark that they should leave. They nodded to the seated circle of Elders and walked down the path from the Elders' shelter.

When alone, the senior Elder turned to his colleagues.

"Now we must consider the Bad Men who threaten the valley. How must we prepare? We have no history of killing men. This is something decent men should not do. Yet we must be ready. How?"

Another Elder spoke slowly.

"Yes, I hear some of our men insist that we should not

kill other men. They were taught that by their fathers. Killing men always led to vengeance, anger, more killings. Now they teach that to their sons. Are we forced to turn our backs on our history and become like Bad Men ourselves?"

"What choice is there?" said another. "We must kill them, or they will kill us. It is the Elders' responsibility to protect families here, to protect the valley. We cannot protect the valley if we do nothing and die."

After a long silence, the senior man spoke what all knew must be their consensus.

"So. We will defend ourselves and our home. Is it agreed? We will kill other men only if we must, but we will now prepare ourselves, in mind and body, to shed blood if . . . when . . . we are attacked."

Reluctantly, his four friends nodded agreement. It was a hard decision none had ever expected to make in his lifetime.

Mark was glad he'd finally convinced Um-see that he should wear his Nike workout suit. He needed it this morning. A cold wind whipped down the game trail they followed to the north. His three companions were also covered head to foot. Um-see wore a soft leather vest next to his body, a loose jerkin that covered his arms, and shapeless pants that reached his ankles. His "boots" were moccasins with extensions on top, tied below the knees.

Um-see's grandson and his hunting companions also were dressed in deerskin coverings and, in addition, the younger men had long trousers tucked into the tops of their boots and tied above their ankles. Both carried the eight-foot poles they'd need to haul home heavy game, plus spear-throwers. Rough ropes were tied around their waists. Their four-foot hurling spears were carried in pouches on their backs. None had head coverings.

Seebo joined the hunting party as it left Um-see's shelter, sometimes paralleling the group on the mountainside, some-times leading it. Um-see had explained to Mark that Seebo was more effective when he was the only hunting dog, that he did not function well when there were other dogs in the party.

"Seebo fight with other dogs?" Mark asked.

"Seebo not friend to most dogs, and no wolves." Um-see smiled.

Mark smiled to himself. That monster didn't like any-body—dogs, wolves, or people. Only Um-see. Mark couldn't figure out why Seebo hadn't taken a chunk out of him. *Maybe he's biding his time,* Mark thought.

Um-see's grandson led the hunters into a cold breeze, un-der cloudy skies. For the first time in his life, Um-moh felt the weight of great responsibility, and it left him deeply wor-ried. Unexpectedly, the Elders had called him in last night to say he had been picked to organize the valley people to defend themselves. It came as a shock to the young man. He was told to gather men in groups, send out hunting parties, make sure the Bad Men did not catch them unprepared. His authority, he was assured, was that of the Elders themselves, and all villagers would obey his orders.

Um-moh made his way to all shelters immediately, asking the best hunters, the most vigorous men he knew, to go hunt-ing at daybreak. He divided them into groups of four, with instructions to move quickly through the mountains and passes in different directions. They were to observe, try and find the men who threatened them, but not to attack them. And the hunters were to return by nightfall with game, if possible, so that the village would be well supplied, and quickly. He also made sure there were good men posted around the village, moving from spot to spot, observing, ready to sound the alarm, in case of attack.

For their part, the women were told to keep ample water supplies at hand, and keep children close to the shelters. No one, for today at least, was to venture down the valley to bathe in the hot springs. And the travelers there were alerted to the danger of the Bad Men coming. Some chose to move their shelters closer to the village, since the Elders had given permission for this.

Um-moh valued his grandfather's wise counsel, and also his intimate knowledge of the mountains. No one knew every part of the forest better than Um-see, and his grandson was proud that the elder man still had fire in his eyes and agreed to hunt today.

For his part, Um-see wanted to show his confidence in his new bow, so he did not bring his spear-thrower.

Mark brought up the rear of the hunting party, watching the trail, the moving trees, as wind swirled leaves through the underbrush. Um-see, over the past two days, had fashioned waist quivers—deep hide pouches that were tied around each man's middle. A dozen arrows nestled in the pouch on his right hip. Mark also carried a pouch across his left shoulder, a catchall container, that held his "bear rock"— as he thought of it—and extra bowstrings, dried meat and his stone knife. How strange it felt to wear his Nike shoes after having accustomed his feet to the thin sandals Um-see had made for him. He had to admit that jogging shoes now felt heavy by comparison.

Mark was not clear on their mission. Um-see had simply said they would hunt today. They needed to, with most of their meat gone. But Mark noted Um-see was not cheerful; nor were the other two younger men. They were grim, in fact. When they went right by a herd of deer grazing below them in a meadow, Mark remembered Um-see's explanation last night of what happened after they'd appeared before the Elders.

"Elders decide valley people be ready," Um-see said to Mark, as they ate supper. He spoke slowly, choosing simple words so Mark would fully understand their grave situation. He was deadly serious as he went on. "Bad Men come. Hurt man say they one day walk north of valley. All valley men get weapons, keep families close to shelters. Elders say we kill Bad Men if they try hurt us." Um-see shook his head sadly. He could remember nothing so unpleasant as this, he made clear. The idea of using a weapon deliberately to kill another man was disgusting to him.

Mark tried to quiet his mind. He couldn't believe that he had stumbled into the middle of a little war, one where people had been killed already. There was a certain mad, grim humor here, he had to admit. He'd left the twentieth century, the bloodiest in mankind's history, only to find himself in the middle of more human violence, up close and threatening. So now what was he doing out here in the boondocks, looking for trouble, and maybe even death?

Certainly it seemed clear that young Um-moh was carefully looking for much more than wild game this day. He led the four in single file along game trails that hugged the sides of low mountains, arching to the northeast. At times he held up his hand, and they stopped and listened, looking carefully through whipping foliage toward lower meadows in the east. A thin, high layer of clouds obscured the sun, giving the wind a sharp bite.

They moved and stopped, observed, moved on. No one spoke. They climbed to the mountaintop, found an open area that gave them a good observation post, and rested, looking in different directions for any sign of movement. Since they ignored small groups of deer, Mark knew they weren't simply after game. They were hunting *people*. Not a pleasant thought. He didn't think he could use his bow to shoot a human being.

Um-moh held up his hand as the hunting party headed back toward the hot springs valley. It had been a fruitless search, with no signs at all of any Bad Men. Now, at midafternoon, he decided they should not return empty-handed. Um-moh and his friend had both spotted the elk herd moving slowly down the mountain, grazing. They were dimly seen, in open timber, and the hunters had a problem. The wind was from their backs and the big animals would catch their smell if they went closer. Um-moh kept them kneeling on the trail until the elk disappeared from view on the downslope.

Then he motioned them forward quickly. He set off at a trot down the trail, passing well beyond the point where the elk had disappeared, and making a wide flanking swing down the mountain. Coming back, they had the wind in their faces. They spread out and moved slowly toward the meadow, where the great beasts had paused. Um-moh hoped for a clear shot, at close range, if the elk moved across a sloping glade down to a small creek slightly below them.

They saw moving antlers. While the hunters stood perfectly still, six elk slowly appeared and grazed downhill, toward them. The last animal was a great bull with the biggest rack of antlers Um-moh or Um-see had ever seen. At the shoulder, he was taller than they were. Um-moh concluded this shaggy animal must be the aged sire of the herd.

Seebo, growling softly, stayed close by Um-see's side, moving in a part crouch as they edged closer to the grazing animals, in shadowy timber, the wind hitting their faces.

Yet conditions still were poor for a kill. The hunters were at least seventy paces away, and to step into the open meadow with the elk would be to announce their presence. Um-moh had only seconds to decide, although the elks' distance vision was not as keen as their smell sense. The leading bull elk paused, raised his head, looked around, then continued grazing.

Um-moh knew they must try, even though he felt sure it was futile at this distance. He gestured to Um-see, offering him the first shot, in respect to his seniority.

Um-see sighted on the older, biggest bull, pulled the arrow carefully, and released.

Mark and the others had their weapons ready as Um-see's arrow flew. It whispered just under the big bull's neck, and Mark's arrow a second later went above the animal, by inches. The two other men's spears, launched at a higher trajectory, straddled the animal. It stopped, startled, began turning.

Um-see's second arrow, already in flight, struck the bull in the left flank. Mark drew and held a second as he saw the elk squeal and pivot around to face his attackers. Mark released at that instant, and quickly nocked another arrow. He glanced up just in time to see his arrow buried up to the fletching in the bull's chest. The arrow had arrived just as the animal turned and caught the elk at the base of the neck. Snorting, it whipped around, seemingly unaware of its wound, and began stumbling away.

At that moment, Um-see barked "Seebo . . . kill."

A golden blur, the wolf-dog raced into the clearing, overtook the wounded elk, launched himself at the huge animal's neck. Seebo's jaws sank into the soft flesh of the neck, all four feet off the ground.

The elk stopped, whipped out, swinging Seebo in a wide arc, but the wolf-dog held tight to the animal's jugular. Snorting, blood running from its two arrow wounds, the elk dropped to its knees in front, the hindquarters swaying. Moments later, it fell on one side, kicking, still snorting, trying vainly to shake Seebo's death grip.

Mark felt himself in shock. He stared amazed at the dying animal. He knew he'd made a lucky shot . . . but somehow he'd expected the elk to survive, to escape. Killing such a magnificent beast seemed awful.

With no such guilt problems, the other three men ran to the downed elk. Mark walked up behind them as the bull stopped convulsing, and its eyes glazed over. He doubted he ever would develop any killer instinct. All he felt at this moment was sick.

Um-see had to put his hand on Seebo's head before the wolf-dog released his bloody jaws.

It was dark when they got back to the village. All were exhausted. It had taken hours of unremitting hard work to butcher the monster elk with skinning knives. The hunters took part of the hide, all organ meats, and and more than a hundred pounds of choice cuts from back to loin. Much had to be left for the scavengers. A great waste, even Mark knew.

When the elk meat was tied to carry poles suspended between the men's shoulders, each pair of men strained erect under its weight. Poles bit deep into shoulder blades and hurt, even though they all cushioned the load with strips of hide on their shoulders. Um-see shared one pole and its load with his grandson, while Mark and the other man teamed up.

Um-moh noted that while Mark was the largest man in the group, and presumably the strongest, he needed rest just as often as Um-see. Um-moh was puzzled that such a big man, with his hide coverings of almost magical quality, would not be much stronger than he was. But there was no longer any doubt in Um-moh's mind that this new "bow"—a word he could hardly say—was a superior weapon. He was pleased to learn that Mark had agreed to share its secrets with the village men.

When they reached the valley, Um-moh asked others to take care of the elk meat and hide while he quickly set about getting reports from his hunting parties. He soon learned that of five groups sent out, only one had spotted what might be the Bad Men. At least five fires had been seen close together far to the east, where no one lived. It was too late in the day to explore closer, and that hunting party, too, had killed a deer and hauled home meat and hides.

Um-moh felt certain that they now knew the enemy's approximate location. So many fires had to mean a large group of people were in motion. He quickly scheduled more hunting parties to search that area tomorrow. Meanwhile, he must tell his best hunters how Um-see and Mark had felled an elk at more than seventy paces. They, like he, would want to learn more immediately about this powerful new weapon.

It could, he concluded, change their entire way of life. Perhaps forever.

THIRTY

She was dizzy and sick in her stomach, and had trouble getting up off the pallet of hides. But she had to go outside to pass her water. She had been stretched out on her back all day, too sick to eat, too disheartened to move.

Only her two children gave the woman any will to live. Her man was dead. She was a captive of savage men. She suffered headaches from the fierce blow to the back of her head. Blood was still caked on her upper thigh where the man's knife had bitten deep.

Her son and daughter came to her side and helped her through the shelter entrance, to a nearby bush. The scowling man outside started to stop her, until he saw what she needed to do. He stood aside, indifferently.

Later, with her daughter's help, she went back into the shelter and collapsed again, thinking what an evil turn their trip had taken. It began happily, as her man finally agreed to travel once again to the valley where she was born, among the hot springs. She had urged him for a long time, but he kept putting it off because their children were small.

"Mee-suh," he had told her, "it is far. It will take many days of hard travel. We must wait until our children are older, and stronger."

And so they had waited, until now. Daughter Mee-fan was ten seasons old, son Um-suh was twelve. Reluctantly, the father had told his friends they would go and see his woman's family, who lived far to the south. He had no close living relatives, Mee-suh knew, and so there was a good chance they would stay and live in the valley of her youth.

She hoped to find her parents still living, although they would be old now if still alive. She also would have an older brother there and many other people of her blood. She tried not to show it, but she disliked the contentious nature of her man's people. They had actually fought with others, with weapons, and some people had been killed, she remembered with distaste. It was peaceful in her home valley, with its green mountains and bounty of water and game all around them.

But it had come to this terrible moment: attacked by these ruthless men, her man killed in the savage fight that followed. She saw him kill one of their attackers, but then he'd been overwhelmed and stabbed to death. She had flown at the men with her own knife, to the screams of her daughter, and had sunk the blade into one of her man's killers. But she was beaten, stabbed in the leg, and knocked unconscious.

The other two people with them, a young couple who had newly come together, had fought also. The woman was subdued but Mee-suh thought the man might have escaped. Either that or he, too, was dead. She wasn't certain.

She was thankful that her children, while terrorized, still lived, and were allowed to tend to her in this small, rough shelter. She made up her mind to live, to try and protect them. One way or another, she told herself, she would get revenge on these horrible killers-of-people, and she must be strong. She looked around and motioned to her silent children. She would eat something now.

Kuh-moh now knew that leadership was just one problem after another.

His growing village of people, some of whom were hurt, was running short of food. He had sent out three hunting parties. One of them got lost in these endless, low mountains and did not get back until almost dark, empty-handed. The other two brought in the remains of a deer, some of which they had eaten, all of it badly butchered. Kuh-moh ground his teeth. If only they still had their hunting dogs.

But they were gone. The previous winter they had camped, unwisely, in an area with little game. When storms came they nearly starved . . . and had to kill and eat their five dogs.

But what was worse, he remembered, was that one of his lookouts today saw a small hunting party looking toward his camp from a distant slope. Did those hunters come from the valley he intended to attack? But that wasn't the worst of it. He now had four captive women. And his men wanted to lie with them—or at least with the three who were not injured. He knew what would happen if he agreed. There would be a fight among his men, and perhaps the women would become violent. He had known women who had killed themselves before submitting to forced love, and these women looked to be determined.

Further, Kuh-moh already had told his men that they must win the women's favor, so that when they captured the valley all of the group could enjoy themselves without more trouble. If they took the women by force, then the women would not cook for them or work on clothes or baskets, or do any of the work that the men had every right to expect.

So, he told them, he would not allow any woman to be taken by force. Once they took the valley, they would divide the women. Kuh-moh concluded that the women they captured in the valley, naturally enough, would resent this at first. But if their men were dead or gone, they would see the good sense of making the best of the new arrangements.

He had never made decisions like this before, and found it strange that he, who had rebelled against authority all his life, was now the authority in this difficult group, and must enforce his will for there to be any peace in camp at all.

If he didn't insist on some kind of civilized order, he knew, the result would be complete disorder that would keep him from his objective. So he warned his men: Try to lie with the women and you will be banished from this group. They muttered and talked, but they knew Kuh-moh's anger, and his willingness to kill, and they unhappily agreed with his demand.

"Our young men want bows," Um-see muttered to Mark, as they stood in the middle of the valley and watched at least twenty of the village men searching through trash piles of broken wood and branches left there by spring floods.

"Yes," Mark nodded. "Seek limb like bow you make," he said slowly. He had to concentrate on each word, still not sure if he was picking the right one. He thought his vocabulary was now at least 150 words, but he still didn't fully understand rapidly spoken conversations around him. He was getting the gist of ideas, though, and he began to see how the small hand movements helped to fill in meanings. He now suspected the language was more complex and complete than he'd thought earlier, but perhaps the hand movements represented descriptive adjectives.

All of the village knew about his and Um-see's shooting of the elk at a distance, and now—two days later—every man and boy in the village sought to make himself a bow. They used Um-see's as their model, and carefully combed every trash pile along both sides of the valley to find four-foot lengths of seasoned oak that could be turned into these new, powerful weapons.

Walking through the village, Mark and Um-see saw that already work was under way to fashion arrows for the bows. The best flint-knappers were making smaller arrowheads. Groups of men and boys were coming back from the swamp area with baskets full of thinner, shorter reeds. Some of the most experienced craftsmen in the group had glue pots heating, but Mark noted they weren't all using pine pitch. Some had shaved up deer hooves, then crushed the material, adding grease to it. When heated, it appeared to be as effective as pitch for attaching feathers to the arrow shaft.

Alongside their men, women and their daughters cut and sewed pouches to carry the arrows.

The entire village, it seemed to Mark, was switching almost overnight from spear-thrower to bow. He knew part of the reason was a growing threat they felt from the Bad Men everyone talked about. Um-see was convinced there would be conflict soon, and he worried that his people—who never had wanted conflict with anyone—would be poorly equipped to hurt or kill other people, however bad they were. He hoped that all these new bows might keep the intruders at a distance, and make them turn away. It was only a faint hope.

Um-moh slept poorly these nights. He could not get to sleep, tired as he was. He had dark thoughts about how the Bad Men would invade his village, kill the men, enslave the women. He'd heard tales of this happening in other places. And it was his responsibility to keep it from happening here.

Why had the Elders called on *him* to be Leader? He did not consider himself to be a great fighter! He was strong and quick and proud of his hunting skills. Already he had made himself a bow like his grandfather's and practiced with it each day. It felt awkward and clumsy, but he began, today, to get the feel of its power. He saw how the taut bowstring stored great thrust and then unleashed the arrow to accurate distances he'd never known with his spear-thrower. With practice he knew he would take more game. But he worried that he had no special knowledge about how to protect his village and people. Aside from his woman, Um-moh never had told anybody what to do. In his village, everyone cooperated in finding food and other supplies, but each man did as he wished. Only the Elders were to be strictly obeyed.

That was why Um-moh needed to talk to his grandfather, in Um-see's shelter, and in Mark's presence. That made him uneasy. Even now, seated by Um-see's fire, he could hardly look at Mark with his shadowed face, those strange white hides, that hairy body, without nervousness. And those markings on the walls! Was this some kind of strange magic? Um-moh wanted to like this big man, but he was . . . so different. Was he bad for the valley? Would he help in the struggle with the Bad Men?

This was one worry in Um-moh's mind. The other was his own need to get Um-see's advice on how to organize the village men. He considered his grandfather the wisest of the older valley men.

"The Bad Men are coming," Um-moh began. "The ones our men saw were only one day to the north. We are not ready. I worry about how we should defend the valley."

Um-see nodded. No one could be braver or stronger than his grandson, but the older man understood his uncertainty. This threat had no precedent in the valley that he'd ever heard of.

"We will watch," he said. "We will practice with our bows, and we will listen at night, so that we won't be surprised."

Mark caught the sense of this. They simply didn't know how to defend themselves, he realized. Any determined enemy could use guerrilla tactics to attack and kill many of the village people, without warning. He knew he should keep his mouth shut. He had no business butting in. They had to settle this conflict in their own way. Mark knew himself to be the world's most timid pacifist; he'd run before he'd fight, any day . . . and yet before he quite knew why, he began to speak, slowly.

"Um-moh," he said. "Where I live before, men fought. Killed. It called *war*," and Mark used the English word. Um-see and Um-moh both pursed their lips to try and pronounce *war*, but the W was hard for them to say.

So Mark added, "Called fight."

"Fite," they repeated, and Mark nodded, then went on.

"Before men fight, they get ready. They *patrol*," and he emphasized this word too. Here was a new sound, and both Indians tried to sound the P, without much success.

"Puh-toe?" said Um-moh. "What means?"

"Mean small group. Men walk and watch. Day and night." Mark held up three fingers. "Three men patrol, walk from camp. One group north, one south, one east, one west look, listen, warn if Bad Men come."

"Puh-toe not sleep?" Um-see asked.

Mark took a stick and drew four groups of three lines each in the dirt. Below that, he drew two more such groups of lines, thirty-six tiny marks in the dirt.

"This group patrol," he said, pointing. "This group sleep. Group patrol sunrise to here," and Mark pointed up, to indicate when the sun was overhead. "Other group patrol to sunset, same with night. Some patrol, others sleep."

"How will groups know where other groups puh-toe?" Um-moh asked. He repeated it slowly so Mark understood.

Mark cleared a larger space in the dirt near the fire. He began to sketch a crude map on the ground, drawing elongated circles to make the three mountains that flanked and capped the valley, and the stream that ran through it.

"Valley here," he said. "West Mountain here. Hot springs here. North Mountain here. Hot water come off mountain here. Here is creek. Flows from north, goes south."

Then Mark drew large semicircles almost touching, on all four sides of the map.

"Patrols here, four sides, walk this way, that way out from valley. Patrols see each other one, two times in walk, each patrol take two hunting dogs . . . see Bad Men, dogs bark, run to village. Make big noise with barking dogs . . ."

Both Um-see and his grandson were shaking their heads.

"No dog bark," said Um-see

"Why not?" Mark was astonished. It was an important alert mechanism.

Um-see then patiently explained that the village dogs were bred and trained not to bark. Only those dogs were allowed to live and breed that rarely, if ever, barked, that their only mission was to hunt, to attack and help kill animals for food. Dogs could be counted on to growl at the approach of strangers, Um-moh added, but this would not be enough to alert the village instantly.

Weird, Mark thought. Then he remembered that some twentieth-century dogs were also bred not to bark—pointers and setters, for example. Then a thought made him smile.

"We make drum," he said.

"Dum?" his listeners said at once. "What is dum?"

Mark quickly got up and looked in the back of the shelter. He returned with the biggest empty pot he could find.

"Where I live, we have drum. Make big noise. Cover top with hide. Stretch hide. Then hit hide with stick. Make noise."

He tried to stretch a piece of hide across the foot-wide mouth of the pot, to illustrate. Both the other men understood. Um-see reached for the pot.

"Get big pot," he said. "Knock out the bottom, cover bottom and top with hide. Make better noise?"

Mark laughed and nodded. "OK, you got it," he said in English.

"What means OK?" asked Um-see.

"Mean yes," said Mark. "Mean good yes. Mean big yes."

Um-moh nodded. "Umm. Oh-kay. Make dum. For big noise."

Then there was a long moment of silence. Um-see and Um-moh both stared at all the marks on the ground, counting. Each group of four three-man patrols . . . that would mean a lot of men. It would take all the men of the village, and the older boys.

Would everyone agree to take part? Um-moh knew the plan made sense, that it should give warning in case the Bad Men approached. He looked at Um-see, who slowly nodded. Very well, his grandfather approved. But Um-moh felt insecure. He knew the older men thought him young to be their Leader. He could not *make* everybody obey him, no matter what the Elders said. He would have to explain to everyone how serious the danger was they faced. And he must lead patrols himself, to set an example. Then he looked at Mark curiously.

"Marrk," he said, mouthing the strange name with difficulty. "You puh-toe? You help?"

Mark groaned to himself. He knew the valley needed every man it could recruit—even the friendly neighborhood

Bigfoot. *That's me*, he thought, *Ace Patroller. I'll probably fall off the damn mountain.*

"Yes," Mark said, after a pause. "I help."

Seebo peered into the shelter later when he saw that Um-see and the big stranger were alone. He stared in for a time, then gave a muted "woof." Um-see looked up, rose, and came out on the porch with a slice of dried meat. He beckoned for the big animal to come inside, but Seebo picked up the meat, turned, and moved into the underbrush.

Um-see sighed. He missed Seebo's nightly companionship, and he had left the animal's sleeping skins where they had been before Mark had come to stay. But Seebo rarely if ever entered the shelter now. He appeared to feel that he was an outsider and unwelcome. He stayed in his den up on the mountain.

Um-see explained to Mark how the wolf-dog came to him. He spoke slowly to make it clear.

"You saw big brown dog in village with Seebo?" he asked.

Mark nodded. Yes, he remembered Seebo's strange subservient actions toward that crippled female dog.

"That dog Seebo's mother," Um-see explained. "She would not stay close to village. Ran away and stayed away long time. We find her hurt much later. She had pups. Seebo was only one of litter to live. Sire was wolf. She had been in fight. She allowed to live in village again since she was good hunting dog. Now she used for breeding. Seebo still knows her. She is only animal he likes."

"Why Seebo live here . . . near shelters?" Mark could not understand the animal's odd isolated status.

"Seebo could not be trained," Um-see explained. "He was to be killed, but I spoke for him and brought him with me when I became Helper. He will not wear harness, and will not obey commands. He only lives to be hunter, and will help me when I hunt big animals."

"Would he help against Bad Men?"

"I don't know," Um-see answered. "Seebo never attack men that I see. He would not know Bad Men from other men. To him, we all look same." Then he looked at Mark. "Except you. You look different. He not decide yet you are friend or enemy."

Mark winced. "Tell me about it."

Kuh-moh knew he could not move all of his people rapidly and surprise the villagers if he had to take his sick and injured with him. They would slow everyone. Three of the women and their children could move with the group. But the one hurt woman must stay behind with two of his men who could not walk fast enough. Would they all attempt to escape? If so where would they go, hurt as they were?

He hated to lose people, so hard had it been to gather this band in the first place. And the woman pleased him. She might survive, and he could come back and get her later. The two men also might recover from their wounds. The men were barely able to stand, so they should not molest the woman if left alone with her. Yes, that would have to be it.

He counted his men, pressing his fist together six times, counting. Yes, six squeezes of five fingers. Not nearly as many as he wanted . . . but if he attacked suddenly with determination, it should be enough to kill most of the men of the village. He had heard they had never had to fight and did not know how. He exulted at the thought of his people moving into already-prepared shelters, with plenty of food and women who would, eventually, do as they were told. It would be a glorious day, he told himself, and worth the trouble he now had trying to move this dangerous band of men over trails and through mountains they hardly knew.

He allowed anger to fill his mind. It was easy for Kuh-moh to stay angry now. He enjoyed the power of leadership but did not like all the small problems that kept coming up. When he found men he could trust, he would not have to make every small decision, he told himself. It would be good to sleep all night, for a change.

* * *

When Mee-suh awoke again it was dark. There were no sounds in the camp. No men talked or laughed, as they had in recent nights. Her head hurt. When she had gone to sleep it had been midday, and she was ill. Her daughter had fed her thin soup. It must have contained the herb she carried that helped dull pain. She had taught her daughter what it was and how to use it.

She must have slept all night, and now she knew instantly that she was alone. Her children both were gone. Light filtered in the shelter entrance, as a faint trace of dawn appeared in the eastern skies. She choked off her cry. It might arouse others. None of her children's possessions were there. No clothes, no pallet, nothing. She wanted to scream. Her headache kept her from it.

Mee-suh climbed to her feet, swaying. She pulled one of her sleeping hides around her and went out to pass her water. A soft, cold wind swept through the camp site, and it appeared deserted. Almost. From the shelter next to hers came a man. He shuffled rather than walked. She knew him now. He was short, only slightly taller than Mee-suh, and stocky. He came up to her and stared, then spoke softly. He was one of the Bad Men.

"The others have all gone," he told her. "We were left here because we are hurt and would make them move slow. You want some food?" She nodded.

The man ignited embers by blowing on them and started a fire. Mee-suh moved to the fire and looked at this man, who sat silently on the ground.

"Where are my children?" she asked, trying to be calm.

"They were taken with the rest. Forced to go, the girl crying. But none were hurt," he added, trying to be reassuring. Mee-suh slumped to the ground.

In her distress and anger, Mee-suh could not help seeing that this did not seem like a bad man. If she were to survive, she must be friendly to him.

"May I know your name?" she asked.

"I am Foh-man," he said. "You are called Mee-suh?"

She nodded and looked around. "Are we alone here?"

"No, another man is in that shelter. He is hurt and may die. He sleeps now."

Foh-man rose stiffly, went to his shelter, and returned, unrolling a wrapped hide. He took out dried meat and nuts, cut the meat in two, pierced each slice with sticks, and gave one to Mee-suh. They held them over the fire until crisp, then ate. The sun sent its first sliver of warmth into their camp.

Mee-suh turned to the man. He was not ugly but not too attractive. His nose was flatter than most men's, his eyes wide-set. He was calm, she noted, and did not stare at her like those other men. He was more dejected than injured, she concluded.

"Foh-man," she said, "I was born near here in a valley to the south. I will go there now, and get help to find my children. I know the way, I think. Will you go with me?"

He looked at her in surprise. Few women would speak so, telling a man what they intended to do, not asking permission. Kuh-moh had told him to stay here until sent for. That might be a long time.

Foh-man was not an angry man, but deeply unhappy. He had joined this group only to survive, and because they gave him no choice. Join or they would kill him, he had been told. His parents had died when he was small, and those who raised him were unkind. He was beaten and sometimes abused in other ways. He had left home one night, never to return, not understanding how hard it would be to survive alone in the wilderness.

After two seasons of wandering alone in the forests, barely able to stay alive, he had joined a traveling group of traders. Sturdy, honest men they were, traveling from north to south, then north again, trading skins for stone points and knives, decorated pots for bone tools. They spent cold seasons in the south, hot ones in the north. They were welcomed by all families since people were hungry for new things and information from afar. It had been a good life, if hard.

So it had been a grim day for Foh-man when Kuh-moh's men had attacked the traders in a remote area, killing one and sending the others running for the forests. Foh-man had been hurt and captured. He thought he would be killed until Kuh-moh found that he was a stone-shaper of great skill. The long knife that he had made from shining green stone caught Kuh-moh's eye, and he took it for his own, along with all the other trading goods Foh-man's little band had accumulated. So Foh-man was allowed to live if he joined the group. He did so, with misgivings. But he had never killed a man, and spent most of his time hunting and shaping spearpoints.

Now he had this opportunity to escape, but to go where? And with a sick and injured woman?

"How will you find your children?" he asked.

"I don't know. But I will find them if I can stay alive. My children are my life now. I must do all I can for them."

She got up and walked around the small clearing, testing her leg to see if it would support her weight. She needed a forked stick to help her walk. She would find one.

She looked at Foh-man.

"You will come?" she asked. He pushed himself to his feet. Neither of them could move very fast, but they could help each other.

"I will come," he replied. And he began to gather his tools, spear-thrower and spears, his small store of belongings. The sun was hazy now, the sky growing overcast, and he sensed that snow was coming. They would need hides to protect themselves. Mee-suh knew this also. They quickly gathered up all that they could carry, made up crude carry packs, and prepared to leave camp.

As they left, Foh-man built up the fire. It was the least he could do for the injured man in the shelter. Big cats or wolves would probably kill him anyway, within hours. Foh-man did not tell Mee-suh that the sleeping man was the one who had killed her own man two days before. She would be upset even more than she was by the loss of her children.

They moved off down a trail, Mee-suh limping and Foh-man shuffling as fast as he could to keep up. He hoped Mee-suh knew where they were going. He did not. He had little hope of staying alive for long.

THIRTY-ONE

The old woman shook her head in disgust. Men were some-times a little crazy when they got excited. They wanted her to break open a big pot, cover it with hide, and create a noisemaker?

Foolish, she decided. It wouldn't make much noise and would ruin a good pot.

They want noise, she knew how to make noise. She smiled, recalling the flutes, rattles, and whistles she'd played with in her youth. She looked for the biggest old basket she could find. It would take work, but she and her daughters could do it quickly. It would take hides, a few sticks, pitch from the scarred tree, and work.

She found most of what she wanted in her shelter, told her daughters what needed to be done. Um-see had called it a "dum." To her it was simply a loud toy, and she could not imagine, with all the important things that needed doing, why they should waste their time. But she set to work. At least it was something different to make, something the young people probably had never seen before.

Um-moh was glad to get away from the valley. He was tired of so much talking and telling people what to do. Organizing the families' men into patrol groups had not been easy. Some men did not want to take part. Older men, especially, said they needed to stay in the village to protect their families and shelters. Um-moh patiently explained the need for patrols, to spot the oncoming Bad Men. A few villagers were so stubborn that he had to mention the reaction of the Elders if everyone did not cooperate. He assigned the most reluctant of the men to day patrols, those most eager to help were put on the night patrols.

He was pleased when Mark found a large old piece of hide, and made marks on it that—Mark said—showed which men were to patrol and where. Um-moh hoped he could remember all of it. Mark agreed to help him keep track of the schedule. No one in the village had, ever before, engaged in an effort like this. Um-moh could see one problem: Only Mark knew what all those painted scratches on the hide meant. Without him to explain it, the patrols would not happen as planned.

In the past, by tradition, everyone took care of food and hunting needs cooperatively. Everyone felt responsible to see that no one lacked food or shelter, Um-moh reflected. It was assumed that all would share on the basis of need. Every family saw that neighbors and friends were not lacking in necessities. It was considered a bad thing not to share, so children were taught this. They also learned obedience, silence when adults spoke, and to speak only when they had something important to say. Rarely did the village's way of life change much, and this was how everyone wanted it. So this patrol was a new, unsettling thing, agreed to from a sense of desperation caused by those Bad Men. Most annoying to Um-moh was that it not only depended on cooperation, but on him ordering things to happen, to tell men, in some cases, to do as *he* knew must be done. As he'd expected, it did not go down well with men much older than he, no matter how respected he was for his size, strength, and hunting skills. He discovered that while he was recognized as temporary Leader, his responsibilities and problems were things he had never dreamed of in the past. This was terribly serious business that he hoped would never be repeated.

One problem remained. Um-see sulked and muttered when Um-moh asked his grandfather to stay behind and make sure the young men practiced with their bows and that the new "dum" got finished. Mark urged them to make another "dum" as well. Um-see expected to go on this first patrol, and his grandson was relieved when Mark helped convince the older man that he was more badly needed in the village. Um-moh knew that his grandfather's fiery nature needed to be put to use in less physical ways, or else his body would fail him.

Mark, too, was relieved that Um-see had been talked out of coming on this first patrol. He knew the older man was not up to the rigors of six hours out in the cold. In fact, he was not sure that he himself could keep up with these hard, lithe men. Even those of middle age were trim, with no body fat, and had spent their lives climbing mountains, exposed to all kinds of weather. Mark still felt himself big and cumbersome by comparison, and he hoped he would not simply collapse on the trail from exhaustion. It was interesting to him that Um-moh had *wanted* him to wear his white workout clothing. Apparently the younger man felt that, if they should see any of the Bad Men, the color of Mark's "hides" might spook or frighten them into thinking he was some sort of spirit, evil or otherwise.

It was early afternoon, and snow was falling as Um-moh took his patrol up a game trail from the valley, going north. Um-moh led, with Mark in the middle, and Um-moh's friend Um-can, bringing up the rear. They walked about ten paces apart and slowly, to be sure they missed nothing in the surrounding trees.

Visibility quickly shrank, as the snow intensified, and soon they could not make out anything beyond a hundred yards. Mark and Um-moh carried their bows, while Um-can, his bow not yet finished, carried a spear-thrower. All were dressed for the cold, had soft hides wrapped around their heads, tied at forehead and neck, with a small opening in front for vision. Snow blew into the opening and stung Mark's lips and eyes. The Indians' hands were bare while Mark kept his thrust into jacket pockets. He decided then and there that gloves would be his next "invention."

It was going to be a long cold day, and Mark turned his mind to other thoughts to make time pass quickly. He was worried, for one thing, about the patrol schedule he'd devised.

These people have no way to tell time, he reminded himself. *No way to measure it exactly, no real math at all.* He shook his head. That Mickey Mouse schedule he'd worked out would last about two days, then fall apart. He just knew it.

Confronted with the instant need to organize the village men into patrols, Mark had finally—in desperation—drawn a big circle in the dirt, as everyone gathered around. He pointed to the east, then marked a spot on the circle, to the east.

"This, sunup," he said. "Four patrols start." And he motioned in all four directions to show they would go out and circle the village at a distance. Then, pointing overhead, he said. "Sun above, patrols come back to village. Second patrol starts."

He saw the men nodding. Thank goodness they understood his frantic efforts to find the right words. "Second patrol come back village, sundown," and he pointed to the west. "Third patrol start."

Again, men nodded. Mark was pleased. *Good. They realize that's half the night.*

"Night patrol walks trails?" someone asked. "How to see?" Mark nodded. Good point.

"Not walk. Sit. Watch. Watch trails," he replied. "Not let Bad Men see you. They come, they pass by, you run village, fast."

He was relieved at the nodding heads. "Okay?" he asked, grinning.

Laughter all around him. "Hoh-kay." Several men grinned. Um-see must have told that word to everybody.

Then Mark painted on the large scrap of hide with his crude brush and thick black paint. He assigned a number to each patrol area—one for north, two for west, three for east, and four for south. He marked the hide with single vertical strokes, much like Roman numerals—I, II, III, and IIII. He repeated the numbers aloud, pointing to each sector and its number, hoping everyone would catch on. They appeared to. He shivered inwardly, knowing how inept he felt, making this up as he went along.

Then, with Um-moh's help, he wrote the names of the patrol leaders on the hide, putting a Roman numeral I, II, III, or IIII beside each name, to show which area that leader would take his men to patrol. No one could read the written names, he realized, but as he repeated each man's name, and pointed to the name written on the hide, he saw more nods. They knew these scratches represented their names, and they knew where to patrol. Or so he hoped. They all were fascinated to see their names represented by Mark's painted symbols. Later, several men came up and felt of the drying paint.

Then Um-moh assigned patrol leaders to periods when they would walk the woods. Everything was committed to memory, Mark noted. He already had found these people's memories were prodigious. They *had* to be, he knew. With no written language, over centuries they'd learned to listen intently and they remembered whatever they needed to remember. It was a matter of totally focusing their attention. Mark thought that Um-see probably remembered every important thing he'd ever heard.

Mark also understood enough of the talk between Um-moh and the others to know that arrangements were made for patrols coming off duty to wake up patrols that were scheduled to start. Sure enough, Um-moh quickly caught the one big hole in Mark's patrol plan: the midnight to dawn shift. Mark was glad the gap had been seen. Um-moh pointed to the circle on the ground, between the south and east marks.

"No patrol here?" Um-moh asked.

"No," Mark said. "One man here, here, here, and here," he added, pointing to areas around the village on four sides." Men watch, move small distance. Stay awake. Not patrol."

He thought he needed to add more reassurance.

"When Bad Men come," Mark said, "maybe sunup or sundown. Or big snow, or rain. Try surprise village. Village be ready always."

Um-moh nodded. He understood the plan. His mouth tightened in a straight line. Since it involved so many men, in so many different places, how could he control them all? How could he find time to sleep? He had the dismal feeling that he could not do all this very well, and it showed in his expression and stance.

Mark had understood. He smiled grimly to himself. *I don't know if it'll work either, my friend. It's not much of a plan, but it's the only one we've got. Maybe it'll keep everybody alert and watching, waiting for whatever disaster will happen to us . . .*

Mark jerked himself back to the present. His feet were cold, and they were still following a white and slippery trail, seeing little but snowfall. Ahead, he could barely make out a small herd of deer cross the trail, moving down to the valley nearby. All he could see close up were tree limbs bending with the weight of the snow covering, a panorama of brush sloping up the mountainside.

They'd only been walking for an hour, Mark estimated, and there was little chance they'd find anything out here today, given the weather. He wished he could think of some excuse to go back to the village, but he knew Um-moh would not agree. What a total waste of time and energy this was becoming! Later, Mark would remember that thought and decide how wrong you can be when you try to guess what's going to happen in a war. Even a small one.

True to his assignment, Um-see urged all the men of the village out into the snow to practice with their bows. The intensity of the falling flakes made visibility poor, and Um-see finally had everyone shooting at bushes and small targets on a section of West Mountain that was free of snow.

Those men who had practiced for several days were starting to get the feel of it, Um-see was pleased to see. They released their arrows well and were reasonably close to the targets at fifty paces. Those with new bows sent arrows in all directions. One man's bow broke in two. Another's bowstring snapped as he released an arrow, cutting his hand slightly.

Um-see heard a distant noise. It sounded like a rhythmic *boom-boom* of someone striking a hollow log. He had not heard such a sound in years. Then he realized it was the sound of the "dum" that Mark wanted made, to warn the village if any Bad Men were sighted. He left the line of practicing bowmen and hastened to the tent of the old woman.

When he saw her handiwork, he was irritated. This was no pot. It appeared to be . . . a basket? He looked at it in surprise. It was round, like a big tree log, but light, and seemed to be woven like a basket. But firm inside, and as long as his arm. On both ends were tightly stretched hides, wrapped around with strips of twisted thongs. He looked at the old woman questioningly.

"You want to make noise?" she told him. "A pot won't do that well. This will make noise. Listen."

She used two small sticks with rounded heads to strike both ends of the drum simultaneously. The noise reverberated so loud that Um-see winced.

Women, he told himself. *They change things. Won't do what you want. But . . . well,* he admitted to himself, *this thing is loud.* He forced a smile.

"Good," he said. "Yes, it will work. Now we need one more dum, Mark said. We must have two dums."

The old woman rolled her eyes.

"Two? One is not enough? Why two?"

"Two," replied Um-see firmly. Then he saw her evident unhappiness. "Our village needs warning if the Bad Men come. Everyone needs to hear at the same time. These dums can be important."

With Um-see's help she rose stiffly, and spoke crossly to her daughters. He left quickly and did not hear her mutter some of the bad words she had heard men use when they were upset. It made her feel a little better.

For his part, Um-see had gotten an idea from the sound of that noise-making basket. It seemed foolish at first. But he would think about it some more. He would not mention the idea unless . . . he chuckled to himself.

Going farther was pointless, Mark felt, since the heavy snow-fall made visibility impossible beyond fifty yards. Mark thought Um-moh knew this also, but he knew the young man did not want to cut the mission short. It would not set a good example for the other patrols if he—the Leader—returned to the village early.

The trail was slippery now, snow turning to mud under-foot, close to freezing, Mark guessed, and the only way to keep warm was to keep moving. But he hoped Um-moh wouldn't stretch this out much longer. Then another thought hit him: He wasn't really all that tired. In fact, Mark realized, he felt good. Except for cold hands, he wasn't hurting at all. He didn't feel wiped out or winded as he had months earlier. He chuckled. *Clean livin' m'boy. No chance for much else.*

He knew that he'd continued to lose weight in recent weeks since eating was now almost perfunctory. He felt arm and shoulder muscles developing from his daily bow practice and knew that his leg muscles were stronger from hurrying up and down hillsides each day. Now, for the first time, he became aware that his stamina was far greater then he could ever remember in the past. Then he saw Um-moh stop ahead of him. The younger man raised his hand, as though in greet-ing. Peering around him up the trail, Mark could barely make out three dim figures of men.

They had come around a sharp turn in the path less than fifty paces away, and stood motionless, staring at Um-moh's party. Was this another village patrol?

Mark walked up behind Um-moh and stepped to one side. For the count of five, no one moved. Then two of the three men raised their arms and threw spears, directly at them. For a split second, Um-moh and his companions were frozen in shock. They dived for cover just as the missiles arrived. One went two feet to their right, the other zipped above Mark's head, missing him by inches, and there was a howl of pain from behind him. By the time Mark jumped to his feet, behind a tree, Um-moh had stood, pulled, and released an arrow. He quickly drew and released another, just as Mark heard one of the three men up the trail cry out in surprise.

Um-moh released his third arrow as two more spears clattered through the branches above Mark's head. He ducked and stepped out into the trail, but as he drew his bow he looked up the trail, and it was empty, the attackers gone. Or at least two of them were. A dark figure was on the ground at the crest of the trail. And he did not move.

Um-moh, another arrow at the ready, moved carefully up the trail, and Mark followed. No movement, but a lot of color. Red. As in blood. The man was on his back, arms outstretched, Um-moh's arrow protruding from the middle of his chest. Blood pumped from the wound, running down the man's hide jacket, painting the snow a deep purplish red. They knelt, Um-moh felt his neck. The man was dying. Um-moh shook his head slowly.

Then Mark whipped around. Um-can. Was he hurt? He was, and was sitting in the trail, holding his leg, making no sound but swaying back and forth, clearly in great pain.

Hastening to him, Mark now knew for sure: *We do have a war here*, he told himself—and he was in the middle of that war. He'd become a combatant, like it or not.

Kuh-moh's face was hot with anger. His black eyes glittered. He clenched and unclenched his fists as he walked up and down outside his shelter. Another of his men gone, probably dead. The two who returned were frightened. They had seen strange things, they said, when they hurried into camp.

"We saw this great animal, or man, and it wore white hides," they told Kuh-moh. "It was much bigger than a man, up to here," and they motioned above their heads. "They had weapons that shoot small spears, fast. The first spear killed our friend. That white thing is evil . . . so we came back quickly, to tell you, before it killed us, too."

It was all Kuh-moh could do to keep from striking these two cowards. They ran away! Ran from people who never fight! He knew he was not mistaken. Everyone said people of hot spring valley were helpers, not fighters. He had heard outcasts tell about going through that valley and getting food and temporary shelter when many families would not welcome them in their villages.

Now this. If these two cowards told all the other men what they had told him, he might find his band of outcasts slinking away into the mountains. He needed every man, and he could not kill these two—not yet. He leveled his most ferocious stare.

"You lost your wits in the cold. You saw things that were not there," snarled Kuh-moh. "The other men will laugh at you if you tell such things. I will call you cowards before all the men if you tell that story. You stay silent about what you *thought* you saw, and I will let you stay in our family. You tell that story, and I will banish you. Do you understand me?"

Both men—ashamed and intimidated—nodded. They knew how awful it was to be alone in the endless wilderness. They would remain silent. But both knew what they saw had been real. And they shivered to think of that manlike creature in white hides. Kuh-moh also decided something else. There was no time to lose. The snowstorm must not stop his preparations to move the camp close to the valley, so his men could attack soon. He would make up in boldness and ferocity what he lacked in numbers. The more miserable the weather became, the more his men should want to fight and kill, out of cold and anger. He must move them, make them upset, promise them great comfort and pleasure, and he must do that within two days.

* * *

Mark and Um-moh watched and worried as the healing woman worked over Um-can's leg wound. She got the stone point out of the flesh, just below his knee. It had lodged in the fatty part of the calf, causing an agony of pain. By wrapping it with thongs, Mark and Um-moh had stopped the bleeding temporarily out on the trail, but Um-can still lost a lot of blood by the time the two men had half carried him back to the village. He drank soup and some herbal fluid the tiny woman gave him, then fell into a fitful sleep, awakening from time to time with mutters and grunts.

Um-see earlier had told Mark the older woman was Meesoon, "a friend of my youth." Mark had seen her treating others. She now wrapped Um-can's wound with clean, soft deerskin, after giving it another treatment of honey. Which reminded Mark of food. It was nearly dark, and he had not eaten since morning.

He felt weak, still unnerved at the death of that man on the trail. Mark knew that he himself might well have ended up with a four-foot spear in his chest, that the spear which narrowly missed his head might have been aimed high because he was so tall, compared to these smaller man. Could his white suit and size have spooked those other men, causing them to attack? It worried him that his appearance might have ignited a situation in which a man had died. He glanced at Um-moh.

The young Leader was wrapped in his own morose thoughts. It shocked him how easily and quickly he had sent that arrow into the Bad Man. Yet he already had learned that nobody blamed him for his act. He was not congratulated, but neither was he criticized. He had immediately reported to the Elders.

They were saddened by what he'd had to do and shook their heads. But to a man they agreed that a Leader must defend himself and his men. And they urged him to continue preparing the village to fight the Bad Men. All felt it was only a matter of time now, in view of Um-moh's encounter.

THIRTY-TWO

Foh-man knew he would be dead if he didn't hurry. It was nearly dark, and wolf packs were starting to move, looking for their nightly kills. Already he heard their distant voices although it was not yet dark.

He and Mee-suh were on their knees, butchering the deer as fast as they could. They did not want the hide, simply a few large chunks and organ meats inside. Foh-man had given the woman a small knife, and together they hacked out the food they would need for that night and the next day. As a skilled hunter, he hated to waste the hide, but at any minute he might have to take up his spear-thrower and defend them against four-footed night hunters. If the wolf pack caught them in the open, Foh-man knew they would be surrounded and, in a fight, they would die.

Ignoring bloody hands and arms, they wrapped the meat in hide scraps and limped away down the game trail. They needed a place of refuge before dark came and a stream where they could wash off the blood. A blood smell could draw animals to anywhere they hid.

Foh-man's foot pained him, and he could hardly walk any faster than the limping woman. But it felt better than the day before and no longer bled. He winced as he thought of how he got that wound. Kuh-moh had ordered him to go on that last raiding party, the one in which Mee-suh's man was killed.

Foh-man did not want to go, nor kill a man. Men should kill only animals, not other men. Although he went as ordered, he hung back when Kuh-moh's men attacked the travelers. It was probably Mee-suh's man who threw the spear that hurt him. The man the spear was aimed at ducked, and it fell at Foh-man's feet, slicing into his left foot just below the ankle. He thought it must have broken some small bones since he could hardly make his way back to camp, so great was the pain.

He did not tell Mee-suh this since it would only make her more upset. Already she wept as she thought of her children and muttered to herself much of the day as they followed mountain trails, going south. She did not know exactly how to get to her birth home, he saw, but knew only that it was south—and these mountains seemed much like she remembered them in her youth, she told him.

They ate the last of their food at midday, and it was late afternoon before he could get close enough to a small deer herd to make a kill.

It seemed to him the distant wolf calls were closer. He saw a stream ahead. They must wash and hide themselves, or they would not be alive when the sun rose again.

As Mark had feared, the village patrol system unraveled slightly the second day after it started. Six hours, he knew, was a long time for even the most seasoned woodsmen to walk up and down trails, watching for people who weren't there. And at night, or under daylight's overcast skies, they had no exact way of telling time. Some patrols returned early, and Um-moh voiced quiet complaints to their leaders. This did not create any good will, Mark noticed, and Um-moh wore a scowl on his young face much of the time.

Two of the patrols got bored before their time was up, and took small game—rabbits, squirrels, even a big possum—to make the time count for something. The only part of the patrol they enjoyed, it was clear, was the chance to hunt with their new bows. The men were now talking about their marksmanship, and Um-moh had to remind them that all their lives might depend on how observant they were. If the Bad Men sneaked past, it could mean death for everybody in the village, he told them sternly. If the situation wasn't so serious, Mark might have been amused.

Command is tough, he would have liked to tell his young friend. Mark didn't envy him. Um-moh could end up the most unpopular guy in the valley, especially if the Bad Men never showed up. *They might see the size of this town,* Mark reflected, *and decide they didn't want any High Noon on Main Street. God,* he prayed, *I sure hope so.*

As he expected, Um-moh didn't get much sleep. His woman heard him coming and going all night, trying to make sure the night watchers were vigilant. Some were not, he discovered, when he found one of the older men sound asleep at his position. Um-moh had carefully picked lookout spots where the men had trees to climb in case they were attacked by wolves—which rarely happened near the village. So this man had climbed a tree and slept there. Another man had wandered off to another position, and Um-moh spent much time finding him. It sorely taxed his patience.

Wearily, Um-moh related this next morning to Mark and Um-see, but to no one else. He had no wish to cause more trouble than he had to, but it was obvious to Mark that the easygoing, informal village life that had existed here for generations was hopelessly at odds with any sort of military discipline, even in a time of absolute crisis.

Kuh-moh was glad to see the snow stop falling and the sun appear. His spirits rose. His hunters began bringing in deer. He kept them busy skinning and working on their weapons. They found they could make good stone points from the white rock they found around them in abundance. Some of the men almost appeared to be in good humor, Kuh-moh noted, as the smell of roasting meat filled the air.

But Kuh-moh knew the hard part was still ahead. He did not trust any of his patrols to seek out the village silently and learn what must be done to capture the valley. He also knew he was the best stalker and hunter among all his men. So Kuh-moh decided he must find out himself what others could not.

"You will watch the camp tonight," he told Kuh-so, the big man who looked most like himself. "I go to find the village, find out what we must do to surprise and capture the valley. I will be gone all night. The men are not to fight, and are to leave the women alone. Can you control them?" Kuh-so nodded.

"If bad things happen here," the burly leader snarled, "I will blame you. You hear my words?"

Kuh-so swallowed and nodded.

A full moon lit the forest, reflecting blue-white light off the snow-covered trail before him. Kuh-moh walked slow, his eyes and his movements in harmony with the deep shadows cast by trees and tall weeds. He felt at peace here and admired the dangerous blue-white beauty of the night. This was his element, one that he had trained himself for during all those seasons alone, cut off from other men. At first he had almost gone mad with loneliness, but then—watching how big cats stalked their prey, silent and deadly—he had become like a night-hunting animal.

He moved into shadows and stayed there, motionless for a long time. The air was cold. No breeze blew, and all was perfectly still. He had slept much this past day, and his senses were keen and alive to every movement around him.

Kuh-moh passed the spot where his man had been killed recently. Looking off the trail, he could see only darkened bones, a skull appearing to grin at him from reflected moonlight, all that remained after predators finished.

He moved on, sometimes along the edge of the trail, at other times drifting through the trees, around large rock outcrops. There were occasional night sounds from birds, scurryings of small animals, the distant howls of coyotes. Kuh-moh listened for his own sounds . . . he made none.

Once he rested and drank from a small stream and ate

some dried meat. He came at last to a large fork in the major game trail, but did not approach it. It seemed to him that he heard—or perhaps smelled—other men. He became invisible, part of a big tree's shadow, for a long time. His wait was rewarded finally as two men came slowly down the slope ahead of him. One stopped and sat down on a large rock, the other continued down the trail, to another position, where he, too, stopped and waited.

So, he said to himself, *they know I will come, have put out watchers to catch me.*

When a light breeze sprang up, moving the branches of trees and whipping up small snow flurries off nearby bushes, Kuh-moh drifted silently up the mountain, circling around the village men, who mostly watched the trails, along which they could see a great distance. Kuh-moh smiled to himself at how easily he moved without being detected. The villagers would be easy to kill. He considered them prey, to be simply eliminated.

Before light began to appear in the east, Kuh-moh had scouted much of the hot springs mountain. He had come down to the trail above the steaming hot springs, looked down at the sleeping village, noted the few men who moved about partially banked fires under the trees. Twice he saw men moving through the forest, watching for him or his men. He froze into, and became, another shadow, and was not seen. He memorized how the valley was laid out, the positions of the springs, the village of shelters, the trails leading into and out of the valley. He did not attempt to cross open spaces to the other, western mountain, but he had in his mind a full picture of what he must do to conquer this beautiful valley.

He was back at his camp before dawn, saw that Kuh-so had carried out his instructions to keep the camp quiet, then went to sleep. By this time tomorrow, he told himself, he would be the ruler of everything he had seen this night. His plan was complete. He needed only to carry it out, kill or chase away those men, capture the women. He slept.

* * *

Sunlight brought warmth but only brief freedom from worry for Mee-suh and Foh-man. They had found a secluded hole in some rocks, high on the side of a mountain, uptrail from a stream. There they had slept while the wolves devoured the rest of the deer they had killed. Foh-man had heard them before he went to sleep, and hoped there was enough to satisfy the wolves' appetites.

Mee-suh got a fire started and roasted some of their meat. She had slept fitfully. At first she was afraid that Foh-man would put his hands on her as they lay in the hide shelter, huddled together for warmth. Then she noted that he was sound asleep. Fears for her children kept waking her up. She shuddered at the thought of them both being captives of foul men, although she told herself that all those men were not bad. She was coming to see that Foh-man was like any other. He was concerned for her safety, she knew, and had no bad intentions. She began to think of him as more friend than enemy.

Mee-suh looked out over the valley ahead of them, but it gave her no sense of where they were. She knew only that they must go south, and as the sun rose higher, they moved slowly along a trail, above the valley floor. Her leg wound did not hurt as much this morning, and the man's wound did not seem to bother him as much as the day before. She hobbled along with her crutch, and he had a short walking stick to aid his movements.

Before midday, the sky clouded over, and a breeze came up. Again it looked like it might snow. In early afternoon, they found a depression in the valley floor and moved across it to the other side, following a streambed down in the decline. They did not want to be seen by any of the Bad Men who might be about. Foh-man had decided that the mountain to the east would have better trails than the one where they'd spent the night. They labored slowly south all afternoon.

Soon light snow was falling, and they knew that before dark they must find another place where they could hide from wolves and the big, silent cats. Above all, they must not be found by the Bad Men. Both knew they would be killed by Kuh-moh. They were no longer of any use to him.

It was dark and Foh-man was silently desperate about finding a safe place to spend the night. Snow fell, the sky was overcast, and there was no moon. Only faint light behind the clouds allowed them to follow the trail up the mountain. They expected to hear the snarls of hunting wolves at any time.

Instead, they smelled something. Roasting meat they agreed silently, looking at each other. Someone was cooking, nearby. Should they move away and go no closer to this possible threat? Or were these people other than the Bad Men? Their decision could be worth their lives, both knew, and they stepped off the trail, sank down, and considered what to do.

"We will sleep now," Kuh-moh told his men. "We will get up in the middle of the night, leave camp, and go to the village. I will lead, and we will attack just before the sun rises. We will kill all those who resist us."

He explained his plan in great detail, as the men eagerly gathered about him. The captive women, cleaning up after the evening meal, stayed well away from the men and kept the children at a distance.

Kuh-moh had decided they could not move fast enough encumbered by women and children. So those must stay behind, guarded by two men that he must select—two who would not be good fighters, anyway, he decided. *That one there*, he thought, *could not move fast, and the older boy nearby, who didn't seem too bright. They could guard the women.*

And one other thing. He would take along that boy from the wounded woman they'd left at the last camp. He smiled at the thought. He was a big strong boy and could keep up. The boy would be killed, he would tell the women, if they did not stay in camp and wait for his return. That should prevent them from trying to sneak away when the two men weren't looking. Then he could put the boy among the hostages he planned to take.

Those were his weapons, he had decided. He would use a ruse, a trick, to get the men away from their shelters, then he would attack and capture the women. He would demand the men leave the valley or else he would kill the women and children. He did not think he would have to kill more than two or three of them before the men agreed to leave, to save their families' lives.

He told his men what they must do. They would position themselves as he directed, and at the proper moment would descend on the shelters while a few of his men attracted attention at a different spot, drawing the village men, along with their dogs away from their families.

Some of the men seemed puzzled by this information. It was such a totally new idea for them, Kuh-moh could see, that they found it hard to cope with the thought of a mass assault and the possible killing of women or children. Kuh-moh knew he must arouse their bloodlust at the right moment for his plan to succeed. These might be bad men, he concluded, but they could not all kill, as he could, without remorse. They would have to change or die, he thought contemptuously.

He then told the women that Mee-suh's boy would sleep with the men this night, that he would go with them—"hunting" as Kuh-moh put it—in the morning. They must not leave the camp, he warned them, or the boy would be killed when they returned from the hunt. The women nodded. They knew this man was capable of doing such a dark deed.

Kuh-moh's camp was quiet as Foh-man moved carefully toward it. Only glowing embers from three fires in a clearing showed where shelters were located. He counted eight shelters on one side of the clearing, three on the other.

Yes, this was the Bad Men, since he remembered this was

how the other camp was organized. Men sleeping here, women there.

He waited, not knowing exactly why he waited. When a small dark figure stumbled from one of the shelters, Foh-man decided what he must do. The man came walking, half-asleep, to the edge of the clearing, to pass his water. Foh-man moved closer, then he recognized the man. He did not know him well but knew his name, Kuh-nah. As the man splashed the side of a big tree, Foh-man moved silently behind him. He turned to go back to his shelter and Foh-man struck, hitting him on the side of the head with a rock. There was hardly a sound as the man slumped into Foh-man's arms. He picked up the unconscious figure and limped back down the mountain to where Mee-suh waited. She was astonished to see Foh-man carrying someone.

"Have you killed him?" she asked, fearfully.

"No, I hit him with a rock. He should wake up soon. We will take him away and find out what he knows about where Kuh-moh plans to go next. We must leave now, so we won't get caught again."

"If he does not tell us," Mee-suh asked, "will you kill him?"

There was a cold silence as Foh-man thought about that.

"I don't know," he finally said. "I . . . hope not."

"My children . . ." Mee-suh began.

"Yes," Foh-man nodded. "We must see what this man knows. Then we decide what to do. Kuh-moh will not hurt your children. He wants children in his new family. Don't worry."

Neither of the two was convinced, however, that anyone in the camp was safe from Kuh-moh's wrath. Foh-man had seen his blazing rages and his lack of concern for another man's death.

He helped the semiconscious man slowly down the trail, his own foot hurting with each step. He wanted to hurry away from this place, from the bloodthirsty leader asleep in the camp. Yet he knew the anguish Mee-suh felt for her children. It would be hard to decide what to do.

The boy sat as quietly as he could in the cold, dark forest, near the trail. He did not want to admit being frightened, so he kept reminding himself of his responsibility. He had lived only fifteen seasons, yet he had been given a man's job—to stay wide-awake until the sun rose, to warn the village if the Bad Men came.

He was grateful to the village people for allowing him, his mother, and wounded grandfather to stay there. The Elders told them they were welcome to become part of the community, and his mother had shed tears at the good news. Now he wanted to repay this great trust, be watchful, and make sure the village knew if any Bad Men came this way.

Despite his good intentions, Um-so-mee almost ran when he saw three dim figures moving down the trail, in his direction. He raised his spear-thrower. . . . No, he remembered, he was not to attack, but warn the village. He must sneak away, quietly . . . but he hesitated.

One of the dark figures was small. A woman? The other two were unsteady on their feet. If these were Bad Men, they did not act like it. So he waited, moving silently behind a large tree, the better to watch. He was fascinated, when the people drew closer, to see that the one in the rear was indeed a woman, limping on a forked stick, to support herself. The boy simply knew these could not be Bad Men, but perhaps people like his own family who had been attacked by those men.

Waiting until they were just beyond his position, he called out quietly: "Wait. Stop there. We must talk."

The bulky man in the middle of the three people whirled around, his spear-thrower rising.

"No," the boy said loudly. "I am not an enemy. I mean no harm. I come from the village. Let us speak, please."

Lowering his weapon, Foh-man motioned. "Good. Come

here. I will not hurt you. We travel to the village in the valley. Can you help us?"

There was a long moment as the boy considered this.

Then, reassured, he hurried down the slope to meet the strangers, hoping he was doing the right thing. He knew his life might depend on it.

Running feet and excited voices awoke Um-moh, and he climbed wearily from his sleeping skins. A small crowd of people gathered around the largest of the village campfires, which he had ordered be kept going through the night.

As he approached, Um-moh recognized the boy he'd placed in the important watcher position on the north mountain. Why had he left his post?

The boy, eager to explain, blurted out the full story, and pointed to the three seated people. "They come on the trail . . . they know where the Bad Men's camp is, and they seek safety. They can tell you much that is important," the youngster summarized quickly, still not sure if he'd done the right thing.

Um-moh nodded and dropped wearily at the fire, staring in turn at the exhausted trio.

"My name is Mee-suh," the woman offered. "I was born here in this valley, and I left long ago with my man . . . do you know my father, Um-see?"

Um-moh's mouth fell open. This was his blood relative, his dead father's sister! He motioned to one of the village boys nearby. "Run fast," he told the boy. "Bring Um-see here. Tell him it is important. Go quickly!"

Um-see's reunion with his daughter was both happy and sad. She hugged him tightly, tears on her cheeks, and her father's eyes watered. He never had expected to see her again. Then he had to tell her about the deaths of her mother and brother. Her only solace was finding that the tall, handsome young man standing next to them was her brother's son. Mark had followed Um-see and stood watching, saying nothing. He could not help noticing how attractive Um-see's daughter was, even in her distraught condition.

She was a tall, strong girl. Her loosened hair hung around her shoulders in a lustrous swirl. Mark guessed her age at about thirty. Her full figure was obvious even through her loose clothing, She was the finest-looking female he'd seen since coming to the valley, but now she barely glanced at him.

They all sat by the fire, Mee-suh holding her father's hand, trying not to cry. Her physical ordeal, her missing children, the news of her mother and brother . . . she thought she must have done something dreadfully wrong, and this was the Spirits' punishment upon her. It was a while before she could speak.

Foh-man told, briefly, how he and Mee-suh had left the deserted camp, found the Bad Men's camp, and taken away this other man, who sat silent and fearful, not wanting to be here, knowing full well that the fearsome Kuh-moh would kill him if he could. Now Kuh-nah was exhausted and was afraid that he was going to be killed anyway. He stared in astonishment at the tall, hairy man in the white hides who had walked up, and who acted like he belonged in the group. He had heard stories of such a man from the camp talk. Others who had seen this huge figure thought he must have special powers and might not even be a real man.

When Foh-man had finished, Um-moh turned to the man they had captured, and spoke in a friendly way. He did not wish to frighten the man, since he wanted to know the Bad Men's plans. Foh-man already had identified their leader as Kuh-moh.

"You know what Kuh-moh will do?" Um-moh asked.

The man hung his head just long enough for it to be obvious to those around the fire that he knew something. After a long pause, Um-see spoke up softly. "You must tell us what you know." The threat behind his words was clear.

Kuh-nah looked at the faces around the fire, fixing his attention on Mark. Light from the fire threw shadows across

Mark's growing black beard, his hair again almost straight up on his head, arms folded across those strange white hides on his chest.

Mark saw the man's indecision and obvious fear of him, so he nodded, then looked directly in the man's eyes and said, "You tell!"

Kuh-nah began speaking slowly, recounting as best he could the words he'd heard from Kuh-moh only hours before. He rambled through the plan, and his listeners let him speak until he was finished. He explained how Kuh-moh intended to divert the villagers off down the valley by a diversionary attack. Then Um-moh spoke.

"So Kuh-moh will attack us, here, before the sun rises? This day?"

Kuh-nah nodded. "He wants to capture the village and all of the valley. He plans to hold the women and force the men to leave, and he will kill those who don't obey. I don't want to kill other men . . . will you kill me?"

There was a long silence. Um-moh spoke slowly.

"If you have told a true story, you will live," he said. "If you lied . . ." and Um-moh shrugged, sadly.

Kuh-nah nodded eagerly. "I have told the truth. I have told you everything Kuh-moh told us. I will not help him. I will help you."

Mark found it difficult not to smile. The impassive faces of his listeners had unnerved the exhausted man, and he was happy to explain again all the details of Kuh-moh's plan he could remember.

He was questioned at length. In the course of it, Mee-suh was distressed to learn that her son was due to be part of the attacking force at dawn, forced to accompany the Bad Men. She looked at her newly found nephew, Um-moh, and asked, "What happens to my son, if the village men fight with the Bad Men?"

This thought already had crossed the minds of the sober men at the fireside, and there was no quick answer. If the villagers defended their homes, as surely they must, how could anyone recognize a large boy among the other attackers and avoid killing him?

Um-moh called for two men to take the captive Kuh-nah to a nearby shelter and keep him there, to sleep. There was work to do this night, he knew, and decisions to make, if the village was to survive the attack they now knew would come by daylight. He understood Kuh-moh's plan of action. He shook his head about the question of Mee-suh's son and turned to his grandfather and Mark. They would have good counsel. He felt their lives depended on finding answers. "What do you think we should do?" he asked his grandfather.

Um-see stared into the fire. He had been turning his strange idea over in his mind. He felt foolish suggesting such a thing, but he explained his idea anyway. When he had finished, both Mark and Um-moh were smiling.

Kuh-moh awoke to find that it had begun snowing and that another of his men was missing. There was no trace of the man Kuh-nah, the older man that he had intended as one of the women-watchers during his attack on the village. Why would such a man—slow and with no courage—put himself back into the wilderness, alone? Kuh-moh shook his head, and shouted his orders.

"Eat now! Prepare your weapons! Take all your spears! We will go soon!"

He then instructed the single man he would leave behind not to let the women escape, on fear of death. He also threatened the women again about what would happen to Mee-suh's son if they left the camp before his return.

Wrapped in extra hides, only his dark eyes showing, Kuh-moh finally signaled to his men that it was time to start their journey. "Follow me," he told them. "Move quietly on the trail. I know where the watchers wait for us. We will kill them if they see us."

He stared at them a moment in silence.

"You must attack quickly when I give the signal and run into the village. Kill the dogs if they don't run away. You may strike the women if they resist—but don't kill them.

"Later," he concluded, "we will have a great feast. There will be food and women for everyone."

He turned and started up the trail, showing his men how much space to leave between themselves. The snowfall had intensified, and Kuh-moh was pleased. That would soften the noise of their approach. A great fire rose in his chest as he began to celebrate his victory in his mind.

THIRTY-THREE

It was odd, Kuh-moh decided. The village watchers he'd seen the night before were gone.

Leaving his men to rest, he had carefully scouted the spots where watchers had been stationed. Nothing. Did the villagers think they were safe just because it was snowing? He chuckled deep in his throat.

Rejoining his men, he led them slowly along the trail. He stopped often, his excellent night vision picking out and examining suspicious forms or shadows. He knew they were nearing the wooded slope behind the village. Here was the fork in the trail he remembered.

He called Kuh-so to him, and told him again of his plan. He pointed up the other trail and told Kuh-so how far to go along that trail and what to do. Kuh-so was to find and attack the village watchers off to the south, just before the sun rose. Make much noise, throw spears, he was told, and cause the village men to run down the valley—away from their shelters—to help the others.

"What should I do if the watchers don't appear?" Kuh-so asked.

Kuh-moh had thought about that.

"If you don't see them," he said, "you run down from the mountaintop to the valley. You shout, wave your spears, make it seem that you are going to attack the valley. But you stay there and make all the noise you can, to get attention," he said.

Kuh-so nodded, then led his three men up the branching

trail, heavy snowfall covering their tracks within minutes.

Allowing some time to pass, Kuh-moh then signaled for his men to move slowly toward the crest of the hill, behind which, he knew, the village shelters were located. When dawn came they would be ready to descend quickly to the valley below. He smelled the wind. Good. In his face. The village dogs should not smell them too soon.

All the fires had been put out. Um-moh knew where everyone was positioned. His voice was raw and hoarse since he'd talked to almost everyone in the village, after they had made their plans. He was tired but not sleepy, the excitement of what was ahead keeping him alert, on edge. He looked across the valley and knew where Um-see was supposed to be but, through the heavy snowfall, could not see him. He hoped his grandfather was equal to the dangerous plan Um-see had just laid out. Um-moh worried that his grandfather would not survive this day. It would be too much for a younger man, what he intended doing.

Mark, beside him, looked even more strange than he usually did. Um-moh had to smile: Mark had rubbed thick grease on his hair, so that it all stood straight out from his head. He wore all his white hides and carried his bow, trying to look serious but looking embarrassed instead.

Mark indeed felt idiotic as the first dim light began to illuminate the valley. Snow fell with blizzardlike intensity and laid a deep coating of soft white powder over all the trees and bushes in sight. Silence was broken only by a light breeze that whipped the snow around and swished tree branches overhead. Mark could not remember ever having a nightmare so unreal as this. If he could only wake up before the trouble starts . . . back to his old life, fat and happy, on his couch, a cold Lone Star in one hand, his channel-changer in the other. How on earth had he gotten mixed up in all this? All these people thought him to be some sort of Superman, and his guts turned to jelly when he thought of what he was supposed to do . . . yet he couldn't run, couldn't hide.

If he didn't try to do his part, he'd be out of Dodge, on his ass, maybe not even alive.

Mark forced himself to think of something pleasant: Mee-suh. He'd spent the early-morning hours fantasizing about that dark-haired doll, thinking how it would be to share a shelter with her, make love to her . . . He gritted his teeth. Where was he getting such thoughts?

Kuh-so and his three men crouched at the trail, overlooking the end of the mountain, where the last of the gushing springs sent hot water cascading down the mountainside.

Despite clouds of steam rising from hot pools below, he could clearly see much of the valley floor, as the snow lifted momentarily. Nothing moved, and it was almost full daylight. No village watchers appeared, nothing he could attack. All was quiet, and the total silence made him nervous. It was time for him to do something, but he wasn't sure exactly what.

Go down to the valley, Kuh-moh had told him. Make a big noise, get village men to run toward him, throw spears, then get away, luring the village men to follow. He signaled his men, and they started down the trail, toward the valley floor. At that moment, four tiny spears flashed by them. One of his men was struck in the shoulder, and cried out, falling down. They jumped off the trail and got behind trees. More small spears hurtled through the trees, close to where they hid.

Kuh-so peered out from behind his tree and a quick glance showed four dim figures a great distance away, barely visible through the snowy mist. They had strange-looking sticks in their hands, bending those sticks, and now more of those little spears whipped through the trees.

Could he send his own spears that far? No, too far away. This was bad.

He crouched, thinking—but not about Kuh-moh's instructions. He thought about how he could get away from those small spears without getting killed.

*   *   *

Kuh-moh was cold, his hands numb, his face crusted with
falling snow. His men muttered unhappily. Daylight revealed
all the shelters far down the slope and no sign of anyone
moving about. No smoke came from the tops of shelters.
There was utter silence through the open forest. Kuh-so still
had made no noise off down the valley. He quietly cursed
the man. Cowardly fool must have gotten lost, took the
wrong turn. Now he, Kuh-moh, must do this with no help
from anyone.

He stood, waving both arms, flexing cold fingers around
his spear-thrower. "Come," he called quietly to his men,
lined up on both sides of him. "We attack now and kill any
who fight. Make the men run away. Quick! Now! Move!"

He began to walk rapidly, then trot, through the woods,
down toward the shelters. His men hurried to keep up,
stretched in a ragged line across the forest, dodging around
bushes and trees, avoiding rock outcrops, finding it hard to
run straight through the drifting snow and soft powder under
their feet.

Kuh-moh reached the first shelter, his spear-thrower ready
in his right hand, and jerked the shelter flap open. Nothing
moved. Empty. His men followed his example. They ripped
open shelters, found no one. The sleeping skins were gone,
each shelter bare. They raced from one to another, breathing
hard, looking for someone, anyone . . . the village was deserted.

Kuh-moh stopped to get his breath and glared around him.
They had been warned! They had fled, the entire village! No
women or children. No men to kill or drive away. He felt
cheated and angry. But then he had another thought. What
did it matter, after all? The village was his now! He must
make sure that the villagers weren't hiding nearby. How
could all the women have moved everything so quickly, leaving their shelters unprotected? He called his men around him.

"We will move down the valley, spread out, and find

those who hide from us. Don't kill the women, kill only the men. Come, quick!"

He led the way down the slope from the shelters and out onto the flat valley floor, straining to see through the snow any signs of life on the western mountain to their right, or through the fog of the hot water pouring off the mountain to their immediate left. They all jogged alongside the fast-flowing creek that ran beside the base of the hot springs mountain.

There came a loud, dull sound. Then another. Thunder? Kuh-moh stopped, as did his men. More sound . . . a booming noise.

Repeated . . . slowly. *Boom. Boom. Boom.* Coming from different directions. The sound was steady, threatening, and it continued without pause.

Someone was making this noise, Kuh-moh knew. Was it a signal between the villagers? He knew of signals between hunters . . . he must be ready for an attack, so he called to his men, motioned, then led them at a run into a grove of trees at the base of the steep mountain alongside the springs, close to where the first line of steaming streams of water cascaded from the rocks high above.

Louder now came the booming noise, reverberating off the snowy mountainsides, filling the valley with a heavy, threatening beat. *Boom . . . boom . . . boom . . . boom . . .*

Kuh-moh's men sensed this was not the way things were supposed to happen. Something was going wrong.

Moments later, their fears were confirmed. On the far side of the valley, at the base of the western mountain, a line of men walked down out of the trees and stood quietly. The long line seemed to stretch off as far as Kuh-moh's men could see, through the snowfall. More numerous than Kuh-moh's band. Each of these silent men held a long branch in his hand. Now each one put a little stick against the branch, pulled it . . . and in the next instant a blizzard of small spears whistled over their heads, striking trees, bushes close by, thudding into the snow-covered mountain slope behind them.

Kuh-moh's men took cover behind anything solid, and they looked at him. Those distant men were beyond the range of their spear-throwers, but Kuh-moh—knowing that—quickly decided to try and scare them anyway.

He ordered his men to step from cover and hurl their spears, high. "Cast high," he shouted, "and make our spears go far." And he hurled his short spear up into the sky. His men quickly followed, flung their spears up at a sharp angle, watched as they fell . . . short of the village men. The villagers did not run or retreat but simply bent those slim branches again, and another flurry of little spears flashed across the snowy valley . . . and one of Kuh-moh's men cried out, hit in the shoulder. Kuh-moh saw blood gushing from the wound as the injured man slumped behind a tree.

Kuh-moh growled in his throat. His mouth was dry, and his breath came in short gasps. That booming noise, he knew, was supposed to frighten him. He shook his head. He must attack, but he knew that his men, now looking around in fear, would not survive a run across the valley. Too many would die.

Behind Kuh-moh rose a steep wall of thick vegetation, and the snow coating would make it hard to climb. To his left, falling, steaming water blocked his path. Only to his right, back up the slope to those shelters, could he and his men escape . . . but he would not allow himself to run away.

He gritted his teeth, knowing that if he tried to escape, his men also would run—and never would he claim this valley or conquer its people. He would again be alone in the forests. At that moment, more spears hummed through the air around him, and he saw with disgust that his men had dropped to the ground to avoid being hit.

Silence then.

The terrible *boom-boom* noise stopped. Kuh-moh saw that distant line of men motionless in the drifting snow. Then a tall, snow-covered figure walked from among them and plodded across the valley floor toward where the Bad Men were gathered.

Well within Kuh-moh's spear-throwing range, the big man stopped. Kuh-moh now saw his features. His hide coverings were white. He had a snow-flecked mass of black hair on his face, and his hair rose straight up and went out to the sides. Kuh-moh stood erect also, in plain view.

The tall, white-clad figure raised both hands to show that they were empty, then he slowly pointed his right hand and index finger at Kuh-moh, and shouted, in a strange accent.

"Kuh-moh is a coward! Kuh-moh hides from fight. Kuh-moh will run away! All men spit on Kuh-moh."

And with that the white giant turned and spit into the snow.

Kuh-moh, his mouth open in astonishment and anger, could hardly believe his ears. He was being called a coward in front of his men! Then reason seeped into his mind.

This was a trick. When he moved ahead from the shelter of these trees, those little limbs would all bend again, and he would be showered with small spears. He moved a step forward and shouted, "You play a trick! You try to get me in the open, then kill me with the small spears!"

The tall white figure shook his head. "No. You fight, you kill me, the village will not kill you or your men. You can leave the valley. If you not fight me, you must run now, or you die! Is Kuh-moh fighter or coward?"

Kuh-moh clenched his jaws, growling deep in his throat. He must take the chance. Big as this man was, he knew that he himself was stronger.

No man could stand against his savage strength. None ever had. He could not remember how many men he had killed who thought they could kill him.

Now, he decided, he would go out and kill this strange thing—for all to see. The village men would lose heart, and his men would follow him in chasing them all away. He stepped out, his right hand brushing along his back to be sure that his long green knife was there, ready for the killing stroke.

As he started forward, the *boom-boom* noise began again,

only faster now. But Kuh-moh did not falter or hesitate.

"They wish to scare me," he smiled to himself. "Do they think I will run from noise? Noise cannot hurt Kuh-moh."

Then he had a thought. He would make sure this was no trick. He turned and ordered one of his men to bring forth the boy they'd captured, the son of that hurt woman.

In a moment, his man appeared, hurrying the frightened boy forward so that he was visible to the villagers . . . who, to Kuh-moh's surprise, stood silent, with no reaction. "You play a trick," he shouted, so all could hear, "and this boy dies. We kill him if you lie." Kuh-moh's man drew a knife high, as though he would plunge it into the boy's chest.

Then Mark began a slow, deliberate walk toward the stocky outlaw leader. The drums boomed again in unison, and he tried to move in a slow cadence to the *boom, boom, boom* that filled the valley.

Kuh-moh was delighted that the big hairy figure was coming to him. He balanced on the balls of his feet, thinking of himself as a great human cat, just before the kill, and he began to hum to himself, feeling his strength swell with anticipation of combat. Nothing so released all Kuh-moh's ferocity than the final moments before he killed a man. He could almost feel the surge of pleasure that he knew would come as he plunged his long green knife into this big man's chest. His hand would move like lightning . . .

Mark, for his part, felt sweat trickle down his spine. He was close to panic. Only the throng of people at his back kept him to his role. He stared in horror at the violent killer only about sixty yards ahead of him, growing in menace and ferocity with each step Mark took. His mind cried, *Foul! Time out!*

Hey, nutcase, this wasn't part of the program. You and your guys were supposed to run like hell, scared shitless. Now what do I do? I sure as hell can't run or Um-moh and his boys will shoot ME . . . come on, Um-see, do your thing, buddy, or your cavemate is gonna be history. . . .

Um-see was trying to carry out his assignment, but it

wasn't easy. He had heard the drums' quickened beat—his
signal to start the breakoff of the overhanging stone ledge,
up on the mountain. It was shaking, as he and his brother's
grandson jumped up and down along the edge. Each of them
wore a loose harness of ropes around his chest, tied to trees
close by, so that when the rock ledge broke away, the ropes
would prevent their fall. Um-see and the boy jumped higher,
harder, dancing along the very edge, high above the valley.
Movement. Vibration. More movement. They jumped harder,
faster. Um-see's bad leg hurt him, but he kept hopping.
Seebo, unable to help, paced, growling up and down the trail
nearby.

Then the stone dropped from beneath their feet, with only
a small crunch, and began sliding down . . . almost in slow
motion, it seemed to Mark, as he noted the giant rock's
downward tilt. The Bad Men, and Kuh-moh, absorbed in
Mark's slow steady walk toward them, apparently heard
nothing over the drum's constant booming.

Then Mark stared in horror. Through the snowfall, he
clearly saw Um-see and the boy, suspended by their ropes,
as the great rock dropped beneath them . . . but he also saw
now the huge stone's path. As big as a ten-ton truck, it
seemed to Mark, it had hit something, turned over, changed
direction slighty . . . and was aimed directly at the man holding Um-see's terrified grandson. In seconds, it was clear, that
huge rock would crash upon them.

When they had planned this, it was simplicity itself. All
agreed, Mark remembered, that the Bad Men—confronted
by superior force, without the element of surprise—would
flee. The women and children were quickly evacuated to
crowd into Um-see's shelter overnight, the men were organized in the brush along West Mountain's forested base. The
Elders were sure that Kuh-moh's men would run . . . would
take shelter at the mountain base, beneath the giant rock
overhang. They hadn't counted on Um-see's grandson being
thrust into danger.

Move, Mark told himself, and began to walk faster

through the ankle-deep snow. His mind raced, he had only seconds, yet the realization flashed to him that he, Mark Lewellyn, full-time wimp of long ago, was now jogging into battle and death against a madman hungering for his blood. Mark closed his mind, broke into a run. Kuh-moh backed a step, ready to meet Mark's charge, drawing his long knife from behind him.

To Kuh-moh's rear stood his man clutching the wide-eyed, struggling boy, and they, too, moved back a step, all clearly unaware of the huge rolling, tumbling boulder coming down the mountainside with increasing speed, aimed directly at them.

At twenty yards from Kuh-moh Mark began to shout unintelligible curses, waved his arms, ran at full speed—then launched himself, feetfirst, into Kuh-moh, slamming his shoes into the stocky man's chest.

Both fell in the snow, scrambling to rise, Kuh-moh slashing at Mark with his knife. The captive boy kicked back against the man holding him as Mark, rolling, grabbed the boy's arm with both hands and dived with all his remaining strength to his right, Kuh-moh two steps behind.

Mark felt flying snow in his eyes, he was shoved by air pressure, then the ground shook as the great chunk of tufa rolled over one last time and almost grazed Mark's shoulder as it shuddered to a stop.

He was aware of a hoarse shriek at the moment of impact. Then movement . . . running feet, shouts as Kuh-moh's men raced away. Mark looked around, brushing snow from his face, expecting attack. He pulled the boy to him, swiveled around, his back to the great boulder. No attack came. The enemy had disappeared.

Then he understood. Kuh-moh was buried. Entombed. He had hungered for this valley, wanted it for his own. Now the valley owned him, and he would rest here beneath this rock. Forever.

As Mark looked down, something green glittered against the white snow. He picked up Kuh-moh's knife, marveled at its length and terrible beauty. It had flown from his hand as he died.

Then came reaction. Mark went down on one knee, got his breath, ran his hands through greasy hair, coughed, sick to his stomach. Shouts in the distance pulled him erect. His friends across the valley ran in different directions, some coming to be sure he and the boy were safe. He took deep breaths of cold air. And a crazy thought. Now he knew how the Duke of Wellington felt right after the Battle of Waterloo. Yeah, Duke, this was another one of those "close-run things."

Um-moh knew that somehow he had to get control of his men. When they saw Mark's close-call rescue of the boy, and the tumbling boulder come to rest, they began hurrying about, talking excitedly, unsure what to do next.

Everyone could see the Bad Men trying to escape in three directions. One group ran around the mountain base, toward the village huts. Others clambered up a steep path they had found alongside the first shower of hot water that spilled off the mountain. Still others raced into the mists of the steam at the base where hot water cascaded down into Hot Springs Creek. Um-moh noted where each group went and shouted instructions to as many of his best bowmen as he could.

It was clear to all that if the Bad Men escaped, they could easily return, even if their leader was dead. Everyone had seen the big stone smash him into the ground, as though the Spirits themselves had ordered this to be done.

Without any instructions from Um-moh, some of the village men began chasing one group of Bad Men toward the shelters, pausing to discharge arrows.

Um-moh led five of his most trusted friends in a dead run down the valley floor south toward the central area of hot springs that fell off the smoking mountain. Through the mists, he could just make out a line of hurrying figures trying to reach a trail up on the mountain above the springs.

Um-see, meanwhile, limped quickly along a game trail, leading down off the mountain. He found an area of dense underbrush, hid his brother's grandson deep in its folds, instructed him to stay there until someone came to get him.

Then, with Seebo at his heels, he hurried along the trail as he saw the Bad Men approaching the shelters below him. Stopping where he had good visibility, he realized the Bad Men would reach the edge of thick woods before any villagers could catch them. Um-see had no choice. Quickly, he pulled and released two arrows. Missed. Um-see corrected for distance, found the range with his third arrow, which buried itself in a man's shoulder. He fell shouting, tumbling in the snow. As Mark had shown him, Um-see did not try to aim but tracked the running figures for a moment, then released. His heart leaped, then grew sad as his next arrow thunked into a man's leg, and he fell face forward, struggling on the ground. Without pause, Um-see forced himself to continue, and his next arrow penetrated a man's neck, protruding out the other side.

Carefully, Um-see released his last two arrows, and one found a running man's thigh. He fell in the snow, got to his feet, fell again, and began screaming. Um-see was proud of his skill with the weapon, but as he saw the villagers converge on the wounded men, holding them down, stone axes rising and falling, he found his eyes watering. It was horrible, and Um-see shut his eyes tight in sadness and fatigue. Then he became conscious of shouting down the valley, to the south. Seebo started down the trail . . . then stopped, whirled, growling.

Um-see had not seen the man quietly approaching from behind him—a man desperate to get by Um-see and the wolf-dog and escape to the woods beyond. He whipped up his spear, then decided at the last instant that the animal now approaching was more threat than the old man. The spear flashed by Um-see and brought a scream of pain and rage from Seebo as it found its mark. Snarling and twisting, the wolf-dog fell into nearby underbrush.

Um-see whirled, the man upon him, spear handle up-
raised. The old man threw up an arm, groping for his knife
. . . knew it was too late . . . as his attacker swung down viciously, trying to split Um-see's skull open.

And would have, except that Seebo still lived. The
wounded animal, blood streaming down his back, shot in a
straight line for the man's throat. As Um-see fell, dazed by
the glancing blow, he saw powerful jaws snap shut with an
audible crunch deep in the attacker's throat. He lost consciousness, thinking both he and Seebo were dying together.
A good death, Um-see thought, as darkness closed in.

Looking for the quickest way into dense forest above them,
the five Bad Men who'd raced into the steaming hot-water
clouds began climbing. Between the hot-water channels was
a narrow trail.

They slipped in loose snow, recovered, scrambled frantically upward, finally saw that they were just above where
much of the steaming water boiled from the ground. Only a
few hot springs were above them . . . but an intersecting trail
led south. They turned and ran as hard as snow and mud
would allow.

Um-moh, watching from the valley floor, could almost
read their minds as they stumbled along. He knew exactly
when they would arrive at the muddy place they must cross.
There the footing would be slippery, and all villagers avoided
it fearfully. One wrong step and you could slide off the
mountain and fall to the rocks far below. The five men, he
could see, did not know this. He and his bowmen were ready,
as the Bad Men ran toward the muddy area, clearly visible.

Um-moh called to his men then to aim carefully. They
knew it was an impossible bowshot—farther than Mark's
amazing kill of the elk recently—but Um-moh knew what
might happen.

Six bowstrings thrummed as one, lofting arrows in a high
arc through rising hot-water mists, descending into the frantic
midst of Bad Men. None was hit, but they stared down at

their attackers, and tried to run faster—across the deepening mud underfoot.

Then the first fleeing man cried out, scrambled to keep his footing . . . and lost it. He grabbed frantically for a bush, a limb, anything to stop his slow, inexorable slide downward. There was nothing to hold to. He shouted, then screamed, as his body flew down the side of the water-slick rock, then into space, down into the mists—where his screams stopped.

His body was still in the air when another six arrows arched toward the frightened Bad Men, who now picked their way forward, trying not to slip. One arrow found its mark in a man's leg. He shouted, and sat down quickly to avoid the fate of the fallen man.

The two men behind him nearly fell over his seated form, as he blocked the muddy trail—and another volley of arrows dropped among them. Um-moh saw one man grab his arm, another ducked an arrow and fell to one knee. The man on the ground was next hit, in the arm. He jerked erect, grabbing at his companions, succeeded in pulling them off-balance . . . slowly then, all three began the deadly, unstoppable slide down across the steaming, slippery rocks.

As they shouted and clawed the air, their bodies disappeared into the hot steam below. Arrows now fell around the sole survivor, who knelt, shocked, on the muddy trail. Um-moh saw an arrow graze his thigh, another ripped through the sleeve of his jacket, but he stoically stood, walked ahead carefully, placing each foot down to be sure of his footing. The six bowmen stopped shooting, astonished at the man's courage, sickened at the deaths of the other four men. They silently watched the lone survivor on the trail above reach solid ground, turn, and limp up into the forest.

With those wounds dripping blood, Um-moh told himself, *That man will be dead before the night is over. Wolves will find him quickly, and he has no spear-thrower.* Then Um-moh steeled his heart and led his men, trotting, down the valley to the south. More Bad Men had preceded them, headed down the creek toward the big river. They must be found . . . and, regrettably, killed.

Mark ran to Mee-soon's shelter when he heard of Um-see's injuries. The man who had shouted the news to Mark said he thought Seebo was dead, but Um-see lived.

He found his friend stretched on sleeping skins with the medicine woman wiping his bloody face clean. examined the gash down the side of his head, and . . .

"His head will hurt," she said, "but he will live." Moments later, Um-see tried to sit up, groggy and dazed, looking around for something.

"Seebo?" he asked.

Mee-soon pointed to a dark form nearby.

"Seebo is hurt," she said. "The spear entered the skin on his back and the wound is deep. I have filled it with herbs and honey. He is still unconscious and may die."

Mark understood enough of this to turn and examine the big animal, whose breathing was fast and shallow. The bleeding had stopped.

Another animal then appeared in the shelter door, and Mark saw it was Seebo's mother. She limped to the wolf-dog's side, sniffed him, then lay down, her head between her forelegs.

Mark had never been so tired in his life. He lay in Um-moh's shelter, trying to listen as the young man told in a low voice of chasing and catching the Bad Men, just south of the valley. The six villagers were faced by seven desperate men, five of whom still had spear-throwers and spears at hand.

They were backed up to the swamp where reeds were found, and they had no cover or concealment. They stood defiantly at the swamp's icy edge, knowing there was no escape in that direction. They brandished stone axes, shouted threats, then hurled their few remaining spears—all of which fell short of Um-moh and his hard-breathing companions. They spread out, took their time and used their bows with a skill and confidence they had never before experienced, advancing steadily. The Bad Men tried to run and to dodge arrows. But it was no use. Um-moh's men moved carefully forward, pulling and releasing, killing men as they never dreamed they would have to do.

Within a few terrible minutes, all seven of the Bad Men were corpses, lying in pools of their blood. Two of Um-moh's men walked a few paces away from the group to vomit. Um-moh himself had never felt so sick. They rested and tried to recover their wits before starting back up the valley.

Um-moh sat silently, his eyes on the ground, as he finished telling his story. For a few minutes there was only the soft sound of branches swaying in the trees outside, dropping a fine snow powder on the shelter. It was clear to all that Um-moh was not proud of his day's work. He must live with all that deliberate killing for the rest of his life. He did not want to admit it to himself, but he had the urge to weep.

He shook himself and rose. Work must still be done, and quickly.

"We must get the women held by the Bad Men, in the mountains," he said.

"Marrk, you will go? Take my men and find the women and children?"

Mark nodded. Tired as he was, he had no choice but to agree, even though he could barely force himself to stand. Um-moh said he would also send the former Bad Man, Fohman, to guide them to the mountain camp, and hurried out.

Groggily, Mark picked up bow, arrows, shoulder pouch, and followed Um-moh. *This has to be a dream,* he told himself, and when he woke up, he'd be on his couch, a cold beer at his elbow, watching reruns of *Leave It to Beaver.*

But as he walked out of the shelter, a handful of snow slid off the hide above and went down the back of his neck. He yelped. It was no dream.

As things turned out, it was a bloodless liberation. Foh-man led the way into camp amidst heavy snowfall, and the one man left there—an older boy, really—was asleep in his shelter. Women and children in other shelters also slept.

Upon being awakened, the lone guard recoiled from the sight of Mark in his white clothing and shrank back as though he saw a ghost. Then Foh-man told him of Kuh-moh's death and that he was free to go into the forests. Alone. He was a mild young man, Foh-man remembered, who joined the Bad Men because he was alone in the forests. He wanted a family now—any family that would take him in.

"Can I go with you to the village?" the boy asked. "I wish to hurt no one and want only for a place to live."

Foh-man shrugged. He wondered indeed whether he himself would get to live in the village.

"I cannot tell you that," he answered. "You can return with us, if you wish. The village Elders will decide your fate." The boy hesitated, then agreed to go with the rescue party and take his chances.

Gathering all the shelter poles and hides they could carry, the entire group was on the trail quickly, Foh-man leading, the women and children in the middle, the other men and Mark bringing up the rear.

The snow at midafternoon had lessened, but a breeze, whipping along the mountain trail, increased in strength, chilling everyone. They were about to make the final turn up toward the village when Foh-man stopped suddenly, jumped off the trail, and waved his arms, motioning for Mark to move forward.

Coming toward them down the trail were three men, recognized by Foh-man as remnants of Kuh-moh's band. There seemed to be no fight in them. They stood silently, waiting to see what the larger group would do. The village men fanned out so they could have bow-shooting room, if the Bad Men attacked them.

Foh-man looked at Mark, expecting the big man to take some sort of action. *Oh great*, Mark thought, *now I'm the damn Leader . . . how am I supposed to keep these guys from getting killed?* He breathed a long sigh. He was so bone-tired he could hardly stand erect, but the moment of decision could determine life or death for those around him, and he had to take an action . . . something . . .

He stepped forward, walking stiffly erect with great dignity, up the trail until he was no more than twenty paces from the motionless men. They eyed his height, his white hides, black beard, stiffened hair, and looked fearfully at each other.

After a long pause, Mark spoke, raising his voice.

"Kuh-moh is dead! Other Bad Men die! You die if you stay near village! Spirits protect village from men who kill! You go now, I let you live. You stay, you die." Mark raised his arm, pointing his finger directly at the men, then moving his pointing finger down the trail that branched off to the east, leading away from the village.

"Go now! Go . . . or die!"

Mark stepped back a pace, nocked an arrow to his bow-string, and slowly began to raise his bow. Instantly, the men began running across the snow, to the eastbound trail and underbrush there. They were gone within seconds, down the mountain, looking back only once.

Mark marveled at their flight. They all had spear-throwers, yet not one weapon was raised defensively. *Well, if that don't beat all,* he mused, in some wonder. *They're more scared than I am!* Then he had another horrible thought: *I have to take a leak, right now, fast. But I can't do it with everybody watching,* he thought, and he hurried quickly into the bushes, almost falling into a soft hole filled with only snow.

It was almost like having his own family, Mark reflected, as he sat back against the stone wall on his sleeping hides. They had just finished eating a huge meal, and he felt sleepy and mellow. Around the big fire in their shelter sat Um-see, smiling at his newly met grandson and flanked by his daughter. Mee-suh, Mark had discovered, was a much better cook than her father, and they had dined well on roast turkey, rare strips of venison, and some kind of flat bread that was new to Mark's palate.

All eyes were fixed on the long green knife that Mark held up to the firelight, reflecting sparks of light off the stone walls.

"I found this was made by Foh-man," Mark explained, "and when I returned it to him, he asked me to keep it, as a gift." It was the handsome dagger that had fallen from Kuh-moh's hand at the instant of his death, as everyone now knew, and Mark wondered whether it might bring him good luck or bad. Um-see's grandson could hardly wait to handle it. Um-see turned it over slowly, clearly awed by its workmanship.

"If Foh-man can make knives and points with this skill . . . will he do it for our families?" Um-see seemed a bit skeptical since he still thought of Foh-man as one of the Bad Men.

"He says he will stay, if allowed to, and teach others his skills," Mark said, choosing his words carefully. "He speaks in an honest way, I think, and he may be helpful here."

"Yes," spoke up Mee-suh. "I think he is a good man. He helped me to live and reach the valley, and I thank him for helping me find my children." She hugged her daughter, who leaned tiredly against her mother, clearly ready for sleep.

Mark found himself studying Mee-suh with both curiosity and admiration. Her face, by firelight, shone with pleasure. Mark stared, finding that face increasingly attractive. Unlike some of the village women, Mee-suh had a slight ski-nose, her lips were nicely formed, her eyes large and dark. She smiled often now, yet Mark could see these were forced smiles, and the sadness was obvious from her slow movements.

No wonder, he thought. *This woman was with her man for what, thirteen years? Suddenly he's dead, she's wounded, her kids stolen. You've got to be tough to get over that in a hurry. I want to know her better*, he decided, *see if she likes*

me. He had to admit to himself the attraction was also physical on his part. Mee-suh was a full-bodied, mature woman
who would want and need a man in her life after some suitable time had passed. Would he be that man? He smiled to
himself. Maybe he'd better ask Um-see to shave him again.

Mee-suh knew very well that Mark's eyes were gently
caressing her face and figure. She found she did not object,
although it was not possible now to think of anything except
her happiness at having her children back and being safe
among family and friends. She began turning occasional
glances toward the big man in the strange hides. He seemed
gentle, and she knew her father's high regard for Mark. But
he was so different from other men. Could he treat a woman
with kindness? She felt doubly sad to recall that in the final
few seasons of living with her man, now dead, he had
seemed uninterested in her and the children. He had good
qualities, she quickly reminded herself, but some of his families' bad habits—fighting among themselves—had rubbed
off on him, and he quarreled often, even with old friends.
She hoped that once in this peaceful valley where she had
grown up, her man would resume his former peaceful ways.

She then noted Mark had dozed off, his head back against
the wall. She smiled. She realized she didn't mind that hair
on his face. Mee-suh decided then that she liked this big man.
He was kind and knew how to control himself. She would
get to know him better. Then . . . who knows? She glanced
at her father and saw him smiling at her.

Um-see, who rarely missed much that went on around
him, had observed his daughter's and Mark's exchange of
glances, and he found it pleased him very much. Perhaps he
might tell Mee-suh about some of Mark's skills and . . . then
he chuckled and shook his head. *No, keep out of it, you old
fool*, he reprimanded himself. *Men and women will decide
these things themselves.*

THIRTY-FOUR

When the phone rang, Eleanor reluctantly picked it up, putting aside her sales reports. Even on weekends she would not let her office work fall behind.

"Mrs. Lewellyn?" a man's voice asked.

"Yes. Who's calling?"

"Is this the home of Mark Victor Lewellyn?"

"It is. Now tell me who you are."

"I'm Professor Harold Hampton, and I'm calling from Arkansas. From Hot Springs. Do you expect Mr. Lewellyn in shortly? I'll be glad to leave my number . . ."

"Professor, I'm sorry to tell you my husband has been a missing person since last October. We have no idea where he is and . . . how did you get my name and number? It's supposed to be unlisted."

"Well, um, that's why I'm calling. Let me explain, if I can. I'm an archaeologist, Mrs. Lewellyn, and we found your husband's name in a site we're excavating, and it has the word *Dallas* next to it, along with this telephone number, so . . ."

"Are you telling me you found Mark's name in a . . . a what? An archaeological site? Do I understand you correctly?" Eleanor realized she suddenly was perspiring freely.

"That's right," Hampton replied. "But let me start at the beginning. This is not just unusual, it's really bizarre. Are you familiar with Hot Springs?"

"Oh, yes. My husband and I were there several times. Nice place. But go on . . ."

"Well, on West Mountain, just above—and across from—the old Bathhouse Row, is where we've been working. What happened just recently, some large trees blew down in a high wind. They fell on, and caved in, what was once a kind of ancient Indian structure, formed by rocks and logs. A jogger called and reported seeing some kind of writing on one of the interior stone walls, so we sent someone over to have a look."

Eleanor sat up straight, hardly daring to breathe. "Go on," she said quickly.

"It took a week or so of excavating, but we got the place cleaned out and found some very faint remains of wall writings. We're still analyzing them but—and here's where it gets very strange—the writing is in English with some kind of phonetic words alongside. And then, in another area . . ."

"This could be important," Eleanor broke in, excited and sick at her stomach. "How long ago would you say all this was written?"

"Ah, now there's the real puzzler." Hampton sighed. "Our preliminary reports are just back . . . and we found enough organic materials to enable us to run carbon-dating tests, and as near as we can tell, this wall writing dates to somewhere between the first and third centuries. A.D., I mean. My own guess is about A.D. 200."

Eleanor was stunned into silence, trying to frame some response. Then she found herself cold and angry.

"Professor, is this some kind of sick joke . . . ? If it is . . ."

"Mrs. Lewellyn, I assure you this is not a joke. I'm quite serious. I was hoping I could learn from your husband how his name and all this other information could possibly be in such a place. Believe me, I know what you're thinking. Our first assumption was that someone has tried to stage an elaborate hoax . . ."

"And now you don't think so?"

"Frankly, we don't know what to think. All the evidence suggests this site was covered over entirely for at least fifteen hundred years. It is not possible that anybody could have dug it up, done that writing, not without being seen on this busy mountainside, then reburied it . . . besides which, the carbon dating of paint flecks from the wall pretty well nails down the time frame. But let me also tell you . . ."

"Do many people know about this?" Eleanor interrupted.

"Oh no, very few. We hope the media doesn't hear about it. You can imagine how foolish we'd look since, on the face of it, what we seem to have here has no rational explanation. It could promptly become a national joke, so no, only a handful of people are aware of the site, for now. There's something else important, Mrs. Lewellyn . . ."

"What is it?"

"Your first name. Would it happen to be Eleanor?"

"Yes, how would you know that?"

"That's the other part of this . . . uh, this strange business. Some of the dimmest lettering at the base of one wall is apparently a message to someone named Eleanor. I have to assume that person may be yourself . . ."

"What does it say?"

"We have only been able to make out scattered letters, until today. We photographed it with various kinds of light, and are using digitally enhanced lab techniques to bring up the rest. I should have the text, or most of it, in my hands this afternoon. I can fax it to you, or . . ."

"No, Professor, I'm coming to Hot Springs immediately—this morning, in fact—and I can be there by midafternoon. I want to see this writing, the site, everything about all this. If I come up, will you take me to the, uh, this location?"

"Oh, yes, of course," Hampton replied quickly. "And one more thing. Would you happen to have any samples of your husband's handwriting, or printing, on hand?"

"I'll look," said Eleanor. "Now tell me where I can locate you in Hot Springs."

Six hours later Eleanor was shaking hands with her caller in the lobby of the Arlington Hotel in downtown Hot Springs. Eleanor was visibly surprised. He didn't look like your stereotypical academic or scientist; he looked like he might have once played linebacker for the Green Bay Packers. Which, as it happened, he had. It always amused Harold Hampton to be introduced as an archaeologist since people, for some reason, expected those of his ilk to be a little under six-four.

The professor too was surprised—pleasantly. He couldn't help but admire this fine-looking woman, despite her obvious nervousness. She stood slim, trim, and erect in a snug-fitting business suit, staring him straight in the eyes. And she announced she would like to go, immediately, to the "dig" he had told her about on the phone.

He agreed. They left the hotel and began walking along Central Avenue, in the city's historic district. Hampton explained to Eleanor in neutral tones how he had initially concluded that somebody had gone to great lengths to perpetrate an involved, expensive hoax. But the carbon dating had thrown him. There seemed no way that what they had in the strange site could have been put there—except by the passing of the centuries.

For her part, Eleanor explained the details of Mark's sudden, baffling disappearance. Never, she said, had there been the slightest hint of what had happened to him . . . and now here was at last some clue. Eleanor walked briskly to keep up with Hampton's long strides as they turned up a narrow street to the West Mountain foothills. Hampton then explained his own deep professional interest in this situation.

"We were tremendously excited to find this site," he said. "It may be unique. The people who once occupied this area were early predecessors of the large Caddo Indian Nation. They lived in what's called the Woodland Era, from roughly 500 B.C. to about A.D. 900, and were part of the Fourche Maline culture. We've found only a few graves and some of their middens—their garbage dumps. But nothing ever found even comes close to this site.

"We know these people were hunter-gatherers who, in their entire lives, seldom went much beyond twenty-five miles from where they were born. They lived off the land, eating mostly nuts, fish, wild fruit, and animal meat. They made pottery but didn't decorate it, as later peoples did. They must have had a pretty good diet, though, since the few skeletons we've found show an almost complete set of teeth."

Now they walked up a broad path onto the sloping mountainside, pausing briefly so Eleanor could catch her breath. She expressed pleasure at the lush, green look of the mixed pine-and-oak forest. Hampton was glad that she had worn good walking shoes, as they moved along a rock-studded path up to the excavation site. Fresh dirt, boulders, and tree stumps surrounded a large hole in the mountain where a makeshift roof had been erected over a tangle of rocks and brush.

Inside the excavation were two of Hampton's assistants, a man and woman, both on hands and knees, sifting through dirt and rocks. Battery-powered lights illuminated the scene, including rough stone walls on three sides.

"We've found some fine artifacts," Hampton explained. "Animal hides, stone tools of all kinds, some made from bone . . . and pieces of carbonized wood that appear to have been bows. And that surprised us. This is the earliest time we've found remains of a bow in this culture . . . several centuries earlier than any found elsewhere. And also remnants of leather gloves . . . well, it's been full of surprises."

"And this is the wall?" Eleanor asked, looking up at the dark rocky surface, nearly ten feet tall, clearly showing faint outlines of letters several inches high. She could identify the English letters but not the odd letter combinations alongside.

"Yes, this is it," said Hampton. "Notice how the printing is more legible near the wall's base, where it was protected from air and rain and wind."

Eleanor got down on her knees to look at the very bottom, and could easily read "Mark Victor Lewellyn," then a dim word that looked like "Dallas," and—with a shock—Eleanor was looking at the crude strokes of her unlisted telephone number. She stared, disbelieving. Yet she knew it had to be. Mark had lived here in this cavelike place. He had to have written this on the wall . . . but centuries ago? This was madness, and she fought back tears.

Hampton cleared his throat, hurriedly explaining things to cover Eleanor's obvious emotion. He did hope she wouldn't go totally to pieces.

"We think this place and this writing survived because when the roof caved in, the shelter was deserted, and nobody made any attempt to make repairs. So dirt, leaves, brush all covered the site over before the writing was obliterated."

Eleanor removed a large folded card from her purse and showed it to Hampton. "It's a poster Mark painted years ago, when our son was in middle school. I was in the PTA and got Mark to do this, to advertise a school debate Charles was in. Mark painted it with acrylic paint and a small brush."

Hampton held the card down next to the wall lettering and turned a light more directly on it. Instantly it was obvious to everyone that the same hand had done both poster and wall lettering.

"Yes, it was Mark," said Eleanor. She put her hands to her face and stood quietly, in a kind of numbed shock. *It must be true, he was here*, she told herself. *Right in this cave. Was he safe here? And well? Had he been hurt?*

Hampton turned to one of his assistants. "Do you have that lab report that came over?"

He took a manila folder to Eleanor and opened it, pulling out a sheet of heavy photographic paper. He used it to motion toward the back of the excavation.

"Look over here, Mrs. Lewellen," he suggested. "This is where we found what seems to be a message." And he aimed one of the lights toward the base of the back wall of soot-covered rock. A large portion had been carefully cleaned off, and Eleanor could see the faint outlines of more lettering.

"You can't read it with the naked eye," Hampton said. "But we've had the lab enhance it repeatedly, and this is what they've come up with." He handed Eleanor the enlarged print, and she moved closer to a light to read it. Some of the letters were barely legible, but the message still seemed to jump off the page as Eleanor read it.

> ELEANOR: I SURVIVED LIGHTNING. WAS THROWN BACK IN TIME TO PREHISTORIC ERA. BEFORE 500 AD. LUCKY TO BE ALIVE. LIVE HERE WITH GOOD FRIENDS. I LOVE YOU AND CHARLES, ALWAYS WILL. BUT NO WAY BACK TO OUR TIME. WE MUST MAKE NEW LIVES, GO ON, DO BEST WE CAN. REMEMBER ME AS I WILL YOU, LOVINGLY, YOUR HUSBAND MARK

Later, at the hotel, Professor Hampton ordered coffee in the lobby for an exhausted Eleanor.

The poster that Mark had painted years before lay on the table between them. Hampton planned to have the wall writing analyzed by an expert, although it was obvious that what was on the wall matched what was on the poster. The brushstrokes were identical. "So, what happens now?" Eleanor asked. She wanted to weep but resisted the urge. She would do her crying later.

"So now we try and figure how the writings of a twentieth-century man turn up in a prehistoric cave, occupied eighteen centuries before he was born."

Hampton shook his head.

"It won't be easy."

"You're satisfied, then, that this is no hoax?" Eleanor asked.

"Hard to figure how it could be. My colleagues and I have been over the ground repeatedly. Before those trees fell, the mountainside had been undisturbed for centuries, and was seen every day by hikers and joggers going by.

"We've dated the few paint flakes from those letters on the wall—the process is accurate—and we know it was a mixture of carbon black and animal fat, and it matches the time frame of other artifacts we found in situ." He sighed. He knew that he, too, now believed exactly what Eleanor believed: Somehow Mark Lewellyn *had* been hurled back

through time. But did he have proof? Hardly. Was he com-
pelled to put his career and reputation on the line in a vain
effort to prove it? Senseless.

"Mrs. Lewellyn—or Eleanor, if I may call you that—I'm
not suggesting that your husband didn't do that wall writing,
or didn't live in this valley. I just don't know how it was
done, and I'm frustrated because I can't put my hands on
any real proof. Our evidence is circumstantial. I'm a scientist
and just hate it when I can't solve puzzles in my own spe-
cialized field."

"Me too." Eleanor smiled. "And this is a doozy, but you
do agree that Mark did go back in time and ended up here?"

"My practical side says, of course." Hampton grinned.
"I'll tell you privately that must be what happened. Publicly,
I cannot hold or express that opinion. We have no skeleton,
no bones, nothing but that writing on the wall. It's maddening."

"Professor, I know this may seem dumb, but have you
asked yourself this question: If you had excavated here a year
ago—well *before* Mark disappeared—do you really think
that wall writing would have been there, *then*?

Hampton's eyebrows went up. "Well, no, I don't suppose
it would have been, since . . ."

He stopped and began to chuckle deep in his throat.

"Now there's an interesting question—and you caught me
off base for a minute. Of course: The wall writing *had* to
have been there since we've established its age, when it was
done, how it was done. So, yes, the writing was there even
before Mark vanished from his home."

"I don't understand," Eleanor said, shaking her head.
"You're saying that if you'd found Mark's wall writing a
year ago—*before he disappeared*—and you'd called our
house as you did, and Mark had been at home, you would
have been able to ask him about this wall writing—which
he wouldn't have known anything about? Come on."

Hampton smiled and studied his coffee cup. But he nodded. "Yes, I think that's about it. That wall writing had to

have been there a year ago, a century ago, ten centuries ago, all the way back to when Mark wrote it . . ."

"This is crazy," Eleanor said, putting her hands to the sides of her head. "What if Mark, the morning of the lightning strike, had told me, No, he would not go outside for that screwdriver . . . and he hadn't gone? Then the lightning wouldn't have caught him, and he wouldn't have been thrown back in time. You mean the writing would *still* have been on the wall?"

Hampton hesitated. He didn't want to get this lovely woman upset. Women mystified him much of the time anyway.

"I think the answer is he *did* go outside that morning, and *did* get sent back in time. It doesn't matter what *might* have happened . . ."

"So, if somebody had discovered this site back in, say, 1945—before Mark was born—that wall writing would be just as we saw it today?" Eleanor was so incredulous that all color had drained from her face. Hampton shrugged regretfully.

"I'm afraid so. That writing wouldn't look as it does now unless it had been right there, untouched, all this time. So, yes, it *was* there at least sixteen or seventeen centuries before Mark, or even his immediate ancestors, were born."

"I've gotta tell you this," she gasped. "Just before I called down to Mark to go outside and get that damned screwdriver, I had to go to the bathroom . . . and I was on the verge of going into the bathroom when I said to myself, oh well, tell him now and he'll get it while you're in there . . . what if I'd gone to the bathroom first? Then Mark would never have gone out into the backyard, never got between the lightning strikes, never gone back." She stopped, out of breath, looking distraught. There was a long moment of silence.

"Same result," said Hampton. "You *didn't* go to the bathroom, Mark *did* go outside. You see, those lightning strikes started this chain of events. Once Mark went back in time and wrote on the walls, that writing was there to stay, for us to find. The deed was done . . . you might call it a time paradox. Yes, it's confusing. There's no way to prove any of this. However, I have a bigger, more immediate problem."

"Which is?" Eleanor asked.

"I don't think there's any way I can publicize my findings. If I do, we all know how the world will react. I'll stand accused of being party to a giant hoax. Every supermarket tabloid, even the mainstream press, will headline this thing and make us all into celebrities, charlatans, or worse. I think it might be best to preserve the evidence and consider Mark's experience to be our personal business."

"What happens to the site?" Helen asked.

"That's up to the National Park Service. This is federal property . . . my report can concentrate on the artifacts and leave out this business of time travel, and our, ah, circumstantial evidence. So, are we then agreed that we want no publicity on the wall writings, or what apparently happened to Mark Lewellyn?"

Eleanor nodded, silently. Then she looked through the lobby doorway toward the small part across the street from the Arlington Hotel.

"Professor, what's that big rock over there—the one those people are standing around? I get an odd feeling about that thing."

"That's called De Soto Rock, for the early Spanish explorer who's supposed to have come through here in the sixteenth century," the professor explained. "It's a big chunk of tufa, a rocklike material, and it must have fallen off the mountainside up near the hot springs centuries ago."

Eleanor held Mark's poster, and her eyes misted. "So Mark knew this place. He must have lived in this valley. I hope so. It would have been a beautiful place to live. I'm only sorry I wasn't with him."

She stopped suddenly. *You're lying, Eleanor,* she told herself. *You're no cavewoman type and never will be. Yes, you loved the man, and you'd like him back. But if he went to some awful ancient place, with all those hardships they must have faced, you want none of it. This, right here, is your century, lady. You like it just fine. You do what you want to do, and you're good at it. So, no time-travel fantasies for you, my girl.*

Feeling guilty, she added aloud, "Wherever he is, or was, I hope he made a good life for himself. What he wrote on the wall is correct. I've got to get on with my life." Then she added, wistfully; "But I do hope somebody looked after him. He was a sweet man but, well . . . not too practical . . . you know, just not a physical sort of guy."

At which point she studied Professor Hampton. His square chin, broad shoulders, those riveting gray eyes behind rimless glasses. Late forties, probably. Quite a hunk, she suddenly realized.

As if reading her mind, the big academic grunted and stretched, then looked at her. "Eleanor, I know you're exhausted. If you'd like, I would be pleased to take you to dinner, then you can probably get a room for the night here at the hotel."

He had been thinking that it would be a pleasant way to spend the next hour or two, talking about other things to this forceful, attractive woman. He had been a lonely man since his wife's death, and he rarely found the females around to be very stimulating. Eleanor, on the other hand, was like a sleek, tightly wound . . . umm, *Face it*, he told himself, *you'd like to take her to bed. Poor timing, though . . .*

Eleanor stood up. "I'll go check in, then take my overnight case to my room and freshen up. Yes, I'd like dinner. I'm hungry all of a sudden."

"Good, and over dinner I'll tell you about some other really fascinating things we found in the dig. Like, well . . . did Mark play golf, by any chance?"

Mark had been out at dawn, hunting with Um-moh and Foh-man and Mee-suh's son, Um-suh. The boy was showing promise with the bow. They returned at noon with a fine big buck, and for much of the day they'd been dressing the carcass, cutting up meat for those who needed it. They talked of going out again tomorrow, this time to the west, where the largest of the elk herds usually grazed. They would take a hunting party of six, Mark suggested. Hauling a mature elk back to the village, even in pieces, was a long, tough job. He had found that he had a taste for elk meat, and the antlers furnished a good supply of tools for the village's stone-knappers.

After a hot bath in the valley, Mark was relaxed as he climbed the vines to the shelter, ready for some sit-down conversation with Um-see. He'd heard several phrases this morning he wanted to ask about. A small surprise awaited him as he pulled up on the rock porch and drew aside the shelter's hide curtain.

Um-see looked up, startled. He had company. She was Mee-soon, the attractive little healing woman who administered to everyone's health. She and Um-see sat side by side at his fire circle, sipping thin soup. She smiled and looked down as Um-see coughed.

"Mark . . . ah, Mee-soon is here to treat my wound," he said, motioning to the livid scar down one side of his head. "We need more water," he added, handing Mark the water basket. "Also, see if you can find Seebo. Mee-soon says he left her shelter two days ago. He may be in his den, up the mountain . . ."

Mark nodded, trying not to smile too broadly, as he backed out, lowering the hide cover, trying to keep from chuckling too loud. *Well, that horny old bastard.* He laughed to himself. *He's got a lady friend and wants me gone. OK, buddy, I'll stay gone . . . if you'll return the favor sometime.*

He then turned and walked to the edge of the rock porch. He still couldn't get over this view of the distant falls. Then it struck him: What a magnificent golf shot this would be. You'd be able to see the ball at least two hundred yards down into the valley if you teed off right here. Crazy idea, and he grinned. But, well, if he got the time, he might make himself a sort of crude driver . . . no, he could never hit a driver.

Maybe a three iron . . . oops, no iron here . . . OK, a three wood, if he could find the materials. . . .

Mark pulled himself up to the shelter on the vines—easily now, he realized—and stretched, breathing deeply as he looked out across the valley. Wonderful. He felt great after that hot bath. This was a lovely time of year. Brisk air smelled of pine needles with a hint of woodsmoke from the village. He adjusted his new hip-length vest over his chest. Its smooth, cured inside felt soft against his skin. The outside still contained black hair of that great bear he and Um-see had killed. Village women had only finished it yesterday and, in the presence of Um-moh and his circle of friends, put it on Mark with great ceremony. He had been deeply touched and quickly used up all his thank-you words in gratitude.

Um-see came climbing up the vines from the trail below, and Mark saw he was pleased about something.

"The Elders have decided," he said. "Everyone can stay in the valley and live here. Foh-man can stay forever, the others, who were with the Bad Men, can stay one season . . . if all goes well, they can stay longer." He hesitated, smiling, drawing it out.

"You wish to stay?" he asked.

Mark laughed. Um-see was teasing him.

"Yes. Yes! You know I wish to!"

"Ho-kay. The Elders say you can stay, too."

Then Um-see's smile faded slightly.

"You wish to stay forever?"

Oops, thought Mark, *commitment time. Do I plan to stay here the rest of my life? A great place. But forever is a tough call.*

"Um," Mark mused, choosing his words with care, "stay . . . a long time." Then he grinned. "I make sure bears do not get Um-see."

For the first time Mark could remember, the older man threw back his head and laughed. "I will teach Mark," he chuckled, "not to use soft wood on fires." It was their running joke.

There was a long moment of silence between them. Both men were comfortable with silence. Um-see never spoke pointlessly, Mark had observed. This was a moment for introspection, and his mind wandered over the life he had made for himself. In the weeks since the Bad Men came and went, Mark had found himself accepted by the village families. He was one of the heroes of the battle, esteemed for his courage in helping to rid the valley of Kuh-moh. Then he was recognized as one of the families' hunters. Groups he hunted with rarely returned home without meat. What drew everyone to Mark also was his obvious determination to learn the village language. Everyone could tell from his questions, and his increasing use of small hand motions, that he wanted to know the tongue and speak it without error. He felt himself making complete sentences.

Rarely did he wear his white clothing, since Mark knew that only the same "hides" that other men wore would identify him as a villager. Um-see had used the sharp green knife to shave him recently, with fewer nicks this time, but now everyone was no longer concerned when his beard grew back, as black as ever.

Mark smiled as he recalled another event. Two nights ago Seebo had appeared at the shelter entrance, just at dark. The big animal stood looking in, and made no sound. Um-see grunted as he acknowledged the wolf-dog, while Mark remained silent.

Then Seebo walked inside with only a glance at the two men. He had lost weight, and the wound along his back still showed, raw and ugly. But he was steady on his feet, and made his way to the rear of the shelter, where his sleeping hides were still laid out.

Sniffing the skins, then circling them, Seebo settled down with his eyes looking toward the fire. His great tail looped around his head, and he began breathing heavily.

He was asleep.

Um-see smiled at Mark, who chuckled, silently. Seebo had accepted Mark, it appeared, and was back. Perhaps to stay.

There was, of course, a downside. Often at night, Mark lay awake, staring up at the rock walls, faintly lit by glowing fire embers. His former smooth, untroubled life filled his mind. His fine son—one that every man would be proud of—and his old comforts, luxuries . . . God, how he'd love to drive his Volvo again! He could almost taste a cold beer, and imagine himself slumped down in front of his big-screen TV set, watching the Cowboys play . . .

And Eleanor. Their past life together was like a dream. But Mark no longer worried about her. She'd manage her finances, make money, find another husband if she wanted one. A tough-minded, modern woman, and also—he reminded himself—a good mother to their son. Mark was glad now he'd written that extra message on the back wall of the shelter, although he didn't think anybody would ever find it. But . . . worth a try.

He had no choice since, indeed, there was no way back. No way home. He had to adapt to this new life . . . yet even if he had a choice, he'd be torn. Now he would not want to change this new man he'd become. He liked feeling strong and confident, enjoying the respect of those around him. Never had he felt more energetic . . . loving the smells of forest, clean air, the sparkling chill of cold mountain streams.

Mark glanced toward the village, where people moved about, busy with their daily chores. They might not have yet learned to plant crops, he mused, but they lived a vigorous, harmonious life, at peace with themselves, in tune with their environment. It was a beautiful but, at times, harsh environment, with danger present each day from predatory animals and few real cures for serious health problems. Little wonder they had a short life expectancy.

However, as Mark had learned the language, he found these were not the simple savages he'd first assumed. Their language was full of nuances. They were intelligent people, with amazing memories, and they lived by a strong "Do-unto-others" moral code that he found admirable. Further, Mark knew they had a system of spiritual values, although he didn't yet know the language well enough to understand their relationship to their "Spirits." He smiled then, recalling that the villagers also had a lively sense of humor. The men Mark saw daily had begun to joke with him about small things, and he became the butt of some ribbing when they found he did not take offense.

In turn, he kidded them about being "strange" because they had no hair on their faces. Um-moh and another hunter had found this so hilarious they had almost fallen down laughing. Mark smiled to himself at the memory. These were good guys to be with, once you knew them . . . and they knew *you*.

Um-see sighed audibly. He, too, had been thinking. He knew how good his life was now that he had this strange but agreeable young man to share his shelter. It was better than before. He was no longer lonely and saw that his new en-thusiasm for living had to do with Mark. Um-see could tell this man had power in his mind, knew many things he could not explain. He liked helping Mark to become part of the valley's life, and he was proud of the younger man's skills and family acceptance. Mark had filled some of the bad space in his life since his son had died.

Then Um-see was surprised and irritated to find moisture in his eyes. *You're getting like an old woman,* he told himself, and cleared his throat noisily.

"Come," he said, getting up. "There is work to be done. We need firewood, and water. We must also search the brush piles . . . I promised my new grandson to help find the right limb for a bow."

He flipped rope and basket to Mark, picked up his own, and moved toward the vines. Seebo, he noted, waited down on the trail below, ready to accompany them.

As Mark grabbed the vines he looked down and froze in surprise. Seebo was looking up. The big wolf-dog had gained weight and seemed on the mend. But Mark could hardly believe it when he noticed his tail. Slowly, it moved back and forth.

Seebo was wagging his tail. Perhaps for the first time in his life. Mark laughed aloud and slid down. *Who knows?* Someday, it came to him, he might even try to pet the big animal. Very, very carefully.

Mark knew that night was a special evening when two things happened. First, Um-see entered the shelter to tell him that Mee-suh was cooking dinner for Mark at her shelter—roasting a fresh-killed turkey one of her neighbors had given her. She would expect Mark before sunset.

Then, shortly thereafter, Um-see's two "new" grandchildren came climbing up to their shelter, laughing and calling out. It turned out they were spending the night with their grandfather at the shelter, and he would cook their dinner, and . . . Mark was surprised at the unspoken implication that he, Mark, would be gone until tomorrow. He would? *Ah*, he thought . . . *and I'm to sleep, where? Oh, at* her *shelter? Well, what* do *you know!*

He almost ran across the valley to take a hot bath, then back up to the shelter to put on his loose-fitting deer-hide trousers and his handsome bearskin jacket. His hair had grown long, and he tied it behind his head with a strip of thin hide, then he put on the comfortable shoes Um-see had made him. Mark also had a deerskin scabbard for the long, green knife, which he wore at his waist.

Well before sunset he was striding up the valley, amused to notice as he left that Um-see was drawing intersecting lines on the shelter floor. Mark had collected over a dozen small rocks, half white, half black . . . and he had taught Um-see to play checkers. For kings Mark had scratched an X on one side of each rock, so it could simply be turned over. Um-see loved it, and now his grandchildren would learn this new game from another time and place.

Tonight Mark carried no bow, but he did have a shoulder

bag. Inside were two presents for Mee-suh, and perhaps she would be impressed.

One was a long stout reed, to which Mark had attached a flat, thinned-down square of wood, sharp along the forward surface. It was a wooden spatula, and it worked. Mark had fried some pigeon eggs only yesterday after building a fire under a thin slab of novaculite. When the animal grease on top was popping hot, he'd cracked and fried the eggs, and the spatula turned them perfectly. Soon he'd show Mee-suh how to make an egg omelet. Or maybe an egg-and-venison omelet.

His other present to her was a pair of wooden forks, that had taken hours of work to carve from oak. Each had a long handle and two tines that came to sharp points. It would seem strange to her, but when she got used to it . . . oops. Then he realized. He'd have to make some wooden plates; otherwise, there'd be nothing for the forks to hold the meat *against* while he cut it. Damn. He should have thought of that. Well, he'd get around to it.

As he started up through the shelters of the village, several of his hunting buddies waved to him.

"Mark! Ho-kay," one friend called out. "Ho-kay," Mark laughed, and waved back. Then up the pathway, he saw Mee-suh. She stood quietly before her new shelter, hands folded before her, the cookfire giving off a tiny trickle of smoke, and—as Mark drew near—wonderful smells.

He stopped for a moment, to preserve this picture in his memory. He knew now that he loved this woman, and as time had passed Mark realized that she returned his affection. But he had dared make no move toward Mee-suh, to show his love, fearful of upsetting any village courtship rules, about which he still knew little.

Tonight, as he slowly approached her, Mee-suh was at peace with herself. She felt sure, somehow, that this man was to be hers. She wore a knee-length deerskin garment with a narrow belt around her waist. There was no avoiding the swell of her hips, the well-tapered legs, tiny ankles, the full bosom. Her dark hair hung at her shoulders. The setting sun reflected highlights in her eyes.

Then she smiled softly and held out her hand in greeting. Mark took it, then saw the care with which she had laid out clean sit-down mats around the cook fire, where two pots of warming food were suspended. The smells were mouthwatering.

This was more than just a dinner, Mark knew. It was an invitation to a whole new life. It offered him love and respect . . . and a settled future, like these other men here. He would have real responsibilities to help feed, clothe, and protect human beings, the hard and primitive life of a hunter, with no Social Security at the end of it.

He looked long and hungrily at Mee-suh's beauty, the open flap of her shelter, where, inside, piles of soft skins had been spread out invitingly. Then he glanced down to the valley and the beauty of those waterfalls, the steaming hot ponds. He smiled and nodded slightly. His spending the night here was no accident. It had been arranged by people who cared for him, loved him, and wanted him to settle here as a member of these families. He had the feeling he was about to become "engaged," or something. Whatever it was, he was willing, even eager, for it to happen.

So, he decided, *it looks like I'm home.* He seated himself before the fire, and Mee-suh settled down beside him. *Who knows,* Mark thought, *maybe this is what they mean by . . . forever?*

ACKNOWLEDGMENTS

Long before organized Indian tribes or "nations" were formed, Woodland Era prehistoric communities (1000 B.C.– 700 A.D.) in the southwest were composed of families, large and small, working hard simply to survive. Increasingly, archaeologists are learning more about them, as "digs" proceed in places like Arkansas's Ouachita Mountains. My book's characters of eighteen centuries ago lived near the end of the hunter-gatherer period. They had begun to plant small gardens. They were skilled hunters. They ate what nature provided, and they ate well. Little is known of their language or culture but what remains is ample to give an author's imagination free rein. Helping me imagine them was Dr. Ann Early of Arkadelphia, Arkansas, a survey archaeologist with the University of Arkansas. She knows they were not prehistoric hillbillies but intelligent people with a language fully as complex as our own. I'm indebted to her for her patient, insightful reading of the manuscript's drafts, and for her thoughtful suggestions.

Pancho Rowe and Wayma Rowe of Hot Springs aided immeasurably in the long process of plotting, character development, and manuscript editing. Their encouragement and constructive criticism constantly urged me forward. It was Pancho who personally led me to the Balanced Rock quarry where Um-see's people shaped their stone for tools and weapons, scarcely an hour's hike from downtown Hot Springs. Incredibly, the site looks as though the Indians have just walked away, despite the passage of centuries. Chipped stone is everywhere.

Mark Blaeuer, anthropologist and Park Ranger with Hot Springs National Park, aided substantially with his on-the-ground explanation (during a freezing winter day) of how the valley's quarter mile of hot-water falls could have looked as it cascaded into what logically became known as the "valley of the vapors." Mark, too, read my manuscripts with an informed eye and a constructive pen.

Tom Free, botanist with the Garland Park Forest Preserve near Dallas, introduced me to a world that no longer exists: a carefully managed wilderness preserve that reveals the kind of virgin forest our hero Mark woke up to when he suddenly disappeared from his backyard. This spot may be unique in the United States. Another scientist most generous in answering questions about prehistoric wildlife in Texas was Dr. D. Gentry Steele, physical anthropologist and zooarchaeologist at Texas A&M University. I should note here that I alone am responsible for the interpretations I drew from these well-informed sources.

And of course my family provided the practical support every author knows and values. My wife, son, daughter, and granddaughter gave priceless counsel in navigating that strange realm where some ideas work and some don't. Most helpful too were Virginia Amos, Ann Beck, John Turner, and Billie Funderburke. They asked me questions I'd never otherwise have been asked—often forcing me back to the typewriter at 4 A.M. So did my editor, Joe Veltre, a constructive voice for fewer words and clearer reading. Then there's Henry Morrison, my literary agent. My obligation to Henry is simply put: Without his conviction, this book might never have seen the light of print.

Robert Steele Gray
Houston, November 1998

TURN THE PAGE
FOR AN EXCERPT
FROM COLIN HARRISON'S
EXCITING NEW NOVEL,
AFTERBURN—

AVAILABLE SOON IN HARDCOVER
FROM FARRAR, STRAUS & GIROUX . . .

CHINA CLUB, HONG KONG

SEPTEMBER 7, 1999

He would survive. Yes, Charlie promised himself, he'd survive *this*, too—his ninth formal Chinese banquet in as many evenings, yet another bowl of shark-fin soup being passed to him by the endless waiters in red uniforms, who stood obsequiously against the silk wallpaper pretending not to hear the self-satisfied ravings of those they served. Except for his fellow *gweilo*—British Petroleum's Asia man, a mischievous German from Lufthansa, and two young American executives from Kodak and Citigroup—the other dozen men at the huge mahogany table were all Chinese. Mostly in their fifties, the men represented the big corporate players—Bank of Asia, Hong Kong Telecom, China Motors—and each, Charlie noted, had arrived at the age of cleverness. Of course, at fifty-eight he himself was old enough that no one should be able to guess what he was thinking unless he wanted them to, even Ellie. In his call to her that morning—it being evening in New York City—he'd tried not to sound too worried about their daughter Julia. "It's all going to be *fine*, sweetie," he'd promised, gazing out at the choppy haze of Hong Kong's harbor, where the heavy traffic of tankers and freighters pressed China's claim—everything from photocopiers to baseball caps flowing out into the world, everything from oil refineries to contact lenses flowing in. "She'll get pregnant, I'm sure," he'd told Ellie. But he wasn't sure. No, not at all. In fact, it looked as if it was going to be easier for him to

build his electronics factory in Shanghai than for his daughter
to hatch a baby.

"We gather in friendship," announced the Chinese host,
Mr. Ming, the vice-chairman of the Bank of Asia. Having
agreed to lend Charlie fifty-two million U.S. dollars to build
his Shanghai factory, Mr. Ming in no way could be described
as a friend; the relationship was one of overlord and inden-
tured. But Charlie smiled along with the others as the banker
stood and presented in high British English an analysis of
southeastern China's economy that was so shallow, optimis-
tic, and full of euphemism that no one, especially the central
ministries in Beijing, might object. The Chinese executives
nodded politely as Mr. Ming spoke, touching their napkins
to their lips, smiling vaguely. Of course, they nursed secret
worries—worries that corresponded to whether they were en-
trepreneurs (who had built shipping lines or real-estate em-
pires or garment factories) or the managers of institutional
power (who controlled billions of dollars not their own). And
yet, Charlie decided, the men were finally more like one
another than unlike; each long ago had learned to sell high
(1997) and buy low (1998), and had passed the threshold of
unspendable wealth, such riches conforming them in their
behaviors; each owned more houses or paintings or Rolls-
Royces than could be admired or used at once. Each played
golf or tennis passably well; each possessed a forty-million-
dollar yacht, or a forty-million-dollar home atop Victoria's
Peak, or a forty-million-dollar wife. Each had a slender young
Filipino or Russian or Czech mistress tucked away in one of
Hong Kong's luxury apartment buildings—licking her lips if
requested—or was betting against the Hong Kong dollar
while insisting on its firmness—any of the costly mischief
in which rich men indulge.

The men at the table, in fact, as much as any men, sat as
money incarnate, particularly the American dollar, the euro,
and the Japanese yen—all simultaneously, and all hedged
against fluctuations of the others. But although the men were
money, money was not them; money assumed any shape or

color or politics, it could be fire or stone or dream, it could summon armies or bind atoms, and, indifferent to the sufferings of the mortal soul, it could leave or arrive at any time. And on this exact night, Charlie thought, setting his ivory chopsticks neatly upon the lacquered plate, he could see that although money had assumed the shapes of the men in the room, it existed in differing densities and volumes and brightnesses. Whereas Charlie was a man of perhaps thirty or thirty-three million dollars of wealth, that sum amounted to shoe-shine change in the present company. No, sir, money, in *that* room, in *that* moment, was understood as inconsequential in sums less than one hundred million dollars, and of political importance only when five times more. Money, in fact, found its greatest compression and gravity in the form of the tiny man sitting silently across from Charlie—Sir Henry Lai, the Oxford-educated Chinese gambling mogul, owner of a fleet of jet-foil ferries, a dozen hotels, and most of the casinos of Macao and Vietnam. Worth billions—and billions more.

But, Charlie wondered, perhaps he was wrong. He could think of one shape that money had not *yet* assumed, although quite a bit of it had been spent, perhaps a hundred thousand dollars in all. Money animated the dapper Chinese businessman across from him, but could it arrive in the world as Charlie's own grandchild? This was the question he feared most, this was the question that had eaten at him and at Ellie for years now, and which would soon be answered: In a few hours, Julia would tell them once and forever if she was capable of having a baby.

She had suffered through cycle upon cycle of disappointment—hundreds of shots of fertility drugs followed by the needle-recovery of the eggs, the inspection of the eggs, the selection of the eggs, the insemination of the eggs, the implantation of the eggs, the anticipation of the eggs. She'd been trying for seven years. Now Julia, a woman of only thirty-five, a little gray already salting her hair, was due to get the final word. At 11:00 a.m. Manhattan time, she'd sit in her law office and be told the results of this, the last in-vitro attempt. Her *ninth*. Three more than the doctor pre-ferred to do. Seven more than the insurance company would pay for. Good news would be that one of the reinserted fer-tilized eggs had decided to cling to the wall of Julia's uterus. Bad news: There was no chance of conception; egg donor-ship or adoption must now be considered. And if *that* was the news, well then, that was really goddamn something. It would mean not just that his only daughter was heartbroken, but that, genetically speaking, he, Charlie Ravich, was fin-ished, that his own fishy little spermatozoa—one of which, wiggling into Ellie's egg a generation prior, had become his daughter—had run aground, that he'd come to the end of the line; that, in a sense, he was already dead.

And now, as if mocking his very thoughts, came the fish, twenty pounds of it, head still on, its eyes cooked out and replaced with flowered radishes, its mouth agape in macabre broiled amusement. Charlie looked at his plate. He always lost weight in China, undone by the soy and oils and crusted skin of birds, the rich liverish stink of turtle meat. All that duck tongue and pig ear and fish lip. Expensive as hell, every meal. And carrying with it the odor of doom.

Then the conversation turned, as it also did so often in Shanghai and Beijing, to the question of America's mistreat-ment of the Chinese. "What I do not understand are the American senators," Sir Henry Lai was saying in his softly refined voice. "They say they *understand* that we only want for China to be China." Every syllable was flawless English, but of course Lai also spoke Mandarin and Cantonese. Sir Henry Lai was reported to be in serious talks with Gaming Technologies, the huge American gambling and hotel con-glomerate that clutched big pieces of Las Vegas, the Missis-sippi casino towns, and Atlantic City. Did Sir Henry know when China would allow Western-style casinos to be built within its borders? Certainly he knew the right officials in Beijing, and perhaps this was reason enough that GT's stock price had ballooned up seventy percent in the last three months as Sir Henry's interest in the company had become known. Lai smiled benignly. Then frowned. "These senators say that all they want is for international trade to progress without interruption, and then they go back to Congress and raise their fists and call China all kinds of names. Is this not true?"

The others nodded sagely, apparently giving consideration, but not ignoring whatever delicacy remained pinched in their chopsticks.

"Wait, I have an answer to that," announced the young fellow from Citigroup. "Mr. Lai, I trust we may speak frankly here. You need to remember that the American senators are full of—excuse my language—full of shit. When they're standing up on the Senate floor saying all of this stuff, this means nothing, *absolutely* nothing!"

"Ah, this is very difficult for the Chinese people to understand." Sir Henry scowled. "In China we believe our leaders. So we become scared when we see American senators complaining about China."

"You're being coy with us, Mr. Lai," interrupted Charlie, looking up with a smile, "for we—or some of us—know that you have visited the United States dozens of times and have met many U.S. senators personally." Not to mention a few Third World dictators. He paused, while amusement passed into Lai's dark eyes. "Nonetheless," Charlie continued, looking about the table, "for the others who have not enjoyed Mr. Lai's deep friendships with American politicians, I would have to say my colleague here is right. The speeches in the American Senate are pure grandstanding. They're made for the American public—".

"The *bloodthirsty* American public, you mean!" interrupted the Citigroup man, who, Charlie suddenly understood, had drunk too much. "Those old guys up there know most voters can't find China on a globe. That's no joke. It's shocking, the American ignorance of China."

"We shall have to educate your people," Sir Henry Lai offered diplomatically, apparently not wishing the stridency of the conversation to continue. He gave a polite, cold-blooded laugh.

"But it is, yes, my understanding that the Americans could sink the Chinese Navy in several days?" barked the German from Lufthansa.

"That may be true," answered Charlie, "but sooner or later the American people are going to recognize the hemispheric primacy of China, that—"

"Wait, wait!" Lai interrupted good-naturedly. "You agree with our German friend about the Chinese Navy?"

The question was a direct appeal to the nationalism of the other Chinese around the table.

"Can the U.S. Air Force destroy the Chinese Navy in a matter of days?" repeated Charlie. "Yes. Absolutely yes."

Sir Henry Lai smiled. "You are knowledgeable about these topics, Mr."—he glanced down at the business cards arrayed in front of his plate—"Mr. Ravich. Of the Teknetrix Corporation, I see. What do you know about war, Mr. Ravich?" he asked. "Please, tell me. I am curious."

The Chinese billionaire stared at him with eyebrows lifted, face a smug, florid mask, and if Charlie had been younger or genuinely insulted, he might have recalled aloud his war years before becoming a businessman, but he understood that generally it was to one's advantage not to appear to have an advantage. And anyway, the conversation was merely a form of sport: Lai didn't give a good goddamn about the Chinese Navy, which he probably despised; what he cared about was whether or not he should soon spend eight hundred million dollars on GT stock—play the corporation that played the players.

But Lai pressed. "What do you know about this?"

"Just what I read in the papers," Charlie replied with humility.

"See? There! I tell you!" Lai eased back in his silk suit, running a fat little palm over his thinning hair. "This is a very dangerous problem, my friends. People say many things

about China and America, but they have no direct knowledge, no real—"

Mercifully, the boys in red uniforms and brass buttons
began setting down spoons and bringing around coffee.
Charlie excused himself and headed for the gentlemen's restroom. Please, God, he thought, it's a small favor, really. One
egg clinging to a warm pink wall. He and Ellie should have
had another child, should have at least tried, after Ben. Ellie
had been forty-two. Too much grief at the time, too late now.

In the men's room, a sarcophagus of black and silver marble, he nodded at the wizened Chinese attendant, who stood
up with alert servility. Charlie chose the second stall and
locked the heavy marble door behind him. The door and
walls extended in smooth veined slabs from the floor to
within a foot of the ceiling. The photo-electric eye over the
toilet sensed his movement and the bowl flushed prema-
turely. He was developing an old man's interest in his bowels. He shat then, with the private pleasure of it. He was
starting to smell Chinese to himself. Happened on every trip
to the East.

And then, as he finished, he heard the old attendant greeting another man in Cantonese.

"Evening, sir."

"Yes."

The stall door next to Charlie's opened, shut, was locked.
The man was breathing as if he had hurried. Then came some
loud coughing, an oddly tiny splash, and the muffled silky
sound of the man slumping heavily against the wall he shared
with Charlie.

"Sir?" The attendant knocked on Charlie's door. "You
open door?"

Charlie buckled his pants and slid the lock free. The old
man's face loomed close, eyes large, breath stinking.

"Not me!" Charlie said. "The next one!"

"No have key! Climb!" The old attendant pushed past
Charlie, stepped up on the toilet seat, and stretched high
against the glassy marble. His bony hands pawed the stone

uselessly. Now the man in the adjacent stall was moaning in Chinese, begging for help. Charlie pulled the attendant down and stood on the toilet seat himself. With his arms out-stretched he could reach the top of the wall, and he sucked in a breath and hoisted himself. Grimacing, he pulled himself up high enough so that his nose touched the top edge of the wall. But before being able to look over, he fell back.

"Go!" he ordered the attendant. "Get help, get a key!"

The man in the stall groaned, his respiration a song of pain. Charlie stepped up on the seat again, this time jumping exactly at the moment he pulled with his arms, and then *yes*, he was up, right up there, hooking one leg over the wall, his head just high enough to peer down and see Sir Henry Lai slumped on the floor, his face a rictus of purpled flesh, his pants around his ankles, a piss stain spreading across his silk boxers. His hands clutched weakly at his tie, the veins of his neck swollen like blue pencils. His eyes, not squeezed shut but open, stared up at the underside of the spotless toilet bowl, into which, Charlie could see from above, a small sil-ver pillbox had fallen, top open, the white pills inside of it scattered and sunk and melting away.

"Hang on," breathed Charlie. "They're coming. Hang on." He tried to pull himself through the opening between the wall and ceiling, but it was no good; he could get his head through but not his shoulders or torso. Now Sir Henry Lai coughed rhythmically, as if uttering some last strange code—"Haa-cah . . . Haaa! Haaa!"—and convulsed, his eyes peering in pained wonderment straight into Charlie's, then widening as his mouth filled with a reddish soup of undigested shrimp and pigeon and turtle that surged up over his lips and ran down both of his cheeks before draining back into his wind-pipe. He was too far gone to cough the vomit out of his lungs, and the tension in his hands eased—he was dying of a heart attack and asphyxiation at the same moment.

The attendant hurried back in with Sir Henry's bodyguard. They pounded on the stall door with something, cracking the marble. The beautiful veined stone broke away in pieces, some falling on Sir Henry Lai's shoes. Charlie looked back at his face. Henry Lai was dead.

The men stepped into the stall and Charlie knew he was of no further use. He dropped back to the floor, picked up his jacket, and walked out of the men's restroom, expecting a commotion outside. A waiter sailed past; the assembled businessmen didn't know what had happened.

Mr. Ming watched him enter.

"I must leave you," Charlie said graciously. "I'm very sorry. My daughter is due to call me tonight with important news."

"Good news, I trust."

The only news bankers liked. "Perhaps. She's going to tell me if she is pregnant."

"I hope you are blessed." Mr. Ming smiled, teeth white as Ellie's estrogen pills.

Charlie nodded warmly. "We're going to build a terrific factory, too. Should be on-line by the end of the year."

"We are scheduled for lunch in about two weeks in New York?"

"Absolutely," said Charlie. Every minute now was important.

Mr. Ming bent closer, his voice softening. "And you will tell me then about the quad-port transformer you are developing?"

His secret new datacom switch, which would smoke the competition? No. "Yes." Charlie smiled. "Sure deal."

"Excellent," pronounced Mr. Ming. "Have a good flight."

The stairs to the lobby spiraled along backlit cabinets of jade dragons and coral boats and who cared what else. Don't run, Charlie told himself, don't appear to be in a hurry. In London, seven hours behind Hong Kong, the stock market was still open. He pointed to his coat for the attendant then nodded at the first taxi waiting outside.

"FCC," he told the driver.

"Foreign Correspondents' Club?"

"Right away."

It was the only place open at night in Hong Kong where he knew he could get access to a Bloomberg box—that magical electronic screen that displayed every stock and bond price in every market around the globe. He pulled out his cell phone and called his broker in London.

"Jane, this is Charlie Ravich," he said when she answered. "I want to set up a huge put play. Drop everything."

"This is not like you."

"This is not like anything. Sell all my Microsoft now at the market price, sell all the Ford, the Merck, all the Lucent. Market orders all of them. Please, right now, before London closes."

"All right now, for the tape, you are requesting we sell eight thousand shares of—"

"Yes, yes, I agree," he blurted.

Jane was off the line, getting another broker to carry out the orders. "Zoom-de-doom," she said when she returned. "Let it rip."

"This is going to add up to about one-point-oh-seven million," he said. "I'm buying puts on Gaming Technologies, the gambling company. It's American but trades in London."

"Yes." Now her voice held interest. "*Yes*."

"How many puts of GT can I buy with that?"

She was shouting orders to her clerks. "Wait . . ." she said. "Yes? Very good. I have your account on my screen . . ." He heard keys clicking. "We have . . . one million seventy thousand, U.S., plus change. Now then, Gaming Technologies is selling at sixty-six even a share—"

"How many puts can I buy with one-point-oh-seven?"

"Oh, I would say a huge number, Charlie."

"How many?"

"About . . . one-point-six million shares."

"That's huge."

"You want to protect that bet?" she asked.

"No."

"If you say so."

"Buy the puts, Jane."

"I am, Charlie, *please*. The price is stable. Yes, take this one . . ." she was saying to a clerk. "Give me puts on GT at market, immediately. Yes. One-point-six million at the money. *Yes*. At the money." The line was silent a moment. "You sure, Charlie?"

"This is a bullet to the moon, Jane."

"Biggest bet of your life, Charlie?"

"Oh, Jane, not even close."

Outside his cab a silky red Rolls glided past. "Got it?" he asked.

"Not quite. You going to tell me the play, Charlie?"

"When it goes through, Jane."

"We'll get the order back in a minute or two."

Die on the shitter, Charlie thought. Could happen to any-one. Happened to Elvis Presley, matter of fact.

"Charlie?"

"Yes."

"We have your puts. One-point-six million, GT, at the price of sixty-six." He heard the keys clicking.

"*Now* tell me?" Jane pleaded.

"I will," Charlie said. "Just give me the confirmation for the tape." ·

While she repeated the price and the volume of the order, he looked out the window to see how close the taxi was to the FCC. He'd first visited the club in 1970, when it was full of drunken television and newspaper journalists, CIA people, Army intelligence, retired British admirals who had gone na-tive, and crazy Texans provisioning the war; since then, the rest of Hong Kong had been built up and torn down and built up all over again, but the FCC still stood, tucked away on a side street.

"I just want to get my times right," Charlie told Jane when she was done. "It's now a few minutes after 9:00 p.m. on Tuesday in Hong Kong. What time are you in London?"

"Just after 2:00 p.m."

"London markets are open about an hour more?"

"Yes," Jane said.

"New York starts trading in half an hour."

"Yes."

"I need you to stay in your office and handle New York for me."

She sighed. "I'm due to pick up my son from school."

"Need a car, a new car?"

"Everybody needs a new car."

"Just stay there a few more hours, Jane. You can pick out a Mercedes tomorrow morning and charge it to my account."

"You're a charmer, Charlie."

"I'm serious. Charge my account."

"Okay, will you *please* tell me?"

Of course he would, but because he needed to get the news moving. "Sir Henry Lai just died. Maybe fifteen minutes ago."

"Sir Henry Lai . . ."

"The Macao gambling billionaire who was in deep talks with GT—"

"Yes! Yes!" Jane cried. "Are you sure?"

"Yes."

"It's not just a rumor?"

"Jane, you don't trust old Charlie Ravich?"

"It's dropping! Oh! Down to sixty-four," she cried. "There it goes! There go ninety thousand shares! Somebody else got the word out! Sixty-three and a—Charlie, oh Jesus, you beat it by maybe a minute."

He told her he'd call again shortly and stepped out of the cab into the club, a place so informal that the clerk just gave him a nod; people strode in all day long to have drinks in the main bar. Inside sat several dozen men and women drinking and smoking, many of them American and British journalists, others small-time local businessmen who long ago had slid into alcoholism, burned out, boiled over, or given up.

He ordered a whiskey and sat down in front of the Bloomberg box, fiddling with it until he found the correct menu for real-time London equities. He was up millions and the New

York Stock Exchange had not even opened yet. Ha! The big American shareholders of GT, or, more particularly, their analysts and advisers and market watchers, most of them punks in their thirties, were still tying their shoes and kissing the mirror and soon—very soon!—they'd be saying hello to the receptionist sitting down at their screens. Minutes away! When they found out that Sir Henry Lai had died in the China Club in Hong Kong at 8:45 p.m. Hong Kong time, they would assume, Charlie hoped, that because Lai ran an Asian-style, family-owned corporation, and because as its patriarch he dominated its governance, any possible deal with GT was off, indefinitely. They would then reconsider the price of GT, still absurdly stratospheric, and dump it fast. Maybe. He ordered another drink, then called Jane.

"GT is down five points," she told him. "New York is about to open."

"But I don't see *panic* yet. Where's the volume selling?"

"You're not going to see it here, not with New York opening. I'll be sitting right here."

"Excellent, Jane. Thank you."

"Not at all. Call me when you're ready to close it out."

He hung up, looked into the screen. The real-time price of GT was hovering at fifty-nine dollars a share. No notice had moved over the information services yet. Not Bloomberg, not Reuters.

He went back to the bar, pushed his way past a couple of journalists.

"Another?" the bartender asked.

"Yes, sir. A double," he answered loudly. "I just got very bad news."

"Sorry to hear that." The bartender did not look up.

"Yes." Charlie nodded solemnly. "Sir Henry Lai died tonight, heart attack at the China Club. A terrible thing." He slid one hundred Hong Kong dollars across the bar. Several of the journalists peered at him.

"Pardon me," asked one, a tall Englishman with a riot of red hair. "Did I hear you say Sir Henry Lai has *died*?"

Charlie nodded. "Not an hour ago. I just happened to be standing there, at the China Club." He tasted his drink. "Please excuse me."

He returned to the Bloomberg screen. The Englishman, he noticed, had slipped away to a pay phone in the corner. The New York Stock Exchange, casino to the world, had been open a minute. He waited. Three, four, five minutes. And then, finally, came what he'd been waiting for, Sir Henry Lai's epitaph: GT's price began shrinking as its volume exploded—half a million shares, price fifty-eight, fifty-six, two million shares, fifty-five and a half. He watched. Four million shares now. The stock would bottom and bounce. He'd wait until the volume slowed. At fifty-five and a quarter he pulled his phone out of his pocket and called Jane. At fifty-five and seven-eighths he bought back the shares he'd sold at sixty-six, for a profit of a bit more than ten dollars a share. Major money. Sixteen million before taxes. Big money. Real money. Elvis money.

It was almost eleven when he arrived back at his hotel. The Sikh doorman, a vestige from the days of the British Empire, nodded a greeting. Inside the immense lobby a piano player pushed along a little tune that made Charlie feel mournful, and he sat down in one of the deep chairs that faced the harbor. So much ship traffic, hundreds of barges and freighters and, farther out, the supertankers. To the east sprawled the new airport—they had filled in the ocean there, hiring half of all the world's deep-water dredging equipment to do it. History in all this. He was looking at ships moving across the dark waters, but he might as well be looking at the twenty-first century itself, looking at his own countrymen who could not find factory jobs. The poor fucks had no idea what was coming at them, not a clue. China was a juggernaut, an immense, seething mass. It was building aircraft carriers, it was buying Taiwan. It shrugged off turmoil in Western stock markets. Currency fluctuations, inflation, deflation, volatility—none of these things compared to the fact

that China had eight hundred and fifty million people under
the age of thirty-five. They wanted everything Americans
now took for granted, including the right to piss on the shoes
of any other country in the world.

But ha! There might be some consolation! He pushed
back in the seat, slipped on his half-frame glasses, and did
the math on a hotel napkin. After commissions and taxes,
his evening's activities had netted him close to eight million
dollars—a sum grotesque not so much for its size but for the
speed and ease with which he had seized it—two phone
calls!—and, most of all, for its mockery of human toil. Well,
it was a grotesque world now. He'd done nothing but understand what the theorists called a market inefficiency and
what everyone else knew as inside information. If he was a
ghoul, wrenching dollars from Sir Henry Lai's vomit-filled
mouth, then at least the money would go to good use. He'd
put all of it in a bypass trust for Julia's child. The funds
could pay for clothes and school and pediatricians' bills and
whatever else. It could pay for a *life*. He remembered his
father buying used car tires from the garage of the Minnesota
Highway Patrol for a dollar-fifty. No such thing as steel-
belted radials in 1956. You cross borders of time, and if people
don't come with you, you lose them and they you. Now it was
an age when a fifty-eight-year-old American executive could
net eight million bucks by watching a man choke to death. His
father would never have understood it, and he suspected that
Ellie couldn't, either. Not really. There was something in her
head lately. Maybe it was because of Julia, but maybe not. She
bought expensive vegetables she let rot in the refrigerator, she
took Charlie's blood-pressure pills by mistake, she left the
phone off the hook. He wanted to be patient with her but could
not. She drove him nuts.

He sat in the hotel lobby for an hour more, reading every
article in the *International Herald Tribune*. Finally, at midnight, he decided not to wait for Julia's call and pulled his
phone from his pocket and dialed her Manhattan office.

"Tell me, sweetie," he said once he got past the secretary.

"Oh, Daddy . . ."

"Yes?"

A pause. And then she cried.

"Okay, now," he breathed, closing his eyes. "Okay."

She gathered herself. "All right. I'm fine. It's okay. You don't have to have children to have a fulfilling life. I can handle this."

"Tell me what they said."

"They said I'll probably never have my own children, they think the odds are—all I know is that I'll never hold my *own* baby, never, just something I'll never, ever do."

"Oh, sweetie."

"We really thought it was going to work. You know? I've had a lot of faith with this thing. They have these new egg-handling techniques, makes them glue to the walls of the uterus."

They were both silent a moment.

"I mean, you kind of expect that *technology* will work," Julia went on, her voice thoughtful. "They can clone human beings—they can do all of these things and they can't—" She stopped.

The day had piled up on him, and he was trying to remember all that Julia had explained to him about eggs and tubes and hormone levels. "Sweetie," he tried, "the problem is not exactly the eggs?"

"My eggs are pretty lousy, *also*. You're wondering if we could put *my* egg in another woman, right?"

"No, not—well, maybe yes," he sighed.

"They don't think it would work. The eggs aren't that viable."

"And your tubes—"

She gave a bitter laugh. "I'm *barren*, Daddy. I can't make good eggs, and I can't hatch eggs, mine or anyone else's."

He watched the lights of a tanker slide along the oily water outside. "I know it's too early to start discussing adoption, but—"

"He doesn't want to do it. At least he says he won't," she sobbed.

"Wait, sweetie," Charlie responded, hearing her despair, "Brian is just— Adopting a child is—"

"No, no, *no*, Daddy, Brian doesn't *want* a little Guatemalan baby or a Lithuanian baby or anybody else's baby but his own. It's about his own goddamn *penis*. If it doesn't come out of *his* penis, then it's no good."

Her husband's view made sense to him, but he couldn't say that now. "Julia, I'm sure Brian—"

"I *would* have adopted a little baby a year ago, two years ago! But I put up with all this shit, all these hormones and needles in my butt and doctors pushing things up me, *for him*. And now those *years* are— Oh, I'm sorry, Daddy, I have a client. I'll talk to you when you come back. I'm very— I have a lot of calls here. Bye."

He listened to the satellite crackle in the phone, then the announcement in Chinese to hang up. His flight was at eight the next morning, New York seventeen hours away, and as always, he wanted to get home, and yet didn't, for as soon as he arrived, he would miss China. The place got to him, like a recurrent dream, or a fever—forced possibilities into his mind, whispered ideas he didn't want to hear. Like the eight million. It was perfectly legal yet also a kind of contraband. If he wanted, Ellie would never see the money; she had long since ceased to be interested in his financial gamesmanship, so long as there was enough money for Belgian chocolates for the elevator man at Christmas, fresh flowers twice a week, and the farmhouse in Tuscany. But like a flash of unexpected lightning, the new money illuminated certain questions begging for years at the edge of his consciousness. He had been rich for a long time, but now he was rich enough to fuck with fate. Had he been waiting for this moment? Yes, waiting until he knew about Julia, waiting until he was certain.

He called Martha Wainwright, his personal lawyer. "Martha, I've finally decided to do it," he said when she answered.

"Oh, Christ, Charlie, don't tell me that."

"Yes. Fact, I just made a little extra money in a stock deal. Makes the whole thing that much easier."

"Don't do it, Charlie."

"I just got the word from my daughter, Martha. If she could have children, it would be a different story."

"This is bullshit, Charlie. Male bullshit."

"Is that your legal opinion or your political one?"

"I'm going to argue with you when you get back," she warned.

"Fine—I expect that. For now, please just put the ad in the magazines and get all the documents ready."

"I think you are a complete jerk for doing this."

"We understand things differently, Martha."

"Yes, because *you* are addicted to testosterone."

"Most men are, Martha. That's what makes us such assholes."

"You having erection problems, Charlie? Is *that* what this is about?"

"You got the wrong guy, Martha. My dick is like an old dog."

"How's that? Sleeps all the time?"

"Slow but dependable," he lied. "Comes when you call it."

She sighed. "Why don't you just let me hire a couple of strippers to sit on your face? That'd be *infinitely* cheaper."

"That's not what this is about, Martha."

"Oh, Charlie."

"I'm serious, I really am."

"Ellie will be terribly hurt."

"She doesn't need to know."

"She'll find out, believe me. They always do." Martha's voice was distraught. "She'll find out you're advertising for a woman to have your baby, and then she'll just flip out, Charlie."

"Not if you do your job well."

"You really this afraid of death?"

"Not death, Martha, oblivion. Oblivion is the thing that really kills me."

"You're better than this, Charlie."

"The ad, just put in the ad."

He hung up. In a few days the notice would sneak into the back pages of New York's weeklies, a discreet little box in the personals, specifying the arrangement he sought and the benefits he offered. Martha would begin screening the applications. He'd see who responded. You never knew who was out there.

He sat quietly then, a saddened but prosperous American executive in a good suit, his gray hair neatly barbered, and followed the ships out on the water. One of the hotel's Eurasian prostitutes watched him from across the lobby as she sipped a watered-down drink. Perhaps sensing a certain opportune grief in the stillness of his posture, she slipped over the marble floor and bent close to ask softly if he would like some company, but he shook his head no—although not, she would see, without a bit of lonely gratitude, not without a quick hungered glance of his eyes into hers—and he continued to sit calmly, with that stillness to him. Noticing this, one would have thought not that in one evening he had watched a man die, or made millions, or lied to his banker, or worried that his flesh might never go forward, but that he was privately toasting what was left of the century, wondering what revelation it might yet bring.

How the Camel
Got His Hump

Rudyard Kipling

Illustrated by Jonathan Langley

PHILOMEL BOOKS

ow this is the next tale, and it tells how the Camel got his big hump.

In the beginning of years, when the world was so new-and-all, and the Animals were just beginning to work for Man, there was a Camel, and he lived in the middle of a Howling Desert because he did not want to work; and besides, he was a Howler himself. So he ate sticks and thorns and tamarisks and milkweed and prickles, most 'scruciating idle; and when anybody spoke to him he said "Humph!" Just "Humph!" and no more.

Presently the Horse came to him on Monday morning, with a saddle on his back and a bit in his mouth, and said, "Camel, O Camel, come out and trot like the rest of us."

"Humph!" said the Camel; and the Horse went away and told the Man.

Presently the Dog came to him, with a stick in his mouth, and said, "Camel, O Camel, come and fetch and carry like the rest of us."

"Humph!" said the Camel; and the Dog went away and told the Man.

Presently the Ox came to him, with a yoke on his neck, and said, "Camel, O Camel, come and plough like the rest of us."

"Humph!" said the Camel; and the Ox went away and told the Man.

At the end of the day the Man called the Horse and the Dog and the Ox together, and said, "Three, O Three, I'm very sorry for you (with the world so new-and-all); but that Humph-thing in the Desert can't work, or he would have been here by now, so I am going to leave him alone, and you must work double-time to make up for it."

That made the Three very angry (with the world so new-and-all), and they held a palaver, and an *indaba*, and a *punchayet*, and a pow-wow on the edge of the Desert; and the Camel came chewing milkweed *most* 'scruciating idle, and laughed at them. Then he said "Humph!" and went away again.

Presently there came along the Djinn in charge of All Deserts, rolling in a cloud of dust (Djinns always travel that way because it is Magic), and he stopped to palaver and pow-wow with the Three.

"Djinn of All Deserts," said the Horse, "*is* it right for any one to be idle, with the world so new-and-all?"

"Certainly not," said the Djinn.

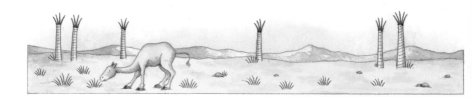

"Well," said the Horse, "there's a thing in the middle of your Howling Desert (and he's a Howler himself) with a long neck and long legs, and he hasn't done a stroke of work since Monday morning. He won't trot."

"Whew!" said the Djinn, whistling, "that's my Camel, for all the gold in Arabia! What does he say about it?"

"He says 'Humph!'" said the Dog; "and he won't fetch and carry."

"Does he say anything else?"

"Only 'Humph!'; and he won't plough," said the Ox.

"Very good," said the Djinn. "I'll humph him if you will kindly wait a minute."

The Djinn rolled himself up in his dust-cloak, and took a bearing across the desert, and found the Camel most 'scruciating idle, looking at his own reflection in a pool of water.

"My long and bubbling friend," said the Djinn, "what's this I hear of your doing no work, with the world so new-and-all?"

"Humph!" said the Camel.

The Djinn sat down, with his chin in his hand, and began to think a Great Magic, while the Camel looked at his own reflection in the pool of water.

"You've given the Three extra work ever since Monday morning, all on account of your 'scruciating idleness," said the Djinn; and he went on thinking Magics, with his chin in his hand.

"Humph!" said the Camel.

"I shouldn't say that again if I were you," said the Djinn; "you might say it once too often. Bubbles, I want you to work."

And the Camel said "Humph!" again; but no sooner had he said it than he saw his back, that he was so proud of, puffing up and puffing up into a great big lolloping humph.

"Do you see that?" said the Djinn. "That's your very own humph that you've brought upon your very own self by not working. To-day is Thursday, and you've done no work since Monday, when the work began. Now you are going to work."

"How can I," said the Camel, "with this humph on my back?"

"That's made a-purpose," said the Djinn, "all because you missed those three days. You will be able to work now for three days without eating, because you can live on your humph; and don't you ever say I never did anything for you. Come out of the Desert and go to the Three, and behave. Humph yourself!"

And the Camel humphed himself, humph and all, and went away to join the Three. And from that day to this the Camel always wears a humph (we call it "hump" now, not to hurt his feelings); but he has never yet caught up with the three days that he missed at the beginning of the world, and he has never yet learned how to behave.

Published in the United States by Philomel Books, a division of
The Putnam & Grosset Group, 200 Madison Avenue, New York, NY 10016.
Illustrations copyright © 1988 by Jonathan Langley. All rights reserved.
Originally published by Methuen Children's Books Ltd., London.
Printed in Hong Kong by Wing King Tong Co. Ltd.   First impression

Library of Congress Cataloging-in-Publication Data
Kipling, Rudyard, 1865–1936. How the camel got his hump. "The
Just so stories." Summary: When the world was new, the camel, a
creature of 'scruciating idleness, said "Humph!" too often and
received for all time a hump[h] from the Djinn of All Deserts.
[1. Camels–Fiction] I. Langley, Jonathan, ill.   II. Title. PZ7.K632Hf
1988   [E]   87-29156   ISBN 0-399-21553-0

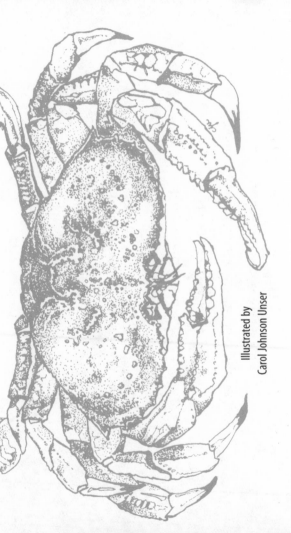

All About Crab

by Nancy Brannon

Illustrated by
Carol Johnson Unser

Also by the Author:

Feasting in the Forest
with husband, Dave Brannon
(ISBN 0-9623036-0-7)

The Lighter Side of Italy
(ISBN 0-9623036-5-8)

Glorious Soups and Breads
(ISBN 0-9623036-4-X)

First Edition, 2000

Library of Congress Catalogue Number 00 135212

Original Illustrations by Carol Johnson-Unser

Published by ConAmore Publishing, 1655 35th Street, Florence, OR 97439

Lithography by R.W. Patterson Printing, Benton Harbor, MI 49022

For my Sisters

My oldest sister, Linda, introduced me to the Oregon Coast and the unforgettable experience of my first Dungeness.

My youngest sister, Sue, recently shared some wonderful sunny days with me crabbing in Alsea Bay.

Their friendship and encouragement means more to me than they know.

Foreword

by Nick Furman, Executive Director
Oregon Dungeness Crab Commission

Dungeness crab is meant to be enjoyed. Whether it is served up on yesterday's newspaper, still steaming from the cooking pot and cracked in the company of good friends and family, with nothing more than melted butter, a glass of wine and one's sleeves rolled up...or as a featured ingredient in an elegant creation that lingers in the memory long after the candles have been extinguished, and the china put away.

In "All About Crab", Chef Nancy Brannon captures this appeal in recipes that range from the simplest appetizer, to tantalizing entrées with an ethnic twist. In each, she demonstrates her appreciation for the flavors of the ingredients as they compliment one another and enhance the sweet, white crabmeat...considered a delicacy in culinary circles around the world. From "Asian Dungeness Crab Cakes with Wasabi Mayonnaise" to the "Classic Deviled Dungeness", Nancy's approach to Dungeness will excite the appetite of crab lovers everywhere.

Whether you are fortunate enough to catch your own crab off the dock, as many here on the coast, or purchase a bright orange whole-cooked crab off a mound of ice at the seafood market, this cookbook will help you enjoy an experience that none other than Oregon's own James Beard once called "...sheer, unadulterated crab heaven".

Arguably the most dangerous job in the world....

Black skies, and angry winter seas have taken many lives since men began crabbing off the western coast of the United States in the late 1800's....many of them leaving families back on shore. Those who earn their livelihoods from crabbing, are certainly a 'breed apart'. We thank all the commercial fleet for the beautiful product they put on our tables.

PHOTO BY BRET YAGER

Table of Contents

Introduction

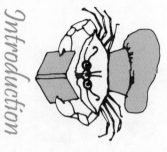

Of all the wonderful foods in the world, the prized Dungeness has to be among the most delicious, and versatile. While serving Dungeness warm, right from the pot with lots of drawn butter, or chilled with a great cocktail sauce rank among my favorites, the creative possibilities are limitless. It is my hope that, in the pages of this little book, you'll find some new and flavorful uses for this 'royal' member of the crustacean family!

If you are fortunate enough to be able to catch your *own* Dungeness, the instructions for cleaning it and removing the meat are given in the following pages...and cooking crab is a breeze! Live crabs should be boiled or steamed for 15-20 minutes, then immersed in cold water (unless, of course the crab is to be served hot, right from the steamer). Fresh, whole cooked crab can be reheated in a steamer, boiling water, or broiler.

Fresh, whole, cooked crab should be refrigerated at 33°-35°F...and can be kept for approximately 7 days. Dungeness *can be* frozen, although I recommend first vacuum sealing the meat (whole crabs can be broken into leg and body sections and placed in a ZipLok® freezer bag)...then defrosting it over night in the refrigerator. (Release the vacuum seal first.) Do not refreeze crab. Frozen, the shelf-life of the whole crab is 6-9 months (not vacuum sealed)...or 10-12 months for vacuum-sealed crab meat.

Any way you serve this wonderful product...you're going to LOVE it!

Comparative Nutritional Information*

	DUNGENESS CRAB	BEEF TENDERLOIN	CHICKEN BNLS. BREAST
Calories	94	179	140
Protein	19	24	26
Total Fat	1.06 gr.	8.5 gr.	3 gr.
Saturated Fat	Less than 1 gr.	3.2 gr.	1 gr.
Monounsaturated Fat	Less than 1 gr.	3.2 gr.	1 gr.
Polyunsaturated Fat	Less than 1 gr.	0.32 gr.	1 gr.
Omega-3 Fatty Acids	0.3 gr.	0.03 gr.	0.05 gr.
Carbohydrates	0.81 gr.	0 gr.	0 gr.
Cholesterol	64 mgs.	71 mgs.	72 mgs.
Sodium	321 mgs. **	54 mgs.	63 mgs.
Calcium	50 mgs.	6 mgs.	13 mgs.
Magnesium	49 mgs.	26 mgs.	25 mgs.
Potassium	347 mgs.	356 mgs.	218 mgs.
Zinc	4.7 mgs.	5 mgs.	1 mg.

* Based on 3-ounce cooked portions.

** It is recommended that the average adult consume no more than about 3000 mgs. of sodium per day. Therefore, while the amount shown here sounds like a lot, it clearly does not present a problem, as it represents little more than 10% of the daily allowance.

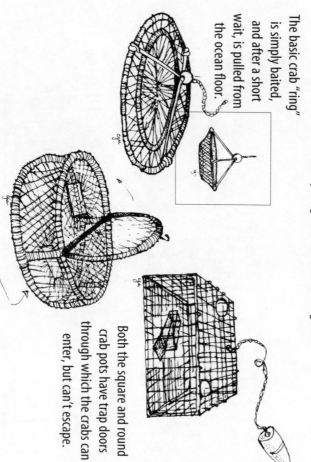

Catching a Dungeness

There are many devices used to catch Dungeness...here are some of the more common ones. Any of these can help you bring home a feast your guests won't soon forget!

The basic crab "ring" is simply baited, and after a short wait, is pulled from the ocean floor.

Both the square and round crab pots have trap doors through which the crabs can enter, but can't escape.

Sexing and Sizing your Catch

Females are easily distinguishable from the males by their wider 'aprons'. Females and smaller males are never to be taken, thus insuring healthy stocks for future harvests.

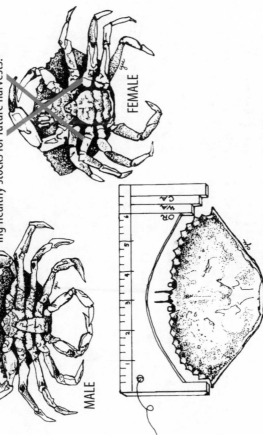

MALE

FEMALE

Shells must measure at least 5³/₄" across for Oregon's recreational crabbers...6¹/₄" for commercial harvesting. Measuring devices like this one are readily available, but Oregon recreational crabbers have it easy...a dollar bill is exactly the right size!

Cleaning a Cooked Dungeness

1. Holding the base of the crab in one hand, remove the upper shell.

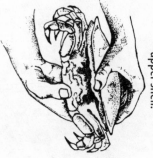

2. Using your fingers, or with the help of a spoon, remove the leaf-like gills.

3. Rinse well under cold running water, washing away the "butter" from its center.

4. Remove each of the legs, separating the claws, at the center joint. With a mallet or nutcracker, crack the claws and remove the meat. Repeat with all the legs. Then, break the body portion into 2 pieces, and with your fingers (and maybe the aid of a nut pick), remove the wonderful body meat.

Appetizers

Crab Empañaditas

Crabby Tomatoes

Dungeness Crab Butter

Chilled Crab and Artichoke Dip

Dungeness Torte

Tijuana Crab and Spinach Dip

Dungeness Crab Puffs

Ginger Crab Phyllo Cups

Dungeness Stuffed Mushrooms

Crab Empañaditas

For the pastry:

3 Rounds of Pillsbury All-Ready Pie Crust
(or your own home-made pie crust dough)

For the filling:

1 tablespoon Butter
1/2 cup finely chopped Onion
1 cup ripe Tomato, seeded and finely chopped
1 pound fresh Dungeness Crab Meat
1 tablespoon chopped Cilantro
1 teaspoon minced fresh Garlic
Salt and Pepper to taste

The egg wash:

1 Whole Egg lightly beaten with 1 tablespoon Water

Have the pastry at room temperature while you make the filling. Melt the butter in a medium skillet and sauté the onion and tomato until soft. Add the rest of the filling ingredients and continue cooking for 5 minutes, stirring often. On a lightly floured board, cut the dough into 4" circles. Place a teaspoon of the filling in the center of each pastry. Brush one half of the circle edge lightly with water. Fold in half, and crimp with the tines of a fork to seal. Put the pastries on a greased baking sheet (or baking parchment lined) and refrigerate until ready to bake. Preheat oven to 375°. Brush the tops of the pastries with the egg wash, and bake for 15-20 minutes, or until golden brown. Serve hot. Makes 36 appetizers.

Serving Size: 1 piece   Calories: 100   Total Fat: 6 grams   Saturated Fat: 1.5 grams   Cholesterol: 15 mgs.
Sodium: 150 mgs.   Total Carbohydrates: 7 grams   Dietary Fiber: 0 grams   Sugars: 1 gram   Protein: 4 grams

Crabby Tomatoes

For the filling:

1/2 pound Dungeness Crab Meat

4 ounces Cream Cheese, softened

1/2 teaspoon finely minced Red Chili Pepper

1 tablespoon finely sliced Green Onion (green portion only)

2 tablespoons finely minced Granny Smith Apple

1 teaspoon minced fresh Garlic

Dash of Tabasco®

1 teaspoon fresh Lemon Juice

---

1 pint Cherry Tomatoes, (about 12 - 18) washed, stems removed

Combine all the filling ingredients in a small bowl and cover with plastic wrap. Refrigerate while you prepare the tomatoes. Cut the tops off the tomatoes, and remove the seeds and pulp from the inside. Rinse well, and invert onto paper towels to drain. With a teaspoon, fill the tomatoes with the crab mixture. Serves 4.

Serving Size: 1 tomato Calories: 50 Total Fat: 3 grams Saturated Fat: 2 grams Cholesterol: 20 mgs.
Sodium: 85 mgs. Total Carbohydrates: 2 grams Dietary Fiber: 0 grams Sugars: 1 gram Protein: 4 grams

Dungeness Crab Butter

1/2 cup (1 stick) Butter, at room temperature
1/2 cup (4 ounces) Dungeness Crab Meat
1 teaspoon grated fresh Lemon Peel
Dash of White Pepper
2 tablespoons chopped fresh Parsley

Combine all the ingredients in the work bowl of a food processor fitted with a steel blade. Pulse a few times to begin the blending process, scraping down the sides to incorporate all the ingredients. . . . . . . then process for 1 minute. Store in the refrigerator in an airtight container for up to 3 days. Let stand at room temperature for 30 minutes before serving. Makes 1 cup, or about 16 tablespoons.

Serving Suggestion: Spread on toasted slices of French bread, dark rye or foccacia.

Serving Size: 1 tablespoon   Calories: 70   Total Fat: 7 grams   Saturated Fat: 4 grams   Cholesterol: 25 mgs.
Sodium: 90 mgs.   Total Carbohydrates: 0 grams   Dietary Fiber: 0 grams   Sugars: 0 grams   Protein: 1 gram

Chilled Crab and Artichoke Dip

1/2 cup Mayonnaise

1/2 cup Sour Cream

3/4 pound (12 ounces) Dungeness Crab Meat

1 14 1/2 ounce can Artichoke Hearts (not marinated), drained and coarsely chopped

2 teaspoons chopped fresh Dill Weed (or 1 teaspoon dried)

1/2 cup thinly sliced Green Onion

2 teaspoons freshly squeezed Lime Juice

Dash of Tabasco®

Salt and freshly ground Black Pepper to taste

Combine all the ingredients (except 1/4 cup of the crab meat) in a medium bowl, mixing well. Taste and season with the salt and pepper. Refrigerate and chill (covered) 2 hours or overnight. Just before serving, top with the remaining crab meat, and if you like, a few sprigs of fresh dill. Serves 8 - 10.

Serving Size: 1/2 cup   Calories: 220   Total Fat: 16 grams   Saturated Fat: 4 grams   Cholesterol: 50 mgs.
Sodium: 690 mgs.   Total Carbohydrates: 8 grams   Dietary Fiber: 2 grams   Sugars: 1 gram   Protein: 13 grams

Dungeness Torte

8 ounces Cream Cheese, at room temperature

¼ teaspoon Garlic Salt

4 tablespoons finely chopped fresh Parsley

8 ounces Boursin® Cheese(seasoned with herbs)

1 pound Dungeness Crab Meat

5 large leaves of Red or Green Leaf Lettuce, cores removed

Line an 8" springform pan with plastic wrap. Set aside. Blend together the cream cheese, garlic salt, and 1 tablespoon of the chopped parsley, then spread it evenly in the bottom of the springform. Place the remaining chopped parsley in a plastic bag in the refrigerator. Spread half the crab meat evenly over the top. Next, spread the Boursin® atop the first layer of crab...then top with the remaining crab. Cover with plastic wrap and refrigerate for 2 hours. (May be made to this point the day before.) When ready to serve, remove the outer ring of the springform, and peel away the plastic wrap from the sides of the torte. Using your fingers, press the remaining parsley into the sides of the torte. Transfer the torte to a serving platter lined with the lettuce leaves. Serve with the Bremner® Wafers

(or other crackers). Serves 8-10.

Serving Size: 1 tablespoon.   Calories: 40   Total Fat: 2.5 grams   Saturated Fat: 1.5 grams   Cholesterol: 15 mgs.
Sodium: 110 mgs.   Total Carbohydrates: 1 gram   Dietary Fiber: 0 grams   Sugars: 0 grams   Protein: 4 grams

Tijuana Crab and Spinach Dip

2 tablespoons Olive Oil
1 cup finely chopped Onion
1 teaspoon minced fresh Garlic
1 10-ounce package frozen Chopped
Spinach, defrosted and squeezed dry
1 4 1/2-oz. can Chopped Mild Green Chilies
1 8-ounce package Cream Cheese,
at room temperature
1 cup Half and Half
2 cups shredded Monterey Jack Cheese
(or Pepper Jack, if you prefer)
8 ounces Dungeness Crab Meat
Salt and freshly ground Black Pepper to taste

Preheat oven to 400°. Spray an oven-proof baking dish with non-stick vegetable spray. Set aside. Sauté the onion and garlic in the olive oil until tender. Add the spinach and chopped green chilies, and sauté for 2 more minutes. Stir in the cream cheese and the half and half. Bring to a simmer. Remove from the heat, and stir in the shredded Monterey Jack cheese and the crab meat and season to taste. Pour mixture into the prepared baking dish and bake, uncovered for 20-25 minutes, or until heated through. Serve with tortilla chips. Serves 6-8.

Serving Size: 1 tablespoon.   Calories: 40   Total Fat: 3 grams   Saturated Fat: 2 grams   Cholesterol: 10 mgs.
Sodium: 65 mgs.   Total Carbohydrates: 1 gram   Dietary Fiber: 0 grams   Sugars: 0 grams   Protein: 2 grams

Dungeness Crab Puffs

6 ounces Dungeness Crab
1 cup Mayonnaise
1 cup grated Swiss Cheese
1/2 cup finely chopped Onion
1 package frozen Puff Pastry (2 sheets), defrosted
1 Whole Egg beaten with 1 teaspoon Water

Preheat the oven to 400°. Combine the crab, mayonnaise, Swiss cheese and onion in a medium bowl, blending well. Flatten the sheets of puff pastry and lightly roll them out. Cut each of the sheets into thirds lengthwise, and then into fourths along the short side, making a total of 12 squares per sheet. Brush lightly with the beaten egg and water. Put a teaspoon of the filling in the center of each square. Fold the squares in half diagonally, and seal them by pressing the tines of a fork around the edges. Brush the tops with more of the beaten egg mixture. Place the puffs on a baking sheet lined with baking parchment (or a non-stick baking sheet) and bake for 10-12 minutes, or until puffed and golden brown. Let cool for 5 minutes or so before serving. Makes 24 appetizers.

Serving Size: 1 puff   Calories: 210   Total Fat: 19 grams   Saturated Fat: 3 grams   Cholesterol: 20 mgs.
Sodium: 140 mgs.   Total Carbohydrates: 10 grams   Dietary Fiber: 0 grams   Sugars: 1 gram   Protein: 5 grams

Ginger Crab Phyllo Cups

1/4 pound Dungeness Crab Meat, roughly chopped
1 large Green Onion, thinly sliced
(white and green parts)
1/2 cup peeled, seeded and diced Cucumber
1 tablespoon Slivered Almonds, toasted
1 tablespoon finely chopped Sweet Red Bell Pepper
1 teaspoon grated fresh Ginger
1 tablespoon chopped fresh Cilantro
1 teaspoon Sesame Oil
2 tablespoons Rice Vinegar
1 teaspoon Soy Sauce

8 sheets of Phyllo dough, at room temperature
6 tablespoons Butter

In a medium bowl, combine the first 10 ingredients. Mix thoroughly. Refrigerate in an air-tight container. Meanwhile, preheat the oven to 400°. Lay the stacked sheets of phyllo on a clean, dry countertop. Cover with plastic wrap. Place one sheet on another section of the countertop. Brush it with melted butter, starting from the outer edge, and working your way towards the center. When completely coated, place another sheet on top of that and butter it. Continue with the remaining 6 sheets. When all the sheets have been buttered and layered, cut them using a sharp knife or a pizza cutter into 24 equal squares. (The easiest way, is to cut it in half lengthwise...then each of those long sections in half lengthwise...then cut all four strips in half the short way, and then each of those in thirds.) Ease each of the squares into mini-muffin tins, and bake for 8-10 minutes, or until crisp and golden. Place on a rack and allow to cool completely. Then fill with the crab mixture. Makes 24 appetizers.

Serving Size: 1 piece   Calories: 30   Total Fat: 3 grams   Saturated Fat:1.5 grams   Cholesterol: 10 mgs.
Sodium: 55 mgs.   Total Carbohydrates: 1 gram   Dietary Fiber: 0 grams   Sugars: 0 grams   Protein: 1 gram

Dungeness-stuffed Mushrooms

24 fresh White or Brown Mushrooms, about the size of a fifty-cent piece

4 tablespoons Butter, melted

1/2 cup finely sliced Green Onions

1/2 pound (8 ounces) Dungeness Crab Meat, flaked

2 tablespoons fresh squeezed Lemon Juice

1/2 teaspoon Curry Powder

1 cup Sour Cream

3 tablespoons grated Parmesan Cheese

4 ounces (1 cup) grated Swiss Cheese

Paprika for garnish

Preheat oven to 375°. Carefully remove the stems from the mushroom caps. Finely chop the stems and set them aside. Dip the mushroom caps in the melted butter, shaking off the excess. Place the caps up side down on a baking sheet. Mix the chopped stems with the green onion, crab meat, lemon juice, curry powder and sour cream. Using a teaspoon, fill each cap with the crab mixture. Combine the Parmesan and Swiss cheeses. Top each cap with a generous sprinkling of cheese and a dash of paprika. Bake for 5-6 minutes, or until hot and bubbly. Serve hot. Makes 24 appetizers.

Serving Size: 1 piece   Calories: 80   Total Fat: 6 grams   Saturated Fat: 3.5 grams   Cholesterol: 20 mgs.
Sodium: 90 mgs.   Total Carbohydrates: 2 grams   Dietary Fiber: 0 grams   Sugars: 1 gram   Protein: 5 grams

Soups

Hot and Sour Crab Soup

Lemon–Avocado Soup with Crab

Crab Bisque

Cajun Crab Soup

Brodetto di Granchio

Fresh Corn and Crab Chowder

Creamy Crab and Spinach Soup

Crab and Wild Mushroom Chowder

Caribbean Crab and Spinach Soup

Hot and Sour Crab Soup

8-10 fresh or dried Shitake Mushrooms* (about 6 ounces fresh)

1 cup matchstick** Carrots

1 cup matchstick** Leeks

6 cups Chicken Stock

1 tablespoon fresh Ginger Root Juice
(made by grating one 2"-3" piece fresh ginger root
and then squeezing out the juice)

1/4 cup Rice Vinegar

1 tablespoon White Vinegar

1 tablespoon Sesame Oil

1 teaspoon freshly ground Black Pepper

1/2 cup thinly sliced Green Onions (white and green portions)

1 stalk Lemon Grass cut into 2" pieces (or 1 teaspoon grated lemon zest)

3 tablespoons Corn Starch mixed with 3 tablespoons Cold Water

1/2 pound Dungeness Crab Meat

1/2 teaspoon Hot Pepper Flakes

2 Whole Eggs, beaten well

Remove the mushroom stems and discard them. Thinly slice the caps and set them aside with the carrots and leeks. Bring the stock to a boil, and add the mushrooms, carrots, leeks, ginger juice, rice vinegar and white vinegar. Return to a boil and add the sesame oil, pepper, green onions and lemon grass (or lemon peel). Remove 1 cup of the stock from the pot, and stir it into the corn starch/water mixture. Stir until blended, and then return it to the pot. Add the crab meat and the hot pepper flakes and stir thoroughly,returning again to a slow boil. Turn off the heat and drizzle the beaten eggs into the soup in a thin stream. Let stand for 5 minutes. Remove the lemon grass stalks before serving.

Serve hot. Serves 6-8.

* If you are using dried shitake mushrooms, place them in a small bowl, and pour 3 cups of boiling water over them. Let stand for about 20-30 minutes, or until soft. Discard the water, and rinse the mushrooms thoroughly before proceeding.

** To cut the carrots into "matchstick" pieces, simply make thin, diagonal slices of a peeled carrot. Then, stacking a few slices at a time, cut them into thin shreds. As for the leeks, just cut the white portion into 2" pieces...then cut those in half lengthwise and then into shreds.

Serving Size: 1½ cups   Calories: 100   Total Fat: 2.5 grams   Saturated Fat: 0 grams   Cholesterol: 20 mgs.
Sodium: 420 mgs.   Total Carbohydrates: 10 grams   Dietary Fiber: 1 gram   Sugars: 2 grams   Protein: 8 grams

Lemon~Avocado Soup with Crab

6 cups Chicken Broth

1/4 cup chopped fresh Flat-Leaf Italian Parsley

1/2 cup Dry White Wine

1/4 teaspoon Coarse Sea Salt

1 large Lemon, washed and cut into thin slices

1 large, ripe Avocado, seeded, peeled, and sliced into long strips

1/2 pound Dungeness Crab Meat

In a stock pot over medium-high heat, combine the chicken broth, parsley, white wine and sea salt and bring to a boil. Reduce the heat to low, and simmer for 5-7 minutes. Meanwhile, divide the lemon slices, avocado and crab meat between preheated bowls. Ladle the hot broth over the top, and serve immediately. Makes 8 servings.

Serving Size: 1 1/2 cups   Calories: 90   Total Fat: 4.5 grams   Saturated Fat: 0.5 gram   Cholesterol: 20 mgs.
Sodium: 470 mgs.   Total Carbohydrates: 3 grams   Dietary Fiber: 1 gram   Sugars: 1 gram   Protein: 7 grams

Crab Bisque

2 tablespoons Butter
1 tablespoon minced Shallot
2 tablespoons Flour
2 cups Chicken Broth
1/4 cup Tomato Paste
2 cups Heavy Whipping Cream
1 pound Dungeness Crab
2 tablespoons Sour Cream
1 tablespoon chopped fresh Parsley

In a stock pot over medium heat, sauté the shallot in the butter for 2-3 minutes, or until soft. Remove from heat and stir in the flour until well blended. Return to heat, and cook until mixture is bubbly (1-2 minutes). Gradually add the chicken broth and then the tomato paste. Whisk until smooth. Next, add the whipping cream and crab. Bring to a boil, then reduce the heat to a simmer. Cook for 3-4 minutes. Serve hot, with a teaspoon of sour cream and a sprinkling of parsley for garnish. Makes 6 servings.

Serving Size: 1½ cups   Calories: 420   Total Fat: 35 grams   Saturated Fat: 21 grams   Cholesterol: 180 mgs.
Sodium: 590 mgs.   Total Carbohydrates: 8 grams   Dietary Fiber: 0 grams   Sugars: 3 grams   Protein: 20 grams

Cajun Crab Soup

1 tablespoon Butter
1 tablespoon Olive Oil
$^1/_2$ cup *each* chopped Red, Yellow and Green Bell Pepper
1 cup chopped Onion
$^1/_2$ cup sliced Celery
1 tablespoon minced fresh Garlic
2 tablespoons Flour
2 Fish-flavored Bouillon Cubes (Knorr® makes an excellent one) dissolved
in 2 cups Boiling Water
4 cups Water
$^1/_4$ cup chopped fresh Parsley
2 tablespoons Worcestershire Sauce
$^1/_4$ teaspoon Cayenne Pepper
1 teaspoon Paprika
Dash of Tabasco®
2 Bay Leaves
2 teaspoons dried Thyme
$^1/_2$ cup uncooked Long Grain White Rice
1 pound Dungeness Crab Meat
Salt to taste

Sauté the vegetables in the butter and olive oil until soft. Add the flour and stir well. Gradually add the fish-flavored broth, then the water, parsley, worcestershire, cayenne, paprika, Tabasco®, bay leaves and thyme. Bring to a boil, then reduce the heat and simmer, uncovered, for 30 minutes. Add the rice and cook an additional 30 minutes. Add the crab and heat through. Taste and add salt if desired. Serves 8.

Serving Size: 1$\frac{1}{2}$ cups   Calories: 150   Total Fat: 4.5 grams   Saturated Fat: 1.5 grams   Cholesterol: 45 mgs.
Sodium: 840 mgs.   Total Carbohydrates: 13 grams   Dietary Fiber: 1 gram   Sugars: 3 grams   Protein: 14 grams

Brodetto di Granchio
(Italian Crab Soup)

1 tablespoon Extra Virgin Olive Oil
1 tablespoon Butter
1 tablespoon minced fresh Garlic
1 cup finely chopped Onion
1 cup finely sliced Celery
$1/2$ cup finely shredded Carrot
2 $14^1/2$-ounce cans Diced Tomatoes(with juice)
1 8-ounce can Tomato Sauce
4 cups Water
1 8-ounce bottle Clam Juice
$1/2$ cup Dry White Wine
1 pound Dungeness Crab Meat
2 tablespoons roughly chopped fresh Basil Leaves
1 tablespoon fresh Oregano Leaves
1 large Bay Leaf
Salt and freshly ground Black Pepper to taste

In a large stock pot over medium-high heat, sauté the garlic, onion, celery and carrot in the olive oil and butter until soft. Add the remaining ingredients in the order given. Simmer, uncovered, for 40-50 minutes, adding salt and pepper to taste. Serves 10 - 12.

Serving Size: 1¹/₂ cups   Calories: 100   Total Fat: 2.5 grams   Saturated Fat: 1 gram   Cholesterol: 30 mgs.
Sodium: 590 mgs.   Total Carbohydrates: 7 grams   Dietary Fiber: 1 gram   Sugars: 4 grams   Protein: 10 grams

Fresh Corn and Crab Chowder

12 ears fresh Corn, husks and silk removed
4 ounces Salt Pork, rind removed and cut into 2 pieces
1 tablespoon Butter
1 cup chopped Onion
2 teaspoons minced fresh Garlic
6 cups Chicken Broth
3 cups diced Red Potato (skins on...about 1 pound)
$1/2$ teaspoon dried Thyme Leaves
Dash of Cayenne Pepper
2 tablespoons minced fresh Parsley
2 cups (1 pint) Heavy Whipping Cream
1 teaspoon Salt (or to taste)
$1/4$ teaspoon ground White Pepper
Enough Gold Medal Wondra® to thicken as desired
1 pound Dungeness Crab Meat

Using a chef's knife, cut the kernels from 4 of the ears of corn by standing them on end, and cutting with a downward motion. You should get about 3 cups of corn. Set aside. Next, using a box grater, grate the corn from the remaining ears and place in a separate bowl. Then with the back of the knife, scrape the cobs to remove the "milk", adding it to the grated corn. In a large stock pot over medium-high heat, sauté the salt pork until it is crisp and golden, using tongs to turn it...pushing down to render the fat. Reduce the heat and add the butter, onions and garlic, and sauté until the onions are soft. Remove the salt pork and discard. Next, add the chicken broth,grated corn and "milk", diced potatoes, thyme, cayenne and parsley. Bring to a boil, then reduce the heat and simmer until the potatoes are tender...8-10 minutes. Stir in the heavy whipping cream and return to a simmer. Add the corn kernels, salt and white pepper, and return once again, to a simmer. Adding the Wondra© and allow it to thicken the chowder as desired. Finally, add the crab meat and heat through. Serve hot, garnished with a little chopped fresh parsley. Serves 8.

Serving Size: 1^1/$_2$ cups   Calories: 270   Total Fat: 17 grams   Saturated Fat: 10 grams   Cholesterol: 85 mgs.
Sodium: 460 mgs.   Total Carbohydrates: 18 grams   Dietary Fiber: 1 gram   Sugars: 3 grams   Protein: 12 grams

Creamy Crab and Spinach Soup

2 tablespoons Butter

$^1/_2$ cup finely chopped Onion

$^1/_2$ cup finely slivered Sweet Red Bell Pepper

4 cups roughly chopped fresh Spinach (well rinsed and drained)

1 8-ounce package Cream Cheese

$^1/_2$ teaspoon Salt

$^1/_4$ teaspoon freshly ground Black Pepper

$^1/_2$ teaspoon Bouquet Garni Seasoning

4 cups Milk

Enough Wondra® to thicken as desired (2-3 tablespoons)

8 ounces Dungeness Crab Meat

4-6 Spinach Leaves for garnish

In a large stock pot, melt the butter over medium heat and sauté the onion and bell pepper until soft. Add the spinach and continue sautéing until the spinach is wilted. Remove from the heat and add the cream cheese, stirring until melted. Season with the salt, pepper and bouquet garni. Then add the milk and return the pan to the heat. Bring the soup to a simmer while adding the Wondra® a little at a time. When the soup is hot, and has begun to thicken, add the crab meat and stir through. Taste, and adjust the seasoning. If it is too thick, add a little extra milk...if too thin, add a little more Wondra®. Stack the remaining spinach leaves, and then fold them in half lengthwise. With a sharp knife, cut them into fine shreds, and set aside. To serve, ladle the soup into bowls, and top with a few of the spinach shreds. Serve hot. Makes 6 servings.

Serving Size: 1^1/$_2$ cups   Calories: 340   Total Fat: 24 grams   Saturated Fat: 14 grams   Cholesterol: 105 mgs. Sodium: 560 mgs.   Total Carbohydrates: 15 grams   Dietary Fiber: 0 grams   Sugars: 10 grams   Protein: 18 grams

Crab and Wild Mushroom Chowder

2 tablespoons Butter
1 cup coarsely chopped Onion
1 cup thinly sliced Celery
1 cup coarsely chopped fresh Wild Mushrooms (any variety you like)
(or you may substitute $1/2$ cup dried)
3 cups diced Red Potatoes, skins on
6 cups Chicken Broth (or Fish Stock)
$1/2$ cup chopped fresh Parsley
1 cup frozen Corn
$1/2$ pound Dungeness Crab Meat
$1/4$ teaspoon White Pepper
1 pint (2 cups) Heavy Whipping Cream
Enough Gold Medal Wondra© to thicken as desired (about 2 tablespoons)
2 tablespoons fresh Lemon Juice
Salt to taste

In a large stock pot over medium heat, sauté the onion and celery in the butter until limp. Add the mushrooms and continue sautéing for 2-3 minutes. Add the potatoes, broth, parsley, corn, crab and white pepper. Bring to a boil, and add the whipping cream. Reduce the heat and simmer until the potatoes are tender...about 30 minutes. Add the Wondra© a little at a time, stirring well. Add the lemon juice and salt. Return to a boil, stirring frequently. When the Wondra© is cooked, it will thicken the soup. If you like it thicker, simply add more Wondra© ...a little at a time, until you reach the desired consistency. If too thick, add a quarter cup or so of broth. Makes 10 - 12 servings.

Note: If using dried mushrooms, reconstitute them first, by pouring boiling water over them and letting them stand for 15-20 minutes. If you like, replace 1 cup of the chicken broth with an equal amount of mushroom water strained thru a coffee filter.

Note: Gold Medal Wondra© is readily available at most supermarkets. It's great for thickening soups, sauces and gravies, and I recommend it highly.

Serving Size: 1$\frac{1}{2}$ cups   Calories: 230   Total Fat: 17 grams   Saturated Fat: 10 grams   Cholesterol: 75 mgs.
Sodium: 440 mgs.   Total Carbohydrates: 15 grams   Dietary Fiber: 2 grams   Sugars: 3 grams   Protein: 7 grams

Caribbean Crab and Spinach Soup

3 tablespoons Butter
1 cup chopped fresh Onion
1 teaspoon minced fresh Garlic
6 cups fresh, washed and coarsely chopped Spinach
5 cups Chicken Broth (or fish stock)
1 13^1/$_2$-ounce can Unsweetened Coconut Milk
1 teaspoon Salt
^{1}/$_2$ teaspoon Coarse Ground Black Pepper
2 teaspoons Tabasco©
^{1}/$_2$ pound Dungeness Crab Meat

In a large stock pot over medium heat, sauté the onion and garlic until soft. Add the remaining ingredients in the order given (except the crabmeat). Bring to a boil over high heat, then return to medium heat, and simmer, uncovered for 30 minutes. Add the crab and simmer an additional 5 minutes.

Serving Size: 1^1/$_2$ cups   Calories: 160   Total Fat: 12 grams   Saturated Fat: 10 grams   Cholesterol: 25 mgs.
Sodium: 610 mgs.   Total Carbohydrates: 6 grams   Dietary Fiber: 3 grams   Sugars: 2 grams   Protein: 8 grams

Salads

Dungeness Salad Niçoise

Alsea Bay Dungeness Crab Salad

Thai Crab and Cucumber Salad

Dungeness and Wild Rice Salad

Dungeness Crab Salad with Cantaloupe

Warm Chèvre, Crab and Spinach Salad

Crab and New Potato Salad

Confetti Crab Salad with Lime Dressing

Dungeness Salad Niçoise

For the vinaigrette:

$^1/_4$ cup Champagne Vinegar
1 tablespoon Dijon Mustard
2 teaspoons minced fresh Garlic
$^1/_2$ cup Extra Virgin Olive Oil
Salt and freshly ground Black Pepper to taste

For the Salad:

8 small New Potatoes
$^1/_2$ pound fresh Green Beans,
tips and stems removed
4 cups mixed Spring Greens,
washed and patted dry
4 ripe Roma Tomatoes,
sliced (tops and bottoms discarded)
1 cup Yellow Pear "Cherry" Tomatoes (optional)
4 Hard Boiled Eggs, peeled and sliced
4 thin slices of Red Onion (about 2-3" in diameter)
1 pound Dungeness Crab Meat
$^1/_2$ cup Niçoise Olives (or other oil-cured olives)

47

8 small Cornichons (tiny tarragon vinegar flavored pickles)
Anchovy Filets (optional) and Lemon Wedges to garnish

For the vinaigrette, combine the vinegar, mustard and garlic in a small bowl and whisk together. Add the olive oil in a slow stream, whisking constantly to produce a creamy, emulsified dressing. Cover and chill. Steam the new potatoes in their skins for 10-12 minutes, or until tender. Set aside to cool. Steam the green beans for about 10 minutes, or until tender-crisp. Plunge them quickly into ice water to stop the cooking, and preserve the color. Drain. On individual chilled plates, place about 1 cup of the greens slightly off center. Then arrange the remaining ingredients attractively in clusters around the plate, overlapping the greens. Drizzle the vinaigrette over the top. Garnish with the lemon wedges and anchovy filets, if you like them, and serve immediately with a crusty loaf of French bread.
Makes 8 to 10 servings.

Serving Size: 1 cup   Calories: 270   Total Fat: 15 grams   Saturated Fat: 2.5 grams   Cholesterol: 120 mgs.
Sodium: 490 mgs.   Total Carbohydrates: 17 grams   Dietary Fiber: 3 grams   Sugars: 4 grams   Protein: 15 grams

Alsea Bay Dungeness Crab Salad

I named this salad for a wonderful time spent crabbing in that bay with my youngest sister!

$1/3$ cup Mayonnaise
1 tablespoon finely chopped Sweet Red Bell Pepper
$1/2$ cup finely chopped Celery
2 tablespoons Dijon Mustard
2 teaspoons Worcestershire Sauce
$1/4$ teaspoon EACH Salt *and* Tabasco®
1 tablespoon fresh Lemon Juice
1 teaspoon freshly grated Lemon Peel
1 pound Dungeness Crab Meat
8 large leaves of either Butter Lettuce, or Radicchio
1 tablespoon finely chopped fresh Parsley
6 Lemon Wedges

Combine the Mayonnaise, red pepper, celery, mustard, worcestershire, salt, tabasco®. lemon juice and lemon peel in a large bowl. Mix thoroughly. Fold in the crab, taking care not to break it up into pieces that are so small that they will "disappear" in the salad. Place the butter lettuce or radicchio "cups" onto chilled plates. Mound the salad in the cups...top with a little chopped parsley, and garnish with lemon wedges. Serve immediately. Serves 4.

Serving Size: 1 cup   Calories: 270   Total Fat: 16 grams   Saturated Fat: 2.5 grams   Cholesterol: 95 mgs.
Sodium: 900 mgs.   Total Carbohydrates: 3 grams   Dietary Fiber: 0 grams   Sugars: 1 gram   Protein: 26 grams

Thai Crab and Cucumber Salad

A little twist on a traditional Thai dish.

2 large Cucumbers, halved and seeded
2 Red Chili Peppers, seeded and chopped
1 teaspoon minced fresh Garlic
3 tablespoons freshly squeezed Lime Juice
$1/4$ pound Dungeness Crab Meat
A little salt to taste

With a large grater, shred the cucumbers (with peel). You should end up with about 6 cups.
In a large bowl, combine cucumbers and all the remaining ingredients, tossing lightly. Salt to
taste, but beware...salt will bring out the "heat" of the red peppers!
Serve immediately. Serves 6.

Serving Size: $3/4$ cup   Calories: 45   Total Fat: 0 grams   Saturated Fat: 0 grams   Cholesterol: 15 mgs.
Sodium: 140 mgs.   Total Carbohydrates: 6 grams   Dietary Fiber: 1 gram   Sugars: 3 grams   Protein: 5 grams

Dungeness and Wild Rice Salad

For the dressing:

$^1/_2$ cup Sour Cream
$^1/_2$ cup Mayonnaise
$^1/_4$ cup freshly squeezed Lemon Juice
1 teaspoon Dijon Mustard
1 tablespoon Ketchup

For the salad:

3 cups cooked Wild Rice
$^1/_2$ cup thinly sliced Green Onions
$^1/_2$ cup thinly sliced Celery
1 cup peeled, seeded and diced Tomato
1 pound Dungeness Crab Meat
4-6 large Radicchio Leaves

To garnish:

2 tablespoons chopped fresh Cilantro

Chill 4 plates in the freezer. In a small bowl, whisk together the dressing ingredients.
Refrigerate, covered, while you prepare the salad. Then, in a large bowl, combine the wild
rice, green onions,celery, tomato and crab meat, tossing well. Place the radicchio leaves on

the chilled plates and mound the crab/rice mixture inside. (If the leaves are small, simply split the stems of the leaves and use 2-3 per serving.) Top each salad with a little chopped cilantro. Serve the dressing in a small container on the side of the plate.

Makes 6 servings.

Serving Size: 1 cup   Calories: 360   Total Fat: 20 grams   Saturated Fat: 5 grams   Cholesterol: 75 mgs.
Sodium: 470 mgs.   Total Carbohydrates: 24 grams   Dietary Fiber: 2 grams   Sugars: 3 grams   Protein: 22 grams

Dungeness Crab Salad with Cantaloupe

1 pound Dungeness Crab Meat
$1/4$ cup finely diced Red Bell Pepper
$1/4$ cup finely diced Green Bell Pepper
$1/4$ cup diced Granny Smith Apple
$1^1/2$ cups Melon Balls (cantaloupe, or other)
2 tablespoons finely sliced Green Onion
1 tablespoon chopped fresh Mint Leaves

$1/2$ cup Mayonnaise
$1/2$ cup Plain Yogurt
1 tablespoon Honey
1 tablespoon fresh Lemon Juice
Dash of Tabasco®
Dash of Worcestershire Sauce
Salt and freshly ground Black Pepper to taste

---

4 cups shredded Romaine Lettuce
Sprigs of fresh Mint to garnish

In a large bowl, combine the first 7 ingredients, tossing well. In a small bowl, combine the mayonnaise, yogurt, honey, lemon juice, Tabasco® and worcestershire. Season with salt and pepper to taste. Pour the dressing over the crab mixture and combine well. Place a generous portion of shredded lettuce onto each of four chilled plates. Mound the crab salad on top and garnish with sprigs of fresh mint. Serve immediately. Makes 6 servings.

Serving Size: 1 cup   Calories: 270   Total Fat: 16 grams   Saturated Fat: 2.5 grams   Cholesterol: 70 mgs.
Sodium: 460 mgs.   Total Carbohydrates: 12 grams   Dietary Fiber: 1 gram   Sugars: 9 grams   Protein: 19 grams

Warm Chèvre, Crab and Spinach Salad

1 Egg Yolk
1 teaspoon Dijon Mustard
1 tablespoon Balsamic Vinegar
1 teaspoon fresh Thyme Leaves (or fi teaspoon dried)
$^1/_2$ teaspoon Salt
A generous grinding of Black Pepper
$^1/_2$ cup Extra Virgin Olive Oil
6 cups washed and stemmed Spinach, patted dry
3 strips Thin Bacon , cooked and crumbled
$^1/_2$ pound Chèvre (Goat Cheese) with Herbs
1 teaspoon Olive Oil
1 pound Dungeness Crab Meat

In a small bowl, whisk the egg yolk, mustard, vinegar, thyme, salt and pepper. Drizzle in the olive oil a little at a time. Whisk until emulsified. Place the spinach and the bacon bits in a large bowl, an toss thoroughly with the dressing. Divide among four chilled plates. Next, cut the goat cheese into 8 rounds. Place the olive oil in a medium non-stick skillet over medium-high heat. Place the rounds of chèvre in the skillet and sauté for 30 seconds on each side. Remove with a flat spatula, placing 2 rounds atop each salad. Surround the chèvre with Dungeness, using the leg meat to form an attractive pattern. Serve Immediately.

Makes 6 servings.

Serving Size: 1 cup   Calories: 290   Total Fat: 21 grams   Saturated Fat: 10 grams   Cholesterol: 105 mgs.
Sodium: 650   Total Carbohydrates: 3 grams   Dietary Fiber: 1 gram   Sugars: 1 gram   Protein: 23 grams

Crab and New Potato Salad

For the potato salad:

1½ pounds small new Red Potatoes
2 tablespoons Extra Virgin Olive Oil
1 tablespoon minced fresh Parsley
1½ cups sliced Leeks, white portion only, rinsed and drained
Freshly ground Black Pepper to taste
Coarse Salt to taste

Cook the new potatoes in boiling water until tender (15-20 minutes). Set aside. to cool. Then slice. In a medium skillet over medium-high heat, sauté the parsley and leeks until tender (5-7 minutes). Combine the potatoes with the leeks and parsley, and season with salt and pepper to taste.

For the salad dressing:

½ cup loosely packed Basil Leaves
1 tablespoon minced Shallots
1 teaspoon minced Garlic
3 tablespoons fresh Lime Juice
½ cup Extra Virgin Olive Oil
Salt and freshly ground Black Pepper to taste

Combine all the ingredients in a blender or food processor and process
until smooth and emulsified.

To complete:

1 pound Dungeness Crab Meat
6 cups mixed fresh Spring Greens

Divide the greens between 4 chilled plates. Place a mound of the potato salad on top...then divide the crab equally between the plates. And lastly, drizzle the dressing over the top of each salad. Serve immediately. Serves 6 to 8.

Serving Size: 1 cup   Calories: 330   Total Fat: 19 grams   Saturated Fat: 2.5 grams   Cholesterol: 45 mgs.
Sodium: 340 mgs.   Total Carbohydrates: 23 grams   Dietary Fiber: 5 grams   Sugars: 3 grams   Protein: 17 grams

Confetti Crab Salad with Lime Dressing

For the dressing:

3 tablespoons freshly squeezed Lime Juice
$1/2$ cup Extra Virgin Olive Oil
1 teaspoon Dijon Mustard
$1/2$ teaspoon Coarse Sea Salt (or more, if desired)

For the Salad:

1 pound Dungeness Crab Meat
$1/2$ cup chopped Yellow or Orange Bell Pepper
$1/2$ cup chopped Red Onion
$1/2$ cup diced Roma Tomatoes
$1/4$ cup thinly sliced Green Onion (white and green portions)
$1/4$ cup diced Radishes
$1/2$ cup peeled, seeded and diced Cucumber
2 tablespoons chopped fresh Cilantro
1 cup finely shredded Hearts of Romaine Lettuce

Combine all the dressing ingredients in a blender. Set aside. In a large bowl, combine all the remaining ingredients, tossing well. Pour the dressing over the salad tossing well, and mound the salad onto chilled plates. Serves 4.

Serving Size: 1 cup   Calories: 280   Total Fat: 20 grams   Saturated Fat: 3 grams   Cholesterol: 55 mgs.
Sodium: 410 mgs.   Total Carbohydrates: 6 grams   Dietary Fiber: 2 grams   Sugars: 3 grams   Protein: 8 grams

Lunch and Brunch

Simple Crab Soufflé

Crab-filled Soft Tacos

Crêpes Dungeness

Dungeness Crab Mornay

Dungeness Crab Rolls

Crab and Avocado Sandwiches

"Crabby Gourmet Cafe" Crab Melt

Crab, Swiss and Almond Quiche

Crab and Bacon Fritatta

Crab Brunch-wiches

Simple Crab Soufflé

3 tablespoons Butter
$1/4$ cup Flour
$1/2$ teaspoon Salt
Dash of Cayenne
1 cup Milk
3 Egg Yolks, beaten
2 tablespoons chopped fresh Parsley
2 tablespoons finely minced Onion
1 tablespoon freshly squeezed Lemon Juice
1 pound Dungeness Crab Meat
3 Egg Whites

Melt the butter in a saucepan over medium heat. Then blend in the flour and seasonings. Gradually add the milk and cook until thick and smooth, whisking frequently. Remove from heat. Add a few spoonfuls of the hot mixture into the beaten egg yolks to gradually raise the temperature of the eggs. Then, add the egg mixture back into the cream sauce. Stir well. Add the parsley, onion, lemon juice and crab meat and stir. Set aside. Beat the egg whites until stiff, then carefully fold into the crab mixture. Place the mixture in a well greased $1^1/2$ quart soufflé dish (or casserole) and bake at 350° for 1 hour, or until the soufflé is firm in the center. Serve immediately. Serves 4.

Serving Size: $1^1/2$ cups   Calories: 330   Total Fat: 16 grams   Saturated Fat: 8 grams   Cholesterol: 275 grams
Sodium: 650 mgs.   Total Carbohydrates: 11 grams   Dietary Fiber: 0 grams   Sugars: 4 grams   Protein: 33 grams

Crab-filled Soft Tacos

1 tablespoon Olive Oil
2 cups Jicama, peeled and julienned
2 Large Sweet Bell Peppers (1 Red, 1 Yellow),
cored and thinly sliced lengthwise
1 small Red Onion, thinly sliced
1 large Pasilla (or other mild green chili pepper)
3 tablespoons Lime Juice
$1/2$ pound Dungeness Crab
Dash of Cayenne Pepper (optional)

6 Medium (8") Flour Tortillas
1 cup shredded Monterey Jack, Pepper Jack, or Cheddar Cheese

In a large skillet over high heat, sauté the jicama, bells, onion and pasilla in the olive oil for 6-8 minutes, or until limp. Add the lime juice and the crab, and sauté for 2-3 minutes more, or until crab is hot, and juices are evaporated. Add the cayenne, if desired. Heat a large heavy skillet over medium heat. One by one, heat the tortillas, flipping a few times until they are soft and pliable. Fill each one with the crab/vegetable mixture, and top with cheese. Fold one end of the tortilla over, and then starting from the opposite side, roll up, "burrito" style. Serve hot. Makes 6 soft tacos.

Serving Size: 1 taco   Calories: 320   Total Fat: 12 grams   Saturated Fat: 4.5 grams   Cholesterol: 45 mgs.
Sodium: 500 mgs.   Total Carbohydrates: 36 grams   Dietary Fiber: 4 grams   Sugars: 4 grams   Protein: 19 grams

Crêpes Dungeness

For the Crêpes:

3 Whole Eggs, beaten
2 Egg Yolks
3/4 cup All Purpose Flour
1 tablespoon Sugar
1/4 cup (1/2 stick) melted Butter
1 teaspoon grated fresh Lemon Peel
4 cups Whole Milk
Dash of Salt

Combine all the ingredients in a blender, or the work bowl of a food processor, blending thoroughly. Set aside for at least 30 minutes. Spray an 8" non-stick skillet with vegetable spray. Place over medium-high heat, and place a scant / cup of the batter in the pan...tilting so as to cover the entire bottom. Let the crêpe bake until the edges are lightly browned, and beginning to peel away from the sides. There is no need to turn the crêpe over, for at this point it is fully baked. The pretty browned side will be on the outside when you roll them up. Stack the crêpes with sheets of waxed paper in between, until all are completed, and you are ready to assemble the dish. Continue until all the batter is gone.

For the Sauce:

2 tablespoons Butter
2 tablespoons Flour
1 cup Whole Milk

$^1/_2$ cup Heavy Cream
Dash of White Pepper
Salt to taste
1 cup shredded Swiss Cheese

Melt the butter in a 1 quart saucepan over medium heat. Stir in the flour, blending well. Cook for 1 minute. Gradually add the milk, cream, white pepper and salt. Bring to a boil and cook until thick and creamy. Remove from heat and stir in fi cup of the Swiss cheese.

For the Filling:

1 tablespoon Butter
1 pound of fresh Dungeness Crab Meat
1 tablespoon minced Shallots
$^1/_4$ cup Dry White Wine
$^1/_2$ cup of the Sauce

Sauté the crab and shallots in the butter in a skillet over medium heat. Add the wine and continue to cook until the wine disappears. Add the sauce, and stir well.

To assemble, spray a baking dish with non-stick spray. Fill each crêpe with some of the filling and roll them into cylinders, placing them in the dish. Top with the sauce, and the remainder of the Swiss cheese, and bake in a preheated 375° oven until bubbly and lightly browned. Serve hot. Makes 8 to 10 crêpes.

Serving Size: 1 crêpe   Calories: 360   Total Fat: 23 grams   Saturated Fat: 13 grams   Cholesterol: 205 mgs.
Sodium: 370 mgs.   Total Carbohydrates: 17 grams   Dietary Fiber: 0 grams   Sugars: 8 grams   Protein: 21 grams

Dungeness Crab Mornay

6 frozen Puff Pastry Shells, baked according to package directions
1 tablespoon Butter
1 cup thinly sliced fresh Mushrooms
1 teaspoon minced Garlic
1/2 cup thinly sliced Green Onion
2 tablespoons Flour
1 cup Heavy Cream
1 cup Chicken Broth
2 tablespoons Dry Sherry
Dash of White Pepper
1/2 cup shredded Swiss Cheese
1/4 cup grated Parmesan Cheese
1 pound Dungeness Crab Meat
Salt to taste
Snipped fresh Chives to garnish

In a large skillet over medium-heat, sauté the mushrooms, garlic and green onion until most of the liquid from the mushrooms has evaporated, and they begin to brown lightly. Remove from the heat and add the flour, stirring well. Gradually add the half and half, sherry and white pepper. Stir well to blend. Bring to a boil and cook, stirring frequently, until sauce is thick and smooth. Stir in the cheese and crab meat and heat thoroughly. Taste, and salt as desired. Place the baked pastry shells onto warmed plates. With the tip of a small knife, remove the center of the pastry. With your fingers, gently hollow out the centers. Fill each pastry with the crab mixture, and serve, topped with a sprinkling of snipped chives for garnish. Serves 6.

Serving Size: 1 shell + filling   Calories: 450   Total Fat: 26 grams   Saturated Fat: 9 grams   Cholesterol: 95 mgs.
Sodium: 680 mgs.   Total Carbohydrates: 25 grams   Dietary Fiber: 5 grams   Sugars: 3 grams   Protein: 26 grams

Dungeness Crab Rolls

4 - 6 large leaves of Romaine Lettuce, finely shredded (about 2 cups)
1 pound of Dungeness Crab Meat, cut into chunks
$1/2$ cup Mayonnaise
2 tablespoons Ketchup
2 teaspoons Yellow Mustard
$1/2$ cup finely chopped Celery
$1/2$ cup finely chopped Red Onion
2 tablespoons fresh Lemon Juice
Salt and freshly ground Black Pepper to taste
2 tablespoons softened butter
4 Hot Dog or Hoagie Rolls

In a large bowl, toss the lettuce and crab meat, then set aside. In another bowl, combine the mayonnaise, ketchup, mustard, celery, onion and lemon juice. Season with salt and pepper to taste. Pour the dressing over the crab and lettuce and toss well. Butter the rolls and then toast them in the broiler until golden. Fill each roll with the crab mixture.
Serve immediately. Makes 4 servings.

Serving Size: 1 roll   Calories: 380   Total Fat: 21 grams   Saturated Fat: 5 grams   Cholesterol: 75 mgs.
Sodium: 820 mgs.   Total Carbohydrates: 26 grams   Dietary Fiber: 0 grams   Sugars: 2 grams   Protein: 22 grams

Crab and Avocado Sandwiches

1 crusty French Baguette, about 18" long
Mayonnaise to taste
4 large Red Lettuce Leaves
1 cup finely shredded Radicchio
1 medium Red Onion, sliced wafer thin
1 large, ripe Avocado, peeled, pitted and sliced lengthwise
2 large ripe Tomatoes, preferably Yellow
1 pound Dungeness Crab Meat
Cornichons for garnish

Split the baguette in half lengthwise. Spread generously with mayonnaise. Arrange the lettuce, shredded radicchio, red onion, avocado and tomato evenly over one half of the bread. Distribute the crab over the other half. Close the sandwich and divide into 4 equal portions, cutting them with a serrated knife. Serve garnished with Cornichons.

Serving Size: 1/4 baguette   Calories: 300   Total Fat: 13 grams   Saturated Fat: 2 grams   Cholesterol: 90 mgs.
Sodium: 640 mgs.   Total Carbohydrates: 17 grams   Dietary Fiber: 5 grams   Sugars: 5 grams   Protein: 28 grams

"The Crabby Gourmet" Crab Melt

If this was a favorite of yours from my "Crabby Gourmet Cafe" in
Winchester Bay, OR, now you can make them at home!

1 pound Dungeness Crab Meat
$^1/_2$ cup Mayonnaise
$^1/_4$ cup Parmesan Cheese
2 tablespoons finely sliced Green Onion
(green portion only)
1 teaspoon grated fresh Lemon Peel
Dash of Cayenne Pepper

4 Thick Slices of Italian Bread
4 ounces grated Cheddar Cheese

Preheat the oven to broil. In a medium bowl, combine the first 6 ingredients. Divide the crab mixture equally between the four slices of bread. Top with the grated cheese. Arrange the sandwiches on a baking sheet, and place them under the broiler. Broil for 5-7 minutes, or until hot and bubbly. Serves 4.

Serving Size: 1 sandwich   Calories: 540   Total Fat: 36 grams   Saturated Fat: 11 grams   Cholesterol: 135 mgs.
Sodium: 1030 mgs.   Total Carbohydrates: 15 grams   Dietary Fiber: 0 grams   Sugars: 2 grams   Protein: 38 grams

Crab, Swiss and Almond Quiche

1 9-inch Pie Crust, fitted into a deep-dish quiche pan
1 cup grated Swiss Cheese
$^1/_4$ cup thinly sliced Green Onion Tops
6 ounces Dungeness Crab Meat
3 Extra Large Whole Eggs
2 cups Half and Half
$^1/_4$ teaspoon Salt
$^1/_2$ teaspoon Lemon Pepper
Dash of Dry Mustard
$^1/_2$ cup Sliced Almonds

Preheat the oven to 325°. Spread the cheese and green onions over the bottom of the pie crust. Top with the crab meat. In a medium bowl, lightly whisk the eggs, half and half, salt, lemon pepper and dry mustard. Gently pour the mixture into the pie shell. Evenly distribute the crab, cheese and onions. Sprinkle the top with sliced almonds, and bake for 1 hour, or until firm in center. Let stand for 10 minutes before serving. Serves 8.

Serving Size: 1 piece   Calories: 300   Total Fat: 20 grams   Saturated Fat: 9 grams   Cholesterol: 140 mgs.
Sodium: 360 mgs.   Total Carbohydrates: 12 mgs.   Dietary Fiber: 0 grams   Sugars: 3 grams   Protein: 15 grams

Crab and Bacon Fritatta

8 Whole Eggs
$1/2$ cup Half and Half
$1/2$ cup finely chopped Green Onion (white and green parts)
1 tablespoon Butter, melted
$1/8$ teaspoon Salt
4 ounces grated Cheddar Cheese
4 slices Pepper Bacon, cooked, drained and crumbled
1 cup Dungeness Crab Meat, flaked

Spray a 10" non-stick skillet (with a heat-resistant handle) with vegetable spray. Whisk the eggs and half and half together in a medium bowl. Stir in the green onion, melted butter, salt, cheddar, bacon and crab. Pour the mixture into the skillet, and place it over medium heat. Redistribute the ingredients evenly over the bottom of the skillet. Cover and let cook (without stirring) for 8-10 minutes, or until the center is firm. Meanwhile, preheat the broiler to high heat. When the center is firm, place the skillet under the broiler for a few minutes to brown the top. Let cool for 5-10 minutes. Serve warm, cut into wedges. Serves 6.

Serving Size: 1 piece   Calories: 270   Total Fat: 19 grams   Saturated Fat: 9 grams   Cholesterol: 335 mgs.
Sodium: 400 mgs.   Total Carbohydrates: 2 grams   Dietary Fiber: 0 grams   Sugars: 2 grams   Protein: 19 grams

Crab Brunch-wiches

2 tablespoons Butter
8 Extra Large Eggs, well beaten
2 tablespoons Heavy Whipping Cream
2 tablespoons grated Parmesan Cheese
Salt and White Pepper to taste
6 English Muffins, split and toasted
2 large vine-ripened
Beefsteak Tomatoes, sliced
1/2 pound Dungeness Crab Meat
2 ounces grated Swiss Cheese

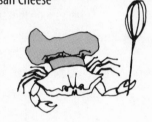

In a large , non-stick skillet, melt the 2 tablespoons of butter over medium-low heat. Add the eggs and cream, and with a rubber spatula, gently stir the eggs, scraping the bottom of the pan as you go. Scramble the eggs to a "soft" stage, as they will finish cooking later. Remove the skillet from the heat, and stir in the Parmesan, and season with salt and white pepper to taste. Place the toasted, buttered muffins on a baking tray and top each with a slice of toma-to. Then add the scrambled eggs, and top with the crab and then the grated Swiss. Place under a preheated broiler for 3-4 minutes, or until the cheese is melted and lightly browned. Serve hot. Makes 6 servings.

Serving Size: 3/4 cup filling + muffin   Calories: 370   Total Fat: 17 grams   Saturated Fat: 8 grams   Cholesterol: 340 mgs.
Sodium: 560 mgs.   Total Carbohydrates: 29 grams   Dietary Fiber: 0 grams   Sugars: 2 grams   Protein: 26 grams

Entrées

Crab and Artichoke "St. Jacques"

Angel Hair Pasta with Crab Sauce

Trinidad Curried Crab

Crab-stuffed Chicken Breasts

Classic Deviled Dungeness

Dungeness Gratinée

Crab-stuffed Peppers 'Barbados'

Dungeness Enchiladas

Dungeness Crab Backs

Crab and Artichoke "St. Jacques"

6 large Scallop Shells, washed, dried and lightly buttered
4 cups Rock Salt
2 tablespoons Butter
1 15$^1/_2$-ounce can Artichoke Hearts, (NOT marinated) drained and coarsely chopped
4 ounces fresh Oyster Mushrooms, roughly chopped
1 pound Dungeness Crab Meat
4 ounces Prosciutto, thinly sliced
$^1/_4$ cup Dry Sherry
1 cup Heavy Whipping Cream
1 cup Half and Half
Salt and freshly ground Black Pepper
$^1/_2$ cup grated Swiss Cheese
1 tablespoon chopped fresh Parsley

Distribute the rock salt evenly over the bottom of a jelly roll pan. Nestle the buttered scallop shells into the salt, so that they will not tip. In a large skillet over medium-high heat, sauté the artichoke hearts, mushrooms, crab meat and prosciutto in the butter for one minute. Add the cream, half and half and sherry and bring to a boil. Reduce the heat and simmer for 8-10 minutes, or until the sauce is reduced to about 3 cups. Season with salt and pepper to taste. Preheat the broiler to high. Divide the mixture evenly among the 6 shells. Top with the grated Swiss cheese and parsley. Broil for 1 to 2 minutes, or until bubbly.

Serve hot. Makes 6 servings.

Serving Size: 1 cup   Calories: 420   Total Fat: 27   Saturated Fat: 16   Cholesterol: 160 mgs.
Sodium: 960   Total Carbohydrates: 13 grams   Dietary Fiber: 4 grams   Sugars: 4 grams   Protein: 29 grams

Angel Hair Pasta with Crab Sauce

1 tablespoon Extra Virgin Olive Oil
1 tablespoon Butter
$^1/_2$ cup minced fresh Onion
2 teaspoons minced fresh Garlic
2 14$^1/_2$- ounce cans diced Tomatoes with juice
1 teaspoon Anchovy Paste
$^1/_4$ cup Red Wine (Chianti, Merlot, Cabernet Sauvignon, etc.)
1 pound Dungeness Crab Meat
1 pound Angel Hair Pasta (Capellini)

In a large skillet over medium heat, sauté the onion and garlic in the olive oil and butter for 2-3 minutes. Raise the heat to medium-high, and add the diced tomatoes with juice, the anchovy paste and the red wine. Bring to a boil. Reduce the heat to medium-low and simmer for 15-20 minutes, uncovered, or until the sauce begins to thicken. Then, stir in the crab and heat thoroughly. Reduce heat to low and keep the sauce warm. Meanwhile, bring a large stock pot of salted water to a rolling boil over high heat. Cook the pasta about 5 minutes, or until "al dente" Drain the pasta well, and divide among 4 heated plates. Top with sauce. Serve hot, topped with a little Parmesan, if you like. Serves 6.

Serving Size: 2 cups   Calories: 330   Total Fat: 7 grams   Saturated Fat: 2 grams   Cholesterol: 65 mgs.
Sodium: 710 mgs.   Total Carbohydrates: 39 grams   Dietary Fiber: 8 grams   Sugars: 11 grams   Protein: 26 grams

Trinidad Curried Crab

$^1/_4$ cup Olive Oil
$^1/_4$ cup Butter (fi stick)
2 cups chopped Onion
2 teaspoons minced Garlic
3 tablespoons Curry Powder
1 Jalapeno, finely chopped (optional)
1 14$^1/_2$-ounce can Diced Tomatoes (including juice)
2 cups Water
1$^1/_2$ pounds Crab Meat
Salt and freshly ground Black Pepper to taste
4 cups Cooked White Rice

Heat oil and butter in a deep skillet. Add onions and garlic and cook for 5-7 minutes, or until onions are soft. Add curry powder and Jalapeno (if desired), and stir. Next, add the tomatoes and water. Bring the mixture to a boil, then reduce the heat and gently stir in the crabmeat, taking care to leave the meat as whole as possible. Season to taste with salt and pepper. Simmer 8-10 minutes more. Serve over hot rice. Serves 8.

Serving Size: $^1/_2$ c. Rice + 1 c. Crab   Calories: 350   Total Fat: 14 grams   Saturated Fat: 5 grams   Cholesterol: 80 mgs.
Sodium: 490 mgs.   Total Carbohydrates: 31 grams   Dietary Fiber: 2 grams   Sugars: 4 grams   Protein: 22 grams

Crab-stuffed Chicken Breasts

1 4-ounce package Cream Cheese, at room temperature
$^1/_2$ teaspoon dried Thyme Leaves (or 1 teaspoon fresh leaves)
$^1/_2$ teaspoon dried Marjoram Leaves (or 1 teaspoon fresh leaves)
1 teaspoon minced Shallots
1 teaspoon minced Garlic
1 tablespoon finely chopped fresh Parsley
$^1/_2$ pound Dungeness Crab Meat
4 Boneless-Skinless Chicken Breast Halves
Enough Flour to coat breasts (approximately $^1/_4$ cup)
2 Whole Eggs, well beaten
$^3/_4$ cup Seasoned Dry Bread Crumbs
1 tablespoon Olive Oil
1 tablespoon Butter

Cream together the cream cheese, thyme, marjoram, shallots, garlic and parsley. Gently fold in the crab, taking care to leave it in fairly large chunks. With the point of a sharp knife, make a slit along the side of each of the breasts, creating a little pocket. With a spatula, fill each of the pockets with the crab mixture and secure with a toothpick. Next, roll the breasts in the flour and then dip them in the egg. Finally, roll them in the bread crumbs. Set aside. Preheat the oven to 350°. Heat the olive oil and butter in a large non-stick skillet over medium heat. Lightly brown on both sides, turning once (about 10 minutes). Transfer the chicken to a 9X13-inch baking dish and bake, uncovered for an additional 15 minutes, or until the chicken is no longer pink. Remove the toothpicks and serve hot. Serves 4.

Serving Size: 1 breast half   Calories: 410   Total Fat: 18 grams   Saturated Fat: 8 grams   Cholesterol: 200 mgs.
Sodium: 520 mgs.   Total Carbohydrates: 15 grams   Dietary Fiber: 0 grams   Sugars: 1 grams   Protein: 46 grams

Classic Deviled Dungeness

6 large Scallop Shells, buttered

---

1 pound Dungeness Crab Meat
1$^1/_2$ cups Cracker Crumbs (I prefer Ritz® brand)
$^1/_2$ cup minced Celery
$^1/_2$ cup minced Onion
2 tablespoons chopped fresh Parsley
2 tablespoons chopped Green Onion
1 teaspoon Dry Mustard
$^1/_4$ teaspoon Salt
Dash of Cayenne
6 tablespoons Butter, melted
$^1/_4$ cup Whipping Cream

Combine all the ingredients in the order given. Toss to combine. Pile into buttered shells and bake at 350° for 25-30 minutes. Serves 6.

Serving Size: $^3/_4$ cup   Calories: 310   Total Fat: 21 grams   Saturated Fat: 10 grams   Cholesterol: 100 mgs.
Sodium: 530 mgs.   Total Carbohydrates: 12 grams   Dietary Fiber: 0 grams   Sugars: 3 grams   Protein: 19 grams

Dungeness Gratinée

2 tablespoons Butter
$^1/_2$ cup thinly sliced Green Onion (white and green portions)
2 tablespoons chopped fresh Parsley
2 tablespoons Flour
Salt and freshly ground Black Pepper to taste
2 cups Whole Milk
$^1/_4$ cup Dry Sherry
1 pound Dungeness Crab Meat
1 cup Shredded Sharp Cheddar Cheese
3 cups cooked White Rice

Preheat the oven to 350°. In a medium skillet over medium heat, sauté the green onions and the parsley in the butter until soft. remove from the heat, and stir in the flour, making sure all the lumps are well blended. Season with salt and pepper. Return to heat, and gradually add the milk and the sherry. Distribute the crab meat evenly over the bottom of a glass baking dish sprayed with non-stick vegetable spray. Top with the sauce, and then the grated cheddar. Bake for 20-25 minutes, or until the cheese is melted and the sauce is bubbly. Serve hot over rice. Makes 6 servings.

Serving Size: 1 c. + $^1/_2$ c. rice   Calories: 370   Total Fat: 14   Saturated Fat: 8   Cholesterol: 100 mgs.
Sodium: 540 mgs.   Total Carbohydrates: 30 grams   Dietary Fiber: 0 grams   Sugars: 5 grams   Protein: 27 grams

Crab-stuffed Peppers 'Barbados'

6 Yellow (or Orange) Bell Peppers
1 pound Dungeness Crab Meat
2 cups Cooked White Rice
1 14$^1/_2$ -ounce can Diced Tomatoes (drained and rinsed)
1 cup finely chopped Onion
1 teaspoon minced Garlic
1 tablespoon chopped fresh Parsley
1 tablespoon fresh Thyme Leaves (1$^1/_2$ teaspoons dried)
1 ripe Banana, roughly chopped
2 teaspoons fresh Lime Juice
2 cups Chicken Broth

Preheat oven to 375°. Cut the tops off the peppers and discard them. Remove the seeds and membranes from the inside of the peppers. Cut a tiny bit from the bottom of each one, so that it will stand upright. Rinse and drain upside down on paper towels. Set aside. Gently mix all the ingredients (except the broth) in a large bowl, and then stuff the peppers.

Place the peppers in a baking dish, and top with the pepper tops. Pour the broth into the bottom of the baking dish. Cover the dish with foil, and bake for 30 minutes, or until peppers are tender-crisp, and hot all the way through. Makes 4 servings.

Serving Size: 1 pepper   Calories: 230   Total Fat: 1.5 grams   Saturated Fat: 0 grams   Cholesterol: 60 mgs.
Sodium: 600 mgs.   Total Carbohydrates: 34 grams   Dietary Fiber: 4 grams   Sugars: 11 grams   Protein: 21 grams

Dungeness Enchiladas

8 White Corn Tortillas (6^1/$_2$")
2 tablespoons Butter
^{1}/$_2$ cup chopped Red Onion
2 teaspoons minced Garlic
1 teaspoon ground Coriander
^{1}/$_4$ teaspoon freshly ground Black Pepper
3 tablespoons Flour
8 ounces carton Sour Cream
2 cups Chicken Broth
12 ounces Dungeness Crab Meat, flaked
1 4^1/$_2$-ounce can Chopped Green Chili Peppers
1^1/$_2$ cups shredded Monterey Jack Cheese

Toppings:

^{1}/$_4$ cup each Red Onion
^{1}/$_4$ cup chopped fresh Cilantro
^{1}/$_2$ cup diced fresh Tomato

Wrap the tortillas in foil, and place in a 350° oven for 10 minutes, or until softened. Meanwhile, in a medium skillet, sauté the onion, garlic, coriander and pepper in the butter until tender. Set aside to cool. In a medium bowl, combine the flour and the sour cream. Then add the cooled onion mixture, and the broth, combining well. In a separate bowl, com-

bine 1 cup of the sauce, the crab meat, chilies, and 1 cup of the jack cheese. Spray a baking
dish with non-stick vegetable spray. Place / to fi cup of filling in each tortilla and roll
up...placing each roll seam side down in the baking dish. When all the rolls are filled, top
with the remaining sauce and sprinkle with the rest of the cheese. Bake for 30-35 minutes,
or until heated through. Let 'rest' for 10 minutes before serving. To serve: Place 2 enchiladas
on each of 4 warmed plates. Top with a little of each of the garnishes. Serves 8.

Serving Size: 1 enchilada   Calories: 280 calories   Total Fat: 16 grams   Saturated Fat: 10 grams   Cholesterol: 70 mgs.
Sodium: 520 mgs.   Total Carbohydrates: 15 grams   Dietary Fiber: 2 grams   Sugars: 2 grams   Protein: 17 grams

Dungeness Crab Backs

4 fresh whole Dungeness Crab, cooked, shells on
2 tablespoons Butter
1 cup finely chopped Onion
1 cup chopped Roma Tomatoes
3 tablespoons chopped Green Onion, green portion only
1 tablespoon Worcestershire Sauce
Salt and freshly ground Black Pepper to taste

2 tablespoons Butter, melted
1 cup fresh White Bread Crumbs
1 tablespoon finely chopped Fresh Parsley

Remove the meat from the claws, legs and body of the crab, as shown in the introduction, discarding all but the main body shell. Rinse it thoroughly. Set aside. Sauté the onion in the butter for 3 to 4 minutes, or until limp. Remove from heat, and add the shelled crab meat, the tomatoes, green onions and Worcestershire sauce. Taste and then add salt and pepper as desired. Divide the crab mixture evenly between the "crab backs" and place them on a baking sheet. Toss the remaining ingredients and place atop each of the crab shells. Brown under a preheated broiler for 3 to 4 minutes, or until heated through. Serve hot.

Serving Size: 1 crab back   Calories: 330   Total Fat: 14 grams   Saturated Fat: 8 grams   Cholesterol: 130 mgs.
Sodium: 720 mgs.   Total Carbohydrates: 19 grams   Dietary Fiber: 2 grams   Sugars: 5 grams   Protein: 31 grams

Crab Cakes

Just a sampling...

Dungeness Crab Cakes Parisian

Crispy Crab Cakes

Asian Dungeness Crab Cakes
with Wasabi Mayonnaise

Crab Cakes with Apple

Crab Cakes with Avocado Salsa

Dungeness Crab Cakes Parisian

1/4 pound (4 ounces) Bay Scallops
2 tablespoons Mayonnaise
1 tablespoon Heavy Whipping Cream
2 Large Eggs, well beaten
3/4 pound (12 ounces) Dungeness Crab Meat, flaked
1/4 cup Fresh Bread Crumbs
1 tablespoon Green Onions, green portion only, finely chopped
1/2 teaspoon Celery Salt
1/4 teaspoon White Pepper

---

1 cup Dry Bread Crumbs
Vegetable Oil for frying

Purée the scallops in a food processor fitted with a steel blade. Combine the scallop purée in a large bowl with the mayonnaise, cream and eggs and blend until smooth. Add the next 5 ingredients and fold until well combined. Shape into 12 small oval cakes about fi" thick. Dip them into the dry bread crumbs, coating all sides. Heat about /" of vegetable oil in a large skillet until quite hot. Sauté each cake for 2-3 minutes on each side, or until golden brown. Serve hot. Serves 6.

Serving Size: 2 cakes   Calories: 260   Total Fat: 13 grams   Saturated Fat: 2.5 grams   Cholesterol: 135 mgs.
Sodium: 590 mgs.   Total Carbohydrates: 14 grams   Dietary Fiber: 0 grams   Sugars: 1 gram   Protein: 22 grams

Crispy Crab Cakes

1 pound Dungeness Crab Meat
2 tablespoons chopped fresh Parsley
$1/4$ cup thinly sliced Green Onion
1 cup *fresh* Bread Crumbs
1 large Egg
2 teaspoons Dijon Mustard
2 tablespoons Mayonnaise
1 tablespoon fresh Lemon Juice
3-5 drops Green Tabasco®
Salt and freshly ground Black Pepper to taste
3 tablespoons Olive Oil

In a medium bowl, combine the crab meat, chopped parsley, green onion, and ½ cup of the fresh bread crumbs. Set aside. In a small bowl, whisk together the egg, mustard, mayonnaise, lemon juice and Tabasco®. Fold the dressing into the crab mixture, taking care to leave the meat as whole as possible. Taste, and season with salt and pepper to taste. Shape into 8 small cakes, and coat with the remaining bread crumbs. Heat the oil in a large skillet over medium-high heat. Fry the cakes on the first side until golden brown. With a wide spatula, carefully turn the cakes, and brown on the second side. Serve hot, sandwiched between two halves of a toasted English muffin...or topped with a poached egg and zesty salsa... or just plain, with a fresh garden salad on the side.

Makes 4 servings.

Serving Size: 2 cakes   Calories: 320   Total Fat: 16 grams   Saturated Fat: 2.5 grams   Cholesterol: 145 mgs.
Sodium: 740 mgs.   Total Carbohydrates: 13 grams   Dietary Fiber: 0 grams   Sugars: 2 grams   Protein: 29 grams

Asian Dungeness Crab Cakes
with Wasabi Mayonnaise

For the Wasabi Mayonnaise:

1 cup Mayonnaise
$^1/_2$ teaspoon Wasabi paste (or $^1/_4$ teaspoon Wasabi Powder), or to taste

Combine ingredients and refrigerate until ready to serve.

For the Crab Cakes:

1 pound Dungeness Crabmeat
1 tablespoon minced Parsley
$^1/_4$ cup finely chopped Green Onion
1 tablespoon fresh Lemon Juice
1 teaspoon grated fresh Ginger
$^1/_2$ teaspoon Sesame Oil
$^1/_2$ cup fresh Bread Crumbs
2 Egg Whites, lightly beaten
$^1/_2$ cup Mayonnaise
Salt and freshly ground Black Pepper to taste
Pinch of Old Bay Seasoning, if desired

1 tablespoon Butter

Preheat oven to 350°. Combine all the ingredients in a large bowl, taking care not to break up the crab meat any more than necessary. Using the tablespoon of butter, coat the bottom of a baking dish. Shape mixture into 8 cakes. Bake for 25-30 minutes, turning once. Serve hot. Makes 4 servings.

Serving Size: 2 cakes + 2 tsps. mayo   Calories: 400   Total Fat: 28 grams   Saturated Fat: 6 grams   Cholesterol:110 mgs. Sodium: 750 mgs.   Total Carbohydrates: 8 grams   Dietary Fiber: 0 grams   Sugars: 2 grams   Protein: 28 grams

Crab Cakes with Apple

$1/2$ pound Dungeness Crab Meat, chunked
$1/2$ cup diced Sweet Red Bell Pepper
1 tablespoon chopped fresh Tarragon
(or $1 1/2$ teaspoons dry)
1 tablespoon chopped fresh Flat-leaf Italian Parsley
$1/2$ cup minced fresh Onion
1 cup peeled and coarsely grated Granny Smith Apple
1 teaspoon fresh Lemon Juice
A dash or two of Tabasco© Sauce
$1/2$ cup Mayonnaise

$1/4$ teaspoon ground White Pepper
Salt to Taste
1 cup Dry Bread Italian Crumbs
2 tablespoons Butter

Combine the first 9 ingredients in a large bowl, blending lightly, so as to keep the crab meat as whole as possible. Add the pepper, and season with salt as desired. Divide into 4 large cakes (or 8 small appetizer size), pressing carefully, to a thickness of about $3/4$". Roll each cake in the bread crumbs. Melt the butter in a large skillet over medium-high heat, and sauté the cakes for 3-4 minutes on the first side, or until nicely browned. Then turn, and brown on the second side. Serve hot. Makes 4 servings

Serving Size: 1 cake   Calories: 410   Total Fat: 27 grams   Saturated Fat: 6 grams   Cholesterol: 65 mgs.
Sodium: 1050 mgs.   Total Carbohydrates: 26 grams   Dietary Fiber: 3 grams   Sugars: 8 grams   Protein: 17 grams

Crab Cakes with Avocado Salsa

For the Cakes:

2 whole Eggs, beaten
1 pound Dungeness Crab Meat, flaked
2 tablespoons thinly sliced Green Onion
(white and green portions)
1 tablespoon Mayonnaise
2 tablespoons Sweet Chili Sauce
1 1/4 cups fresh White Bread Crumbs

Canola Oil for frying

For the Salsa:

1 cup ripe Roma Tomatoes, chopped
1/2 cup chopped Red Onion
1 cup finely diced ripe Avocado
3 tablespoons fresh squeezed Lime Juice
2 tablespoons roughly chopped Cilantro
Salt and freshly ground Black Pepper to taste

Gently combine all the ingredients for the cakes in a small bowl. Cover with plastic wrap and refrigerate for 30 minutes. Combine all the salsa ingredients in another bowl, mixing thoroughly. Using wet hands, form the crab mixture into 12 small cakes. Heat about $1^1/4$" of the oil in a heavy bottomed skillet until quite hot. Gently slide the cakes one at a time, into the hot oil. Fry 4 to 5 at a time, frying 3 to 4 minutes per side, or until golden. Drain on paper towels. Serve hot, topped with a spoonful of the salsa. Serves 6.

Serving Size: 2 cakes + salsa   Calories: 300   Total Fat: 18 grams   Saturated Fat: 2.5 grams   Cholesterol: 130 mgs.
Sodium: 460 mgs.   Total Carbohydrates: 14 grams   Dietary Fiber: 2 grams   Sugars: 3 grams   Protein: 21 grams

Index

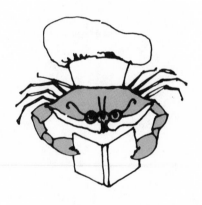